YOU CAN *Trust Me*

SABRINA JONES

WRITERS REPUBLIC L.L.C.
515 Summit Ave. Unit R1
Union City, NJ 07087, USA

Website: *www.writersrepublic.com*
Hotline: *1-877-656-6838*
Email: *info@writersrepublic.com*

Ordering Information:
Quantity sales. Special discounts are available on quantity purchases by corporations, associations, and others. For details, contact the publisher at the address above.

Library of Congress Control Number:	2021934155	
ISBN-13:	978-1-63728-137-6	[Paperback Edition]
	978-1-63728-138-3	[Hardback Edition]
	978-1-63728-139-0	[Digital Edition]

Rev. date: 02/24/2021

I thank God for my life, without him I have nothing. I would like to thank my children who pushed me to write this book, they are my biggest supporters. They believed in me and they encouraged me when I wanted to give up. My children pushed me like I pushed them to go after their dream and never stop setting goals once you have accomplished a goal. I thank yourself for being a go getter and not being afraid to dream big. I thank all my readers. Remember there's nothing that you can't do if you have a long rope and a ladder. Climb up and swing across to the other side.

Contents

Chapter 1

Who can tell my story better than me if not me......?

Yasmeen Blake is a very intelligent, talented, and gorgeous young lady with a heart of gold. She has some short comings but who doesn't. Yasmeen is an administrative supervisor of Social work at the local hospital in California. She is hard working, and she is damn good at her job. Yasmeen is unmarried, single and she is looking for love. If she could change her attitude, she just might find it, but don't hold your breath, old habits die hard. You see Yasmeen's mouth is very spicy sometimes she can be downright rude. Yasmeen is very outspoken which gets her in trouble a lot because tongue biting is not her thing, so what comes up comes out. Yasmeen has a kind heart most people love her, and she has more friends than enemies. Wherever Yasmeen goes, she stands out. It's not because of Yasmeen's attitude it's because she is a beautiful African American woman. Yasmeen stands five feet seven inches tall, with flawless skin like a cup of espresso with just a touch of cream. Her chestnut colored eye captures your soul. Behind her beautiful smile and soft full lips are the whitest set of even teeth that you have ever seen. She had a head full of jet-black shoulder length hair that frames her beautiful face. Her look is exotic, full of wonder. Yasmeen is woman with curves in all the right place. She worked out five days a week, so she's fit. Her long chocolate legs are like the legs of a track star. Slim waist, thirty-six D perky breast, an apple bottom, and a walk like a super model. Nothing was man made everything came from God. Oh yes, she's blessed.

Sabrina Jones

Yasmeen and Aaron Sinclair a doctor at the same hospital are what you call feeling each other. Aaron is a heart doctor. He looks a lot like Boris Kodjoe with smooth light brown skin. His eyes are hazel brown with a killer smile. Aaron is somewhat of a lady's man, but he and Yasmeen has been dating for six months and sex is still on hold. Yasmeen wants to give herself to Aaron but something with in her keeps telling her no. After many nights at Aaron's home during hot and heavy make-out sections. Yasmeen longed for Aaron to be inside of her as he kisses her with so much passion. Yasmeen watches Aaron as he makes his way down to her perky breast. He takes Yasmeen nipples into his mouth one at a time and gently bits them with passion. She moans in ecstasy as Aaron strong hands grip her ass as he grinds his hips and push his erected dick against her pelvis. Yasmeen can feel herself getting wet. She wants Aaron so bad that her mouth water. It has been three years and it was time for a good fuck. Yasmeen grabs Aarons ass as he unbuttons her jeans. Yasmeen pushes him away.

"Wait I thank we should slow down, I'm sorry but I'm not ready for this... not yet".

Aaron buries his face on the side of Yasmeen neck thinking. "What the fuck! Aaron gets up with his erected dick stand at full attention. Yass what wrong is there something that you need to tell me?"

"No Aaron I'm...I'm just scared that's all."

"Scared of what?"

"Aaron, I want you so bad and I know that you want me to but in my own time. Please be patient with me. I promise that I will be well worth the wait."

Aaron smiles and kisses Yasmeen on her forehead. "I can wait but when I get a hold to that ass, I'm going to really put it on you. They both laugh as Aaron pager goes off. Shit work calls."

"Well I know what that means." Yasmeen gets up and Aaron walks her to the door.

"I'll see you in the morning sexy."

When Yasmeen gets home to her townhouse, she calls her best friend Zada Reese a nurse at the same hospital that Yasmeen works at. Zada and Yasmeen have been friends for five years they are like sisters. Zada stands five feet five inches' caramel skin, brown eyes, a beautiful smile, she has a short sexy haircut, and like Yasmeen Zada likes to workout but not as much. Zada and her husband Joshua Reese have two children.

"Hey, Yass, what up chick?"

"Za we really need to talk, are you busy?"

"For you, never. What wrong?"

"I don't know I think that I'm losing my drive."

"Your drive! Girl what in the hell are you talking about?"

"My sex-drive!"

"Huh. what da what?"

"Za you know that Aaron and I have been dating for six months now and we still have not had sex yet."

"Hell, no Yass why not? Girl don't tell me that his dick is too small! Is the Doc not packing?"

"Za… Yasmeen laughs. no that's not it from what I can see or not see he's packing a good eight to ten inches. Anyway, it's not him its me."

"What are you not feeling him or dose he not turns you on?"

"Oh, he turns me on alright. It's just that when we get to the point where we are about to have sex, I push him away."

"Have you tried sucking his dick first?"

"What? No…no I have not tried sucking his dick."

"Well how about him eating you out?"

"No!"

"What so he doesn't eat pussy and you don't suck dick?"

"No Zada that's not it! I'm sure that Aaron would love to eat my pussy anytime and I would love to suck his dick until the sun comes Za that's not…

"Yass give the man the goodies let him fuck the dog shit out of your ass! Baby girl it has been three year what are you waiting for? I know that your ass is horny, and that vibrator is not cutting it, you need some dick!"

"I want to sleep with him, but I can't. It's like something inside of me is telling me that it's not right. Za it's something about him that's makes me ill-at-ease. I don't think that I trust him. I do care for him, but I can't give myself to him not yet.

"Have you talked to him about it?"

"No!"

"Well don't you think that you should?"

"I will"

"Yass, could it be that what you are feeling is from your pass relationship."

"That could be it Za. I'm afraid I just don't want to get hurt all over again."

"Look don't do anything that you don't want to. You know that I'm here for you and whatever decision you make I got you."

"Thanks, good night."

"Good night gets some sleep love you chick."

"Me to."

The next day Yasmeen is at her best friends Todd Robertson and Oscar Davis house. Todd and Oscar are two gay men, at one point they use to date. Things didn't work out, so they decided to be friend and roommates. Todd is a slim white man. He looks like a cross between Johnny Depp and Channing Tatum. Todd had black hair and blue green eyes. He's a smart and successful stockbroker. Oscar Davis is a tall black male with features like Morris Chestnut and a young Daniel Washington with glasses. Oscar is a prominent attorney. The three of them are like brothers and sister. For the past six years, they have had an unbreakable bond with each other.

"Who's cooking dinner tonight Todd I'm hungry?" "Ain't no body cooking for your ass! You Know where the kitchen is."

"Come on Todd don't be like that I thought that you loved me.

"I do but Todd's not cooking. Kissing Yasmeen on her forehead.*"*

Yasmeen looking over at Oscar. *"O…"*

"Don't O me Yass"

"Come on guys I'm depressed, and I need food."

"Depressed…. Why are you depressed?"

"Go fix me something to eat then I will tell you. Oh by the way I'm staying the night and my room had better be clean."

"Well you had better go clean it! Oscar and Todd both laugh. *We don't have a maid around here."*

"Oscar, why do you treat me so bad?"

"Because I love you."

"Whatever!"

Todd comes out of the kitchen with a plate of steak and potatoes. Oscar and Yasmeen get up and sits at the dining room table. Yasmeen puts her hand over her face and she starts to cry. Todd and Oscar look at each other with a puzzled look on their face as they put their arms around her. Oscar kisses the top of Yasmeen's head.

"Yasmeen what's wrong? You know that we don't like to see you cry."

Yasmeen just shakes her head as Todd wipes away her tears. *"Talk to me Yass please."*

Oscar Hold Yasmeen face in his hand. *"Say something. Tell mama Who did it."*

"Did Aaron do something to you? Yasmeen shakes her head."

"What is it? If you don't want steak and potatoes just say so you don't have to cry."

Yasmeen laughs. *"No, it's not that."*

"What the hell is it? Yass you're scaring me? Don't tell me that you are pregnant!"

"No O I'm not pregnant. Even if I was it would be a miracle

Both Todd and Oscar reply. *"Why is that?*

"Because Aaron and I never had sex."

"Yass it's been six months."

"Yes, Todd I know."

"Ok alrighty then…hum why not?"

"I don't know. I mean I want to, but I can't."

Oscar sits back in his chair. *"What do you mean you can't?"*

"It's like every time without fail when we are about to be intimate something inside of me echoes that it's not right, he's not the one for me. I can't explain it. My body says yes but my heat says no. It's like I'm fighting with myself and I don't know who's winning. What I do know is that I'm going to lose Aaron if I continue pushing him away."

Todd looks at Yasmeen. *"Have you Relayed any of this to Aaron Yass?"*

"No not yet. I just keep telling him that I'm not ready yet. He says that he understands but I don't think that he does, and I don't think that he's willing to wait much longer.

Oscar puts his arm around Yasmeen shoulder." *Yass if Aaron really cares about you, he should be willing to wait and not force you into having sex with him. Yasmeen if he does leave then he really wasn't the one for you."*

Todd chimes in. *"Yeah, let him go and you follow your heart. If it is meant to be it will happen in time."*

"Now eat up. You got me and Todd in here boo wooing."

It is Friday morning Yasmeen is in the bedroom looking in the mirror having a conversation with herself. *"Ok listen here you it's the weekend I'm horny as hell tonight we are going to fuck the shit out of Aaron Sinclair. I really need you to cooperate with me ok girlfriend. You and I need to be on one accord. Tonight, you will not back out, as a matter of fact, I'm getting a pair of handcuffs just for you. The drought is over after tonight.* Singing. *Say my name, say my name Yasmeen say it. I'm going to ride his pony so say my name. Aaron I'm your baby tonight."*

When Yasmeen gets to work, she sees Rosetta Copper waiting by her office door. Rosetta is Yasmeen's Puerto Rican assistant social worker. Rosetta is short in statured olive skin, long black waist length hair and dark brown eyes. Rosetta and Yasmeen friendship's rocky at times, but they work past their issues.

Yasmeen unlocking the door to her office. *"Good morning Rosie are you waiting on me?"*

"Yes I am. Holding her chest. *Please tell me that you've seen the new President slash doctor slash owner of this hospital!*

"I can't say that I have. Laughing as she walks into her office. *You know that I have been at that conference all week. This is my first day back."*

"Yass oh my God papi cita is mucho calor. He is so hot. Do you hear me?"

"I hear you."

"That man he can pop my piñata anytime with his tall sexy self."

"Ok what does Mr. Wendell Copper have to say about Mr. tall and sexy new President slash doctor slash owner popping your piñata?

"Now you know that I'm just playing, right?"

"Yeah sure you are."

"Yasmeen the man is drop dead gorgeous. You know who's all over him like flies on shit."

"Who Rebecca?"

"Who else? You know she will fuck anything moving if he got money! That whore just irritates all of my nerves."

"Rosie you know that she's trying to land herself a doctor."

"Yeah all of them. You know that she will be working with him as his nurse practitioner. Old bitch!"

Yasmeen Laughs. *"Rosie listen to yourself. I am appalled by your language young lady."*

"Whatever you know that I'm right. But this is one doctor that she will not be getting."

"Oh, and why not?"

"Because he is already engaged. You see his parents are from Mumbai, but he was raised in London and his parent believes in arranged marriage. In year or so, he will be marring the woman that his parents have picked for him."

"Well damn did you have the man investigated or what. Go head inspector gadget."

"No but I did my homework."

"You need Jesus now"

"I'm not going to tell you want I need. Anyway, how was your week? What have you and Doctor Sinclair been up to? Rosetta raise her eyebrow.

Yasmeen gets up from her desk. *"You know what I have a lot of work to do, so I'm not go to engage in this with you not right now."*

"Come on Yass tell me about your week! Was it good? Did you get some?"

"Girl…girl bye."

"Is that a yes or no?"

"It's an I am not telling you."

Yasmeen is on her way down the hall when Aaron walks up and pulls Yasmeen back into her office, where he kisses her passionately. Yasmeen wraps her arms around his neck as she receives Aaron kisses from his soft full lips. She can feel his manhood pressing up against her pelvis. As Aaron grips Yasmeen ass, as he pulls her skirt up, so he can run his fingers over her soft smooth espresso skin. Aaron holds Yasmeen around her waist with one of his muscular arms as his other hand finds its way to the front of lace red pants, he slides his hand inside. Yasmeen starts to push him away; but before she does, she remembers the conversation that she had with herself. Yasmeen can feels Aaron, finger massaging her clit. Aaron fingers find there way to Yasmeen wet spot. Aaron dips his finger in and out of her juicy pussy Yasmeen starts to moan. "Damn baby you are so wet. Aaron takes his finger out of Yasmeen's wet pussy and put his finger into his mouth. *And you taste so good!"*

The telephone rings its doctor Jacob Baldwin Yasmeen's boss. Jacob is tall medium build with short straight salt and pepper hair and green eyes. He's a family physician.

"Don't answer it let it go to voice mail."

Looking at the caller ID. *I have to its doctor Baldwin."*

Aaron sigh. "Shit Yass I want you so bad."

"Soon sweetie. Answering her phone. Good morning doctor. Yes, I'm on my way I will see you in about three minutes."

"Yass, you know that you drive me crazy!"

"Do I really?"

"You know you do."

Yasmeen kisses Aaron. "I have to go, but I will see you later to night and you can show me how crazy I make you."

"Is that a promise?"

"Yes, it is."

Aaron opens the door for Yasmeen and they walk down the hall to doctor Baldwin's office. As they are walking down the hallway, they pass Rebecca McNair. Rebecca is a nurse practitioner at the same hospital. She is five feet four inches tall with long blond hair, tan skin and single.

"Well good morning."

Yasmeen and Aaron reply. *"Good morning."*

Its seven-thirty Friday night Aaron is calling Yasmeen's cell phone, but she doesn't answer because she is in the shower. *"Come on Yass pick up. Where in the hell are you?"* Aaron gets mad and hangs up the phone without leaving a message. Just as Aaron hang ups his doorbell rings. Aaron smile as he walks to the door. *"Yasmeen that had better be you.* Yanking the door open. *It's about time…What… what are you doing here?*

Rebecca looks at Aaron and smile. *"Well I have some paperwork that I needed you to look over and it couldn't wait until Monday. I hope that I'm not interrupting you. May I come in?"*

Aaron opens the door wide and gesturing for Rebecca to come in. *"Sure come in."*

Rebecca walk in and looks around. "So where's your girlfriend? Is she not here?"

"She not here yet. Please have a seat. Can I get you something to drink?" *"That depends on what you got."*

"What's your pleasure?"

Rebecca smile as she bites her lower lip. "Well I'll have a glass of red wine if it's not too much trouble.

"A glass of wine coming right up."

As Aaron turns to walk into the kitchen Rebecca sits back on the couch as she's admiring Aaron butt.

Licking her lips *"Nice, what a lucky woman you are Yasmeen Mmm yum."*

Aaron returns from the kitchen with a glass of red wine he hands it to Rebecca. *"Here you go.* Sitting down beside Rebecca. *So where is this paperwork that couldn't wait until Monday?"*

Rebecca takes a sip from her glass. *"Oh, yeah here let me get it for you."* As Rebecca leans down to pick her purse up from the floor, her low-cut blouse fells open to reveal her C-cup breast inside of a black Lace bra. Aaron being man looks down her blouse before looking away. Rebecca can feel Aaron looking so she smiles to herself. Pulling some papers out of her purse and hand them to Aaron. *"Here you are. I have already made the necessary correction I just need you to look over them and sign off on them before I send them off in the morning."*

Aaron eyeing Rebecca. *"And this couldn't wait?"*

"No. It's already late. Taking another sip of wine from her glass. *This is good wine. Why don't you have a glass with me?"*

Aaron smiles as he pours himself a glass of wine. "I think that I will."

"I hope that I'm not keeping you from anything doctor Sinclair."

"No...no not at all. Sitting back on the couch."

When Yasmeen gets out the shower, she sees a miss call from Aaron. She smiles as she puts on her pink lace thongs. Yasmeen runs her finger across her freshly waxed pussy.

"Nice, and smooth. No hair Mr. Sinclair. Tonight, is going to be a night of unbridle passion one that you will never forget."

Yasmeen pause as this overwhelming feel wash over her like a wave of fear and sadness. Her heart starts to pound faster. Yasmeen puts her hand over her heart and take a deep breath as her eyes fill with tears.

"Come on Yasmeen don't do this now... Ok I'm not going to think about it. I'm just going to go before I lose my nerve."

Yasmeen starts to get dress in a haste as she tries to divert her thoughts, but she just can't shake the feel of deceit that she feels within herself. Back at Aaron house Rebecca and Aaron are still drinking wine laughing.

"So, Aaron can I ask you a question?"

"Sure, you can."

Rebecca takes a deep breath. *"When was the last time that you had, your dick sucked?"*

Aaron takes a big goop of wine. "What? ... Yeah this is some good wine?"

Rebecca laughs. *"I'll wait."*

Aaron sit back on the couch. *"You, you want me to answer that?"*

"Yes, I do."

"Why?"

Moving closer to Aaron. *"Because I haven't had a dick in my mouth in long time."*

Aaron puts his glass down on the coffee table and smile. *"Oh really."*

"Yes really."

Aaron holds his head back and smile. *"Well today might be your lucky day."*

"I hope so. Rebecca gets down on her knees in front of Aaron and unbutton his pants. *"*

Aaron puts his hand on Rebecca shoulders *"Wait a minute what are you doing?"*

"Shhh don't talk just relax and enjoy."

Rebecca takes Aaron's not so erect dick out of his boxers with both hands as she puts it into her moist hot mouth. Rebecca commences to suck Aaron's dick. Aaron tries to fight back the excitement of getting a head job. After two minutes, he can no longer fight the desire within. Aaron grips the couch as he looks down at Rebecca sucking on his dick. The more she sucks on his dick the bigger and longer it gets as she pulls is his member in and out of her hot mouth. Aaron give into the ecstasy before him. With his eyes rolling in the back of his head he grabs the back of Rebecca's head and push his dick deeper into her mouth as she moans with delight. Soon Aaron explodes in Rebecca's mouth. She smiles as cum drips from her mouth and chin. Rebecca stands before Aaron naked with her nipples hard. Aaron grabs both of her breast and put them in his juicy mouth. Rebecca screams with passion. Aaron pick her up by her ass cheeks and carry's her up to his bedroom. Before long Rebecca is calling out his name as he thrust himself in and out of her wet pussy. The more she screams the harder Aaron fucks her. Aaron and Rebecca are so caught up in their fuck session that they don't hear Yasmeen come in the house. Yasmeen walks into to the living room her smile drops as she looks at the clothes sprawled out on the floor and two wine glasses on the coffee table.

Yasmeen looks around in disbelief. "What the fuck!"

Yasmeen stands in the middle of the floor as she listens to Rebecca screaming out Aarons name. Yasmeen races up the stairs to Aarons bedroom. When she reaches the bedroom door, she prepares herself for what is on the other side. She hesitates and takes a deep breath before busting into the room.

Yasmeen standing in the doorway. *"What the fuck! You cheating son-of-a-bitch! I should fucking kill the both of you."*

Aaron jumps out of the bed as Yasmeen grab a glass vase off the dresser. Rebecca pulls the sheet up over her in fear.

Aaron trying to speak. *"Yasmeen baby please let me explain…please."*

"Don't you Yasmeen baby me! Explain what! You, dumb bitch! Explain why you're fucking this whoring bitch is that what you want to explain?"

Yasmeen throws the vase at Aaron head, he ducks as she picks up another one.

Rebecca starts to speak. *"I didn't…."*

Yasmeen cuts Rebecca off. *"Bitch you shut the fuck up!"* Walking over to Rebecca and dragging her out of the bed by her hair. *Don't you say shit, or I will bust you in your fucking face with this vase? You, didn't what? You are a nasty bitch? You, didn't fucking care? Is that what you were about to say? Bitch, you smile in my face and fucking my man. Now you didn't what? Think I would find out huh…. Bitch answer me!"*

Rebecca just lay on the floor crying, as Aaron stands by the bed frozen with fear.

Yasmeen walks over to Aaron. *"What do you want to explain to me Mr. Aaron Sinclair? I already know that you ain't shit. I just hope that she was worth it! Yasmeen slaps Aaron across the face."*

Yasmeen is about to walk out of the room; she stops and throws the vase against the wall it shattered all all over the floor, Yasmeen starts to cry as she pushes everything on the dresser to the floor. Yasmeen pulls Aarons television off the wall it falls to the floor.

"I can't believe that I actually care for you. You're a filthy dog. Y'all deserve each other."

Yasmeen closes the door behind her as she leaves the room. She walks out of the house and gets into her Gray Mercedes that Aaron paid for. Yasmeen drives away in tears. She's overwhelmed by Aaron partial that she can't console herself. So, she pulls over to the side of the road and cry uncontrollably.

Rebecca gets up and walks over to Aaron. Who is still in disbelief? "Sweetheart are you ok?"

"You need to leave." Aaron sit down on the bed.

In disbelief. *"Excuse me!"*

"I said you need to leave!"

"Aaron, you can't be serious! Are you kidding me?

"Rebecca please get dressed and get out of my house."

"No!... why?"

"This should've never happened! Please leave now!"

"So just like that! You want me out?"

"Yes!"

"What about us?"

Us...us there is no us! Rebecca, we had sex and that's it nothing more! Oh, you thought that we were going to... Pause holding back tears. *This shouldn't have happened."*

"Aaron what about me and my feelings?"

Aaron rest his hands-on Rebecca's shoulders. *"Look Rebecca I'm sorry, please understand."*

"Can I stay with you to night?"

No did you not see what just happened. We... *I fucked up. I fucked up.*

"Aaron."

Interrupting Rebecca. *"Get the fuck out of my house now! Get out! leave!"*

Rebeca runs down stair. She grabs her clothes she and runs out the door without looking back. Aaron calls Yasmeen, she pushes the ignore button. Aaron continues to call so Yasmeen turns her cell phone off. Yasmeen pulls into the driveway of Oscar and Todd's house it's elven o'clock at night, so Yasmeen just sit in her car trying to gather herself, but she can't. she turns her cell phone back on and calls Todd.

"Yasmeen this had better be important."

"Todd..."

"Yasmeen what's wrong? Where are you?"

"I. I..."

Todd go in to wake Oscar. "Yass please talk to me! Oscar get up something is wrong with Yass."

"*What? Where is she?*"

"*I don't know. I can't even understand her. Yasmeen stop crying and tell me where you are.*"

The phone hangs up just as Oscar takes the phone out of Todd's hand. Oscar yells into the phone.

"*Yasmeen, Yasmeen! Hello, hello. Damn it Yasmeen. Todd what the hell is going on where is she?*"

"*'O', I don't know. I'm scared.*"

As Oscar jumps out of bed the doorbell rings. Oscar and Todd both run down stair in a panic. Oscar flings the door open and Yasmeen is stand there sobbing. Todd and Oscar pull her inside just as she falls to the floor still crying unable to control herself as Todd and Oscar try to console her.

"*What wrong? Why are your hands bleeding?*"

Todd speaks. "*Say something please!*"

Yasmeen looks down at her hands she still can't speak she just shakes her head. Oscar helps Yasmeen up and they guide her over to the couch they sit with her until she able to speak. They clean the blood from her hands and wipes her face.

"*Can you calm down and tell us what happened?*"

Yasmeen takes a deep breath as she tries to tell Oscar and Todd what happened.

Wiping her tears. "*Well tonight I decided that I would surprise Aaron by sleeping with him. I told myself that it was time that we had sex. I went over to his place like a fool.* Holding her head back crying. *I was ready to fuck him. I was the one who was surprised, because I caught him in bed with another woman.*"

Todd is speechless. "*Who was it?*"

"*It was Rebecca.*"

Oscar speaks. "*Rebecca from the hospital?*"

Yasmeen shakes her head. "*That's the one.*"

Todd chime in. "*That no good bastard and that bitch.*"

"*How could I be so stupid? I'm a fool.*"

"*Don't you say that you are not stupid and you're nobody's fool.*"

"*Todd look at me, look at me!*"

Todd puts his arms around Yasmeen. "*Honey you are going to be ok. We are here for you and we are going to get through this together. It hurt me to see you like this. I'm so sorry that this happened to you.*"

Oscar to Yasmeen. "Yass what happened to your hands?"

Yasmeen looks down at her hands. *"I'm not sure. I think that It happened when I throw his TV on the floor or something. Oscar, I was so furious. I was out of my mind I couldn't even see or think straight. I'm just trying to wrap my mind around this so that I can... I need a drink."*

"No, you need to rest."

"I can't... I can't, it just hurts so bad!"

Yasmeen starts crying with so much hurt as Oscar hold her in his arms tears start to roll down his face. He looks over at Todd who is still cry. Oscar existed his hand out to Todd and pull him over to the other side of Yasmeen.

"We are going to be ok. God will see us through, this too shall pass."

They all go upstairs to bed Yasmeen falls asleep with Todd and Oscar by her side. The next morning Yasmeen is still asleep when Todd and Oscar look in on her.

Oscar quietly Closes the bedroom door. *"Let her sleep Todd she has had a long night."*

When Todd and Oscar get down stairs, they hear Yasmeen cell phone ring. Oscar looks at the ID display. *It's Aaron, he's been calling all night. "I know this idiot isn't call her after that stunt he pulled last night. He has some nerve! Oscar press the ignore button. Aaron calls back. Really he's calling back."*

"Answer it Oscar. he's not going to stop calling."

"I think that you're right... Hello!"

"Yes, may I speak to Yasmeen?"

"No, you may not speak to Yasmeen. After what you did to her. You're a selfish pig. Where do you get the gumption to call her phone?"

"Please whatever your name is, can you just put Yasmeen on the phone?"

"My name is Oscar and no I can't, and I won't put her on the phone, so stop calling! Why don't you call Rebecca I'm sure she would just love to hear from you? Oscar push the end button. Can you believe that asshole? I mean who in the hell does he think he is?"

Oscar slams the phone down on the counter and go back upstairs. It's now three o'clock in the afternoon Yasmeen is sitting on the side of the bed revisiting her embarrassing event from last night. The event plays over and over in her head like a bad movie that stuck on rewind. Yasmeen is stand in the shower hope that the water will wash away her hurt. Trying to hide her tear she let the water run down her face. Soon Yasmeen is overwhelmed with unfounded emotions that she can no longer control.

Yasmeen slide down the Shower wall sobbing. *"God please help me. I can't do this on my own. Please help me. I don't want to live like this. Please help me."*

After sitting on the shower floor for ten minutes Yasmeen gets out of the shower, she gets dressed. She looks in the mirror and staring back at her is her own reflection. One that she doesn't recognize. All she sees are swollen red puffy eyes filled with tears. Yasmeen pulls her hair back into a ponytail and go down stairs. Zada, Todd, and Oscar are sitting in the living room talking.

"So, how is she?"

Oscar speaks. *"I'm not sure. I went to check on her and she was still asleep. I didn't want to wake her."*

"Why would he do that to her Todd?"

"Who knows. I'm just glad that she didn't sleep with that shit bag."

Oscar speaks. *"I'm just so annoyed that I can't even think. I have never seen Yass like that, my heart aches for her. Some people are just heartless, and to make things worse is the fact that he has been calling her cell all day like some maniac."*

"He's a pathetic moron let him call back I'll answer her phone…"

Yasmeen walks into the room Zada gets up and hugs her. *"Hey honey! How are you?"*

"Numb, betrayed, foolish, hurt. I'm just trying to make sense of it all. I'm at a total lost. All I ever asked of him was to be honest with me that's all."

"Here Yass let me fix you something to eat."

"No that's ok Todd, I really don't have any kind of an appetite."

"You need to eat something."

Maybe later." When did you get here Za?

"About an hour ago."

"Thanks for coming. I'm so thankful for all of you. I know that my life is a mess right now. I'm trying to get it together."

Zada Put her arms around Yasmeen. *"No sweetie your life is not a mess, Yass we love you and we will always be here for each other please don't cry."*

After ten minutes Yasmeen stop sobbing Oscar sets down beside her.

"Yasmeen, I know that last night you were distraught, but I need to ask you do you need an attorney?"

"For what?"

"So, you didn't hurt anybody last night, right?"

Yasmeen takes a long pause. "No, I don't think so, maybe Aarons ego was a little bruised that's all."

"Are you sure?"

"Yes."

"How did you hurt your hand?"

Yasmeen looks down at her hands. "Oh, I think that came from me destroying his room. I didn't hurt him or her but, I wanted to."

Yasmeen cell phone rings its Aaron again. Yasmeen Looks at her phone. *"Why is he calling me?"*

"Is that Aaron?"

"Who else? I don't have anything to say to him Todd." Zada reaches for Yasmeen's cell phone.

"Give me that... Hello!"

Aaron sounding confused *"Hello Yasmeen.".*

"No this is Zada. Yasmeen can't talk to you anymore."

"Zada please let me speak to Yasmeen. I just want to talk to her and to see if she's alright."

"Oh, she is just fine."

"Come on what is your problem?"

"You are my problem. You hurt my friend and now you have the audacity to call her like you did nothing wrong! You're my problem Aaron Sinclair! You should be ashamed of yourself! You made your chance now move on you got the bitch that you wanted!"

"Zada I fucked up big time, I can admit that. I just want to talk to Yasmeen."

"She doesn't want to talk to you!"

"Well, let her tell me that she doesn't want to talk to me! I don't won't to hear it from you!"

"Well you're going to hear it from me…."

"Yasmeen is a big girl, she can speak for herself."

"Well I'm speaking for her and I say don't call her anymore she doesn't have anything to say to your lying, cheating ass. Good bye."

Yasmeen starts laughing. "Thank you, momma."

"Anytime. Really Yass are you going to be ok.

"I'll live. It's going to take some time but, I'm going to take a break from dating."

"That's understandable."

"I think that I will just go home now Oscar…."

"Oh, no you are going to stay right here tonight right Todd!"

"Right. You are going to take yourself back upstairs."

It's now seven-thirty Yasmeen, Oscar, Todd, and Zada are drinking wine at the dining room table. Yasmeen takes a sip of her wine before sitting down in her seat. She looks at everyone and close her eyes tightly. Todd puts his hand on top of Yasmeen's hand.

Are you ok?"

Yasmeen looks down at the table before she speaks. *"Do you all remember to last time. I was this sad?"*

Zada Speaks. *"Yass don't do this."*

Yasmeen looks over at Oscar with tears in her eyes. "Do you Oscar?"

"Honey don't do this to yourself."

Yasmeen closes her eyes before she speaks. *"The last time that I was this sad was. No, sad doesn't even begin to describe how I felt that day…"*

"Yass…"

Yasmeen cuts Oscar off before he can get another word out of his mouth. *"It was the day that Gregg was taken away for me. That was the day that my life changed forever. The day that I lost Gregory."*

Gregory was Yasmeen's fiancé. He was killed in a car accident three years ago. Two months after he and Yasmeen had gotten engaged, he was on his way to his friend's house when a drunk driver ran the red light. Gregory and Yasmeen had been together for two and a half years the night that he died. *"I loved him so much and I still do."*

"You know that Gregg has always loved you Yass."

"Yes, I know Za, he was my everything. He only came second to God."

"We know."

Yasmeen continues to speak uninterrupted. *"Gregg, he was my rock. He always told me that I was his Nubian Queen and he treat me like a queen every day that we were together. He would tell me how honored he was that I chose him to share my life with. There wasn't a day that went by that he didn't tell me or showed me how much he loved me. I know that I was special to Gregg and he was special to me, he was my king. I never wanted for anything, he made sure of that.*

"Yes, Yass he did love you and the two of you complemented each other in every way."

Yasmeen put her index finger on her top lip. *"I never told you guys this, but the day before the love of me was taken from me. We both called in to work and we made love all day. We couldn't get enough of each other. He made love to me like he... Like he would never make love to me again. He promised me that he would always be with me. We talked about having kids after we got married.* Holding back her tears. *That evening his friend came by the house to get him. They were going to go watch the game and hang out. Before he left, he kissed me with so much passion, he held me so tight.* Wiping her arms around herself. *Soo tight and long as he whispered in my ear, I love you my queen. As he walked away, I yelled out I love you too my king. Normally he would look back and blow me a kiss but this time he didn't... he didn't blow me a kiss... They just drove away. About thirty minutes later my phone ringed. It was the Highway patrolmen calling to telling me that there had been an accident and Gregg He was asking for me. Do you all remember when we arrived at the scene?"*

Todd, Zada, and Oscar reply *"Yes"* at the same time as tears streams down their face.

Yasmeen wipes a tear from her eye. *"When we got there my love was laying on the stretcher and EMS was working on him. I can still see his face when he saw me...He smiled at me as to say I'm ok now that you are here. I kissed him, and I begged him not to leave me. He reached up and placed his hand on my cheek...*Touching her face. *He said my queen it's going to be ok. I love you and I will always be with you. We kissed and as we kissed, I could feel him leaving me.* Tears roll down Yasmeen cheeks and they met under her chin. *When his hand dropped down to his side, I knew that he was gone... Why did I let him go? Why did he leave me? We were going to get married..."* Zada tears flows as she spoke. *"Yass, it was his time. You know that Gregg would have never left you if he had a chose. You meant everything to him."*

"Za, it was my fault, because I should have stopped him. I should not have let him walk out that door!"

"It's wasn't your fault. There was nothing you could have done. A careless drunk drive that run the red light, that's whose fault it was not yours."

As Yasmeen continues to speak Zada and Oscar comes to her side. "He's gone, and I miss him so much. There are days where I can still smell his cologne. I still feel him touch on my face when I'm lying in bed. I swear that he's there with me."

"That's because he is. His presents will always be part of you."

"Oscar, I feel as if I cheated on him. Do you think that I cheated on Gregg with Aaron?"

"Oh, no Yass you didn't cheat on Gregg. Gregg is gone, and he would want you to be happy. Honey you didn't cheat so, get that thought out of your head.

"Oscar do you think that the uneasy feeling that I had about Aaron was Gregg way of telling me that Aaron was not the right one for me.

"I don't know, but anything is possible..."

Yasmeen smiles and looks up. "Thank you, my king. I love you."

Chapter 2

Move forward without you

Its Monday morning and Yasmeen is getting ready for work. This is the day that she had been dreading all weekend, and to make things worse is the fact that Aaron has been calling her phone since the incident that took place at his house. Yasmeen gets dressed and starts to put on her make-up. As she looks in the mirror at her reflection. She smiles as her mind flash back to Gregg. In her mind, she can hear him say you can do this my queen. Everything is going to be alright Yass. Remember I will always love you.

Yasmeen reply to herself as she stares into the mirror. *"And I love you more my king in heaven...* Looking down at her cell phone its Aaron. *Not now it's too early for this."* Pushing the end button. Yasmeen pulls up in her parking spot at the hospital. She takes a deep breath before turning off the car ignition. She hesitates as she reaches for the car door.

"I should have called in. It's going to be a long day. I can feel it lord give me strength."

Yasmeen walks down the hall to her office. She's the first one in as usual. Yasmeen puts her purse and briefcase under her desk she turns on her computer and takes some patient files out of her desk draw. Yasmeen cell phones rings, it's Oscar. *"Hey 'O'."*

"Well good morning. How are you?"

"Don't won't to be here 'O'."

"And why not sis?"

"I just don't won't to face them... He has already called me like four times this morning."

"Everything is going to be ok, just call me when you get to the Station. I might be in court, but I'll be there…"

"Yeah my favorite attorney." Yasmeen laugh.

"It's good to hear you laughing."

"It feels good too."

"Well I'm here if you need me and call Todd."

"I will 'O' and thanks for everything love you."

"Anytime. Besides that's what big brothers are for. Love you to Yass.

Yasmeen is working on her computer when Rosetta knocks on her door. She's standing in the doorway with two cups in her hand. *"Good morning."*

Yasmeen looks up from her computer smiling. *"Good morning. Please tell me that's Green tea in your hand!"*

"What else would it be."

"Coming from you I don't know."

"Wait till lunch."

"So how was your weekend Rosie?"

"It was Devine Yass we…"

Aaron walks in. *"Yasmeen can we talk?"*

Yasmeen removes her glasses. *"No, we can't! Can't you see that we're busy."*

"Oh, I can leave."

"No, you can't! Aaron, I need you exit my office before I call security!"

"I just need five minutes please."

"I said get out."

Aaron throws his hands in the air and walks out. Rosetta looks at Yasmeen with a look of confusion on her face. *"hum Yass, what's… what's going on!"* Yasmeen gets up from her desk. She closes her office door. As she fights hard to hold back her tears. Yasmeen sitting on the edge of her desk shaking her head. *"Rosie I'm so hurt right now."*

"Why? What happen? Trouble in paradise."

"Oh, troubles is not the word, more like an atomic boom."

"Yass what did he do?"

Yasmeen walk back to her chair. *"Well to start I planned a romantic weekend with that low life who just left only to find out that he had other plans.*

"What kind of plans?"

Yasmeen fights to hold back her tears. *"Plans like fucking Rebecca!"*

"What?"

"Yeah you heard me right. I went over to his house Friday night, and I found him in bed with Rebecca."

"Are you talking about Rebecca from the main hospital?"

"That would be her unless you know someone else."

"Yass no! I mean does he know that you saw them?"

"Hell, yeah he knows! I walked in on them fucking like jack rabbits!"

"Is she in intensive care? Where is that bitch?"

"I don't know. She's somewhere around here."

"Are you ok?'

"Oh, I'm fine. I just want him leave me alone."

"I just can't believe this. Yass why are you so calm and why didn't you call me?"

"Well first of all you were out of town and I didn't won't to disrupt your weekend. Besides Za, Todd, and Oscar they calmed me down."

"Calmed you down… What did you do?"

"Not much, you know me."

"Yes, I do know you Yass. Now what did you do?

Yasmeen gets up and walk out of her office. *"I said not much."* Rosetta runs out of the office behind Yasmeen. After lunch Yasmeen is sitting in her office when she hears a knock on the door. She looks up from her computer. *"Come in. Please don't let that be Aaron!"*

The door opens it's not Aaron, but to Yasmeen surprise it's Rebecca. She walks in and closes the door behind her. *"Yasmeen, we need to talk."*

"Bitch I know that you did not just walk your ass up in my office. You got a lot of fucking nerves!"

"I just wanted to talk to you."

"There is nothing that you and I need to talk about! What you need to do is to get out of my office, if you don't want your ass beat!"

"I did not come here to fight with you. I just wanted you to know that I'm sorry.

"You're sorry… I know you're sorry! You are a sorry excuse for a woman, you slut!"

"Just hear me out!"

"Hear you out! Yasmeen runs over to Rebecca and slaps her to the floor. *How dare you come in my office with this bullshit. Bitch get out."*

Yasmeen snitches Rebecca up by her arm and pushes her out of her office and slams the door behind her. Rosetta runs into her office. *"Oh, bitch you're back?*

"Yass it's me… I heard the commotion down the hall and I came to check on you."

"I thought that you were Rebecca! The nerve of that slut!"

"What happened?

Yasmeen puts her hand on her hip. *"That bitch going to come up in here talking about we need to talk, just hear her out! Bitch please!"*

"Who Rebecca?"

"Yes. I'm so livid, I just need to go home before I really hurt somebody."

"Calm down."

Yasmeen sits down behind her desk and she calls Oscar. It's now six twenty-five in the evening Yasmeen is at home. She has just gotten off the telephone with Zada who is on the way to her house with Rosetta for girl's night. Yasmeen is in the kitchen cooking when the doorbell rings. Yasmeen runs to the door as she looks down at her watch. *"I know that I said seven o'clock not six twenty-five. I'm not even ready yet."*

Yasmeen opens the door jokingly with a smile. *"Didn't know you all had a jet. Guess y…"* "As Yasmeen opens the door she is flabbergasted to see that it wasn't Zada and Rosetta at her door. It's Aaron instead. *What are you doing here?"*

"I came here to talk to you."

Yasmeen attempts to close the door. *"I'm sorry that you're wasted your time by coming here!"*

Aaron push the door back open. *"Yasmeen please can we talk, please?"*

" You keep calling me, Aaron why won't you leave me alone?"

"Because you are ignoring me. Just talk to me or will you at less listen, to what I've got to say. Yasmeen, I promise to leave you alone.

"Ok, I'm listen. What do you have to say?"

"May I come in?"

"No, I don't think so. You can say whatever you need to say outside!"

"Yasmeen look I'm sorry that I hurt you. You have to believe me. I never intended for this to happen. Can you find it in your heart to forgive me? Yasmeen, I love you and I'm so sorry."

"How dare you come here with that weak ass apology Aaron. To answer your question no I will not forgive you. Aaron the only reason that you are sorry is because I caught you, other than that you're not sorry. You are a pathetic human being. You make me sick." Again Yasmeen attempts to close the door. Aaron push the door back open. *"Yasmeen don't do this. Don't do this to us!"*

"Us... don't do this to us! The day that you went to bed with that bitch that was the end of us! There is no us! Us no longer exist, us ended the moment that you portrayed my trust!"

Aaron puts his hands to his mouth. *"This wasn't supposed to happen."*

"But it did."

"I don't won't you to be bitter."

"I'm not. I'm discussed. There is a difference."

Aaron search for an answer. *"Why is it because she's white?"*

Yasmeen is stunned by Aaron question. *"Because she's white, are you stupid? I could give two fucks about what color she is. The color of her skin doesn't matter to me. I wouldn't care if she was red, yellow, orange, purple, or blue. What matters to me is the fact that you cheated, or do you not comprehend that."*

"But would you have preferred her to be black?"

Yasmeen is dumbfounded. "No, I would have preferred you to be a man. You know what leave, get off my doorstep!"

"I'm sorry I should not have said that. I'm sorry Yass I don't won't to lose you. Not like this."

"It's too late...

"I'm sorry that you caught me in an awkward position..."

"Awkward position! You make it sound like you were playing twister. Don't dress it up asshole, call it what it is. I caught you fucking! Awkward my ass."

Aaron fights to hold back his tears. *"What did you expect from me? Yasmeen I'm a man with needs."*

Yasmeen with tears in her eyes." *You call yourself a man! You're not a man, you don't know how to be a man. A man would have waited... waited for me! Aaron a man you're not...What did I expect from you? Nothing, nothing at all. You don't even have a clue."*

"Were you ever going to sleep with me Yasmeen?"

With tears starting to roll down her face. *"Yes... Yes, Aaron I was."*

"When?"

"The same night that you slept with Rebecca. I had made special plans for us. I wanted it to be a night that we would always remember… ha, I guess we will thanks to you. Yasmeen claps her hands. Give yourself a hand because you deserve it."

"I'm sorry. Yasmeen I'm so sorry." Aaron reach for Yasmeen. Yasmeen steps backwards. "Don't you touch me. Don't you ever touch me."

"Yasmeen, I love you. I screwed up, please tell me what I can do to fix this! I don't won't to lose you. I really love you! Tell me what to do?

Yasmeen slams the door close. Aaron just stands there looking at the closed door before walking away. At seven o'clock Zada and Rosetta arrived with Todd and Oscar. Yasmeen is still cry sitting on the couch. Zada knocks on the door as they enter the house.

"We're here. What wrong? Why are you crying?"

"It's Aaron."

Todd Speaks. *"What about Aaron?"*

"He was here."

"What did he do. Did he hurt you?"

Yasmeen shakes her head no as she tells them what transpired. Afterward Yasmeen washes her face, they continue with their girl's night. Yasmeen doesn't know that this is just the beginning of her new life. She's not sure what her future hold but she's getting ready. Yasmeen sees herself as broken because she lost the love of her life. The only man that she has ever loved. She longs for the day that she will be able to love again with her whole heart and not feel like she is cheating on Gregory. A week later Yasmeen is getting ready for work as she continues to pray out loud to herself.

"Lord it's me Yasmeen. I know that I don't talk to you as often as I should. I'm trying to do better. Lord I come to you this morning in need of your grace and mercy as I go into work this morning. Lord I need you to be with me so that I don't do anything that will get me fired or put in jail. Lord please give me strength, a piece of mind, peace in my heart, and keep Satan out of my path. Lord keep me near the cross. I plead the blood of Jesus over me as I walk out this door. In Jesus name, Amen."

Yasmeen pulls into her parking spot with her radio loud, on the gossip station. As she turns her car off, she looks in the mirror and blew a kiss to herself. Yasmeen steps out of her car with her six-inch red pumps that accentuates her shapely calf's and legs that goes all the way up to her hips. she is wearing her knee length black skirt that enhances all her curves with a red blouse with black buttons that compliments her firm breast that hold a diamond shape heart neckless. Yasmeen goes into her office to prepare for her nine o'clock meeting. With everything that has been going on, Yasmeen has yet to meet the new president of the hospital. When she walks into the conference room everyone is just sitting around the table engaged in their own personal conversation. Doctor Maxwell Khalidah who works with a team of neurosurgeons. He's tall medium built with natural tanned skin. Short black hair that falls on his forehead. Like a silk wave. He has dark green eyes with spots of blue. He speaks with an accent. Doctor Maxwell Khalidah is talking to Doctor Mahmoud Shashivivek the new Owner of the hospital. He is also a neurosurgeon. He stands six feet tall one hundred sixty-five pounds with silky black curly hair the flows down to his shoulders enhancing his strong facial fetchers. His eyes, are as blue as the ocean. His skin is flawless and blemish free like smooth light creamy caramel. His smile is bright like the sun that revels his beautiful pearly white teeth. Mahmoud lip like a dark pink rose. His a physique, better than the Rock, with his eight pack abs, with strong arms and hands. He speaks with an accent that makes your heart quiver. Yasmeen walks into the conference. "Good morning" Everyone replies except for Mahmoud. He looks up as Yasmeen without saying a word. Yasmeen says to herself. *"Well I must be the only one in the room or did he leave his voice at home?"*

Mahmoud whisper to Maxwell. *"She going to be my wife."* Maxwell looks confused by Mahmoud's statement. After the morning meeting Jacob Yasmeen's boss interduces her to Mahmoud who is still talking to Maxwell.

"Dr. Shashivivek I don't believe that you have met Ms. Yasmeen Blake. She is the head of social work and hospital management. She and I work very close as well as other doctors within the hospital."

Maxwell Speaks. *"Oh yes Ms. Blake does an outstanding job here."*

"Nice to meet you and I'm looking forward to working with you. Mahmoud nods his head. *I also understand that you will be working with Rebecca.* Mahmoud just stares at Yasmeen without saying a word. Yasmeen whispers to Jacob. *Can he speak English or is he just an asshole?"*

"Yes, he can speak English" "Ok got it. He's an asshole." Yasmeen walks away.

Jacob puts his one finger on the side of his head and smiles. Mahmoud is still watching Yasmeen as she walks out of the conference room. To himself he smiles. Yasmeen is at the nurse station talking to Cindy a unit secretary at the hospital. When Aaron walks up.

"Good morning Yasmeen."

"Good morning Dr. Sinclair." Yasmeen walks away. She looks at her cell phone it's a text from Aaron. *"You look great. I miss you."* Yasmeen rolls her eyes as she deletes the text. When Yasmeen gets home, she finds two dozen long stem roses outside her door with a note from Aaron. Yasmeen doesn't read the note. She walks over to the trashcan and toss the roses in the trash. Yasmeen is at the gym when her cell phone rings its Todd.

"Hey baby."

Hey dolling, are you still at the gym?"

"Yes. Are you coming?

"No not today. I was just calling to check on you."

"I'm good and work was ok. I saw you know who."

"Huh. What did he have to say?

"He sent me a text, talking about I look good and he miss me. Get this he going to have the nerve to send me flowers."

"Girlfriend no he didn't!"

"Girl Yes he did. I put all twenty-four of them in the trash."

"No, you didn't."

"Yes, I did, and you know how much I like roses!

"He must be smoking that stuff. Todd Yells out to Oscar. 'O' he said that he misses her."

Oscar in the background. *"Boy bye."*

Two weeks later Yasmeen is at work when she sees Anne-Marie. Anne-Marie is a nurse she's married to Chase an IT Manager at the hospital. Anne-Marie and Yasmeen were once friends. Their friendship ended after they got into a fight and Yasmeen beat her ass. Anne-Marie and Rosette are still good friends. Anne- Marie misses her friendship with Yasmeen, but after she and Chase got married, he put a strain on their relationship because he and Yasmeen could never see eye to eye on anything. Anne-Marie wants to speak but she doesn't. Yasmeen smiles to herself and keeps on walking. Anne-Marie and Rosetta are talking at the end of the hall. They are talking about Yasmeen. Wallace a male who work in Environmental services at the hospital over hears their conversation. Wallace likes Yasmeen, because she has helped him with many of his personal problems in the past.

"I know that you have heard about what happened to Ms. Yasmeen."

"I heard bits and pieces, But I know that you got the tea

Rosetta laughs as her mouth takes off. *"You know I do. Anyway, let me tell you. You know how that bitch be walking around her like she's the boss and shit."*

Anne-Marie rolls her eye. *"Girl yes, that black bitch!"*

Rosetta put her hand on her hip. "How about Aaron broke the bitch heart."

"I know that you are lying."

"No"

"You Know I haven't seen them together."

"That because she caught him and Rebecca in the bed together about three weeks ago. That bitch was crying her heart out."

Anne-Marie laughs. *"Rosie, you know I heard a little bit, but I didn't hear any of this."*

"Girl that's not the half of it."

Rosetta starts to tell Anne-Marie everything that transpired between Aaron and Yasmeen. Wallace is hurt by what he hears. He shakes his head and walks away. Later that day Wallace stops by Yasmeen office. Wallace knocks on Yasmeen door. "Come in."

Wallace enters. *"Good evening Yasmeen."*

"Well hello Wallace how are you today."

"Ms. Blake, I… I. "

"What's going on?"

"Ms. Blake, can I talk to you."

"Yes…sure come in and have a seat and call me Yasmeen we've had this talk before Wallace."

"Yasmeen, I need to tell you something, but I don't won't to start no conflict."

Yasmeen sits up in her chair. *"You know that you don't have to worry about that. What you tell me will stay in this office."*

"Are you and Mrs. Rosetta close friends?"

"No, we are associates. I wouldn't call her a friend. Why do you ask?"

"Yasmeen don't trust her."

"I don't. What happened?

Wallace takes a deep breath. *"Well today when I was pulling trash, I overheard her telling Mrs. Brice... I know that I shouldn't be repeating gossip but the way that they were talking about you just made me mad."*

"What were them saying?"

"Mrs. Rosetta was telling her about you and Dr. Sinclair's situation. They were calling you all kinds of... You know the 'B' word. Again, I'm not trying to start any confusion I just wanted you to... Yasmeen that woman don't mean you no good. I mean I know that I can't tell you what to do but you shouldn't trust her."

"Wallace, I can promise you that she will never know about our conversation. Thanks, for your concern and I don't trust Rosetta I never did."

"Ms. Blake, I do consider you as a friend. You have done so much for me and my family and I will always be grateful for that."

"Oh its Ms. Blake now. Really Mr. Thomas." *"You're right my bad."*

"Thanks for being my friend Yasmeen."

"No thank you."

Ten minutes after Wallace leave Rosetta walks into Yasmeen's office joking. *"Hey lady!"*

"Did you forget how to knock?"

No ma'am. What wrong with you?"

"Oh, there is nothing wrong with me. Now what do you want?"

"Did I do something?"

Yasmeen sits back in her chair and cross her long legs. *"I don't know, did you?"*

"No, I didn't... Any way girlfriend..."

Cutting Rosetta off. *"Girlfriend!"*

"Yes. You know that you are my friend."

Yasmeen Laughs. *"Girl...* Yasmeen pauses as she thinks about her conversation with Wallace. *Girl, girl what do you want?*

"I saw your boo."

"You didn't see no boo of mine.

"Yes, I did. Your boo Aaron."

"Don't play with me, you can get out of my fucking office with that!"

"I'm sorry I was just kidding."

"Well I'm not."

"I was just trying to cheer you up."

"Oh, I don't need cheering up! Especially not by you!"

"I just wanted to know what time were you coming over tonight."

"I'm not."

"Yass why not?

"I have plans."

"Plans…what Plans?"

"My plans."

"Now Yass you know that I wanted you come over tonight so that we could have some girl time. We talked about this on yesterday.

"Yeah I know but something important come up."

"What could be more important than your friend?"

"Girl please… you can try to get in my business some other time.

"Get in your business."

"That's what I said."

"I'm not trying to get in your business Yass. I just wanted to make sure that you are ok. I'm your friend and I care

"That's ok I'm good. We don't need girl time, but thanks anyway."

"Yass are you serious?"

"Yes I am."

"So, you're really not coming over."

"No, I'm not coming over."

"But Yass…Ok do you want me to come over to your place than?"

"No, I don't. I told you that I have plans."

Rosetta storming out of Yasmeen office. Yasmeen laughs as she picks up her cell phone to call Oscar. Its eight o'clock Yasmeen is at her townhouse with Todd, Oscar and Zada. They are having dinner out on the patio.

Oscar Speaks as he takes a sip of wine. "I for one I'm not looking forward to going into courting in the morning… Damn Yass this is some good wine! Pick up the bottle to read the label. *Where did you get it?"*

"From that new winery that just opened up. It is good. and why don't you want to go to court?"

"This case is just dragging on. I just want it to be over with."

"They can't speed it up?"

"It doesn't work like that Todd! I wish that it did."

"Yass you're quite tonight what on your mind?

"Oh, Todd it's nothing…It's nothing"

"Yass, you can tell that lie to someone else who don't know you, because I know better. Now what's on your mind and don't say it nothing because something is bothering you."

Yasmeen puts her glass down and props her elbows on the table. She takes a long pause before speaking. *"Guys, I know that this is supposed to be a nice a quite evening and I don't won't to spoil it with nonsense."*

Zada laughs jokingly. *"Too late! Now spill the beans."*

Yasmeen laughs. *"Za you know what, go home."*

I will after you tell me."

"You are so right Za. Oscar hi-five Zada. *We're listing you have our undivided attention."*

"Guys let just forget it."

Oscar eyes widen. 'Yass, don't you make me get out of this chair. You had better start talking. Counting. One…two…"

"Zada you all know Wallace the house keeping guy. Everyone replies yes. *Well he came by my office today to tell me that he that he overheard our girl Rosetta and her sidekick talking about me…And it was not good. He didn't want to tell me, but he did.* Yasmeen repeats everything that Wallace stated to her.

"Yass, I don't know why you associate with that… Person. I have told you repeatedly that she doesn't mean you no good. See you're hard headed!"

Zada speaks. *"Yass see you're good, because I would have punched that trick when she came up in my office like we cool after she had been talking shit about me. Stop fucking with that girl like Todd said! Want until I see her two-faced ass in the morning."*

"No Za I told Wallace that I wouldn't say anything.

"You told him that not me.

"Zada Reese, you better not.

Todd speaks. *"Well what are you going to do Yass? Let her keep smiling in your face and cutting your throat.*

"Not at all dear. You know that I'm her boss. She works for me. I have to be professional right Oscar."

"You are so right Yasmeen. And I see where you are coming from."

"You all know that I got this. They said that I was a bitch, but they haven't seen a bitch yet."

"And I say that we drink to that." Todd holding his glass up.

The doorbell rings. Yasmeen gets up. *"I wonder who that could be."*

Zada reply. *"Your best friend Rosetta. "They* all laugh.

Yasmeen walks inside. *"Don't even play like that."* Yasmeen makes her way to the door. Before she opens the door, she takes a deep breath, praying to herself. *"Please let this be anybody but Rosetta or Aaron. I'm trying to have a peaceful night."*

When Yasmeen opens the door, she is surprised to see Angelina standing there. Angelina Hernandez is Anne-Marie's younger sister. After Anne-Marie slept with her ex-husband and had a child with him they have not been close. Yasmeen was friends with both Anna-Marie and Angelina before their fight. Yasmeen is so happy to see Angelina after not seeing her for a week.

"Hey girl, I'm so happy to see you. Come on in, we all are out back."

"You know that I miss you… How have you been really?"

"I have been better. It's getting easier. Yasmeen and Angelina walk outside. Look who's here Y'all."

Everyone replies. *"Hey Lina bout time you got back. We missed you."*

Angelina hugs everybody. "And I miss y'all."

Zada Speaks. *"You know you had Yass ass terrified as hell to answer the door."*

"Za, why?"

"She was scared that it was Rosie at the door."

"Oh that… she and my bitch sister are at the house talking about you in code. Like I don't know who they're talking about. You do know that you are all kinds of bitches over there.

Yasmeen laughs. *"Yes, I know. But I'm not even worried. Those miserable… Angie, I know that's your sister so I'm not going to…*

Interrupting Yasmeen. *"Hell, I will say it for you… that bitch. I know what they are. Hell, we all know what they are so don't sugar coat it. Let's call it a spade a spade and a bitch a bitch I mean two bitches. All I want to know is Yass why do you still fuck with that bitch Rosetta? Why Yass Why?"*

"We have been asking that question all night."

They all laugh as they drink wine. Yasmeen thinks to herself. that there is nothing like true friends and she is lucky to have them in her life.

Zada Speaks. "Yass… Have you seen the new doctor? Holding her chest. Girl he's fine as hell."

Yasmeen takes a sip of her wine. *"Yes, I have seen him and he's an asshole!"*

"No, he's not Yass. He's really sweet, with his sexy self."

"If you say so. I don't like him. Let me tell y'all when doctor Baldwin introduce him to me this morning that ass didn't speak, he just looked at me like I was crazy. I was like dose he speaks, English. Looking at me like a fish. Oh, and I'm telling Josh your husband about this sexy doctor to see what he has to say Za,"

"Yass don't start. You see how you do me baby girl."

"Baby girl my ass. I'm telling."

Angelina chimes. *"Oh yeah I have been hearing about him from you know who. I did hear that he was hot. He from Mumbai, or Dubai or something like that Right."*

I'm not sure I just know that he's Arabian or Indian. Hell, he sexy!

Yasmeen gets up. *"Let me get some more wine. Za you and Angie can't have any because y'all already drunk. Talking about the new doctor fine."*

Zada interjects laughing. *"Yass don't be like that now. The man looks delicious, mouthwatering, tasty!"*

"Ok tasty."

Todd and Oscar speak. *"He sounds yummy."*

"Oh, he is."

Todd puts his glass down. "Girl do tell. We want to hear everything leave nothing out."

"Now here you go. I've told you all the man's an asshole."

They all laugh as Zada starts to describe doctor Mahmoud. Two days later Yasmeen is at the nurse's station talking to Zada and Cindy when doctor Mahmoud, Maxwell, and Rebecca walks off the elevator. Rebecca has been avoiding Yasmeen, so she walks to the other side of the nursing station. Doctor Mahmoud walks over

"Good morning ladies."

Everyone speaks but Yasmeen. Yasmeen looks up and Mahmoud is looking at her, their eyes lock. Yasmeen can feel her insides turning. Yasmeen heart begins to race, she feels her pussy starts to throb out of control. A door slams and Yasmeen break her eye contact. She walks away without saying a word. Yasmeen make her way down the hall, to the restroom. she can still smell Mahmoud's cologne as it lingers in the air. By the time Yasmeen gets to the restroom her panties are wet. Yasmeen can't think, her body shivers as her legs give way under her. Yasmeen splashes her face with cold water trying to clear her head. Yasmeen looks in the mirror talking to herself. *"What in the hell is wrong with me."* Zada coming into the restroom.

"Now Yass that was rude."

"What?"

"You could have said good morning. He was being nice."

"Who…what?"

"Doctor Hakim."

Yasmeen dries her face. *"Zada…*

"Are you ok Yass?"

"Yeah…yeah I'm ok just a little light headed."

"Come on have a seat."

"Za I'm ok."

"Yass come sit down. Let me get you something to drink."

"Za… Ok Zada but I'm fine."

Yasmeen gets herself together, she tries, to comprehend what just transpired within her. Yasmeen denies herself the lust that she is feeling. Yasmeen cannot give into her overactive hormones. As Yasmeen walks down the hall Doctor Mahmoud and his team are standing in the hall about to start seeing patient's. Mahmoud watches Yasmeen as she walks up. He smiles and looks away. For the past three weeks Yasmeen and Mahmoud has been bumping heads. They can't seem to agree on anything when it comes to patient care. Yasmeen has always fought for her patients. That is one of the quality's that most people love about her. Today is the Monday patient meeting and Yasmeen's ready for the show down. With who it doesn't matter because she likes a good squabble with her fellow counter parts. Yasmeen gets a kick out of ruffing their feathers, but she and doctor Mahmoud disagreements are like firework's that keeps exploding long after the show is over. No matter how much Yasmeen tries to avoid having any kind of conflict with Mahmoud the tension between them is like foreplay. Hot and electrifying Yasmeen heart pounds as if something inside of her is awakened deep within and it longs to get out. Yasmeen wonders is this beast within hate or fear. Yasmeen wants, and she try to be cordial, but her pride gets in the way. How can she be friends with a man who is obviously out to get her or is it all in her mind? Yasmeen walks in the conference room. Doctor Baldwin Yasmeen boss is talking to Maxwell, Mahmoud, and Brandon. Brandon Oakley is another doctor on Mahmoud's team of special care doctors. Doctor Baldwin turns his attention to Yasmeen.

"Good morning Ms. Blake."

"And good morning to you Doctor."

"Don't you look lovely."

Yasmeen cannot help being a smart ass. *"Yes, I am as usual."*

"Good morning Yasmeen."

Yasmeen takes a deep breath. *"Good morning Doctor Shashivivek."*

Brandon cut in just to get under Yasmeen skin. *"Well, well, well if it isn't Yasmeen Blake Ms. Hot head."*

An evil smile grows across Yasmeen lips. *"Well, well, well if it isn't doctor Brandon Oakley with the hot morning breath. Did you not wipe your mouth after taking your morning dump?* Maxwell, Mahmoud, and Jacob look at Yasmeen as she smiles. *Don't look at me like I'm the only one who smells his hot breath!"*

"Yasmeen don't you start with me. I've had a long weekend and I'm not up for it."

Yasmeen smile. *"Yes, I can tell. Your mouth smells like it needs to be flushed."* Yasmeen cannot help laughing.

"Yasmeen…" Brandon pause.

"What? You started it I just finished it." Sitting back in her chair.

After the meeting Yasmeen is talking to Tia a nurse about one of Yasmeen patients. Tia walks away, and Yasmeen walks into the breakroom when Rebecca walks in behind her. *"Yasmeen."* Yasmeen turns around surprised. *"Yasmeen can we please talk?"*

"We don't have anything to talk about Rebecca."

"I think…I think we do."

Yasmeen walks over to Rebecca as she takes a step back towards the door. *"What in the hell do you think we need to talk about?"*

"I just want to clear the air that's all."

Yasmeen puts her hand on her hip. *"Clear the air. Girl my air is clear. Stop wasting my time ok… You know what say whatever it is that you have to say and be quick about it."*

"I just wanted you to know how sorry I am about what happened, and I had no intention on sleeping with…"

"*No... No, you're not sorry. You have no remorse about what you two did. And yes, you had every intention of sleeping with Aaron. You had that intention for a long time. So, don't insult my intelligent with that pathetic bullshit.*

"*Yasmeen can we at least be friends.*"

"*Friends... Did you say friend? We can't and will never be friends. I have no desire to be friends with you Rebecca. The only thing that you and I can be, is two people working in the same hospital That's it. I don't want your friendship.*"

"*Yasmeen please can you find it in your heart to forgive me.*"

"*I forgave the both of you a long time ago. I have moved on and you should do the same.*

"*You have to know that I don't want Aaron.*"

"*Rebecca yes you do. Girl you are probably still fucking him, but I can tell you this for damn sure I don't want him, you can have him, he's yours. Miss lady make this the last time that you come confront me without an appointment. You are dismissed.* Tia and Zada walks in."

"What's going on Yass."

"*Oh nothing. She just wanted to clear her air.*

"*What air?*

Yasmeen laughs. "*Hell, she doesn't know. She's just clueless. She wants to be my friend. I think not.*"

Zada, Tia, and Yasmeen walks out of the breakroom leaving Rebecca standing in the middle of the floor. Two days later Yasmeen is standing at the nurse's station when she over hears Rebecca and doctor Mahmoud talking.

"*You need to let me cook for you.*"

"*That's very kind of you but no thank you.*"

"*Come on. I will not take no for an answer.*"

"*Rebecca, I...*

"*Just think about it.*"

Yasmeen looks at them and walk away shaking her head. Yasmeen to herself. "*Now she's pursuing him. I wonder who's next.*

Wallace walks over to Mahmoud. "Hey Doc."

"*Hey Mr. Wallace, you were hiding from me yesterday*"

"*No Doc I wouldn't do that. I was been busy, all day.*"

"*Yeah if you say so*"

Mahmoud pauses as Yasmeen walks pass and Mahmoud can't take his eyes off her as she stands at the elevator. He watches her until the elevator doors close. Mahmoud smiles. Wallace interrupts his thoughts.

"Hey Doc, I see you."

Mahmoud Smiles. "What… See me what."

"Doc we'll talk later."

"Ok"

Rebecca finally gets Mahmoud over to her house for dinner. They are sitting at the dinner table drinking wine. Rebecca is wearing a little red low-cut dress that shows off her beast.

"I hope that you like lame chops."

Mahmoud smiles nervously. *"It's ok.*

Rebecca puts her hand on top of Mahmoud's hand. *"Would you relax. I don't bite, unless you what me to."*

Mahmoud Eyes widen. "No… No… No biting!"

"You might like it."

"I like a lot of things."

Rebecca leaning forward to show her breast. *"Oh yeah like what?"*

Mahmoud sips his wine. *"Like this wine for one."*

"I have something better than that wine." Rebecca leans in to kiss Mahmoud, but he pulls her back. I'm sorry did I do something wrong?"

"No not at all. It's getting late, so I should be going."

Rebecca puts her arms around Mahmoud neck. *"Don't go you haven't had your dessert."*

Mahmoud looks in Rebecca eyes. *"Dessert."*

"Yes dessert."

Mahmoud is curious. *"And what are you serving for dessert?"*

Rebecca removes her dress. *"Me!"*

Rebecca kneels in front of Mahmoud and starts to unzip his pants. He pulls her up on her feet. Before she can remove his dick from his pants.

"What are you doing?

"If you don't know I promise that you won't forget.

"Rebecca no."

"No… Come on I just what to taste you in my mouth. It'll be our secret."

Mahmoud push Rebecca away. *"This is not going to happen... No, I am not going to engage in this at all. If I would have known that this is what you had in mind, I wouldn't have agreed to this.*

"Why not?"

Mahmoud is annoyed with Rebecca. *"Are you not in a relationship with doctor Sinclair?"*

Rebecca is furious. "Doctor Sinclair! No, I'm not in a relationship with Aaron Sinclair. Who told you that?"

"It's not important. I should go."

Grabbing Mahmoud's arm. *"No don't go. there is nothing between doctor Sinclair and me. He's in a relationship with Yasmeen.*

"Oh, is he really?"

"No not really but he has a thing for her."

"Don't lie to me."

Rebecca tries to make up a cry. *"I'm sorry, but we are not in a relationship."*

"Thanks for dinner, good night."

"Wait please. Let me explain."

Mahmoud leaves and Rebecca falls to the floor wailing naked. After Rebecca finish crying, she calls Aaron over. Before he can get through the door Rebecca is on her knees with his dick in her mouth.

. *"Damn girl it's like that!"*

As Rebecca takes a mouthful of Aaron big dick into her mouth she starts to think about Mahmoud and how she wishes it was his dick in her mouth instead of Aaron. The more she fantasizes about Mahmoud's fucking her mouth the harder she slurps on Aaron dick.

"Oh yeah baby I want you to cum in my mouth. I want to taste all of you." Yasmeen grab Aaron by the ass as she sucks on his balls. Aaron cum in Rebecca mouth. Aaron bends Rebecca over the couch where he fucks her from behind. Rebecca scream as Aaron goes deep inside of her pussy. Yasmeen runs across Aaron mind, he can see her face looking at him. Rebecca cry out in pain as Aaron fucks her uncontrollably. Aaron stop as Yasmeen face fades away and when he looks down, he sees Rebecca looking back at him. His heart drops as his thoughts goes back to Yasmeen. Aaron longs for Yasmeen her name echoes in his head.

"I have to go."

"What? Why Aaron?"

"Because I do."

Aaron kisses Rebecca and leaves. Rebecca calls Mahmoud but he doesn't answer. After an hour, she cry's herself to sleep thinking about Mahmoud. Aaron is sitting in his car outside of Yasmeen townhouse. He longs to knock on her door as he watches her bedroom light go out. Aaron imagine make love to Yasmeen and kissing her breast as she holds him in her arms. Aaron reminisce about the last time he and Yasmeen kissed and how good she tasted. He runs his finger across his lips. His dick begins to get hard. A car door slams and Aarons thoughts are interrupted. He drives off as his mind wonders back to Yasmeen and how he hurt her. He thinks to himself will he ever get her back. Only time will tell.

Chapter 3

The sun on my face...

It is the next morning Mahmoud and Wallace are talking in the hall. Mahmoud motion for Wallace to come to the end of the hall.

"Wallace, you and I are cool, so I can trust you right?"

"Yes Doc. I mean I know that we haven't known each other that long but I do consider you as a friend and yes you can trust me."

Mahmoud rubs his chin. *"I need to ask you something and I need you to be completely honest with me."*

Wallace shakes his head yes. *"Doc I will always be honest with you."*

"I need you to keep this conversation between us."

"Whatever we talk about will stay between us. No one will ever know. Doc I give you my word on that."

"I just want to know something, and I hope that you can tell me."

Wallace puts his hands into his pocket. *"Ask away."*

Mahmoud hesitates. *"Wallace, is Yasmeen and doctor Sinclair dating?*

"Oh no! No, no, no Yasmeen and doctor Sinclair are not dating, not at all."

"They were dating I'm I correct?"

"No, I wouldn't call it dating. They did go out that was it. It wasn't no more than that. Doctor Sinclair, he did like Yasmeen and he pursued her for some time. They went out, but it didn't last..."

"And why not?"

Wallace bits his lower lip. *"Doc you may or may not have heard, that Yasmeen caught him and Rebecca in bed together, so she broke things off..."*

"*So, he cheated on her?*"

"Yes."

"*How long did they go out?*"

"*About six months or so.*"

"*Was it a serious relationship?*"

"*No not at all. I don't think that they even… you know.*"

No, I don't know."

"*Oh, you know Doc. You know exactly what I'm talking about.*

Joking. "No, I don't tell me."

"*Ok Doc come on now.*"

"*So, is it ok to assume that he and Rebecca are now dating?*"

Wallace searches for an answer. "*You know Doc I don't know. I think that they are just having sex. Doctor Sinclair he gets around so does Rebecca. Doctor Sinclair he really wants Yasmeen but...*

Cutting Wallace off. "She doesn't want him."

"*Yes.*"

"*Wallace, I was just curious.*"

"*Doc I'm curious too.*"

"*Oh, you are, about what?*"

About you. Doc you like Yasmeen don't you?"

Mahmoud scratch his head. "What? Who? You know I have patients to see."

"*Yes, I know. So, are you going to answer the question?*"

Clearing his throat. "*What was the question?*"

"*Doc be honest with me. You have a thing for Yasmeen, don't you?* Mahmoud walks away without answering. *So, is that a yes?*"

"*Have a good day Wallace.*"

"*You have a good day too. I know that's a yes. Doc I see how you look at her.*"

Wallace and Mahmoud both laugh as they walk away. Mahmoud is sitting in his office when Rebecca knocks on his door. She walks in. Mahmoud looks up at her as she stands in front of his desk.

"*Good day Rebecca.*"

"*Are you busy? I really need to talk to you about last night.*"

"*About last night. What about last night?*"

"*Well for one thing's really didn't go according to plan.*"

"What was your plan?"

"I really like you and I had planned on us having a beautiful night."

"What about Doctor Sinclair?"

"There is nothing between us. I've told you that. We are just friends that's it. Besides he and Yasmeen are seeing each other."

"Oh, are they."

"Mahmoud I just want to know where you and I stand."

"You do know that I'm engaged, and I will be getting married within a years' time.

"Yes, I do know that, but we can still have some fun in the meantime."

"Let's not do this. Let's just be friends because anything else will not work."

"How do you know that it will not work if you don't attempt to make it work. I tell you what let's plan a weekend getaway. Just you and me."

"No that's not a good ideal."

"Would you at least think about it. Don't answer right now ok please."

Mahmoud sit back in his chair with a confused look on his face. Yasmeen is walking down the hall to her office when Rosetta walks up behind her.

"Hey good looking."

"Girl… You almost got yourself hurt.

"Yeah right. I missed you lady are we still on for tonight?"

"Yes, we are Rosie unless you have other plans."

"No, I don't have other plans. Are we meeting over at Zada's house?"

"affirmative"

Rosetta walks behind Yasmeen into her office. *"Oh, Yass let me give you the tea about old girl Rebecca."*

Yasmeen sit down at her desk. *"What now?"*

"Well, you know that she is on the prowl after doctor Shashivivek."

"Damn already. What Aaron didn't do for her."

"You know how that slut is."

"Well I've heard, but I didn't think that she was just giving that ass up like free lunch."

"That not all she's giving up. You know yesterday she told me that she was going to have doctor Shashivivek over to her house for dinner. I bet that she sucked his dick."

"I wouldn't put it pass her ass. You know that she'll suck dick's out of a box."

"Aaron must not be all that in bed."

"That I wouldn't know, but from what I heard he was putting it down."

"Are you for real Yass?"

"Girl I said that's what I heard. Anyway, back to Rebecca and Mahmoud. What happened?"

"I don't know yet but I'm going to find out and I will give you the full report at two."

"Yeah you do that."

Yasmeen is going over some paperwork when she hears a knock on the door. Yasmeen looks up at the clock on the wall. *"Who could that be. Come in!"* The door opens and in walks Aaron. Yasmeen is surprised to see him standing before her. Her stomach drops as she rolls her eyes. *"Excuse me but did you get lost? What do you want?"*

"I want you." Aaron closes the door."

I don't think so, and you can leave the door open. There will be no closing of doors around here Aaron."

"I just want to talk to you in private."

"There is nothing that you and I need to talk about in private. So, say what you got to say and get out. I'm busy."

"I've missed you."

"Sorry I can't say the same."

Aaron puts his hand in his pocket. *"So, you didn't miss me not even a little.*

"Nope not at all."

"Well I miss us, and I think about you all of the time. Yasmeen, I still care about you."

Getting annoyed. *"Aaron there is no us and I use to care about you but not anymore. I can't miss something that I never had."*

"Don't say that. Yasmeen, you know that I was yours."

"You were mine? Just who in the hell do you think you're talking to? Aaron, you were mine and I caught you in bed with another woman or did you forget about that? Aaron you have got to be the biggest asshole that I know. You betrayed my trust and now you have the audacity to stand here and insult

my intelligent with your bullshit. Where did you get your gumption, from the bottom of your shoe?"

Aaron gets emotional. *"Yass don't do this to me! Why won't you forgive me?"*

"Oh, I forgive you I just do want to have anything to do with you."

"Damn it Yasmeen. Grabbing Yasmeen by her shoulders. *I need you."*

"Get your hands off me! Don't you ever touch me again!"

"I'm sorry. I just want you back."

"Well I don't want you. You know what Aaron I'm going to say to you the same thing that I said to your girlfriend. I bet that y'all are still fucking."

"She's not my girlfriend."

"But you're fucking her like I said."

"You are Wrong."

"I don't think so."

"Yasmeen…"

"Get out."

"Yasmeen."

"I said get out."

"Ok if that's what you want but I will get you back. Yasmeen Sinclair."

"Don't count on it."

Aaron looks back at Yasmeen as he walks out of her office. Yasmeen put her hand over her face and laughs to herself. Yasmeen thoughts shift as she thinks about Mahmoud and what Rosetta told her. She takes a deep breath and close her eyes. "Gregg, I need you my love." Rosetta and Rebecca are in the hall talking.

"So, did Shashivivek come over?

"Yes, he did. We had a lovely dinner."

"Ok and what happened. Did you'll…?"

"No, we didn't! He blew me off.

Rosetta smiles to herself. "No why?"

"I don't know he… I tried to arouse him, but he said no and left. You know I think that he's playing hard to get."

"You know what he might be. So, what are you going to do?

"Oh, I'm going to get him, he will be mine! I will not give up until I get him, he can't run forever."

"Isn't he engaged?"

"Yeah he mentioned that to me but that means nothing to me, I usually get what I want."

"You don't say."

"Oh, I say."

"You are too much. Look I've got to go. call me later."

Rosetta is on her way back to Yasmeen office when she see her getting on the elevator. *"Hold the elevator!"*

"You had better hurry up, and where are you off to?"

"I was on my way to your office, to tell you about Rebecca and doctor Shashivivek.

"Do I want to hear this?"

"Yes you do, so listen. I told you that she invited Doc to her house for dinner."

"Yes, you did noisy."

"Well anyway… I am not noisy."

"Yes, you are."

"No, I'm not I'm helpful. Anyway, he did come over and she try to fuck him, but he wouldn't give up the dick and he left her ass hot and bothered. Oh, that bitch mad."

"Girl no. I know he let her taste the dick."

"Nope not at all. Not even smell it. Bitch talking about she's going to get him. Yeah right. He doesn't want that shit, that pussy trash."

"Oh, speaking of trash. Aaron came by my office today,"

"Oh really."

"Don't even look at me like that!"

"What did he want?"

"He's on some BS. Talking about I want you back I miss you. Man get out of my face with that mess."

" What did you say?"

"I told him to get out of my office. I don't want him. I just want him to leave me the hell alone."

"Yass, he knows that he fucked up."

"I'm glad that he does."

"So."

"So, what? Rosie please don't even think about it, we're done! I'm in a better place now."

"Does he have a chance.

"Not a snowball chance in hell."

The next day Rebecca goes to Mahmoud's office. He is sitting at his desk. She walks in smiling.

"Hey, I hope that I'm not interrupting you. I just wanted to know have you given any thought about what I asked you."

"No, I haven't. You know Rebecca I have been very busy that was not on my list of things."

"So, you don't want to go away with me for the weekend.?"

"It's not that. I just think that you want more than I'm willing to give you. I'm not looking for a romance relationship. Not right now."

"You are not looking for a romance relationship with me."

"With anybody not just you."

"Sorry that I bothered you. It will not happen again."

"Look Rebecca I'm just not interested in an intimate relationship. Not now ok."

"Some other time right?"

"We'll see."

Rebecca turns and walks out of Mahmoud's office. She is hurt by his responds to her advances. Rebecca wants Mahmoud and she will not stop at nothing to get him into bed. Every sense Rebecca rubbed Mahmoud's dick through his pants. She has fantasizing about him plowing himself into to her waiting pussy. All she needs is one night to make him forget all about his upcoming nuptial to a woman who he has never met. It has been over a month Mahmoud and Yasmeen are still at odds with each other. Aaron is still trying to win Yasmeen back. Yasmeen refuse's all Aaron's advances. She rejecting him with the hope that he will move on and out of her life for good. All the while Aaron and Rebecca's affair continues. Zoe comes to visit Mahmoud. Zoe is a woman that Mahmoud dated for three weeks. When Zoe leaves Rebecca rush into Mahmoud's office she is furious to see another woman coming out of his office.

"So, who was that?"

"Excuse me!"

"Who was that woman? And don't say that she's one of your patients?

"No, she is not my patients not that it's any of your business."

"Well if she's not a patient then who is she? Your girlfriend!"

"If you must know yes, we dated…"

"Yes! Did you say yes? How could you? What about your soon to be wife and you not wanting to be in a relationship?"

Mahmoud is vexed by Rebecca questioning. *"I said yes we dated! I don't owe you're an explanation. I dare you come in my office like that. You work for me and that's it, so what I do in my private life is not any of your concern Rebecca. You have over stepped your boundary. Make this the last time you question me about what I do outside of work. do I make myself clear!*

Rebecca hold back her tears as she forces herself to answer. *"Crystal. Sorry that I over stepped my boundary. But…"* *"No butts! Mahmoud walks over to the door. Make this the last time!"*

Rebecca rushes out of Mahmoud's office in tears. Later that day Mahmoud, Aaron, Jacob, and Maxwell are having a conversation at the nurse's station when Yasmeen walks off the elevator. She hesitates as she walks up to the nurse's station. Seeing Aaron pisses her off and seeing Mahmoud makes her weak.

"Good evening."

"Hello dolling."

Yasmeen rolls her eye. *"Yasmeen will suffice doctor Sinclair."*

"Well hello Yasmeen how have you been? I haven't seen you in days."

"Well you know I try to keep myself busy and out of trouble Maxwell.

"Yes, I know."

"So, how is your wife."

"She's great. She asked about you.

"She did.? Tell her to call me. We need to do lunch or something just us girl."

"I will tell her. You know how she feels about you."

Aaron interrupts. *"You didn't ask how I was doing.*

"That's because I don't care. Asshole."

Wallace walks up. Yasmeen greets him as she passes by. Mahmoud keeps his eyes on her as she walks down the hall. To himself he smiles. When he glimpses up Wallace is staring at him smiling. Mahmoud looks away quickly and rubs his hand across his face. He ignores Wallace as he whispers under his breath. *You like that.*

"So, are we on for golf this weekend?"

Aaron reply. *"Yeah absolutely… Who's picking me up, because I plan on drinking a lot after I kick y'all butts.*

Mahmoud laughs. *"We will see about that, but we can all ride together if that's ok."*

Jacob in agreement. *"That's fine with me.*

Maxwell speaks. *"So, we will see you around one doctor Sinclair*

"Ok doctor Khalidah I'll see you all then."

Anyway, I have to go because some of us do work around here."

Jacob reply's jokingly. *"Who might that be?"*

"The same guy who going to whip y'all butt on tomorrow Me!"

Yasmeen walks back pass the nurses station she doesn't see Mahmoud watching her as she gets on the elevator. As the elevator door's close Mahmoud shakes his head and walks away. The next day Jacob, Maxwell, and Mahmoud arrivers at Aaron's house. They knock on the door for five minutes before he answers the door. When Aaron opens the door, he's wearing a bathrobe.

Maxwell speaks. "Come on man get dressed. *Did you forget that we were coming to pick you up?*

Aaron is speechless. "What… What are y'all doing here?"

Jacob is Taken aback. *"We're supposed to be playing golf today remember."*

Before Aaron can answer Rebecca comes up behind him wearing only a sheet. Not knowing who's at the door. Rebecca, pulls on Aaron bathrobe. *"Come back to bed baby I want…"* Rebecca mouth flies open as she looks at Mahmoud, Jacob, and Maxwell standing at the door. Mahmoud smiles as Rebecca runs back upstairs humiliated. Aaron closes his eye tightly. His heart is beating fast like he just finished running a race. Sweat starts to run down his face. They're all surprised to see Rebecca at Aaron's house with almost nothing on. Jacob looks at Aaron and say's *"I guess it's safe to assume that you will not be playing golf with us today."*

Maxwell also joins, he's being an ass. *"Yeah he already got a hole in one or two."*

They all laugh.

"We see that you are busy, so we'll let you get back to who you were doing."

Jacob agrees with Mahmoud. *"Yeah let's go or we're going to be late.* Joking with Aaron. *Are you coming Aaron? Never mind you did already."*

Aaron is speechless standing at the door as he watch them drive away. Aaron closes the door and rest one hand on the door. He doesn't know what to do. He can't speak his mind is in a million places. He can still see their faces in his mind. Aaron looks at his reflection in the hall mirror. He's shaking he can feel himself getting weak, so he sits down on the floor. He thinks to himself. How can he face them better yet how can he face Yasmeen? Aaron gets up and goes up stairs Rebecca is sitting on the bed in silent. She avoids making eye contact with Aaron who is sitting one the opposite side holding his head.

" Should, I leave?"

Aaron looks at Rebecca. *"I don't care what you do!"*

"You should have told me that they were coming over Aaron."

"No, you should not have come down stairs Rebecca. I don't balm you I balm me. I balm me for continuing this whatever this is with you."

"So, I'm a mistake."

"Yes, you are. We're a mistake!"

"Do you still care about Yasmeen?"

"Yes, I do. I still love her.

"After all this time, you still want her."

"Yes, I do."

"Aaron is she better in bed then me"

"I don't know and thanks to you I never will."

Aaron walks down stair and pour himself a drink. He picks up his cell phone and call Yasmeen. she doesn't answer, so Aaron leaves her a message. Rebecca walks up behind Aaron as he tells Yasmeen that he loves her and how he wants her back because he made a big mistake. And to please call him. Rebecca is hurt when Aaron turns around Rebecca slaps him across the face. He grabs her and pushes her down on to the couch. Rebecca begs Aaron to make love to her. Aaron obliges with animalistic passion. As Aaron eruption with ecstasy he yells out Yasmeen's name. Rebecca pretends not to hear him as she in visions Mahmoud's face stand at the door. Her heart aches as she realizes that she will never have him after the event that transpired today. She holds Aaron tight as her body shakes. In her mind, she calls Mahmoud. As Aaron collapse on top of her. Once again, he yells out Yasmeen's name. Aaron gets up without uttering another word. He retreats upstairs and slams the door. It is the Monday morning meeting.

Aaron enter the conference room talking to Ashton. Who is another doctor. Rebecca looks up at Aaron and smiles as he sits down at the far end of the table. Mahmoud, Brandon, Maxwell, and Jacob walk into the conference room. Rebecca looks at Mahmoud. She quickly looks down at the table. Rebecca can't look at him. She can feel her heart beat speed up in her chest as panic sets in, the instant Mahmoud says good morning as he takes his set at the head of the conference table. Yasmeen walks in she is wearing a yellow fitted dress with white trim and black stiletto. She has her hair pulled back to show off her full gloss lips and her smooth chocolate neck. Aaron and Mahmoud take a long glimpse at her as she takes her seat. Aaron peeps at Yasmeen ass as he thinks about how firm it felt the last time, he cupped it in his hands. He smiles. Yasmeen crosses her long shapely legs as she greets everyone at the table.

Ashton replies to Yasmeen. "Well good morning. So where did you get that dress?"

Yasmeen responds. *"Out of your closet next to the blue one that you like to wear."*

"What?"

Yasmeen smiles. *"You know the Blue dress that you like to wear when you visit the prison on Saturday's.*

Ashton is offended by Yasmeen responds. *"I never…"*

"Yes, you do."

Ashton sit back in his chair and rolls his eyes at Yasmeen. As she wickedly smiles back at him. At the end of the meeting Mahmoud and Yasmeen are still at odds with each other about Yasmeen patient. Mahmoud storms out leaving Yasmeen in the conference room. As she bends down to pick up her brief case from the floor Aaron walk up behind her.

"Nice view."

"Excuse me"

"Just saying that I like what I see.

Yasmeen turns around. *"Well I don't."*

"Did you get my message? Damn you smell good baby girl.

"I saw that you called. I deleted the message."

Aaron stands in front of Yasmeen. *"So, you didn't listen to it?"*

"No, I didn't."

"Why not?'

"*Because I didn't want to hear your bull shit. Now get out of my way Aaron.*"

Aaron grab Yasmeen. "*Yasmeen…*"

Yasmeen push's Aaron away. "*Get your hands off me and get out of my way!*"

Aaron holds onto Yasmeen's arm. "*Not until you listen to me.*" Yasmeen files fall to the floor.

"*Move before I scream!*"

Mahmoud hears the commotion as he walks back into the conference room. He sees Aaron hold Yasmeen by her arm as she try's frantically to get away.

"*What's going on? Get your hands off her!*"

Aaron release Yasmeen arm. "*Oh, everything is ok, right Yasmeen.*" "*No that's not right you jerk! Don't you every put your hands on me again.*"

Aaron walks out. Yasmeen start to pick up her file when Mahmoud reaches down to help her. "*You don't have to. I got it.* Mahmoud looks up at Yasmeen as she sits down in the chair with her hand over her face she's shaking with anger. Mahmoud is infuriated as he looks at Yasmeen.

"*Are you alright? Should I call security?*"

Yasmeen gathers herself. "*No doctor Shashivivek. I'm ok.*"

"*Are you sure?*"

"*Yes, I'm sure. But I do need you to change those orders today thank you.*"

"*Yasmeen are you and doctor Sinclair dating?*"

Yasmeen turns around. "*No not at all! Are you dating Rebecca?*"

"*No…no I'm not!*"

"*Alright the No's has it! Now change the orders and stop asking me ridiculous question.*"

Mahmoud shakes his head and smiles. Rebecca has been avoiding Mahmoud all day. After lunch, she decides to go into his office. He is on his computer when she walks in. Rebecca takes a deep breath. "*Doctor Shashivivek are you busy? If so, I can come back.*"

Mahmoud glance up from his computer. "*No not at all come in.*"

"*Are you sure?*"

"*Yes, I'm sure.*"

"*I just wanted to talk to you.*"

"*Oh, what about?*"

"About Saturday."

"Saturday. What about Saturday?"

"You know me and doctor Sinclair."

Mahmoud push's his hair away from is face. *"Oh yeah. You don't have to talk to me about that. Just as long as it doesn't interfere with you work."*

"Yes, I need to explain…"

"No, you don't."

"Yes, I do. I didn't mean to lie to you. I'm sorry."

"Rebecca, you don't owe me an explanation."

"I feel that I do."

"Don't feel like that because you don't. What you do on your time is your business. It doesn't concern me."

"I guess that's all that I have to say then. So that weekend thing is… "

"Not going to happen, although I'm sure doctor Sinclair would be delighted to go away with you."

Rebecca is disappointed as she walks out of Mahmoud's office. She tells herself that she will get him to understand that he is who she wants not Aaron. It is happy hour at Yasmeen's favorite bar. Zada, Todd, Oscar, Rosetta, and Angelina are already sitting at the table eating and drinking, when Yasmeen walk's in. Yasmeen walks over as she pulls her seat out, she takes a long deep breath. *"Hello everyone, I see that you have ordered me two tequilas on the rocks Oscar. I have had the worst day in months!"*

Angelina rubs Yasmeen hand. *"Oh, what happened sweetie?"*

"Well to start it's Monday! Monday means Monday morning meets and that mean Me and doctor Shashivivek morning brawl. Yasmeen takes her drink from Oscar. *That man makes me crazy. I could just strangle him. He and I are like oil and water we just don't mix.*

Angeline sip her drink. *"Yass is he that bad?"*

Rosette joint in. *"No, he's not."*

"Oh yes he is. He does shit just to fuck with me he's a dick. A very small one at that. They all laugh. *Right Za?"*

"Yass, I think that he pretty nice. I get along with him just fine."

Yasmeen take a sip from her drink. *"Who asked you sunshine? Yasmeen giggles as she mock Zada. He pretty nice."*

"Y'all know how Yasmeen is. She walks in ready to get in somebodies, shit."

Todd chimes in. *"Yes, she does."*

Yasmeen picks her drink up. "*I do not. Forget y'all.*"

"*Yass can be a fire starter and that mouth is spicy all the time.*"

"*Todd, I know that you didn't just throw me…*"

"*Yass, you know that I love you with all my heart, but you have no filter on your mouth.*"

"*I thought you all were my friends. I need to rethink this friendship thing. I've been hoodwinked Oscar.*

"*Come on baby girl we love you but the truth hurts. Oscar hugs Yasmeen and laugh.*"

"*Get off me Oscar. I don't like you and lose my number all of you.*

"*She doesn't, mean that.*"

"*Yes, I do. As a matter of fact, I'm deleting you first Rosie.*"

Rosette takes Yasmeen phone. "*Give me that.*"

"*Anyway, as I was saying before the train took off. After me and doctor Shashivivek nice little disagreement had subsided. In walks Aaron Mr. dumb ass. We had some words. How about this fucker grabs me talking about you are going to listen to me! I was petrified. He was acting like a mad man. I tried to get away from him! I was yelling get off me! By pure luck doctor Shashivivek happened to come back into the conference room and asked what's going on, that's when he let me go.*"

Oscar responds with anger. "*Yasmeen why didn't you call me? I don't like this at all. You know what Yass I don't what to talk about this anymore. We will talk later.*"

Zada calls out to Oscar as he leaves the table. He waves his hand as he continues to walk away.

"*Oscar is pissed Yass. You should have call one of us when that asshole put his hands on you. "Todd looks down at Yasmeen he can see bruises on both of her arms. What the fuck Yasmeen look at your arm!*"

"*It's ok Todd! I'm fine.*"

"*No, you are not fine. This is unexpectable.*"

Angelina hugs Yasmeen. "*Yass this is not right.*"

"*Za I know but…*"

"*There are, no fucking but's.*"

Oscar comes back to the table. Todd shows him Yasmeen arm, which add fuel to the fire. Oscar tells Yasmeen that it's time to go. Oscar try to smile as he bids everyone a good night. Oscar pay's the bar tab and they leave. Two days later Yasmeen is at the nurse's station talking to Cindy and Tia when Mahmoud walks up he overhears them talking.

"So, Ms. Blake you have a date tonight are you ready?"

Cindy butts in and ask who has a date? Tia smiles before she replies *"Yasmeen."*

"It's not a date guys."

"Cindy what do you call it when a man and woman go out for a night on the town."

"Tia mind your business."

"Tia yeah it's a date."

"No, it's not! Stop it you two!"

Mahmoud heart drops from hearing their conversation. His heart pounds as he walks over to Yasmeen.*" Excuse me but may I speak with you Ms. Blake?"*

"Sure. Yasmeen whisper to Tia and Cindy. *What did I do? I just got here."*

"I just wanted to let you know that I did change the orders, but I will need to see a full report before I can do anything more.

"Thank you doctor Shashivivek. Now that wasn't too hard, was it? Just kidding and thank you again. I will get you that report before lunch today..."

Mahmoud rubs his head. "It was difficult, but I managed. I also wanted to ask you were you ok?

"Oh yeah. Yeah I'm good thanks for asking."

"Good. Oh, have fun on your date!"

"It's not a date! What is it with you people!"

The next day Mahmoud is standing at the nurse's station when Yasmeen gets off the elevator. He glances at her before walking around the desk. Cindy greets Yasmeen with Good morning and a big smile. Yasmeen asks. *"What are you smiling for?"* Tia and Zada walk up. *"Hey girl so, how did it go?" "*Zada laughs as she ask, *"Did you get busy or what?"*

Yasmeen put her hand on her head. *"Yeah I got busy getting out of there."*

"Why what happened?"

"Y'all this guy was a total douche bag. The first thing out of his mouth was damn shorty you get a fat ass.

Zada chuckle. *"No he didn't Yass.*

"Yes, he did, but that's not the worst part. He had the audacity to ask me. So, are we going back to your place or mine? I said I don't know where you are going but it will not be with me. Za you should have seen me paying that bill and running out of there.

"No Yass! Did you pay the whole bill?

"No, I paid my part and I was out. Oh, and he was not a gentleman. He failed before we got into the restaurant. He didn't open or hold the door, he didn't pull my chair out! And y'all know I'm a lady. Then he asked me can I kiss you. I was like hell no you may not! I don't know who he thought I was, but he found out quick.

"So, are y'all going out again?"

"Cindy don't' play with me. After last night, I'm not dating anymore. This dating thing is not for Yasmeen.

"Don't give up.

"To late. I'm done Tia."

Mahmoud is sitting at the desk laughing to himself. He's happy to hear that Yasmeen date was a disaster. When Yasmeen gets home, she is about to open her door when Aaron walks up behind her. Yasmeen is shocked to see Aaron. Yasmeen can feel her body starting to tremble with fear.

"What are you doing here? Aaron you need to leave!"

"Not until we talk."

"Aaron there is nothing for us to talk about! Why won't you just leave me alone?

"Oh, there a lot we need to talk about."

"Like what a restraining order?"

"Cute! That's fucking cute Yasmeen! Go ahead with your restraining order."

"I will."

Aaron gets in Yasmeen's face. *"Do it."*

"Aaron leave please.

"I said after we talk. Now open the door.

"No Aaron. We can talk out here."

"Open the damn door Yass!

"Aaron why are you doing this. It's over."

"It's not over Yass!"

"Aaron. Aaron please go home."

"Yasmeen sweetie I just want to talk that s all. Will you please give me that?"

"Will you leave me alone after this?"

"I promise I will, now open the door. I don't want to talk out here. Yasmeen I want to talk without everyone interfering."

Yasmeen hesitates before opening the door her hands are trembling with fear. She doesn't know what Aaron is about to do tears start to roll down her face as she opens the door. Yasmeen walks inside and Aaron follows. Yasmeen sit in a chair as Aaron sits on the sofa.

"Why are you sitting over there? Come sit next to me Yasmeen.

"No, I fine over here Aaron."

"Yasmeen please come over here. Yasmeen gets up and sit on the sofa. *That's better."*

"Aaron please think, about your career."

"My career. Yasmeen, I just want to talk."

"Oh...oh, ok let's talk."

"Yasmeen why?"

"Why what Aaron?'

"Why are you playing this game with me? You know that I want you!"

"Aaron I'm not playing a game with you. Aaron, you cheated on me. I should be asking you why."

"I know and I'm sorry. Can we just try to work this out?"

"Are you still sleeping with her."

"I'm not going to answer that."

"So yes, you are? Aaron get out of my fucking house and don't you ever come back! You do know that I'm seeing someone? Aaron, I have moved on and you should do the same."

"What? You're not seeing anybody!"

"Yes, I am, now get out!"

Aaron grab Yasmeen and pins her down on the sofa. Yasmeen screams for Aaron to stop as he forces Yasmeen to kiss him. Yasmeen fights as Aaron pins both of her hand over her head as he puts his hand under her blouse. Aaron fondles her breast with his one free hand. Yasmeen continues to fight as Aaron bits her breast. Yasmeen Sobbing uncontrollably as she begs Aaron to stop.

"Please don't do this. Please. Trying to push Aaron off her. *So, you're just going to rape me?"*

"No, you're going to give yourself to me. Now kiss me!"

"Aaron please stop!

Aaron unzips his pants. *"Stop fighting and make love to me!"*

Aaron takes his eructated dick out of pant as he forces Yasmeen legs apart. Yasmeen begs for Aaron to stop.

Yasmeen screams. *"Aaron stop please stop! Aaron please you're hurting me! Somebody please help me!"*

"Kiss me!"

Yasmeen turns her head crying. *"No Aaron get off me.* Yasmeen try to free her hands, but Aaron is much too strong. *Aaron, you don't have to do this. I promise not to tell. Please don't do this!"*

"Yasmeen, I love you."

"Is this how you prove your love for me, by raping me Aaron. I hate you! I hate you Aaron! I hate you!"

Aaron looks down at Yasmeen crying. Yasmeen frees her hands of Aaron strong grab around her wrist. She pushes Aaron off her. He falls to the floor. Yasmeen leaps off the sofa to her feet. She falls to the floor as Aaron grabs her by her leg, he crawls back on top of her. Yasmeen manages to bits Aaron hand, he releases her. Yasmeen makes a run for the door, but before she can get the door open Aaron grabs her and throws her back onto the sofa. Yasmeen starts kicking her legs and screaming. Aaron pulls Yasmeen off the sofa and they both fall to the floor.

"You are going to have to kill me before I let you rape me you son-of-a-bitch!"

"Yasmeen stop fighting me!

"Get off me! I hate you, get off me!"

"Don't say that. Yasmeen, I love you."

"You don't love me. You hate me as much as I hate you for you to do this to me!"

Aaron release his hold on Yasmeen. *"Yasmeen I'm sorry. I just want you back. Yasmeen, I know that I've hurt you. God knows that I never meant to Yasmeen I'm so sorry. Forgive me! Forgive me Yasmeen!"*

Yasmeen look up at Aaron with tear screaming down her face. *"Is this how you get me back, by forcing yourself on me? Is this how you show your love for me?"*

"Yasmeen please. I don't know why I did this. I just thought that if I made love to you than you would take me back. It was wrong I know, but I was despite. I can't stand the thought of losing you. I guess that you are going to call the cops and put me in jail right? Yasmeen, I don't care... Here call them." Aaron hands Yasmeen his cell phone. Yasmeen reaches for the phone Aaron pulls it away. He sits down on the floor beside her. They both cry Aaron puts his arms around Yasmeen. She flinches in fear. As Aaron rubs her face.

"Sweetheart you don't have to be afraid of me. I'm not going to hurt you anymore. Can you forgive me one day?"

"I can try. Aaron, you didn't have to do this to me."

Aaron holds Yasmeen face with both of his hands. *"Do you want me to kill myself? Just tell me and I will!"* Aaron pulls out a nine-miller meter from is jacket.

Still Crying Yasmeen shakes her head. *"No Aaron I don't want you to kill yourself. I just want you to leave. Leave my house that's all. I promise not to call anyone. I won't call the police. Just don't hurt me."*

"Kiss me!"

Aaron please."

"Kiss me Yass! Kiss me!"

Yasmeen kisses Aaron. He puts his arms around her and squeeze her tight. Tremble with fear. She can't stop crying.

"I won't tell."

"Do you promise."

"Yes! Yes, I promise!"

"I love you Yass ok. I'm sorry."

Aaron gets up and puts the gun to Yasmeen head, she closes her eyes and takes a deep breath. Yasmeen knows that Aaron is going to kill her, so she starts to pray. As she prays, she hears the door slam. Her body jolts and she open, her eyes to find Aaron gone. Yasmeen gets up and runs to the door locking it as her body quivers with uncontrolled fear. She pulls out her cell phone. she can barely compose herself to dial the number on the phone. Her hands can't stop shaking. Yasmeen can't control her tears as they run down her face.

"Hello! Hello please somebody! "

Voice on the Phone. *"Hello Yasmeen, what's..."*

Todd... Todd please I need you, get here now! Please hurry! Please hurry!

"Yasmeen calm down and tell me what's wrong"

"Todd hurry! God help me!"

"Ok I'm on my way!"

Yasmeen stands with her back to door she cry's in horror as she slides down to the floor. She is terrified that Aaron will come back so she runs to the kitchen and grabs a knife. She sits on the floor in front of the door. Yasmeen is exhausted from fighting with Aaron her body aches, Yasmeen continues crying. Yasmeen falls asleep on the floor. Yasmeen is waken by loud banging on the door. Yasmeen grabs her knife and scramble to her feet. Her heart pounds out of control she's frozen with terror as the banging on the door continues. She fears that Aaron has returned. Tears stat to roll down her face as she stands quietly staring at the door.

"Yasmeen open the door it's me Todd."

Yasmeen drops her knife and runs to open the door. She pulls Todd inside and she locks the door back. Her Blouse and skirt are ripped. Yasmeen grab Todd as her body trembles. Todd holds Yasmeen.

"Yass what's wrong? Talk to me! You are really scaring me. Oh, sweetie please talk to me. I can't help you if you don't talk. Looking Yasmeen over. *Who did this to you?"*

"Todd! Yasmeen voice quivers. *Todd please don't leave me please I'm scared!"*

"Yasmeen I'm not going to leave, just tell what's happened? Do you know who the fuck did this?"

"Aaron…Aaron… Aaron! Todd please don't leave me!"

"Aaron! What did Aaron do?" Todd looks at Yasmeen with tears in his eyes. *"What did he do?"*

"He… He…"

Todd franticly calls Oscar. *"Where are you? You need to get over here now! You really need to hurry Oscar."*

"Why Todd? What happened? Is Yasmeen ok?" *"Just get here. Don't rush be careful but get here like yesterday!"*

Yasmeen starts to tell Todd what happened, before she can finish someone starts beating and trying to open the door Yasmeen starts screaming with fear. *"Oh my God he's back!* In a panic. *Todd he's back!* Todd gets up Yasmeen pull him back down on the sofa. *No! No! No don't open the door it's Aaron! Don't! Don't open the door he's going to kill me! Todd don't open the door!"*

"No, it's not Aaron. It's Oscar."

"No, it's Aaron! Todd don't! I beg you! Please!"

"Todd, Yasmeen it's me Oscar. Let me in!"

"See its Oscar, Yass it's ok."

Oscar rush in. "What going on? Where's Yass?"

"'O' it's bad."

Oscar pushes pass Todd. He runs over to Yasmeen who is sitting on the sofa crying. He kneels in front of her and put his hand on the side of her face. His heart breaks from seeing Yasmeen so helpless. Oscar wipes the tears from Yasmeen's face.

"Tell me what Happened. Tell me everything."

"Aaron... Aaron tried to rape me!"

Oscar's heart drops as Yasmeen tells him all the details.

"It was my fault. I should not have let him in. I just wanted him to leave me alone. It's all my fault."

"It's not your fault ok. I'm going to call the police."

"No Oscar don't! Please don't! No one can know about this!"

"You can't let him get away with this Yasmeen!"

"Oscar please! Oscar, he has a gun!"

Oscar puts his hand on Yasmeen knee. "You have to press charges. Yass, you can't let that bastard get away with this shit! Yass, you have nothing to fear I promise."

"Yass, you said that he had a gun. What if he comes back?"

"He will Todd if I press charges. I can't please."

"Ok Yass I tell you what we will talk about this later, but you are not going to stay here. Todd go get her things. Oscar kisses Yasmeen on her forehead. It's going to be ok."

Yasmeen lays her head on Oscar shoulder. Oscar rubs her back as she cry's. Oscar and Todd take Yasmeen back to their house. Oscar is sitting on the couch with his head down when Todd comes back down stairs and sits beside him

"Is she sleeping?"

"Yes finally. Oscar what are we going to do?"

"I don't know. I really don't know. I'm going to leave it up to her. I just hope that she makes the right decision."

"'O' she will. You know she will. She really needs us. So, let's not pressure her. She has been though a lot."

"I know Todd, I know. Todd at Gregory funeral I promised him that we would always take care of Yasmeen, his queen. Oscar fight to hold back tears. I feel like I have failed him not once but twice. Tears start to run down Oscars face. Todd, I intend on keeping my promise from here on out no matter the cost. Even if it means going to prison. Yasmeen will not be hurt by that no-good son-of-a-bitch again! That's a promise that you can take to the bank!"

Oscar get up and goes up stairs. Oscar is sitting on the edge of his bed crying as he thinks about Yasmeen and all the things that Aaron has imposed upon her. Oscar loves Yasmeen like his own sister. So, when she hurt's he hurt's just the same. The next morning Yasmeen is looking in the mirror at her tear swollen eyes and her buried wrist. She turns the water on and wets her face, hoping that the cold water will take some of the swelling away. Yasmeen dry's her face and removes her bathrobe. She touches her breast she's horrified at what she sees. Her breast is bruised from Aaron. She can still see his finger prints. Yasmeen is infuriated as she put on her blue lace bra. She can feel herself trembling. A tear rolls down her face as Oscar enters her room. Yasmeen wipe her tear and reties her bathrobe.

"Yasmeen where are you off to?"

"Work... I'm off to work."

"To work. Yass are you sure that you should be go in today honey?"

"Yes, I'm sure."

"Why don't you call out just to give yourself sometime."

"'O' I'm going to be fine. I promise."

"You promise."

Todd enters the room. *"Good morning sunshine, and where do you think you're going?"*

"I'm going to work Todd."

"Are you sure Yass?

"Yes...Yes, I'm sure. Now let me get dressed." *"Ok but I'm taking you to work so hurry up. I'm not asking you I'm telling you. So, there is no need to debate.*

"Ok Todd if you insist.

"I do."

Todd drops Yasmeen off at work. As Yasmeen walks into her office she starts to regret being there. Yasmeen puts down her purse then she locks the door. Yasmeen is sitting at her desk with her face in her hands when she hears a knock on the door. Her body shivers with fear. Her mind tells her that its Aaron, so she grabs a pair of scissors from her desk drawer. She hears another knock on the door as the knob jiggles. Yasmeen breath, a sigh of relief when she hears Rosette calling her name. Yasmeen opens the door.

"Why are you sitting in here with the door locked?"

"Because I can."

"It's too early for that Yasmeen. I didn't think that you were here where's your car?"

"The repo man got it."

"Ha, Ha, Ha funny so you got jokes?"

"Yes, I do."

"Yass what's wrong with you? Why are your eyes all swollen and shit mama?

"I didn't get much sleep. I have been up all night."

"Doing who?"

"Doing nobody."

"I thought maybe Aaron came over."

Yasmeen Blood boils. *"What the hell is that supposed to mean?"*

"Yass relax I was just kidding."

"Well don't... Don't joke with me about Aaron coming over to my house. You got me?"

"Ok Yass I didn't mean any harm. I'm sorry.

Yasmeen take a long deep breath. *"Look Rosie I've got a lot of work to do, I'm tired ok, and my head hurts so I'm just going to sit here for a little while alright."*

"Ok but if you need anything you know where I'll be."

"Yeah in my office in the next five minutes

Yelp, that right."

"Oh, where's my Tea?"

"Yass, I got you.

"Rosie, you're slipping."

Yasmeen sits back down at her desk. After lunch Yasmeen is in a meeting with Jacob and Mahmoud. It's not long before Yasmeen and Mahmoud's conversation becomes heated. They can't agree on too much of anything. Mahmoud is stubborn, and Yasmeen is determined to get her way. She has no problem being confrontational if it means getting what she wants. At times, she can be downright combative just long as she wins in the end. Yasmeen makes Mahmoud's blood run like fire through his veins like hot coal. His body aches with unknown passion. It's a passion that he can't explain. It washes over him like a huge wave from his head to his toes. He tries to contain himself from the lust that lurks inside. Yasmeen is like a ghost that haunts his soul from the first day that he saw her. Yasmeen's animosity towards Aaron spills over onto Mahmoud. Yasmeen is filled with rage as she storms out of Jacob's office. Her heart pounds as she fights, back her tears. Yasmeen pasties back and forth in her office. Yasmeen wants to apologize but her pride won't let her, not this time. Three days later Yasmeen has just finished cooking dinner at Oscar and Todd's house. She is about to set the table when Todd and Oscar enter the kitchen.

"So, Yass I know that we haven't revisited the subject of Aaron. I... well we, Todd and I just wanted to know what you planed on doing, or have you thought about it anymore? We were just wondering what you've decided if anything."

"Yes, I have decided what I'm going to do. I'm not going to press any charges! I'm going to kill him." Yasmeen walk's out of the kitchen.

Todd and Oscar look at each other than they both rush out into the dining room after Yasmeen. Oscar takes Yasmeen by her arm and leads her out into the living room.

"Yass honey Put that down. Gently pull Yasmeen down on the couch beside him. *Yasmeen sweetheart. Hum what... What did you say? Did we hear you correctly?"*

"Yes, you heard me right. I'm going to kill him!"

"Yass, I...I. *We don't think that's a good idea. Right Todd."*

Todd speaks under his breath. *"Hmm speak for yourself."*

Oscar clench him teeth. *"Todd!"*

"Yeah right, you can't do that. To himself. *But I can."*

Oscar searching for words. *"Yass. Yasmeen just hypothetically speaking. Let's say that you did kill Aaron. God forbid that it should happen. How would you go about doing it? We just want to know."*

"I'm going to shoot him."

Oscar holds his chest. *"Shoot… shoot him! With what, do you have gun?"*

"Yes, I do have a gun."

"You have a what? Todd fall back. *Oh, my goodness. Yasmeen where in the hell did you get a gun from?"*

"Where do you think? From the gun shop Todd."

"Where is this gun?

"It's in my car, would you two like to see it?"

"Yes, we would like to see it!"

Yasmeen gets up to retrieve the gun from her car. Yasmeen remove the gun from its case. *"Here it is."*

"Give me that. Let me hold that thing, Yass, you cannot have a gun.

"And why not Oscar?"

"Because you can't! Yass this is not the answer. As your friend and legal console. You can't just go kill someone. Not only is it wrong but you can go to prison for a long time. Oscar pleads with Yasmeen. Please Yass let's rethink this. *Yasmeen, we don't want you to do something that you will regret.*

"But he hurt me "O". he tried to rape me. Do you understand where I'm coming from?"

"Yes, we understand, but if you kill him then what? This is not a good decision."

"I don't want him to go to jail. I want to hurt him myself Oscar."

"Well beat his ass! Hell, I'll help you but you can't kill him!"

"You will?

"Hell, yeah I will."

"Me too. I'll hit his ass in the head with this damn vase. Then I…

"You know you are not going to do shit Todd.

"Who? Yes, I will just as soon as you knock his ass out.

"Todd I'll punch him in the face and you kick him in his balls."

"That sounds like a good plan."

"That sounds like you both have lost your minds. I'm going to leave I don't want to hear this premeditated shit, and you miss thang I'm keeping this gun. Yasmeen we will figure something out that will not get us all put behind bars.

"Ok if you say so."

"Oh, I say so! Now come on in here I'm hungry!"

A week later Yasmeen is back at here town house. She is getting dressed to go out to the bar. Yasmeen puts on her red silk body dress it has a low cut in the front, but not too low as to show her breast, but just enough for an innocent peak show. Her dress does an awesome job reveal her beautiful round shapely ass. Yasmeen peep toe stiletto compliments her long chocolate sexy legs. Yasmeen talks to herself while admiring herself in the mirror.

"Well I don't want to toot my own horn, but toot, toot. Damn girl you look good, even if I do say so myself. Yasmeen phone ring. She answers. *Hello Todd."*

"Hey sexy are you dressed?"

Yasmeen licks her full soft lip before applying her lip gloss. *"Yes almost."*

"Well are you riding with us?"

"No, I…I can meet y'all there. Y'all go ahead."

"Are you sure Yass because you know that we have no problem with picking you up."

"No Todd I'll be ok. I will meet you at the bar. I'm getting ready to walk out the door now actually."

"Are you sure Hun?"

"I'm sure dolling."

"Well let me hear you jiggle your keys."

Yasmeen laugh as she pick up her keys. *"Really Todd."*

"Let me hear them."

Jiggling her keys. *"Do you hear them daddy?"*

"Yes. 'O' said to stay on the phone until you get in the car."

"What?"

"Do it or we're on the way to your house!"

"Ok, ok give me a minute."

Yasmeen gets in her car and drives off. When Yasmeen gets to the bar, she sees Rosetta, her husband Wendell, Anne-Marie, and her husband Chase whom she does not like in the least. They are all sitting at the table with Jacob, Maxwell, Brandon, and Mahmoud. When Yasmeen walk in she lock eyes with Mahmoud. She can't take her eyes off him. He looks so handsome with his flowing black wavy hair. In her mind, Yasmeen is saying damn you fine, but before she can finish her lusting over Mahmoud, she sees Aaron sitting next to Rebecca. In that instant, a rush of angry takes hold of her. Yasmeen fights hard to control herself but all she can think about is breaking a bottle over his head. Her eyes lock in on Rosette beckoning her over to the table. The last place Yasmeen want to be is at a table with Aaron. Yasmeen has never told Rosetta about the encounter that she and Aaron had, and she never will. Rosetta call's Yasmeen over. *"Yass come sit with us.*

"I know this bitch is not calling me, oh Yes, the hell she is. This big, headed dumb bitch. I'm just going to pretend not to see her ugly ass."

Rosetta walk's over to Yasmeen. *"Hey, Yass I was trying to get your attention."*

Yasmeen mumbles o herself. "I know bitch, I was trying to ignore your ass… Oh, I'm meeting Oscar, but thanks anyway."

"Oh yeah they are sitting over there."

"Thanks, nice seeing you."

"Oh no you're coming with me."

Yasmeen Pulls away. *"Girl are you drunk? You know that I don't like most of the people at that table."*

"Well I'm at the table."

"And I don't fuck with you either."

"Yass stop playing!"

"Rosie I'm not playing. Pulling her hand back. *Let my hand go shit I can walk hell!"*

Yasmeen walks over to the table with Rosetta. She can feel her blood starting to boil.

"Jacob look who came to hang out with us."

"Hello, it's nice to see you, but I'm actually here to meeting some friends who are over there."

"Oh, come on Yasmeen come have a seat. What are you drinking?"

"Honestly Maxwell I can't, maybe next time."

Todd and Zada walks over to Yasmeen. *Oh, here come my friends now. I should go, have a good night and nice seeing you all."*

"We saw you when you came in and the two-face bitch grabbing you. I said let me go get Yass before I have to slap Rosie fucking face."

As Yasmeen walks away her perfume looms in the air Mahmoud watches her with delight. A smile creep across his lips. Yasmeen looks back over her shoulder she can feel eyes watching her. She smiles to herself. Mahmoud keeps his eyes on Yasmeen until she sits down. Aaron is looking at Mahmoud with evil eyes. Their eye lock and Mahmoud raise one eyebrow as he takes a sip from his glass. Aaron looks away.

"Damn Yasmeen is looking good as hell tonight. Why did you and Yasmeen split up again Aaron?"

"You don't need to know that Brandon! Now if you would excuse me, I need to get some fresh air."

"Hell, I was just asking. What's eating him Maxwell?"

The Waiter walks over to Yasmeen's table and hands her a drink. She tells her that it's from the man at the next table and she point to Maxwell and Jacob with a smile. Yasmeen holds her drink up and thanks them with a silent node. For the rest of the night the waiter continues to bring drinks over.

"Man, I have never drink this much in one night. Who in the hell keep ordering all these drinks? Better yet who in the hell is going to pay for this shit?"

Angelina and Yasmeen reply. *"Not you. According to the waitress our tab has already been paid Josh."*

"Y'all fucking with me right Yass and Angie... Because I'm about to take me a couple of drinks and go to the house.

"We are not playing. Yasmeen looks over at Mahmoud. Our boss paid for everything.

"Hell, I'm going over there and thank them personally Za."

"Oh no you are not! Josh sit your ass down!"

Oscar favorite song comes on. He gets up and take Yasmeen by the hand.

"That's my jam come on Yass and dance with me.

"Get him Yass... Za I love watching Yass dance."

"Me too. Y'all look at 'O' he can't keep up with Yass."

"Come on Todd lets show them how it should be done."

"Come on Angie you want some of this? Let's go."

"Don't hurt him Angie.

"No, I'm going to put it on her watch me Za."

Yasmeen is on the dance floor Mahmoud watches her every move with jealousy. Yasmeen and Oscar dance three more songs before going back to their table exhausted.

"Rosetta Who's that? Is that Yasmeen's Husband?"

Rosetta turns in her seat. "Who Oscar? Oh no he's her best friend. Oscar is more like her big brother. Doc you know that Yasmeen is not married." Mahmoud smiles. *"I was just asking."*

At the end of the night as Yasmeen is driving home, she keeps seeing Mahmoud's face. She smiles to herself. She knows that Mahmoud is engage. So, Yasmeen shakes herself back to reality. She let her fantasy go back out of the window and drives home. When Yasmeen get home, she calls Todd and Oscar to let them know that she made it. Yasmeen is in the shower and her mind goes back to Mahmoud. As the hot water cascades down upon her, she lathers soap all over her body. Yasmeen run's her hands over her chocolate breast. She can feel her nipples getting hard as Mahmoud's face runs through her mind. She imagines Mahmoud touching her all over she can feel him inside of her as she pushes her finger deep inside of her wet pussy. As she reaches her climax, Yasmeen screams with passion. She opens her eye and smiles. The next week Yasmeen is at work getting ready for her Monday morning meeting when Ashton, Rebecca, Brandon, and Jacob walks into the conference room. She looks around for Mahmoud. When Aaron walks through the door. Yasmeen turns away she can feel her heart racing with fear, she sits down as her leg tremors under her. Yasmeen closes her eyes, so she doesn't see Mahmoud walk in. When she opens her eyes, Ashton is staring at her.

"You know Yasmeen I was thinking about you this weekend."

"So that's why my ass was hurting Ashton you had your head up in it."

"Ha, ha. You wish. No, I was thinking why you are always in a depressing sad mood and it clicked. Snapping his fingers. *It was like a light bulb came on."*

"Oh really!"

Ashton looks at Rebecca and wink his eye. *"Yes. I figured out what's wrong with you. I don't know why it hadn't dawned on me before.* Ashton put his elbows on the table. *Yasmeen the reason why you are so angry is because you need some dick."*

"Oh well maybe you should give me one of the ones that you keep in your mouth! You know the ones that you love sucking on. I know that you have some extra ones." Everyone looks in Ashton direction.

"Yasmeen how dare you!"

"Dare me what? Yasmeen looks around the room. Oh, everyone knows about you sucking…"

"I hate you!"

"Why? Is it because I don't have something long to put in your mouth?"

"Yasmeen the thing you say to people is just horrible!"

Yasmeen stands up. *"Well you started it and I finished it, so don't you ever come for me! Now, shell we start this meeting, or do you have more light bulbs going off in your head doctor?"*

At the end of the meeting Yasmeen is gathering her belongs in a rush. One of her files drops to the floor as she's picking up the last of the paper from the file Aaron walks back in the conference room, he closes the door and walks over to Yasmeen. Pure Horror takes over her body as she rises from the floor. Yasmeen backs up as Aaron advances towards her.

"I just wanted to tell you how good you looked the other night."

Yasmeen is frozen with terror. As Aaron grabs her by the shoulder, Yasmeen flash back to the day Aaron attacked her and her terror is replaced with overwhelming angry. Before Aaron can say another word Yasmeen knee him in the groin. Aaron falls to the floor in pain.

"Don't you ever put your hands on me again you bastard!"

Yasmeen exits the conference room leaving Aaron wallowing around on the floor in pain. Yasmeen runs down the hall to the elevator. As the door of the elevator close. The fear she had has escaped and the feeling of relief takes hold of her which cause her to laugh uncontrollably. Mahmoud goes back into the conference room where he finds Aaron on his knees with his hand between his leg in excruciating pain he can't speak.

"What happened? Are you ok doctor Sinclair? Helping Aaron up and leading him to a nearby chair. *I'm going to get some help you just sit here."*

Aaron grab Mahmoud hand. *"No…No, I'll be ok. Feeling nauseous. Please just give me the trash can."*

Mahmoud Puts the trash can down in front of Aaron. *"What's wrong? Doctor Sinclair you don't looks so good."*

Breathing hard in pain. *"Thanks, but I'll be fine just give me a minute."*

"Are you sure?"

Aaron shakes his head yes just as Maxwell enters the room.

Is everything ok in here?"

"I'm not sure. I just found him on the floor, he says that he's ok."

Aaron holds his groin trying to stand. *"Look I'm just fine. I just need some fresh air."*

Mahmoud and Maxwell hold Aaron under his arms and leads his outside. Aaron fills his lungs with air as he thinks, back to Yasmeen kneeing him and the pain that he's feeling. In his head, all he can think is what the fuck. Aaron assure Mahmoud and Maxwell that he's ok and they leave him outside. When Yasmeen gets back to her office, she calls Oscar and Todd on three-way to tell them what she did.

"I did it!"

"You did what?"

"I got that fucker! I kneed him right in his no-good balls!"

"Girl who are you talking about?

"Aaron Todd, I got his ass. How about he came after me again."

"Are you kidding me?

"No, I'm serious Oscar! He came after me and I let him have it to. Y'all should have seen his ass on the floor rolling around in pain and I left his ass! I didn't look back!"

"Good for you. Yass, how are you? Are you ok?

"Oh yes I'm over joyed."

"Good but I'm going to meet you at your house when you get off just in case Mr. Aaron pays you another visit."

"Yeah you are right. I think that I should come to your job instead of going straight home Todd.

"Yeah I like that idea better and I'll see you both when I get off.

Yasmeen hangs up with Todd And Oscar. It has been over a week, Yasmeen has just got back from her Social works convention in New York. She is feeling refreshed when she returns to work. Yasmeen hasn't seen or heard from Aaron since the incident and she has been too busy to think about Mahmoud. Yasmeen is eager to move on with her life. Yasmeen and Rosetta are in the hospital auditorium preparing for the nine o'clock lecture that she has put together from her New York trip.

"So, when did you get back Yass?"

"Late Friday night."

"And why didn't you call me this weekend."

"Because I was too tied plus, I was working on this presentation and to be honest I wasn't thinking about calling anyone when I got back."

"I bet you called Todd, Oscar, Angie, and Za."

"Well actually they call me, and they came over. You could've done the same. So, don't bring that attitude."

"I don't have an attitude Yass it's just that you and I don't communicate anymore, and I miss that."

"I was getting things ready for today Rosie ok. Besides we're going out together this weekend right. Unless you made other plans. Yasmeen thinks to herself. *What is this heifer up to?"*

"Oh no I haven't made any plans. I can't wait for all of us to get together, it's been so long since we all hung out."

"Yes, it has been a long time. Anyway, lets finish up in here before everyone starts showing up."

Yasmeen and Rosetta finish setting up. At eight-forty- five people start entering the auditorium. Yasmeen is on stage setting up her laptop when Mahmoud, Maxwell, Brandon, Ashton, Chase, and Aaron walks in. They are engaged in their conversation when Mahmoud and Aaron simultaneously look towards the stage and they see Yasmeen stand there with her head down. she is wearing a long sleeve silk blue shirt and black slacks that show off her muscular frame. Her hair is pulled back into a bun. Aaron's heart drops when he sees Yasmeen. He still cares for her and wishes that he could kiss her lip. Aaron looks away as he thinks how much he hates himself for what he did to her. When Yasmeen looks up to adjust her glasses, she locks eyes with Mahmoud as he takes his seat in front of the stage. She is standing at the podium looking down at the laptop as she smiles to herself. She's happy to see Mahmoud with his sexy self. When Yasmeen looks back up, she spots Rebecca, Anne-Marie, Zada, and Tia walking in. Rebecca and Anne-Marie both sit behind Mahmoud and Aaron. Yasmeen walks from behind the podium to the edge of the stage as she puts on her microphone head-set. Rosetta stands beside Yasmeen as she starts talking.

"Good morning everyone. My name is Yasmeen Blake I am the head Manager of social work here at the hospital and this is my assistant Rosette

Copper. We're delighted to see your smiling faces here this morning… We have some excellent information to share with you. I know that you will enjoy this lecture and we promise to make this as painless as possible. I just ask that you follow along with me and not read head because you will get confused if you do. So, keep up with me and please hold all question until the end. I will speak slowly, and I will explain everything as I go."

Yasmeen walks back to the podium she has been talking for three minutes when Rebecca raises her hand to ask a question. Yasmeen can feel her blood boiling she looks at Rebecca. Yasmeen pauses in annoyance, that Rebecca interrupt her.

"Yes, I'm looking at page six and it states…"

Yasmeen interrupts Rebecca. *"You're on the wrong page. Go back to page two and try to keep up with me. Also, if you look up here at my screen it also shows the page number."* Using her pointer

Yasmeen continues talking. After ten-minute Rebecca interrupts her lecture again. Yasmeen is annoyed by her disrespectful action which she tries to ignore for as long as she can before she explodes in anger.

"Can you collaborate more on the next page; paragraph four, I think. Searching her paper. *Yeah paragraph four."*

Yasmeen to herself. *"This bitch is playing with me right. Yasmeen calm down.* To Rebecca. *Yes, I can when I get to that page and not a second before. If you can't follow along with me maybe you should just listen. Because I see that following directions is not one your attributes.. Again, I ask that all question be held until the end. You may take notes."*

"Oh, I have many attributes."

Yasmeen trying to compose herself. *"If you say so.* To Rosetta. *That's two. One more."*

Jacob. Maxwell, Aaron, Ashton, and Mahmoud look back at Rebecca as she smiles with delight. They all shake their heads in disbelief of her behavior. Yasmeen goes back to her lecture Mahmoud is vexed and he is disappointed with Rebecca. Before Mahmoud can tell her to stop talking, she interrupts Yasmeen's once more. This time Yasmeen is outraged. Rebecca looks at Anne-Marie and smiles. "Excuse me…Yasmeen is beyond heated. *"No, you need to leave.* Calling security. *Security can you please escort this young lady out of here."*

Two security officers walk over to Rebecca.

"What? Are you being serious right now?"

"Yes I am. I want her out of here now.

Brandon to Ashton. *"It's about time. Yasmeen should've been put her out."*

"I know that I would've. She's just rude."

At the end of the lecture Yasmeen apologizes and thank everyone for their participation. When Mahmoud gets back to his office Rebecca is waiting on him.

"I don't know why...

"Your behavior was unacceptable. You were obnoxious. I'm beyond disappointed in you. Rebecca, not only did you embarrass yourself. You embarrassed me and all my colleagues. You will apologize to everyone. Now get out of my office."

Rebecca runs out of Mahmoud's office in tears. Yasmeen is in her office talking to Zada, Tia, and Rosetta. She is livid. She tries to calm herself down by pacing around the room.

"Yass calm down. I know that you are furious, but don't let that bitch get to you."

"I'm just so...Searching for words. Za I can just..."

"Yass don't even give her the satisfaction. Now you held your own. You were very professional when you put that ho out. I was so proud of you girl."

"Za I wanted to strangle that chick. I was about five seconds from jumping my ass off that stage and on her monkey ass!"

"I know you were Yass, but I'm glad that you didn't. Za did you see Yass. She was boss as hell! Mimicking Yasmeen. *Yass said security escort this young lady out of here. I almost cried. I said look at my girl."*

"Tia you know what.? Both of you are silly. Rosetta tell your little friend that she struck out today."

"She's not my friend."

There's a knock at the door. *"Oh yes she is. Let me get that. I hope this is Aaron so that I can get in his ass too! Yasmeen answers the door with attitude. Who is it?"*

When Yasmeen opens the door, she's surprised to see Anne-Marie standing there.

"What do you want."

"I just wanted apologize for today and I wanted you to know that I didn't have anything to do with that. Yasmeen, I didn't know...

Oh, I saw her wink at you. It doesn't matter! Pointing at Rosetta and Anne-Marie *You two can go talk about this and tell that bitch that I said when she crosses me again, I don't care where we're at I'm going to kick her fucking teeth in! The both of you can tell your little friend that she wrote her last check and I'm going to cash in on her flat ass!"*

Anne-Marie looking down at the floor. *"Yasmeen, I'm sorry. I know that you and I are no longer friend, but I would never disrespect you like that. You may not believe me Yasmeen, but I am truly sorry, and I did enjoy your lecture."*

"Yeah thanks."

Anne-Marie leave, and Yasmeen sits down at her desk. She scratches her head. *"I have to let this mess go before I do something foolish Za."*

"I think that will be best Yass. It's over and that bitch didn't stop your show. Hell, if anything she made you shine."

"She did, didn't she. Especially when security put her dumb ass out. Za she was like really you going to just put me out. That bitch looked at Aaron like you not going to help me. Aaron looked at her ass and turned his head like bitch bye."

"Yass, she sure did."

"Yass for real Rebecca is not my friend. I'm serious. You got me over here thinking hard."

"About what?"

"About Rebecca and I being friends."

"Well you and her, do talk."

"Yes, but we are not friends. Yass, I just be getting information out of her ass. That's all."

"Ok Rosie I'm done with this ok. Let's move on. Thank you for your outstanding work today.

"Yass thank you, so are we good?

"Girl we good. so, stop beating yourself up over nothing. Ok now give me a hug and let's get some work done."

As they all exit her office. Yasmeen is going over her report when someone knocks on her door. Yasmeen looks up at the clock.

"Now what? Answering with attitude. *Come in! This better not be somebody with some BS."*

Yasmeen puts her report down when she sees Jacob walk into her office, she doesn't know what to think. So, she immediately puts her guard up.

"Hey Ms. Blake. May I come in."

"I don't know that depends on why you're here."

"Just wanted to talk to you."

"About."

"About this morning. May I sit down?

"Yes, you may doctor Baldwin."

"Well first let me start by saying that you did a fabulous job today, I am proud of you."

"Well thank you! Now what did you want to talk about?"

"Ok so you want to get straight to the point.'

That's, the only way to be right."

Jacob takes a deep breath before he speaks. The last thing he wants to do is quarrel with Yasmeen, so he chooses his words. "Yasmeen, I need to ask you something very important." Yasmeen look confused as she speaks. "Ok ask away."

"Yasmeen are you and Doctor Sinclair still seeing each other.

"What? No and why are you asking me that."

"Are you sure?"

"Well if I was still seeing Doctor Sinclair, I think that I would know that. Is there a point to this question?"

"I think so." "Ok what is it?"

"Yasmeen, I want to disclose something with you. But first I need to know are you and Doctor…"

"I said no! We stopped dating well over two months ago. Look we went out for six months that's it. We never slept together. We kissed, we touched, and we broke up end of story."

"Ok that's a little more than I expected."

"Doctor Baldwin do you want to tell me something or not. Why are you so into me and Doctor Sinclair?"

"Yasmeen this is between you and me. About a month in a half ago I went over to Doctor Sinclair's house and Rebecca was there, she came to the door half dressed. I assume well I know that they had been intimate. Yasmeen, I didn't know if you knew about them or if you found out and that's why…"

"No Doctor Baldwin the incident today had nothing to do with me and Aaron Sinclair. To be honest I don't know what this whole thing was about. No, I didn't know for sure that Rebecca and Aaron were still sleeping together, but I kind of figured that they were. I really don't care."

"What you knew, and you still went out with him?"

"No! What kind of freak do you think I am?"

"Hell, you said that you knew. I was about to say."

"Say what? Don't you even play with me like that!"

"Ok. But you knew?"

"Yes. That's way we broke up. I caught them in bed together, and it was over for me."

"Yasmeen what were they doing?

Yasmeen is dumbfounded by Jacobs question. *"They were playing leap frog. What in the hell do you think they were doing? They were fucking, having sex, doing the nasty. What's wrong with you. You know what they were doing. The same thing that you and your wife be going!"*

Jacob laughs widely. *"No, I mean how? Like…"*

"He was fucking her up the ass!"

Jacob eyes widen. *"What? Up the ass!"*

Yasmeen is render speechless. *"Get out of my office. I can't with you. Listen he had his penis in her vagina. Do you need me to draw you a picture?"*

"No, I got it."

"Are you sure doc?

"Totally. So, you are ok with them…?"

"Yes, I'm just fine just as long as they leave me alone. I don't care. And this little stunt that she pulled today was crazy I don't know why she did it, but she did."

"I don't know myself, but you handled it well. Well I've got to get back to my patients… Oh, Yasmeen let's keep this between us."

"No, I going to tell everybody that you don't know what fucking is."

"Stop it Yasmeen. I do know what fucking is."

"What is it?"

"Have a nice day Ms. Blake."

Yasmeen sit at her desk as she reflects on what Jacob just disclose with her. Yasmeen knows that what she and Aaron had been long over, she struggles with why Rebecca suddenly is out to get her. Did Aaron tell her something or is she a crazy bitch. Yasmeen doesn't know what her problem is, but Yasmeen is sure of one thing she can and will help her solve it. Yasmeen has just got home she is about to get underdressed when her cell phone rings. It's Oscar, he is calling to check up on her. They are in the middle of their conversation when the doorbell rings. Yasmeen's mind starts to race as she wonders who could be at the door. She runs to door and look through the peep hole. Yasmeen is alarmed to see Rebecca on the other side of the door. Yasmeen tells Oscar that he's not going to believe who's at the door. He guesses that its Aaron and he informs her not to open the door. Yasmeen quickly corrected him by telling him its Rebecca. Yasmeen can't imagine what she wants better yet how did she know where Yasmeen lived. Yasmeen doesn't know but she is about to find out. Yasmeen opens the door angrily. *"What in the hell are you doing at my home and how did you know where I live?"*

Rebecca responses with a smartass answer. *"Now is that anyway to answer your door? And for your information I followed you home."*

Rebecca smile which infuriates Yasmeen. Yasmeen thinks to herself that this bitch has lost her fucking mind! Yasmeen is about to close the door as Rebecca put her foot in the door and pushes the door back open on Yasmeen. *"No, you owe me an apology and I'm not leaving until I get it. Yasmeen your actions today were inexcusable and not to mention rude.*

Something inside of Yasmeen snapped and uncontrolled anger takes over her like a category five hurricane on the inside. Yasmeen puts her cell phone up to her ear. She tells Oscar. *"You need to come and get me out of jail because I'm getting ready to beat the life out of this white bitch!"*

Yasmeen tosses her cell phone to the floor as she grabs Rebecca by her hair and pulls her through the door. *"I got your apology bitch!"* Yasmeen punches Rebecca in the face and she falls to floor. Yasmeen straddle Rebecca. She puts her hands around her neck and starts choking her. Yasmeen pulling Rebecca up by her hair and slapping her back to the floor. *"I told your ass not to confront me again didn't I. Your ass thought that I was playing with you. I'm going to show that I'm nothing to play with!"*

Rebecca tries to get away. Yasmeen puts her foot on her back and she falls on her face. Yasmeen pulling Rebecca back to her. *"Where do you think that you are going? Get your ass back here and get this apology!"*

Oscar, Todd, and Zada rushes into Yasmeen townhouse where she and Rebecca are still fighting. Yasmeen is sitting on top of Rebecca banging her head on the floor. Todd and Oscar pull Yasmeen off Rebecca. Zada helps Rebecca to her feet. *"Rebecca what in the hell is wrong with you?"* Yasmeen gets away from Todd and Oscar she runs over and punches Rebecca in the mouth. *"This bitch followed me talking about I own her an apology!"*

Oscar and Todd pull Yasmeen into the kitchen as Zada pushes Rebecca out of the door with her mouth bleeding. *"Girl you better get your ass out of here and don't come back."*

Rebecca runs to her car crying she speeds out of Yasmeen's driveway. Oscar and Todd still has Yasmeen in the kitchen trying to get her to calm down. Zada has never seen Yasmeen so exploitive. As Yasmeen starts to calm down, she realizes what she has done. *"Oscar, I know that I'm going to jail."* Oscar assures her that she's not and that everything is going to be ok.

Rebecca drives like a mad woman down the road. She arrives at Aarons house her hair is all out of place. Her face and lip are swollen, and her eyes are puffy from crying. She runs to Aaron door where she rings the doorbell and knocks on the door franticly. When Aaron opens the door, he's not happy to see her at all. His shirt is unbuttoned as Rebecca falls into his arm. She tells him that she needs to come inside and that she just left Yasmeen's house. Aaron can't believe that Rebecca went to Yasmeen's house. Aaron is furious *"Why would you do something so stupid? You know what you deserve everything that you got!"*

"Aaron who here with you?"

"That not any of your business"

Rebecca tries to push her away in, but Aaron pushes her back out. She begs Aaron to let her in, but before she can tell him about her fight with Yasmeen. A tall light skin woman comes to the door wearing Aarons shirt and nothing else she kisses Aaron on the mouth and pulls him back inside. Rebecca is hurt she feels betrayed by Aaron. She thinks how he could do this to her. Before she can ask who, the woman is Aaron tells her that she need to leave, and he slams the door close in her face. Rebecca doesn't know what to do not wanting to leave Rebecca sits in her car outside of Aaron house for an hour before she drives away.

It's Monday morning Yasmeen walks into the conference room, Brandon and Jacob walks in behind her. Before Yasmeen can take her set, Brandon says to Jacob *"You better be careful what you ask today because Yasmeen will have you kicked out."* He laughs as Yasmeen turns to him. *"Don't start with me today Brandon, with your, stank ass breath. Doctor Baldwin y'all supposed to be his friend. Why don't you tell him that his breath smells like shit? Everybody talking about you behind your back but I'm going to say it to your face. Your breath stank you need to go get your insides checked."* Before Brandon can tell Yasmeen that he was just joking she walks away. Jacob pull Brandon off to the side. The meeting is almost over when Rebecca walks in. she is wearing shades and a lot of make-up. Aaron and Rebecca stare at each other no one is willing to speak on what happened. Rebecca apologies for being late as she sits down. Ashton whippers to her. *"Girl what happened to you? It looks like you got your ass beat or are you into some freaky shit!* After the meeting Yasmeen is walking down the hall when Aaron runs up behind her. Not wanting to get into an altercation with Yasmeen he tells her that he only wants to know what happened. Yasmeen gets defensive as she tells him that he had better keep his bitch in check and away for her house. Yasmeen tells Aaron that Rebecca followed her home. Aaron is outrage he apologies which only make Yasmeen angry. Aaron wants to hold her, but he knows what Yasmeen's capable of doing, so he rejects touching her without her permission. Rebecca is standing at the end of the hall watching Aaron and Yasmeen talking. Just seeing them together hurts her all over again. Should she tell Yasmeen about the other woman or let her find out on her own? For the past two weeks now, Rebecca has been calling Aaron, but he has yet to return or answer her phone calls. At night, Rebecca has been riding pass Aaron's house and sitting in his driveway waiting on him to come home. Most nights Aaron don't come home at all. In Rebecca's heart, she knows that he is back with Yasmeen and he played her like a fool. In her mind, she knows that Aaron and Yasmeen are fucking in his bed, in his BMW, in some hotel, or at Yasmeen townhouse. The one place that she dares go. Why would Yasmeen take him back? Just to get back at her. To hurt her like Aaron did her. How could she have been so blind not to see this coming. Rebecca starts to cry as she thinks to herself. I've lost Mahmoud I can't loss Aaron too. Rebecca puts her hands inside of her panties and touches herself as she thinks about Aaron licking Yasmeen pussy. She images Yasmeen legs around Aaron neck. As he eats her out. She can hear Yasmeen calling Aaron's name as she climaxes in his mouth. How could Aaron be so cruel?

Rebecca can feel Aaron big dick inside of her. Soon Rebecca finds herself back at Aaron's house. When she gets there, she sees Aaron, but he is not alone. She can see that he's with a woman, but who is she? Is it Yasmeen? She watch's them as they enter Aarons house holding hands. Rebecca feels as if her heart has just gotten ripped out of her chest. The next day Rebecca see's Yasmeen walking down the hall and it's not long before Aaron appears. Rebecca knows that they were together, and she can feel it in her gut. Her stomach turns, and it sickens her. Rebecca walks up behind Aaron and pulls him to the end of the hall. She asks him why he haven't returned any of her calls. Aaron smiles "Because I've been busy." Rebecca explodes with anger as she blurts out. *"With who Yasmeen?"* Aaron stops and looks at Rebecca in disbelief. As he replies to her ridiculous question. *"Are you out of your mind?"* Aaron walks away from Rebecca as Yasmeen, Mahmoud, and Jacob walks back down the hall. Yasmeen walks pass without speaking. Rebecca wonders is Yasmeen mad or does she not care? When Aaron gets off work, he drives straight home. He has been bothered by what Rebecca said about him and Yasmeen. He is curious to know has Rebecca heard something? Could Yasmeen really want him back? Aaron needs to know so he drives over to Rebecca's house, with the hope that what he believes is true. When Aaron arrives at Rebecca's house she is not alone. She and her friend Rachel are drinking vodka on the rocks. Rachel is a tall medium built, dark blond hair woman with three kids. She's Rebecca's next-door neighbor. When Rebecca opens the door, she utterly surprised to see Aaron standing there. she invites him in. Rebecca offers Aaron a drink as he sits down across from Rachel. *"Here have, a drink with us."* As Aaron pours himself a drink, he's asks Rebecca *"Why did you asked about me about Yasmeen?"* Like Aaron Rebecca is just curious. Aaron hopes of getting Yasmeen back are crushed. But Rebecca don't care all she wants is Aaron no matter the cost. Just long as he's with her and not Yasmeen Blake. Soon Aaron forgets all about Yasmeen for the time being, when Rebecca starts kissing him on the neck. He whippers for her to stop because her friend is watching. Rebecca looks back at Rachel and smile as she tells Aaron oh, she likes to watch. Aaron finds Rebecca response interrogating, so he asks if maybe her friend would like to participate. Before long Rebecca and Rachel leads Aaron upstairs to Rebecca's bedroom. Aaron smiles with delight. All Rebecca can think about as she pushes Aaron back on her bed is Yasmeen sitting at home waiting for

Aaron. She smiles. Rachel removes Aarons pants she can't wait to taste his dick. As she puts Aaron dick into her mouth Rebecca joins in soon, they are both giving Aaron head. Rebecca pushes Aaron legs up and puts his balls into her mouth. Aaron can't control himself as both Rebecca and Rachel spreads his butt cheeks open and lick his asshole. Rachel climbs in top of Aaron as Rebecca put his dick inside of her. Rebecca will do anything to keep Aaron. As Aaron Fucks Rachel Rebecca licks her pussy. She wants to taste her juices. Rebecca push her finger up Rachel ass while Aaron fucks her from behind. Rachel screams make Rebecca jealous because Aaron has yet to fuck her. Rebecca pushing Aaron off Rachel. "*This dick is mine.*" Rebecca, push Aaron backdown on the bed, she and Rachel starts giving him head once again. Aaron cry's out in ecstasy. Aaron is about to reach his climax, when Rebecca gets on top of him. She screams as she feels Aaron inside of her, she begs Aaron to fuck her up the ass. Aaron pushes her down on the bed and pushes his wet dick in her ass. Rebecca almost passes out from the pain of Aaron big dick in her ass as he pounds her from behind, cum runs down Rebecca thigh. Aaron looks at Rachel smiling as he tells her to lick Rebecca's Pussy. Aaron watches as Rebecca sits on Rachel face. She licks Rebecca's pussy. Aaron gets in front of Rachel and starts fucking Rebecca while she licks Rachel pussy juices. Aaron gets up. Rebecca pulls him back. "*where are you going? We're not done yet.*" Aaron smiles as he gets dressed. "*I've got to go. You two bitches are nasty. But thanks for the fuck session. It was nice meeting you what's your name?*"

Rebecca replies in disbelief. "*Her name is Rachel. So, I guess you are going over to Yasmeen after fucking us both. I wonder what she will say if she knew?*"

Aaron delight erupts in anger as he walks over to the bed. "*I don't know. Why don't you go over and ask her! Rebecca, you think that Yasmeen and I are back together. You are so wrong. I would not be here if I had Yasmeen back. Remember we fucked that up along, time ago. Now why don't you go back to licking your friend's pussy!*"

Aaron walks out of Rebecca bedroom angry. She runs after him apologizing. Aaron drives away furious. Rebecca looks in the mirror at herself she can't put her mind around what she had just done. All for a man just to have him walk out on her. In Rebecca's heart, she knows that she will do anything Aaron what's just to get and keep him happy. Even if that mean's having a three some.

Chapter 4

Better days are coming, so just let go and let God...

It's Friday the last day of the week Yasmeen has just returned from lunch with Zada and Tia. As they are walking across the parking lot, they see Mahmoud hugging Zoe beside his black Jaguar. Seeing this make Yasmeen heart pound with disappointment. Yasmeen can't Explain the emotion that she's feeling. She fights hard to ignore her unwanted feelings as she walks pass Mahmoud and Zoe. Mahmoud is shocked to see Yasmeen he watches her until she is out of his sight. Zada And Tia both frowns. They assume that Zoe is Mahmoud's girlfriend. Tia say out loud. *"I guess he's not faithful either with his fine ass. I know that's not his fiancé with her big face. I guess pussy is pussy no matter where you get it. Right Yass."*

Yasmeen laughs as she replies to Tia not to put her in it. All the while her heart aches. Yasmeen part ways with Zada and Tia. Yasmeen is back in her office thinking about Mahmoud and the lady the she saw him with. Who is this woman? Is she Mahmoud's friend? Yasmeen ponds over the fact that Mahmoud had a new love interest, but why is she worried about what he does he's not her problem. Never was and will never be. Yasmeen must let go of whatever feelings that she has for Mahmoud, a man who she obviously hates. Yasmeen tells herself that she had no business catching feeling for a man who she barely knows, moreover for a man who has the same trendies as Aaron. That is to sleep with anything with a hole between their leg or face. Like Aaron Mahmoud is full of shit and can't be trusted. Yasmeen reminds herself that workplace relationships are now off limits. She will not be hurt again. As Yasmeen ruminates, she starts to feel foolish for even lusting over Mahmoud no matter how good he looks. Yasmeen promises that it won't happen again. As Yasmeen exits her office she runs into Maxwell, Mahmoud, and Aaron coming out of Jacob's office. Maxwell stops her and ask will she be coming to the bar after work. Yasmeen has no desire to share any space with Aaron or Mahmoud, so she smiles as she tells Maxwell that she has a date and she will not be at the bar. She walks away in a haste to keep Maxwell from interrogative her more about this so call date. As Yasmeen disappears down the hall Aaron heart sinks to his stomach. He can feel anger setting in as he tries to smile once he catches Mahmoud looking at him. In Aaron's mind, he thinks why is Yasmeen doing this to him? Aaron knows but he cannot face the truth that Yasmeen has moved on. Aaron still cares a lot for Yasmeen, but he knows that the shit that he did to her and continues to do he will never get her back. That doesn't mean that he will stop trying because one day he will make love to Yasmeen and they together will enjoy it. It had been a long weekend. It's the Monday morning meeting and Yasmeen has not arrived yet. Jacob looks around as Yasmeen enters the conference room singing Bruno Mars *"That's what I Like. Sex by the fire at night. Silk sheets and diamonds all white. Lucky for you, that's what I like, that's what I like."* Yasmeen is in a cheerful mood. Something or someone has Yasmeen walking on air and Brandon can't wait to bust her bubble. He looks at Yasmeen and states not only are you last but you are singing to. Yasmeen stops singing. *"Last I'm not. Yes, I'm in a delightful mood and not even you and rain on it!* Yasmeen pulls some tissue out of her purse. *This is for you, corpse mouth."*

Yasmeen starts back sing. Ashton ask Yasmeen did she get some this weekend. Yasmeen tries to ignore him as best she can but after asking her two more time she answers. *"Well not as much as you got from your boyfriend."* At the end of the meeting Yasmeen is about to walk out of the conference room when Aaron stops her. He asks if he could have a word with her. Yasmeen knows that his question has nothing to do with patients she tells him no and walks out. Mahmoud and Jacob watch Aaron as he exits irritated by Yasmeen response. Jacob and Mahmoud are standing in the hall when a delivery of flowers comes for Yasmeen. At the time same a handsome man walks up to the receptionist's desk and ask for Yasmeen. Mahmoud turns to see the man standing before him. Mahmoud refuses to answer. Yasmeen walks around the Corner just as Aaron walks up. Jacob points to Yasmeen. When Yasmeen sees the tall handsome man, she runs over to him and wipes her arms around his neck and kisses him on the mouth. *I see that you got the flowers.* He smiles at Yasmeen with even white teeth, hazel brown eyes, and smooth brown skin. Yasmeen turns around to see the most beautiful arrangement of flowers. Tears start to form in her eyes as she holds the man tight. Together they walk out holding hands. Mahmoud's face is flushed with anger. Who is this man? Aaron dashes off to find Rosetta. He demands that Rosetta tell him who the man is, but she don't know. Aaron is over taken by rage he knows that Rosetta is lying. Aaron rush pass Mahmoud and Jacob without saying a word. Aaron's on the hunt to find Zada because if anybody knows who this man is it's Zada. To Aaron's surprise Zada is out to lunch. At the end of the day everybody is talking about this sexy man who has Yasmeen walking on clouds. It is ten o'clock at night when Aaron drives over to Yasmeen's house only to see the same gray Tesla from earlier parked in Yasmeen's driveway. He's hurt to see the lights off in her house. His heart aches because he knows that whoever this guy is, he's staying the night with Yasmeen. Aaron calls Yasmeen phone and it goes to voice mail without ringing. Aaron images this man making love to Yasmeen as he grips her ass and she calls out his name. Aaron knows that Yasmeen is only fucking this bastard because she's mad at him. She will do anything to hurt him. Sad to say she succeeded. How could she be so cruel. Aaron sit's outside of Yasmeen house until three in the morning. When Aaron gets to work, he is infuriated to find out that Yasmeen called out of work for the rest of the week. Aaron drives back to Yasmeen house only to see this man putting Yasmeen's suitcase's in his trunk and them driving away. Aaron begs Zada to tell him who this man is, but she won't tell him anything. After a week Yasmeen comes back to work with a big smile. Everybody wants to know about her new man. but she's not talking. Yes Zada, Todd, Oscar, and Angelina knows who he is but they're not talking. Yasmeen goes into Jacobs office for a briefing she is surprised to see Maxwell and Mahmoud. Jacob tells Yasmeen that she will be going to a convention with them for three days and that he's happy to see her back. Maxwell cannot hold his question back any longer. *"Yasmeen who was the tall gentlemen?"* Yasmeen smile, and she starts to cry tears of joy. As she tells them that he's her baby brother. He came home from the military for a week and that she hasn't seen him in over two years. He surprised her. Mahmoud is relieved but happy for Yasmeen at the same time. When Yasmeen gets back to her office Aaron is standing at the door waiting for her. Yasmeen is more than shocked to see him. "What in the hell does he want?" Yasmeen stops when she gets to her door. *"Aaron what do you want?"* Aaron looks at Yasmeen he is beside himself. The only thing that he wants to know is who in the hell did she spend a week with, when he couldn't even get her to stay the night. Aaron steps away from Yasmeen. *"I'm happy to see that you are back. Where did you go?"* Yasmeen is in no mood to play a million question with Aaron. *"Why do you need to know?"*

"I just want to know."

"Well I'm not telling you. Now if you don't mind, I have a lot of work to do Aaron."

Aaron is hurt by Yasmeen blunt responds. *"Well who was he?"*

Yasmeen smile. *"And you don't need to know that either."*

Yasmeen walks into her office and slams the door behind her. Aaron walks away hurt and furious. After two weeks Yasmeen is completely over Aaron and Mahmoud. But things between her and Mahmoud are still the same. They can't agree on anything. Everyday her dislike for him grows stronger. She can still feel the lust that she tries desperately to hind. Yasmeen has just finished talking with one of her patients when Ashton knocks on her office door. Yasmeen looks up to see Ashton standing in her door she rolls her eyes and starts back typing.

"Well hello to you too. May I enter?"

"No!"

"Well thank you. Yes, I would like to sit down."

"Ashton what in the hell do you want? Why are you here?"

"Well I came here to see you."

"For what? No wait! Don't answer that just get out."

"Yasmeen why don't you like me?"

"You don't like you!"

"You are so mean Yasmeen."

"Thanks now leave. Go back into your little hole."

Ashton looks at Yasmeen and rolls his eyes as he sinks deeper into the chair.

Ashton smiles. *"This is really a nice chair. Where did you get it?"*

"Out of your ass!"

"Yasmeen the things that you say." Yasmeen can feel herself starting to loss her cool with Ashton. *"If I get up from this desk, I'm going to kick your ass Ashton. I'm not playing with you!"*

"Why are you so violent. I just want to talk to you damn."

Yasmeen get's up. *"Who do you think you're talking to."*

"Will you please sit down! I just want to talk."

"About what man!"

"I just wanted to know why you are always and I do mean always use gay reference when you talk to me."

"For the same reason, you always talk shit to me. Because I can."

I don't always talk shit to you." "Yes, you do. Now you can just go suck a dick and leave me alone."* Ashton gets upset. *"See that's what I'm talking about, nobody can talk to you!"*

Yasmeen is getting irritated with Ashton. She's trying to figure out why is he in her office trying to do an intervention. It takes, everything in her not kick him in the nuts. Maybe if she ignores him then he will disappear. When she looks up Ashton is still looking at her. Yasmeen sits back in her chair.

"Ashton what do you want?" "Yasmeen do you really think that I'm gay?"*

"Now you and I both know that you like man. Doctor who do you think you're fooling? Not me."

"I'm not gay!"

"The hell you say. Boy-stop."

"Stop what?"

"Your bullshit lies."

Ashton looks away before he asks her how did she know was it that obvious? Ashton is not ashamed of his sexuality but at the same time he likes his privacy.

"How did you know Yasmeen?"

"Because I can see. What are you still in the closet?"

"No, but I am a doctor. You know when people find out they may not want…"

"Want what you to treat them. That some BS You are who you are and if somebody don't like it to hell they can go. Ashton be you the only person you know how to be."

"So, do you like me?"

"*Look Ashton I don't have anything against gay people, but I don't like you.*"

"*Bullshit Yasmeen yes you do.*"

"*No, I don't.*"

"*Fuck you Yasmeen.*"

"*You wish.*"

Ashton rolls his eyes as he and Yasmeen laughs. This is the first time that he and Yasmeen have ever had a conversation.

"*You know Yasmeen you have a good heart. Really you do.*"

"*Now that you know you can get out.*"

"*I'm trying to be serious here, so can you stop playing?*"

"Ashton what do you want. Just spit it out!"

"Ok Yasmeen I saw you out last weekend."

"So, do you want a cookie. Hell, I saw you to."

"*Yasmeen really? No… Anyway I have seen you out with these two guys…*"

"*Stop it right there. I know what you're going to say. Yes, they are gay and no they are not together.*

"*Good now do you think that you can introduce me to the them?*"

Yasmeen lets a laugh so loud that it scares Ashton.

"*I knew that you wanted something with your hot ass.*"

"*Yasmeen, you are insane.*"

Yasmeen and Ashton continue to talk and joke with each other. They find out that they have a lot in common and there is a chance for them to develop a friendship. After Ashton leaves Zada and Yasmeen are walking down the hall together when Rosetta comes up behind them. Before she can ask about the mystery man. Yasmeen cuts her off.

"*Don't ask. That was my brother.*"

Rosetta is surprised, she smiles as she tries to make small talk. Later that day Aaron is in his office. He has been calling Yasmeen all day and she has been ignoring his call. Which infuriates him, because he wants to know who this man is. As Aaron put his cell phone back into his pocket Rebecca enters his office. When she sees Aaron puts his phone away. She becomes enraged. She knows that he is talking to another woman. She approaches Aaron.

"*Was that your little girlfriend?*"

"*What?*"

"*You Heard me. Was that your girlfriend?*"

"Was who my girlfriend?"

"On the phone."

"My phone my business. I don't have to explain anything to you."

"Oh, but you do Doctor Sinclair."

Hearing this tone from Rebecca only escalates Aaron anger. He walks over to Rebecca.

"Let me make something clear to you so that you want make this mistake again coming to my office questioning me. Rebecca, you mean nothing to me now and you never will."

"How can you say that after what I did for you!"

"Did for me! You didn't do a damn thing for me! You must, be out of your fucking mind."

"Oh, so you forgot about Rachel?"

"Rachel! Are you talking about your friend?"

"Yes, my friend the one you fucked."

"The one we fucked. The one who sat on your face, Rachel."

"Whatever I did it for you."

"No, you did it for yourself. I never asked you or your friend to do anything."

"Well it was your suggestion."

"I suggested it! Rebecca, I came over to ask you a question you and your little friend decided to suck me off."

"Oh yeah you wanted to ask about your precious Yasmeen. I know that you are still seeing her."

"You don't know shit."

"I know that you were not home last night because I came by your house."

"What you came by my house? Why?"

"To see you. Guess you had to go get Yasmeen's new man's left overs."

Aaron doesn't know what to think when he hears Rebecca imply that Yasmeen has a new man. All Aaron feels is anger.

"If I were back with Yasmeen, I would be with her now not standing here wasting my time with you. Do you think that if I were back with Yasmeen, I would be fucking with somebody like you Rebecca? Are you obsessed with Yasmeen?"

Rebecca looks away as Aaron smiles.

"Yes, you want Yasmeen, don't you? You want to lick her sweet chocolate pussy, don't you? I bet you fantasize about you with your head between her legs. You're a nasty girl. I'll lick her pussy before you do."

"Fuck you Aaron. I have no desire to be with Yasmeen. I only what you."

"Well I don't want you. So, stop coming by my house unless you have your friend, I like the way she fucks."

Rebecca becomes livid. Her anger heightens as she rushes over to Aaron and slaps him in the face. Aaron pushes her down on to the chair. Rebecca knows that Aaron is going to kiss her. As she Waites her heart races and she can feel her pussy getting wet. She longs for Aaron big dick as he stands in front of her.

"Rebecca get the fuck out of my office!"

Rebecca is stunned when she hears Aaron response to her.

"What?"

"I said get out of my office before I call security. Get your ass out of my office and don't come back!"

Rebecca's body surges with anger as she runs out of Aarons office almost in tears. Aaron pulls his cellphone out of his pocket and call Yasmeen. this time she answers and Aaron heart plunge to his feet when he hears Yasmeen voice. Aaron has a loss of words. He can't remember what he wanted to say. So, he tells Yasmeen that he misses her and that he loves her. Yasmeen hangs up the phone without saying a word. It's Monday morning and Yasmeen has just gotten back from a two week long medical convention in Dallas Texas with Jacob, Maxwell, Brandon, Mahmoud, and Rebecca. For the first time in months Mahmud and Yasmeen agree to disagree in a civilized manor. Yasmeen even let Mahmoud pay for her lunch. But it's Monday anything can happen because Yasmeen is Yasmeen to say the least. When Yasmeen walks into the conference room she can feel Rebecca's, eyes watching her like a hawk. She can feel her animosity in the air. Yasmeen wonders can it be that she's mad because Mahmoud avoided her, and she couldn't get laid even if she set her pussy on the sidewalk men would just step over it. Or could it be that Yasmeen's ass looks good from the back and side and like Rebecca Aarons dirty ass is watching too. Yasmeen drops her pin on purpose as she bends over to pick it up, she smiles to herself. The thought enters her mind. Yasmeen Blake, you are one bad bitch. As she takes her seat Rebecca is still watching her with envy. Yasmeen continues to smile with evil intent. Ashton can read Yasmeen's bad behavior before he speaks.

"So, Yasmeen is all that you back there?"

"Yes, it is Ashton. Why do you ask? Did yours get worn out sweetie? I've told you to keep them men off your back."

"Yasmeen see you didn't have to go there."

"I bet you told him that too."

"Yasmeen, I will talk to you later miss thang. You make me sick."

"love you too."

After the meeting Yasmeen gets up to walk out as she passes by Mahmoud who can't take his eyes off her. He's not looking at her ass. He mesmerized by her walk. Yasmeen walks with such grace and confidence. Mahmoud sees Yasmeen as the most beautiful woman that he has ever seen. She is strong minded and can be intimidating at times. But she hides a secret that Mahmoud wants to uncover. As Yasmeen walks out Maxwell calls out to her. She turns around Mahmoud looks away.

"Yasmeen, I just wanted to remind you of my cookout this weekend. You will be, there right?"

"Wouldn't miss it."

As Yasmeen waits for the elevator, she sees Wallace. Yasmeen walks over to him.

"Good morning Wallace. How are you?"

"Oh, Good morning Ms. Blake. I'm blessed how about you?"

"You know I'm blessed and highly favored. So, did you get the position?"

"Well no I didn't."

"Why not you are more than qualified."

"I know, he gave it to the new guy."

"That's some bull. Don't you worry God has a better plan for you, but that supervisor of yours he's going to get what's coming to him, you mark my word. Don't give up, hang in there ok."

"I will and thank you. Ms. Blake, you really made my day."

Yasmeen shakes Wallace hand as she gets on the elevator. Mahmoud walks over to Wallace and ask him about the position. He's disappointed, as he and Wallace walk down the hall Wallace turns to Mahmoud.

"Hey, Doc, you know Ms. Blake she is really a care lady."

"Oh, is she?"

"Yes, and I'm sure that you know that to. You know she really made me feel better about not getting that position. So, Doc have you asked her out yet?"

Mahmoud stops and looks dumbfounded by Wallace's question. He's rendered speechless. Mahmoud doesn't know what to say.

"What are you talking about?"

"You and Ms. Blake. Doc I know that you have a thing for her. Between me and you, I think that you should ask her out."

"You do know that I'm engaged right, besides me and Ms. Blake are just coworkers that's it."

"Doc this me! You're a man just like me, I know that you're engaged but you want that woman and don't tell me that you don't."

"You know what I was going to ask you to have lunch with me, but I've changed my mind."

"Come on Doc don't be like that."

Wallace and Mahmoud laugh as they walk to the end of the hall. It's the weekend of Maxwell's cookout. Everyone is there. Everyone but Yasmeen. Maxwell and Jacob ask Rosetta where she is. Rosetta has no idea she has been calling Yasmeen, but she has been unable to get her on the phone. Zoe walks in, she hugs Mahmoud and Maxwell. Rebecca is outraged to see her. *"Where did this plastic bitch come from and what does Mahmoud see in her?"* Just as Rebecca is about to walk over to Mahmoud in walks Yasmeen with Oscar and Todd. She has her hair pined to one side. She is wearing a knee length white sun dress with red rose all over it. The dress hugs all her curves with her backless white heels. Yasmeen flashes her beautiful smile that reveals her even white teeth. Rebecca takes a deep breath as she looks over at Aaron who has stopped eating just to gawk at Yasmeen. Yasmeen walks pass Rebecca over to Maxwell and his wife Saidah who admires Yasmeen. Yasmeen hugs and kisses Saidah on her cheek.

"Yasmeen I'm so happy to see you. You are breath taking as always."

"Oh, thank you. You know that I would not have missed this for the world. You two are my favorite people."

"Oh, and it's good to see you both Oscar and Todd it's been a while. You two have been hiding from me."

Both Todd and Oscar hugs Saidah. *"No Saidah you know that last Wednesday I had meetings all day and Oscar was in court."*

"I know but I missed you. I had to eat alone."

Maxwell interrupts. *"Oh, Yasmeen I don't believe that you've met Zoe."*
"No, I don't believe that I have."

Yasmeen reaches out to shake Zoe hand as she introduces herself. Yasmeen has seen Zoe with Mahmoud, so she knows who she is or supposed to be. For now, she's going to play along.

Zoe admire Yasmeen as she shakes her hand. *"Hi I'm Zoe. Please forgive me for staring but you are breath taking Yasmeen you're so beautiful."*
"Well think you and it nice to meet you."

Rebecca intrudes on Zoe and Yasmeen conversation just as Yasmeen is about to introduce Zoe to Todd and Oscar. *"So, Yasmeen I see that you have met Zoe Mahmoud's girlfriend."*
"No, I'm not his girlfriend we're friends! By the way who are you?"

"Oh, I'm Rebecca Mahmoud and I we work very closely together. Forgive me but I thought that you and Mahmoud were a couple. I have seen you at his office a time or two."

"What's your point? Rebecca if you have a question please ask and don't assume ok dear."

Yasmeen see that things are about to get ugly. But to herself she thanks Rebecca for getting the information that she wanted and for bring an asshole. *"Way to go bitch*!" Yasmeen intervenes. *"So, Zoe do you drink. because we do."*
"Yes, I do"
"Well would you like to join us at the bar?"
"Yes, I would because it's getting crowded over here."

Yasmeen, Todd, Zoe, Oscar, and Saidah walk over and join Zada and Tia at the bar. Mahmoud is enraged with Rebecca. The last thing he wanted was for Yasmeen to think that Zoe was his girlfriend. Rebecca tries to apologize to Mahmoud. As he and Maxwell walk away. Rebecca smiles because now that she knows just who Zoe is, Mahmoud is now fair game again, now she just need to get rid of her once and for all! Maxwell knows that Mahmoud is crossed so he tries to get answers.
"What was that all about?"
"I don't know but I will find out. Rebecca is just intrusive."
"I'll say. Maybe she wants you."
"Maxwell don't push me."

All Mahmoud can see is Yasmeen's face. The more that he thinks about what Rebecca did the angrier he gets. For the past hour Yasmeen has been talking to one of Maxwell's guess. He has been occupying all of Yasmeen's time. No one has been able to get him away from her. Mahmoud is about to go crazy watching this man whisper in Yasmeen ear. Yasmeen finally gets away Mahmoud heads over to the bar.

"So, Yasmeen are you enjoying yourself?"

"Yes I am. How about you?"

"Oh yes I am, I wanted to tell you that you look great!"

"Well thank you."

"Well I better let you get back to your boyfriend."

"Yeah and you better get back to your girlfriend, I know that she's looking for you!"

"I don't have a girlfriend."

"And I don't have a boyfriend. I'm a grown woman so if you want to give me somebody, I suggest that you give me a man not a boy doctor Shashivivek!"

"I will remember that."

"You do that. Better yet write it down!"

"Oh, Yasmeen for the record Zoe is not my girlfriend, I too am a grown man and I date women not girls! So, when I get a woman, I'll let you know so you won't have to guess!"

"Oh, I don't guess or assume, you're engaged right? Hopefully she's a woman. Oh, and by the way men don't play childish games. Being a man is not based on how many women you get, it's based on the one you keep."

"What is that supposed to mean?"

"You're a doctor figure it out!"

Yasmeen takes a sip from her drink and walks away from Mahmoud smiling. Mahmoud runs his hand across his face and smiles as he tells himself you are the woman that I will keep. At the end of the night Mahmoud asks Yasmeen if she need a man to walk her to her car.

Yasmeen smiles as she replies jokingly. "Yes, I do. Would you happen to know one?"

"Yasmeen may I walk you to your car?"

"Why. Where is your friend Zoe? That's who you should be walking to their car."

"Well I think that she's back there with her friend."

"So, I assume that she's waiting on you."

"No, she's not waiting on me. Yasmeen, she and I are friends. Didn't you tell me not to assume?"

"You're right, but I can manage on my own thanks anyway."

"Well too late we're at your car."

"Yes, we are. would you look at that."

"Good night Yasmeen. Drive safe."

"I will do that."

Mahmoud closes Yasmeen car door. "Oh, did you tell your boyfriend good night?"

"No, you go tell him for me when you go find your girlfriend!"

Yasmeen laughs as she pulls off. Todd and Oscar follow her. Mahmoud stands in the drive way and watch's Yasmeen as she drives out of sight. Aaron sits in his car watching Mahmoud. He thinks to himself "Is this asshole after his girl or is he just being nice?" Aaron knows that Mahmoud is engaged. Aaron wants to confronting Mahmoud but what would he say? Aaron decides that he will just observe him before he goes after Mahmoud, besides he doesn't want to piss Yasmeen off more than what she is. Aaron tells himself. *"I'll just chill for now."* It is Tuesday morning Aaron has been agonizing for the past two days over Mahmoud and the fact that he might be interested in Yasmeen. He can't ask Yasmeen because it may cause a fight. He can't ask Mahmoud because he might be wrong and he's not willing to risk Mahmoud's friendship over his stupidity and jealousy. Aaron wants to let this idea that he has stuck in his head go but he can't. When Aaron sees Wallace, he can't help but ask because if anybody knows if Mahmoud has a thing for Yasmeen it would be Wallace because they talk a lot. Aaron calls Wallace to the back of the hall. *"Wallace can I ask you something and can you keep it between you and me?*

"Yes, sure doctor Sinclair what is it?"

"Look Wallace I know that you and doctor Shashivivek are pretty close. I see you two conversating just about every day and I'm quite sure that you two share some secrets."

Wallace look confused he's not sure what Aaron is trying to imply. Wallace puts him hands down by his side as he responds to Aaron's question. *"Well we talk just like I talk to everyone else."*

"I know that, but I just wanted to know has he mentioned anything to you about Yasmeen?"

"Mentioned anything like what?"

"Like him wanting to date her."

Wallace can't believe his ears. Why is Aaron asking him about Yasmeen and Mahmoud? Did something happen? Wallace wonders has Mahmoud finally confessed his feeling for Yasmeen? If so, why hasn't Mahmoud told him?

"No doctor Shashivivek never said anything to me about him having feelings for Ms. Blake. As far as I know he thinks that you and Ms. Blake are dating."

Wallace tries to keep his lie and facial expression straight. Wallace knows just how Mahmoud feels about Yasmeen, but he will never tell Aaron. *"Doctor Sinclair I'm not sure about this but I think that doctor Shashivivek is seeing somebody and he and Yasmeen they don't get along at all. I don't know why you would think that.*

"Well Yasmeen and I we are no longer seeing each other. Things just didn't work out."

Wallace thinks to himself. *"Yes, I know what happened you cheated with your lying ass."* He pretends not to know. *Oh, I didn't know that."*

"Yeah, look Wallace can you forget that I asked you about this. I should have known better. I'm just over thinking things that I shouldn't."

"I understand."

"Thanks Wallace. Oh, keep this between us don't tell anybody about what I asked you please."

"Don't worry I won't."

Soon as Aaron walks away Wallace runs to find Mahmoud. Rebecca is sitting at her desk. She is feeling good about herself after the cookout. She knows that Mahmoud is pissed but he'll get over it. In her mind Rebecca thinks that she did him a favor. She finally got Zoe to confess that she and Mahmoud are no more than friends. Maybe fuck friends but friends. Now how will she get Mahmoud to see that Zoe is nothing but a bitch and with her is where he needs to be. Mahmoud enters his office Rebecca goes in behind him.

"Doctor Shashivivek I just wanted to apologize to you about this weekend. I was out of line and I should not have said anything and I'm sorry."

Mahmoud turns to look at Rebecca, he's not angry, he's disgusted by her apology. *"Rebecca, you could have asked me about Zoe and I would have told you that yes we dated very briefly. We parted ways and now we are only friends. I'm disillusioned that you took it a pond yourself to confront her in the mist of doctor Khalidah guest. I know that you are aware that I am engaged, and your actions were uncalled for. I don't know what game you're playing but keep me out of it! Unlike you and doctor Sinclair Zoe and I don't have an intimate relationship now you can stop your little snooping. I've told you that what I do on my time is none of your business. I've told you this once before, don't make me tell you again because the next time won't be pleasant at all."*

"Mahmoud I'm sorry."

"Yes, I've heard you say that but are you really."

"Yes I am. Mahmoud I just want you to see that I am a good person just give me a chance to prove it to you."

"Prove what to me? I can never be with you."

"Why not?"

"Because I'm not attacked to you in that way."

"You could be if you tried."

"No Rebecca I couldn't."

"Why is it because of Aaron? If so, I'll let him go."

"Are you insane? Rebecca listen to yourself. You're no good for me, the things that you do are inappropriate. Rebecca if I were interested in you, you lied you were dishonest."

"Look I know that I hurt you."

"Hurt me! You didn't hurt me I could careless! Why would I be hurt? There's nothing between us and there never will be."

"Why?

"Because I don't want a relationship on that level with you Rebecca so stop trying or I will be forced to make a report. Your advances are unwanted. Now leave my office!"

Rebecca rushes out of Mahmoud's office in tears. It's not long before Wallace knocks on Mahmoud's door. Mahmoud thinks that it's Rebecca, so he hesitates before he say's come in. Mahmoud is surprised to see Wallace walk in.

"Well hello Wallace how may I help you?

"Hey doctor Shashivivek, can we talk.

"Well of course. Sit down and tell me what's on your mind."

"Well Doc between you and I doctor Sinclair approached me in the hall. He asked me if you and Ms. Blake had something going on."

"And what did you tell him?"

"I told him no!"

"Good, but you should have told him yes."

"What? Why would I tell him yes?"

"Because!"

Wallace eyes widens as he smiles. *"Because you do. I knew it Doc!"*

Mahmud smiles.*" What did you know?"*

"That you have the hots for Ms. Blake."

"No." "Yes. You can tell yourself that, but you can't fool me. I know better. Now what happened this weekend?"

"Nothing."

"No...no something happened."

"Wallace, I just walked her to her car like a gentleman, that's all."

"And!"

"And what? We talked that's it."

"About."

"Nothing important. Just Rebecca making an ass out of herself. I guess Aaron saw us."

"So, you didn't tell her that you..."

"I didn't tell her anything."

"You need to make your move before it's too late that's all I have to say."

"What move?"

Wallace looks at Mahmoud with one eyebrow raised. Then he walks out. Mahmoud knows just what Wallace is talking about but how can he tell Yasmeen how he feels about her when she hates his guts. For now, he will keep his feeling to himself and hope that they will subside. It's going to be a challenge because every time Mahmoud sees Yasmeen the deeper his feeling for her gets. Mahmoud find himself thinking about Yasmeen late at night. He longs to kiss he lips both sets. Will Mahmoud ever get the chance to please Yasmeen? He asks himself before Maxwell knocks on his door ending Mahmoud's daydream..

Chapter 5

Let the cards fall where they may and blow your heart away...

After a week Rebecca is still avoiding Mahmoud. She tries to have little to no contact with Mahmoud as possible until he cools off. Rebecca will stop at nothing to get Mahmoud. In time, he will have her anyway he wants, but as of now she has, to wait until Mahmoud comes around. Rebecca reminds herself that she took Aaron from Yasmeen and she will take Mahmoud from Zoe and his fiancé but for now Aaron will have to do. Rebecca has had a long day and she needs to talk to somebody. After work Rebecca decides to go over to her neighbor Rachal's house for a much-needed drink and some girl time. It has been a long time since Rebecca had Rachal in her bed she misses the taste for Rachal's pussy juice. Rebecca wants to feel Rachel long fingers inside her as she cum on her face. When Rebecca arrives at Rachal house she's about to knocks on the door, but the door is half open, so Rebecca lets herself in. As Rebecca enters, she can her Rachel screaming which makes Rebecca excided. Her pussy starts to throb as she thinks about Rachal and her husband fucking. Rebecca wants to get in on the fun. Rebecca makes her way to the back bedroom. Rebecca pushes the door open. Rebecca stands in the door paralyzed. Her heart feels like it exploded as she watches in horror Aaron and Rachal fucking. Rebecca takes her cellphone out to record them. *You two mother fuckers. Aaron how could you. Rachal I thought that you were my friend.* " Aaron jumps up just as Rachal son walks in. *"Come on in kids and look at your bitch of a mother in bed with another man who's not your daddy."* Rachal is mortified as she sees her kids standing in the doorway looking at her. With tears rolling down her face Rachal yells for her kids to get out, Rebecca is still recording.

"Rebecca how can you be so cruel? Get out of my house!"

"Oh, I'll get out as soon as I send this to your husband bitch."

"Rebecca please don't! Think about my kids!"

"Why should I think about your kids? You didn't, and Aaron you're going to pay for this you son-of-a-bitch!"

Rachal Yells for Aaron to do something.

Aaron reaches for his pants as Rachal kids looks at her crying, Rebecca pushes them into the room. *"Come on in kids ask your mother what's she doing? Rachal I bet your husband would love to know what you're up to so why don't I just call him!"*

Rachal begs Rebecca but it is too late, she can hear her husband voice coming from the phone. Aaron rushes to get dress.

Rebecca turning around. *"Oh, and by the way I sent him the video, both of you can go to hell!"*

Rebecca runs out the door crying. Rachal screams for Aaron to get out before her husband comes. Aaron rushes pass Rachel's kids who are standing in the door sobbing uncontrollably. Rebecca sprints to her house where she collapses to the floor weeping. This can't be happening to her why? There's a knock at the door it's Aaron.

"Rebecca open this fucking door!"

"Leave me the hell alone Aaron! Get away from my fucking door!"

"Not until you let me in."

"No Aaron no!"

Aaron continues to beat on the door, but Rebecca refuse to let him in. As she sits on the floor crying, she thinks about how Yasmeen must have felt the day she walked in on her and Aaron. Rebecca's heart breaks, because she knows that she will go back to Aaron one day. Rebecca cellphone rings its Rachel. Rebecca smiles as she hears Rachel's husband yelling in the back ground. *"Rebecca, how could you?"*

"Easy bitch you fucked my man without my permission. I hope your husband leaves you! Pay back's a bitch!"

Rebecca hangs up the phone and wipe her tears away, she calls Aaron, because being alone is not an option. Losing a friend is better than losing Aaron. Four days have passed it is now Friday. Aaron is in the lobby at the hospital he's waiting for Mahmoud and Maxwell so that they can attend a staff lunching. When he sees Yasmeen coming towards him. Aaron still has feeling for Yasmeen and he hopes that she will forgive him one day soon. The closer Yasmeen gets the faster Aaron heart beats. He wonders if she has heard the latest news about him and Rebecca. Aaron steps in front of Yasmeen with caution.

"Good day pretty lady."

"Hey Aaron! Bye Aaron! Get of my way Aaron!"

"I'm just saying hey Yasmeen that's all."

"Hey. Now move!"

"Yasmeen, I really miss you. Do you think that we could go out as friends?"

"I really don't."

"Why not?"

"Because I don't trust you!"

"I know and I'm sorry. Will you at least let me try to win your trust back please?"

"Aaron I've got to be somewhere will you move please!"

Yasmeen is trying hard not to knee Aaron in his junk if it wasn't for all the visitors walking around, she would. Yasmeen will never go out with Aaron again but to get him out of her face she will play along. Besides she has about a minute to bullshit around.

"Ok Aaron you can take me out to dinner."

"Really Yasmeen? When?"

"How about tonight."

"Ok tonight it is. Where would you like to go?"

Yasmeen smiles. *"I'll call you."*

"Ok, ok call me."

Yasmeen walks away smiling as she says to herself. *"That asshole should know that I'm not going anywhere with him. Who in the hell does he think I am? I'll call him alright."*

Aaron walks away feeling like he just won the jackpot. Aaron can't wait to see Yasmeen. Aaron walks into the dining hall where the lunching will being held. It's early and Aaron is the first person to arrive. He doesn't see Rebecca coming in behind him because he is too busy thinking about Yasmeen and his mind is not on anything but taking Yasmeen out. Rebecca grabs Aaron by his arm interrupting his daydream.

"So, Aaron why haven't you returned my calls?"

Aaron pulls away. *"Rebecca!"*

"Yes Rebecca. Why haven't you called me?

"Because I didn't want to!"

"Aaron don't do this to me."

"Rebecca, you did this to yourself!"

"I did this! Are you out of your mind? You and Rachel did this to me!"

"Rebecca this is not the time nor is this the place for us to have this conversion!"

"If not now when?"

"Look Rebecca you choose to make your little video and send it to Rachel's husband like a little girl and for what? To get back at me, that was childish!"

"No, I'll tell you what was childish! For you to go behind my back and fucking my friend!"

"Go behind your back! Who in the hell are you?"

"Apparently I'm not shit to you!"

"Look will you just leave me alone!"

"I will when you tell me how long the two of you have been going behind my back fucking."

"Why? Will that make you happy?"

"No but at least I will know Aaron! Tell me did you and Rachel continue seeing each other after that night we were all together?"

"Why do you need to know that?"

"Because I do. Now did you?"

"Yes Rebecca! Yes, we continued seeing each other. We have been hooking up for weeks. Are you happy now that you know? And for the record we're going to continue fucking! That little stunt that you pulled didn't stop anything, now leave me alone!"

"You, selfish bastard, I hate you! I hope that you both rot in hell."

Rebecca runs over to Aaron and starts hitting him and screaming. Mahmoud, Maxwell, Jacob, and Yasmeen hear the commotion and they all rush into the room as Rebecca is yelling. "How could you sleep with my friend Aaron? I hate you!"

Mahmoud and Jacob grab Rebecca to stop her from hitting Aaron. *"Stop it Rebecca! What is going on in here doctor Sinclair?"*

"I'll tell you! He's has been fucking my friend, my best friend and she's married! Tell them Aaron how I caught you in bed with my friend Rachel!"

Mahmoud holds Rebecca by her arm. *"You need to calm down and go get yourself together. Doctor Sinclair you and I need to talk right now."*

When Aaron turns around, he looks right into Yasmeen's eyes, who's looking at him with a smile on her face. Aaron knows that he has fucked up again with Yasmeen and there is no way that she will go out with him after this. Rebecca runs out, Aaron and Mahmoud follows. Mahmoud is in fury Yasmeen can see it in his eyes. As he walks pass Yasmeen puts her hand on Mahmoud's arm. *"We will take care of things in here."*

"Thank you, Yasmeen. I really appreciate that."

At the end of the lunching Yasmeen is talking to some of the guest out in the lobby, when Rachel walks up to Brandon and Ashton. She asks them if they knew where she could find Aaron. Brandon points to Aaron as he walks out into the lobby with Maxwell and Rosetta. Rachel rushes over to Aaron in a hast and pulls him by the arm. *"Hey Aaron."*

"Rachel what are you doing here?"

"I do apologize for coming up here unannounced, but I needed to talk to you. Is there some place we could go?"

"Yes, hmm let's go down here."

Aaron takes Rachel by the hand and they scurry down the hall before Yasmeen and Mahmoud turns around. They are too busy talking to notice Rebecca when she comes out into the lobby Ashton approaches her. *"So, Rebecca who is that woman that came to see Aaron?"*

"What woman?"

"The Woman who just came looking for him."

"I didn't see a woman, where are they?"

"They went down the hall holding hands girl."

Rebecca take off down the hall trying to find Aaron. Aaron and Rachel are in the parking garage next to Aaron's car. *"So, Rachel what did you need to talk to me about?"*

"Aaron, I need a place to stay."

"You need a place to stay? What do you mean?"

"I mean I don't have anywhere to go, and I need a place to stay"

"You have a house."

"I can't stay there."

"So why are you here? I guess that's my question."

"I'm here because I don't have nowhere to go. Aaron."

"What dose you not having a to place to go have to do with me."

"It has everything to do with you."

"Ok what do you want from me? What can I do for you?"

"I need to crash at your place."

"I can get you a room for about a week."

"Ok and after that, then what?"

"What do you mean then what? Then you go back home to your house."

"I can't go back home. There is no home."

Aaron puts his hand over his face. All he can think about is Yasmeen. He wishes that he had never gotten involved with Rachel or Rebecca. How can he work on getting back with Yasmeen when he's surrounded with all this shit?

"Well get an apartment."

"How? I don't work, and I don't have any money! Look Aaron I was thinking that I could move in with you."

"Move in with me! No…no that's not even an option, you can't move in with me!"

"And why not?"

"Because you can't. Rachel we're not together. We just had a little fun that's it nothing more!"

"Are you, kidding me right now?"

"No, I'm not. Look Rachel I'm trying to get back with my ex and I can't with you living at my house. Now I can put you up in a hotel that's it."

Aaron, I left my husband and kids for you! You ruined my friendship and now you're telling me that you're trying to get back with your ex!"

"Go get them back! Rachel, I didn't tell you to leave your husband for me because I never wanted to be in a relationship with you. So, if you left your family you did it for you not me and if Rebecca was your friend you would have never went to bed with me in the first place!"

"So, I guess that I didn't mean anything to you! You just used me for sex! Sex and a blow job."

"If you want me to be honest, then yes."

"I want you to be a man, Aaron, you used me!"

"Hell, you didn't have to fuck me, remember you came over to my house!"
Slapping Aaron. *"Fuck you Aaron you disgust me!"*

Just as Rachel slaps Aaron across the face Rebecca runs out into the parking garage over to Rachel and pushes her to the ground. Rachel gets up swinging. She and Rebecca start fighting. Rachel and Rebecca are still fighting when Jacob, Zada, Mahmoud, and Yasmeen enter the parking garage.

"What is going on over there isn't that Rebecca Za?"

"I don't know, it looks like her."

Jacob looks over. *"What in the hell?"*

When Mahmoud and Jacob arrivers at Aaron car they help Aaron pull Rebecca and Rachel apart. Rachel struggles to get away. Yasmeen and Zada looks on in utter disgrace.

Rachal screams as tears runs down her face. *"Aaron, I left my husband for you and this is how you do me, you and Rebecca deserve each other! I hope that you both die!"*

"Fuck you!"

"No fuck you too Rebecca! How about you tell your co-workers how you eat my pussy as Aaron watched!"

"Well you ate my pussy too you bitch!"

Yasmeen shakes her head in disgust *"You two need to stop this shenanigan. Y'all out here fighting like two animals embarrassing yourselves out here in front of everybody. Rebecca what are you doing out here. I'm disappointed in all three of you and Aaron you should know better. You should be setting an example. This is a hospital, a place of business. If y'all what to fight and carry-on like fools I suggest taken this foolishness someplace else before I call security."*

"Yasmeen you're right I'm sorry."

Yasmeen walks away. *"This is a disgrace, what if children were out here? The three of you should be ashamed!"*

Yasmeen and Zada gets in her car and drive away. Mahmoud can see that Yasmeen is bothered by this which anger's him. Aaron can't believe that this is happening. As he stands beside his car all he can see is Yasmeen driving out of his life for good. He has nobody to blame but himself. Mahmoud demands Aaron and Rebecca to go to his office and wait until he gets there. Rachel leaves crying. Yasmeen, Rosetta, and Zada are sitting in her office. Yasmeen is still upset by the whole situation. *"I can't believe them! I'm so pissed off right now!'*

" Why because of Aaron?"

"I don't give a damn about Aaron, Rebecca, or that woman Rosetta, I'm pissed because what if some kids happened to be out there in the garage they would have seen those idiots out there fighting!"

"I know right. That would have scared them."

"I know Za, they should have taken that crap to their house! And Aaron he's sick, did you hear what she said?"

"Yes, I did hun, I'm glad that you end things with him who knows what he would have had you eating Yass."

"Oh, hell no, I would have killed his nasty ass! Za that's some sick shit."

Jacob and Maxwell enter Yasmeen office

"Yasmeen, we just came to check on you, we could see that you were upset.

"I'm ok. I'm just mad because today was supposed to be fun day. I'm so glad that it was cancelled because the kids, would have seen all that drama. I was so terrified by that thought, I just don't know what to say Maxwell."

"You're right Yasmeen, I can apologize on behalf of me and Mahmoud."

Maxwell hugs Yasmeen before he leaves. When Maxwell gets back to Mahmoud's office, he's sitting at his desk Maxwell tells him that Yasmeen is ok. Mahmoud is relieved. Two weeks has passed its Monday morning. Ashton walks into the conference room with Brandon, Rebecca walks in behind them. Jacob and Rosetta walk in together. Rosetta sits down next to Ashton.

"And where is Yasmeen?"

"Oh, she is teaching a class off campus today, so I'm sitting in for her."

"Oh, I see." Ashton rolls his eyes.

"Oh, so you're not happy to see me doctor Ward?"

"No not really."

Ashton and Rosetta continue to make small talk when Maxwell, Aaron, Mahmoud, and Uma walk in. Uma Wells is Maxwell's new patient administrator. Uma is a tall brunette with big brown eyes and tan skin with a bitchy attitude. Uma flashes a bright smile as she sits down next to Maxwell. Maxwell introduces Uma.

"And who is that guys? She's a cutie."

"We don't know."

Maxwell speaks. *"Everybody this my new patient administrator Ms. Uma Wells. You will be seeing her around so please make her feel welcomed. Uma is there anything that you would like to say?"*

"As a matter of fact, there is. Hi first things first, I want you all to know that I'm not here to make friends, I'm here to do my job, so If you don't like me oh well. I really don't care, but if I can help you do your job better I will."

"Where is Yasmeen when I need her Rosetta?"

"I know right! Like who is this bitch?"

"Oh, she and Yasmeen are going to get along just fine. I can't wait until she gets back Brandon."

"Doctor Khalidah needs to put her in her place."

Mahmoud looks at Uma he is surprised. *"Ms. Wells welcome aboard and we all will try to get along. That statement was uncalled for."* Mahmoud looks at Maxwell.

"Oh, I was just clearing the air that's all."

At the end of the meeting Mahmoud and Ashton exits the room leaving Rebecca and Uma behind.

"Uma, is it?"

"You can call me Ms. Wells."

"Oh, ok then Ms. Wells I was wondering if you would will like to have lunch with me and I…

"Now why would I do that; did you not hear me? I'm not here to make friends.

Uma walks out of the room leaving Rebecca standing in the middle of the floor. The next morning Yasmeen is in her office when her door is pushed opened and in walks Uma. Yasmeen looks up with total disbelief. Rosetta has already told her about Uma, so Yasmeen attitude goes from zero to one hundred in a quick second.

"So, you're Yasmeen."

"And you must be crazy! Who in the hell are you to come busting in my office like you run shit?"

"Oh, I'm Uma. Uma Wells."

"I don't give five fucks! Let me tell you something! Don't you ever walk your big-headed ass up in my office unless you have two of the three things an appointment, an invite, and you better knock and wait for a reply before you enter! Now get your ass out of me office!"

"Are you serious?"

"Dead ass! Look lady you don't know me and I don't care to know you, but if you ever walk up in my office like you just did you will be sorry! For the last time get your dumb ass out of my office bitch!"

Yasmeen takes Uma by her arm and pushes her out into the hall and slams the door in her face. Uma Stands in the hall looking at the closed door. Rosetta enters Yasmeen office and slams the door closed.

"Yass what did she say?

"That bitch bring her ass up in here like she's the shit. Talking about her name is Uma or some shit. I told that bitch that I didn't give a fuck what her name is, and I put her ass out. She got me twisted.

"You put her out Yass?

"You saw her standing in the hall don't you. I play no games. If you don't know you better, ask somebody!

Uma runs down to Jacob office almost in tears.

"You need to go down there and talk to Yasmeen!"

"You need to knock before you come in my office, I could have had a patient in here."

"I'm sorry doctor Baldwin, but Yasmeen just kicked me out of her office.

"What did you do? Did you just walk in like you just did?"

"Well yes!"

"That's why she kicked you out, you can't do that."

"And why not?"

"Because you can't! Now look you're going to start a lot of problems if you keep this up. Doctor Khalidah really needs to have a talk with you."

"So, are you going to talk to Yasmeen?"

"No but you can."

Jacob walks Uma back into the hall and closes his door. Later that day Yasmeen is standing at the Nurses station talking to Zada, Tia, and Cindy when Mahmoud, Maxwell, and Uma walk up. Mahmoud smiles to himself when he sees Yasmeen.

"Yasmeen."

"That's Ms. Blake to you."

. *"Ms. Blake, I think that you and I may have gotten off to a bad start."*

"Yes, and it's not going to get any better."

"I just wanted to introduce myself to you."

"Why? I have no desire to know you. I don't like you."

"You don't know me."

"Good. Let's keep it that way. Yasmeen waves her hand. *You're dismissed."*

Yasmeen walks over to Maxwell and Mahmoud. Maxwell can see that Yasmeen is in a foul mood when she approaches him. So, he braces himself. Maxwell and Yasmeen are close, and he hates it when she's mad.

"Doctor Khalidah may I have a word with you please?"

"Yes, you may Yasmeen."

"Doctor Khalidah I like you. You know that I do, but I don't know where you got that Uma chick from, she's rude and she has one more time to come up in my office like she crazy and I will be out of a job. My suggestion is for you to have a long talk with her or I will."

"Yes, Yasmeen I will have a talk with her, Jacob also talked to me about her. Calm down and you're not going anywhere. Now stop that crazy talk."

"I'm serious!"

"I know you are and I'm listening to you."

Yasmeen rolls her eyes and walks away Maxwell smiles he knows how Yasmeen is the last thing that he wants to do is to get on her bad side. It is Monday again and Yasmeen is sitting in the conference room when Uma, Maxwell, and Aaron walks in. Uma stops and stands behind Yasmeen's chair.

"May I help you?"

"Yes, you're in my seat."

"Your seat, if you don't get from behind me your seat is going to be in that trashcan little girl don't play with me!"

"Well I sat there last week."

"And I don't care this week now get from behind me!"

"Well where should I sit Ms. Blake?"

"Hell, you can sit on the floor for all I care!"

"I just thought that I should sit next to Doctor Khalidah."

Yasmeen points to the end of the table. *You can if he wants to sit down there."*

"Ok."

"Don't sit next to or across from me because I don't need you looking at me every time I look up with your big eyes and forehead."

Ashton and Brandon cover their face as they laugh. Yasmeen gets up to start her report when Uma interrupts her. Everyone looks at Yasmeen. Mahmoud smiles.

Ashton to Brandon. "It's on now."

"Yasmeen, I have a question."

"I'm sure that you do, just write it down on the paper in front of you and study it like a test."

"But I have a question."

"About what I haven't said anything yet! So, what can you possibly have to say?"

"What are you reporting on?"

"I will tell if you zip it. Look Uma this is not hard all you have to do is sit back and listen. Don't make this a long morning."

"But I...

"Look air head this is not rocket science. Stop talking and listen!"

At the end of the meeting Yasmeen and Mahmoud are having a discussion as usual Yasmeen and Mahmoud can't agree to much on anything. Yasmeen and Mahmoud are going over his new patient orders when Uma reenter's the room.

"Is everything ok Doctor? Do you need me to sit in on this?"

"No, he doesn't!"

"No, I think that we got this, but thanks for asking."

"I can take notes if you'd like. I do have a medical back ground.

Yasmeen looks in her briefcase. *"Here you go."*

"What's that?"

"A piece of candy I don't have a cookie. Doctor Shashivivek this is what I need from you."

"You need what?"

"I'm not talking to you, but I do need you to leave because you are really starting to...

"Uma did you need something?"

"No."

"Well I need you to leave we are discussing patients."

Uma walks out, and Yasmeen gets up.

. "Where are you going Yasmeen?"

"I'm done."

"Well I'm not. Why can't you just try what I've written?"

"Because it's crazy. This Patient needs home care first!"

"Ok Yasmeen we'll try it your way and if it doesn't work."

"Oh, it's going to work trust me!"

Yasmeen strolls out of the room. Mahmoud watches her as she walks out. He smiles with approval because he loves the way Yasmeen walks. Mahmoud doesn't know how much longer he can go before he shares his true feelings with Yasmeen. As Yasmeen walks down the hall, she can still see Mahmoud's face. She smiles because she knows that if nothing else Mahmoud loves the view. It has been two weeks and Yasmeen and Mahmoud still can't come to an agreement they have an attraction for each other. Uma and Yasmeen see things the same way long as Yasmeen has a say in it. It's the end of the day and it's Friday for Yasmeen it has been a great day. She didn't have to fight with Mahmoud over changing his patient orders and not once did she receive an unwanted text from Aaron. As Yasmeen walks to her car she smiles as she hums to herself. Yasmeen is about to get into her car when Uma runs up behind her.

"Hey Ms. Blake, I'm so glad that I caught up to you."

"And why is that?"

"I just wanted to talk to you."

Yasmeen looks confused as she puts her hand on her curvy hip. Yasmeen tosses her hair back as she takes a deep breath. *"Talk about what?"*

"About you and me and the fact that you obviously have a problem with me."

"I know that you didn't just run your little happy ass all the way down here with that bullshit! Yasmeen bites her lower lip. *It's Friday, I'm going home, and I don't have time for you ok!"*

"Yasmeen, I just want to know what it is that I did to you!"

"You didn't do a thing to me and you will never get that chance, but you were the one who come up in the meeting on your first day big and bold as shit talking about you are not here to make friends!"

"What?"

"Oh yeah you said it and I heard all about you, so I feel just like you, we will never be friend so let's make that clear."

"Yasmeen. Ms. Blake, we are co-workers."

"And your point is!"

"*Well at some point our paths has to cross. I may need something, and I have to come to you or vice versa.*"

"*I will not! You can't do anything for me. If I need something, I always go to the source not the help... Look I don't know what your little plot is but don't get your ass fucked up because you don't run shit I do!*"

"*I see that you and I are just alike. So, will you give me a second chance?*"

"*Oh no you and I are nothing alike. You see you are a want-a-be. You talk down to people like your shit don't stank that's not me I tell it like it is. I try to like everybody until they across me like you did that's when the problem begins. I can be nice if you let me and I can be your worst nightmare if you make me, you never get a second chance to make a first impression, because your second impression will just be a lie! So, Ms. Bells...*

"It's Wells."

"I really don't give a damn what your name is. It doesn't matter to me just stay your ass out of my face. And if you ever run up on me after work, I will clean your fucking clock bitch, I don't like you!"

"*But I...*"

"But my ass. You are full of shit and I don't trust your slick ass. I don't like bullies!"

"*I'm not a bully Yasmeen.*"

"*No, you're not but you try to be and for the last time it's Ms. Blake to you. Don't make me tell you that again. I'm only Yasmeen to my friends and a friend you are not. Now get out of my way before I put some tire marks on your back.*"

Yasmeen gets in her car and drives away. Uma stands to the side and watches her as she leaves the parking garage. Uma had hope that she and Yasmeen could come to an agreement, but Uma knows that Yasmeen is a strong woman who she doesn't want any part of her. It's Monday Yasmeen and Ashton are sitting at the table talking. Rebecca is sitting across from Ashton texting on her cellphone when Uma and Maxwell walk in.

"*Good morning all.*"

"*She's in a good mood Yasmeen.*"

"*Yes, and we both know why.*"

Ashton hi-five Yasmeen over the table. "*Ok*"

"*Hi Uma, me and a couple of the nurseries are going out later, you're welcomed to come if you'd like.*"

"Rebecca I'm sorry but what part of I'm not here to make friends did you not understand. I don't socialize with coworkers outside of work."

Yasmeen is outraged by Uma's arrogant response to Rebecca. Yasmeen looks over at Ashton as Ashton mumbles get her. *"Excuse me Uma but when you say that you don't socialize with co works outside of work dose that apply to just woman or men or both.*

"Ms. Blake dear it applies to both."

Yasmeen winks at Ashton. *"Well we saw you on Saturday night. Right doctor Ward hugged up with doctor Sinclair. Is he not considered a man or co-worker? Or are you just a liar?"*

Uma looks at Maxwell. *"You... You didn't see me!"*

Yasmeen pulls her cellphone out. *"Oh yes we did, and I have pictures to would you like to see them?"*

"No!"

"Is that no, you don't want to see them or no we didn't see you? Cause if it's no, that doctor Ward and I didn't see you two, I can pass this picture around because I might be wrong, but I don't think that I am."

Uma rubs her face. *"No, I don't want to see your pictures."*

Rebecca can't believe that Aaron and Uma are sleeping together. She She looks over at Uma wanting to push her onto the floor. Aaron, Mahmoud, and Jacob walks in just as Rebecca is about to confront Uma. Yasmeen sits back in her chair and smiles. Yasmeen intention was not to hurt Rebecca but to put an end to Uma snootiness. Rebecca looks at Aaron with tears in her eyes as he sits down beside Uma. After the meeting Rebecca confronts Aaron.

"So, when were you going to tell me Aaron?"

"Tell you what?"

"About you and Uma? Aaron don't you dare lie! Not only Did Yasmeen see you doctor Ward saw you as well, now when we're you going to tell me?"

Aaron heart skips a beat. The last thing that he wanted was for Yasmeen to find out about his new affair. *"What do you mean Yasmeen saw me?"*

"I mean Yasmeen saw you Saturday night after you told me that you were going out of town with your homies. Aaron, you lied to me!"

"Rebecca let's not do this at work. You know what's at stake! Both of our jobs if any of this gets back to doctor Shashivivek. I'll talk to you later, and please don't call me."

Aaron walks out as Rebecca starts to cry. Yasmeen walks back into the conference room she sees Rebecca crying. Yasmeen feels bad for Rebecca, knowing that she is the cause of her hurt. Yasmeen sits down next to Rebecca.

"Rebecca, I didn't mean to hurt you. That was not my intent. I shouldn't have said anything."

"It's ok Yasmeen I deserve it."

"Rebecca no you didn't. I guess you're still seeing Aaron."

"Yes I am. I know that I'm a fool."

"No… not really but I do apologize for my part in this. Handing Rebecca, a Kleenex. *I just wanted to put an end to Uma's crap. She's so full of herself. But had I known that you were still involved with Aaron I would have went about it in a different way. Forgive me for my actions."*

"Thank you, Yasmeen. I hope that one day you can forgive me for everything that I've done."

Yasmeen smiles as she walks out. Yasmeen tells herself that she has already forgiven her, but she will never forget what she and Aaron did. Yasmeen is not bitter in fact she is thankful that she found out who Aaron was before it was too late. Yasmeen says to herself thank you Rebecca for relieving me from that no-good sack of shit. Yasmeen goes back to her office. She is sitting at her computer when her door flies open and in steps Aaron like a mad man pointing his finger at Yasmeen. *"Can you explain to me way in the hell you told Rebecca about me and Uma!"*

Yasmeen looks up from her computer. *"Yes, I can, right after you explain to me why are you running, up in my office like you Billy bad ass! No, no don't you dare close that door!"*

"Yasmeen, I just want to know why?"

"Me to! Why are you here?"

"Yasmeen do you just want to hurt me? Is that it?"

"Hurt you for what. Aaron I don't give two fucks about you or who you're with, and as far as me telling Rebecca anything is some bullshit. I didn't tell her ass shit I was talking to your new bitch with your punk ass. I was talking to Uma get your facts right. For the record, I didn't know that you were still in a relationship with Rebecca because if I did, I wouldn't have said anything to your bitch!"

"Yasmeen can you lower your voice,"

"*No Aaron I cannot! Since you want to fly your ass up in here interrogating me like you're the police. I want you to hear everything that I say so that you won't have to make that mistake again. Now you should know that I don't care for your new trick. Not because of you because I just found out about you and her this weekend, so don't flatter yourself. No, I dislike her for the way she came off like she was big shit on day one. Talking about she didn't come to make friends and she don't socialize with coworkers. Yes, she has the right to associate with anybody that she chooses to. But when you walk up in my office you had better bring your 'A' game. Especially when you come out the gate giving up ass to the first person who shows you some attention!*"

"*Yasmeen…*"

"*Don't Yasmeen me. just stand your ass right there and listen because I don't want you to get confused. I don't want you, hell I'm glad that you're gone. I wish that I never have to see your face another day in my life. I don't want to hurt you. In fact, I wish you the best. I just don't won't to be bothered by you or your many sex partners. I have moved on and you don't even cross my mind even when I'm taking a shit.*"

Aaron is hurt. He takes a deep breath as he stares in Yasmeen eyes. All the feelings that he had for Yasmeen are still there. Aaron wishes that he could make Yasmeen see how much he cherishes her still.

"*Yasmeen, you know that I still care for you no matter what you say or how you may feel.*"

"*Yeah Aaron I know that you still care about me. You showed me that night that you tried to rape me!*"

Aaron is muted by Yasmeen response as he looks at her, he can see the hurt in her eyes. Aaron is ashamed of himself. He puts his hands over his face. He doesn't know what to say because sorry just won't do not this time. Aaron regrets going into Yasmeen office. He turns and walks out without saying another word. Yasmeen picks up the phone and calls Oscar. Yasmeen, Zada, and Ashton are sitting out on the patio at Oscar and Todd's house drinking wine.

"*Yass, I heard that you had a wonderful day.*"

"*Yes, she did, but Yasmeen I still can't believe that you said that.*"

"*And why not Ashton? You for one should know first-hand.*

"*Oh yes I know, but Oscar I thought that she only talked shit to me.*"

"*Oh no she talks shit to everybody me and Todd included.*"

"*Y'all should have seen Uma's face when Yasmeen said that she had pictures. Knowing damn well that she didn't have not one picture Todd.*"

"*No, she didn't. Ashton what did Uma say?*"

"*Hell, that ho was shaking like a leaf on a tree with the wind blowing. She didn't want nobody to see that picture. She said no I don't. She muted herself. She didn't say one word in the meeting. I forgot that she was there.*"

"*Stop it Ashton you can call me Yass ok.*"

"*Really I can?*"

Oscar pulling Ashton by his Arm. "*How much have you had to drink?*"

"*Not much. Why?*"

"*Cause you getting all sensitive and shit.*"

"*No, I'm not and where are you going?*"

"*Inside to get some steaks for the gill. Come with me.*"

"*Ok sure.*"

Todd and Yasmeen reply. "*You two come right back!*"

"*Mind y'all business. Come on Ash forget them.*"

After ten minutes Yasmeen goes into the kitchen, she sees Oscar and Ashton kissing

Yasmeen smiles and walks back out without say a word. The next morning Yasmeen is

sitting at her desk when Ashton walk in.

"*I know that you didn't just walk in my office!*"

"*What you didn't see me?*"

"*Oh, I see you.*"

"*Yass, I need to talk to you.*"

"*Ok about what?*"

"*You said that you and Oscar are good friend, right?*"

"*Yes, we are. where are you going with this doctor?*"

"*I'm just saying. Yasmeen, you know that he speaks very highly of you and all*"

"*And.*"

"*And I think that I'm crushing on him.*"

"*Crushing my ass, I saw y'all kissing last night.*"

"*Saw who?*"

"*Saw you, oh I got pictures.*"

"*No, you don't. let me see.*"

"You're crazy."

"Yasmeen…"

"Did you stay the night over at Oscar and Todd?"

"Who me?"

"Who me? Yes you, ain't no owls in here. I'm talking to you.
Covering her mouth. You slut.
You did, I can see it on your face! You and 'O got busy."

"Let me go."

"No, where are you going?"

"I got work to do and I don't have time for you today."

"Well I got time for you. Come sit back down Doc!"

"No bye. Thank you."

"For what hell thank Oscar, he's the one who put it on your ass."

"You know what fuck you! I'm not doing this with you."

No, you did that last night.

"This morning."

"Well damn you slut how low did you go?"

"Yass."

Yasmeen can't stop laughing. "Ok, ok come back."

"Yass I'm serious. Thank you for introducing us."

"Aww, you're welcome. Oh, and don't hurt my friend."

"Yasmeen, I promise you that I won't."

A month has passed Yasmeen is on her way back to her office when
Rosetta runs up behind her. "It's about time!"

"What are you talking about?"

"You, hiding out in your office."

"Yasmeen rolls her eyes. *"Hiding out! I'm not hiding. It's called working.
You should try it."*

"Whatever. Anyway what are you wearing to the ball Friday?"

Yasmeen looks up at the ceiling. *"Is it that time already?"*

"Yes, it is now what are you wearing and who are you coming with?"

"I don't even want to think about the Ball and I don't want to go!"

"Well it's not like you have a choice."

"Thanks for reminding me."

"Yass it's not that bad and for the past three year it's been great."

"*Great for who? Rosie, I don't call a room full of fake assholes with money and boring conversation great.*"

"*Ok Yass is it' because of Aaron is that why you don't won't to go?*"

"*Because of who? Aaron! I don't care if Aaron is there or not. I just don't want to go. Anyway why is that you always throwing Aaron up in my face? I'm over Aaron and you need to do the same!*"

"*Look I'm sorry I should not have said that.*"

"*You think.*"

"*Let's talk about last night. Sorry that I didn't make it.*"

"*It's ok we had fun without you.*"

"*What is that supposed to mean?*"

"*It means that we had fun without you being there.*"

"*Thanks, glad to know that I was missed.*"

"*Not by me.*"

"*You know Yass I do have feelings.*"

"*Oh, you do? I didn't notice.*"

Rosetta leaves Yasmeen in her office laughing. Yasmeen knows that Rosetta is not who she says she is, and Yasmeen knows that it's just a matter of time before she brakes, out of her ugly shell, but in the meantime, Yasmeen will just have to wait. Yasmeen mind begins to race as she thinks about going to this event that she knows in her heart will not end well for someone.

Chapter 6

Get the trash from in front of your door
before you sweep in front of mine....

It's Friday the night of the Hospital annual fund-raising Ball. Maxwell, Mahmoud, Aaron, and Jacob are talking when Brandon and his wife Clair join in on there conversation just as Yasmeen walks in with Todd, Oscar, and Ashton. Yasmeen is wearing a long black fitted backless dress coved in sparking rhinestones. Her hair is pulled up into silky black curls on top of her head. Yasmeen smiles with her full glossed lips that shows off her even white teeth and flawless chocolate skin. She pushes her breast forward as she walks across the room. She can feel hundreds of eyes on her. Rosetta and her husband Wendell rushes over to Yasmeen Just as Jacob looks in her direction. Jacob to Maxwell. *"Yasmeen is here. Wow she's beautiful!"* Maxwell, agreeing. *"Yes, she is."* Mahmoud looks up at Yasmeen he chokes on his drink. Mahmoud closes his eyes all he can see is Yasmeen beautiful face smiling at him. when he opens his eyes Yasmeen in standing in front of him. Before Mahmoud knows it, he takes Yasmeen hand and kisses it as he tells her how beautiful she is. Yasmeen thanks him as she gazes in his eyes a wave of lust enters her like ice running down her back. She licks her lips as she put her hand on top of his. In her mind, all she can say is damn. Mahmoud looked better than good in his black tuxedo and bowtie. He looks delicious and Yasmeen more than anything would love to have a taste. Yasmeen can't take her eyes off Mahmoud as she Greets Maxwell and his wife Saidah. She than shakes hands with Jacob and his wife. As Yasmeen mingles, she doesn't notice Aaron, Uma, and Rebecca gazing at her. She continues, to shake hands and make small talk with the other guest. Ashton walks over to Aaron who is standing next to Uma.

"Well hello Aaron. Are you enjoying yourself?"

"Well yes I am. How about you?"

"I must say that everything is just lovely, Oh, did you see Yasmeen?"

Aaron takes a deep breath. "Yes, I did."

"She looks stunning don't you think?"

Aaron looks at Yasmeen. "Yes, she does as always.

At the end of the night Yasmeen is talking to Ashton, Oscar, Todd, Maxwell, and Mahmoud. Aaron is standing behind Anne-Marie and her husband Chase. Aaron longs to kiss Yasmeen and to smell her sweet skin as she covers him in her sweat. Just as Aaron looks up Uma and Rebecca are looking at him, so he looks away. He makes his way over to Yasmeen. Aaron tells her how eye-catchingly beautiful she is and kisses her on the cheek. Brandon and his wife stroll over to where Yasmeen and the others are.

"Sweetheart do you remember Yasmeen. Winking. She had the hots for doctor Sinclair."

Clair smiles as she looks at Yasmeen. "Oh yes I do. She's the one that he dumped right!"

Everyone gasps as Brandon and Clair smiles a, evil grin of delight. Mahmoud looks at Yasmeen who is smiling just as evil as Brandon. All eyes are on Yasmeen. Jacob is disappointed by Brandon action.

"Brandon that was uncalled for!"

"What Yasmeen has thick skin."

Ashton and Oscar whispering to Yasmeen. "No, he didn't! Get his ass before we do."

Yasmeen talks under her breath. "Who I got this. Oh, Jacob it's ok. Besides I remember Brandon's wife Clair fondly, but correct me if I'm wrong. You're the one who's having the affair with Brandon's brother. Oh, and by the way Brandon did you get treated for that STD that you had last week? You know the one that your wife contracted from your brother."

Clair looks at Brandon with her mouth open. "Excuse you! I don't know what you are talking about!"

"Yes, you do. Yasmeen looks over at Jacob. It was just last week when you both had crabs Clair."

"Get your facts right I didn't have crabs last week!"

"Oh, you're right. You both had crabs a month ago. You both had chlamydia last week. Silly me how could I forget. Do forgive me. Oh, and Brandon I am sorry that you found out that your ten-year-old son is really your fathers. I guess he's your stepbrother or is he your stepson? I guess he's your stepbrother or is he your stepson? Yasmeen turns to Jacob and Maxwell. *Talking about keeping it in the family. Oh, where are my manors have you met my two best friends Todd and Oscar?"*

"Get me out of here now Brandon! I can't believe that you said that in front of all these people"

"Oh, believe it sweetie and one more thing Mrs. Oakley are you still caring your husbands brother baby. Sipping her wine. *Oh, this is some good wine."*

Clair runs out in tears as Brandon takes off behind her. Yasmeen looks at Maxwell and Jacob who are rubbing the side of their face smiling.

"Oh, did I tell you that this event is a success Mahmoud and I'm having a lovely time. I'm really enjoying myself."

Mahmoud stares at Yasmeen. *"Thank you I'm glad that you are."*

Yasmeen kisses Mahmoud lightly on the cheek and walks away with a big smile on her face. By the time Yasmeen gets home her phone can't stop ringing. She turns her phone off and goes to bed happy as a child on Christmas day. The Monday meeting was over faster than a flash of light. As usual all eyes were on Yasmeen. All stares but no action. Yasmeen walks out of the meeting smiling to herself because she knows that Brandon would beat the hell out of her if he could. She heads back to her office knowing that today is going to be one for the books. After the meeting Brandon pulls Jacob off to the side. He's still livid about Yasmeen's behavior at the fund-raising event.

"Doctor Baldwin may I please have a word with you?"

"Yes, you can follow me back to my office and we can talk on the way if that's alright with you."

"Ok I think that would be best."

"What is it that you want to talk about?"

"I want to talk about what you're going to do about Yasmeen."

"I sorry but I don't follow! What do you mean?"

"I mean that her behavior Friday night was uncalled for and I want to know just what you intend to do about it!"

"I'm not going to do anything. It's not my place."

"You're not going to do anything?"

"What would you like for me to do?"

Brandon raises his voice. *"Fire or suspend her!"*

"Doctor Oakley I'm sorry but I can't do that."

"You can't, or you won't!"

"I can't, and I won't. Look I have no control over what Yasmeen does on her own time."

"So, you mean to tell me that it's ok for Yasmeen to tell my business to a room full of people and you not do a damn thing about it!"

Jacob cleares his throat. *"Doctor Oakley you are just as much to blame. In fact, you and your wife started in on her. Now you want to play victim!"*

"Doctor Baldwin she was out of place.

"And so were you! So, get over it because I'm not going to suspend Yasmeen over something that you brought upon yourself. Now you have a good day."

Brandon pushes pass Jacob. Jacob shakes his head because he knows that this is not the end of Brandon's rage. After lunch Yasmeen is sitting in her office when her door flies open hitting the wall. Yasmeen heart skips a beat before she looks up to see Brandon rushing towards her with big red eyes. Yasmeen picks up a book from her desks and throws it hitting Brandon in the face, stopping him dead in his track. Brandon puts his hands up to his face to cheek to see if his nose is bleeding.

"You are an evil bitch!"

"And are a no-good son-of-a-bitch!"

"Yasmeen what did I ever do to you?"

"I am the one who should be asking you that question! You and your whore of a wife!

"Yasmeen just who in the hell do you think you are?"

Yasmeen points her finger. *"I know who I am! Who in the fuck are you to come running up in here like the hulk! With your bitch ass! Boy, I will beat your sorry ass!*

"Oh, you think."

"No bitch I know." Yasmeen throws her shoe at Brandon hitting him in the chest.

"Yasmeen, you have assaulted me twice!"

Yasmeen throws her other shoe. *"Yeah because I fear for my life!"*

"Fear for your life I never touched you!

"Prove it asshole! Prove it! You assaulted me when you came into my office uninvited!"

Brandon pauses as he looks at Yasmeen who is smiling as she picks up another book from her desk. She is about to throw it when Brandon runs back and ducks his head. His heart is beating fast not because he's mad but out of fear of what Yasmeen might do. He has never seen her like this before. This is not what Brandon was expecting.

"Please don't throw that book! Yasmeen, I just what to know why would you put my business out like that? Not to mention in front of a room full of people."

"Ok I will tell you after you tell me why you and your wife tried to put my business out…"

"No, you wanted to put on a show for your friends!"

"No, you wanted to put on a show for your friends. You want to give them a laugh, so I helped you out that's all. You were the opening act and I was the head-liner. I gave them want they wanted.

"Yasmeen, you know that was not my intent!"

"Oh yes it was. It was you and your wife's intent to embarrass me, but like a magician I pulled a rabbit out of my hat."

"That…that is not true."

"Oh, it's true alright. Y'all rehearsed y'all lines and you helped her because that bitch don't know me like that. You told her what to say. That's ok because I got the last laugh. Oh, and for the record I never had the hot for Aaron he chased me, and he didn't dump me I out grew him and moved on. Guess what he's still chasing after me so tell your wife that!"

"Yasmeen…"

"Don't lie! I hate a liar. Be the man who you think that you are. Be the little man who rushed up in my office and admit to what you did!"

Before Brandon can answer Jacob and Ashton enters Yasmeen's office. Jacob is enraged. He push's Brandon cross the room.

"What's going on in here? Yasmeen are you ok?"

Yasmeen picking up her shoes. *"Yes, I'm ok."*

"Why are you here? I told you to leave it alone. I promise you that doctor Shashivivek will hear about this. You had no right coming in Yasmeen's office confronting her about anything! You talked to me so that should have been the

end. Now get out before I call security and you are going to fix that fucking wall!"

Ashton puts his arms around Yasmeen as he asks her if she's ok. Yasmeen says to herself *"hell yeah I'm good."* Yasmeen pretends to be crying. Yasmeen is going to ride this until the wheels fall off. Looking at Yasmeen with her face buried in Ashton chest makes Jacob feel sorry for Yasmeen. He wishes that there was something that he could do. Rosetta who called Mahmoud is standing in the door. Mahmoud looks around Yasmeen office he sees Yasmeen who is still pretending to be crying. Sends him into a rage. Mahmoud asks Jacob what happened. Jacob tells Mahmoud everything that transpire that lead up to Brandon confrontation with Yasmeen. Both Jacob and Mahmoud agree that Brandon was wrong.

Mahmoud rubbing Yasmeen's back. *"Could you all give us a moment. I would like to talk to Yasmeen alone.*

Yasmeen holds Ashton tight as she whispers. *No don't you dare leave."*

"Let me get her calmed down first and I'll come get you when she ready."

Mahmoud agrees, he and Jacob exit Yasmeen office.

"I think that I should stay too.

"No, I can handle this alone Rosetta, just close the door behind you.

After everybody leaves the office Ashton push's Yasmeen away.

"Get your ass off me! You're full of shit! Now what in the hell did you do? Your ass is not crying." Ashton calls Oscar.

"He come rushing his ass in here like I'm supposed to be scared or some shit. I hit his ass in the face with that book and my shoe."

"No, you didn't!"

"Yes, I did. I bet he won't bring his ass up in here no more. He talking about you assaulted me twice. I said prove it!"

"Yass, you're crazy. Something is seriously wrong with you. Then you're sitting here pretending to be crying messing up my new shirt."

"Whatever."

"But on a serious note are you really ok."

"Yes, I'm fine but when Oscar gets here, I'm going to start crying again and I'm putting you out."

"Hell, you weren't crying the first time and when Oscar come you are not putting me nowhere. Hell, I got to fix myself up before he comes, and to hell with you Yass.

"He's coming to check on me not you.

"Hell, you good, you're just crazy. Now here wipe your face before Mahmoud comes back in here.

When Mahmoud comes back in Yasmeen is wiping her face, she turns her back to him and hides her face. Mahmoud thinks that she is crying so he sit down beside her not knowing what to do he put his arms around Yasmeen shoulders and pulls her close to him. When Yasmeen feels Mahmoud hand her body shakes she lets out a moan as her vagina start to moisten from his touch. Yasmeen fights with everything in her to keep from pushing Mahmoud to floor and fucking him until his nose bleeds. Yasmeen pushes Mahmoud away and runs out of her office. Mahmoud runs his long finger through his hair as he thinks to himself what did he do wrong or what did he do right. Could Yasmeen feel the same way about him or is he just fooling himself? How would he find out and where would he find the nerve to ask? As Mahmoud leaves his heart tells him to stay. After three days Yasmeen is at the end of the hall talking to Wallace when Chase Anne-Marie's husband approaches her. Yasmeen has no idea why he would want to talk to her about anything, because for one they have never had more than one good word between the both of them to say to each other. To say that they hated each other would be an understatement.

"Wallace, I would like to have a word will Ms. Blake if you don't mind!"

Wallace looks at Yasmeen. *"Ok I will talk to you later Ms. Blake."*

Wallace walks down the hall as Yasmeen says to *herself "What now. What does this moron want?"*

"Yasmeen, I need to talk to you!"

"About what?

"About what you said to Brandon the other night!"

"About what I said to Brandon? What did I say to him?

"You know just what you said!"

"I do?"

"Yes, you do Yasmeen! So, don't play dumb!"

"Dumb never, but whatever I said to Brandon is none of your damn business!"

"It is my damn business!"

"How? He said what he said, and I responded back. I didn't see you attached to his ass. End of story!"

"You were wrong! You were damn wrong!"

"And he wasn't!"

"In my eye's no he wasn't"

"Of course not. I forgot that you are blind to the truth!"

"You can say what you want but you need to apologize to him and his wife!"

"Apologize. You must have a lost whatever's left of your mind.. Look this crap happened almost a week ago and as far as I'm concern it's over like this discussion is!"

"Oh, you will apologize!"

Yasmeen walks over to Chase. *"Oh yeah and who's going to make me? It sure ain't you. You can run up with your, chest out huffing and puffing like a bull all you want to, you still don't scare me partner, but I can tell you this; you had better get your stupid ass back in the basement and work on a computer before I shit on your day!"*

Chase takes a step back. *"Oh, you're tuff!"*

"Very"

"You better be glad that you didn't pull that shit on me!"

"Are you threating me?"

"No because you don't have shit on me!"

"Threaten me again and we will find out. I can promise you that!"

"What…what are you going to do go run and tell your boss?"

"There is only one way to find out."

Chase starting to walk away. *"That's why Aaron dropped your ass cause, you weren't about shit!"*

Yasmeen smiles. *"Really that's why he dropped me?"*

"Yeah you know it!"

"Well you need to go ask him again because obviously you got it wrong."

"No, I didn't get it wrong. But like I said you better be glad that you didn't pull that shit on me."

"No what you better do is tell your wife that you have been having an ongoing affair with her ex best friend who is HIV positive. That's what you better do and go get your ass checked. Oh yeah, she told me about a month ago and she told you too, now tell your wife before I do!"

Chase gasp and his mouth drops open. He is speechless because out of all the things that Yasmeen could have said this is the last thing that he ever wanted to hear. Without saying another word. He walks backwards down the hall just as Tia and Zada approaches.

"Yass what going on? I know Chase bitch ass not back here fucking with you! I'm sick of you all fucking with my friend! What do he do Yass?"

"He was talking shit threating me right Chase!"

When Yasmeen gets home her heart hurt's. She feels bad that she had to tell Chase about his lover and Ann-Marie ex best friend having HIV. All she can think about is Ann-Marie and how she doesn't deserve this. Even though they are no longer friend this is not something that she wanted to fall on her. With all the hate that she has for Chase she hopes that he too is negative for having HIV. This is a secret that Yasmeen has been keeping to herself. She despises Chase for pushing her to the point that it came out the way that it did. This is the one thing Yasmeen wishes that she could take back. But she knows that once it comes up and out of your mouth it can't be unsaid or heard. Yasmeen falls to her knees and starts to pray to God that Ann-Marie is ok just as she has been doing since the day that she found out. The next day Yasmeen is sitting in her office when she hears a knock on the door. Yasmeen heart drops, as she says to herself.

"I should have called out today. Answering. *Come in."*

Yasmeen stares at the door waiting to see who will walk in. When the door opens Yasmeen almost falls out of her chair when Brandon steps into her office. He's closes the door behind him. All Yasmeen can say is not today. Yasmeen tells herself that she's not ready to deal with bullshit not today. Like the last time this too will not end good. All Yasmeen wants to do is avoid any confrontation with anybody.

"Yasmeen can we talk?"

"I'm listening."

"May I sit down?"

"Help yourself."

"Look Yasmeen I know that you and I detest each other."

"Well I don't like you."

"And why is that? What did I do to you?"

"No what did I do to you. Brandon from the first day that we met you had it out for me. I never did anything to you, but you went out of your way to be an ass to me whenever possible. I don't know what your objective was, but I was not going to let you disrespect me and talk to me any kind of way."

"Yasmeen, I did not do that. I only had words with you when you said something off the wall to me first."

"No, you are the one and I quote you saying, "That bitch thinks that she's all that. She thinks that she going to come in here trying to run shit, but I got news for her ass. I'm going to have her ass running out of here in tears before this week is over." Is that not what you said?"

"I may have said something like that."

"No that is exactly what you said. You thought that I was weak. Oh, how wrong were you! You had me fucked up from day one."

"I'm sorry for what I said. I didn't mean it.

"Oh, you meant it. You just don't think I would find out. You're sorry for letting me get the best of you. Now why are you here to lie?"

"No. I'm here to try to make amends with you. Call it truths."

"The truth is you said some bullshit to me and I responded back. Now weather you liked what I said I really don't care. You were always taking cheap shots at me every time you got the chance."

"Yasmeen, you are right. I said somethings to you that I shouldn't have, and the other night was no different."

"Yes, there was a difference. Brandon, you tried to embrace me in front of those people. You and your wife, but your plan back fired. Tell the truth since we are being honest right."

Brandon looks at the floor. *"Yasmeen you're right and I do apologize on behalf of me and my wife. Will you accept my apology?"*

"No... No not now and to be honest with you I don't trust you. And before you ask no I will not apologize for what I said. Brandon, you are foul, and I just can't bring myself to believe one thing that you say."

"Yasmeen I'm here trying to make peace with you that's all.

"That might be true, but I just don't feel it coming from you."

"Why not?"

"Because I think that you're up to something and I'm not going to fall for it."

"Well I'm sorry that you feel that way. Maybe one day you will accept my apology."

"Yeah one day but not today."

"Well thanks for your time."

"You are welcome and have a nice day."

When Brandon leaves Yasmeen puts her hand over her face and laughs. She can't believe that that Brandon thought that she was going to apologize to him after the conversation that she and Chase had, Did Brandon really think that she was that stupid. When Brandon gets back to his office, he can't stop thinking about Yasmeen no matter what he does. All he can see is Yasmeen smiling at him. Could it be that after all this time his feeling for Yasmeen had changed from hate to lust or has these feels always been there? Brandon thinks that he must be out of his fucking mind to be think about Yasmeen in this way. This can't be happing, but the more Brandon tries to push Yasmeen out of his mind the more intense his lust for her gets. All Brandon can think about is Yasmeen's smooth chocolate skin and her full lip's. He thinks how soft they must be. Brandon tries without success to get Yasmeen out of his head. Before long Brandon has his hard dick in his hand. He masturbates as he thinks about him fucking Yasmeen as he sucks on her nipples. Brandon orgasm is so intense that he screams out with passion. When Brandon open his eye's, he realizes that he is calling Yasmeen's name. Brandon looks down at his hand that's covered with his juices.

Brandon smile. *"Damn that was good. Yasmeen, I have to get some of that pussy if my thoughts of you are this damn good."*

Brandon cleans himself off. He gets up from his desk and walks out into the hall Yasmeen and Maxwell are standing in front of his door. He runs back into his office. Brandon can feel an erection coming on. After a week of avoiding Yasmeen Brandon hopes that this thing for her has passed but the moment that he sees Yasmeen his lust returns and all he can think about is fucking her. Yasmeen looks at Brandon and rolls her eyes as she walks away. Before Yasmeen can get down the hall Uma runs up behind her.

"Hey Ms. Blake, may I have a word with you?"

"No, you may not."

"Why not?"

"Because I don't have time for nobody drama today!"

"I just want to talk to you that's all."

Yasmeen blow out air. *"Talk to me about what?"*

"I was thinking that we could talk some place a little more, you know not here."

"Where did you have in mind?"

"How about over lunch today! My treat."

"Ok if I can pick the place."

"Great. So, I will meet you in the parking lot at…"

"At eleven-thirty."

Uma and Yasmeen are sitting in the restaurant. Yasmeen is trying to figure out why in the hell did Uma want to talk to her and why over lunch. What is this bitch up to and why is she so damn happy? Uma tries to make small talk, but Yasmeen is not feeling her.

"This is really a nice establishment."

"Well I like it."

"Me to."

"Let's cut the crap Uma what do you want to talk to me about?"

"Ok just like that."

"Yes just like that. Now spit it out."

"Ok Ms. Blake I wanted to talk to you about doctor Shashivivek."

Yasmeen chokes on the tea. *"Doctor Shashivivek! What about him?"*

"Is he seeing anybody."

"Uma, I don't know anything about his personal life and I hardly think that I'm the one that you should be asking."

"I just thought, that you could like give me some insight on him."

"No, I can't but maybe he can, after all who can tell you better than doctor Shashivivek about himself."

"I just thought that you could tell me just a little something about him."

"Well I can tell you this, he is engaged, and I think that in about a year and a half he is supposed to get married. Other than that, I can't tell you anything."

"So, you don't know of anybody who he has slept with?"

"Like I've said before. I don't know anything about that man's personal life and what he does when he's not at the hospital. I don't know, and I don't care. Ok Uma I have a question for you. Are you interested in doctor Shashivivek?"

"Yes I am. I think that he's so handsome. I get horny just thinking about him, don't you?"

"No, I don't!"

"Really you don't?"

"No! Yasmeen to herself. *This bitch is crazy. Who 's next?* To Uma. *I thought that you and doctor Sinclair were seeing each other or am I wrong"*

"No, you're right. I just like to have more than one option you know a girl must keep a spare or two just in case one blows out."

Yasmeen laughs as she thinks to herself. *"And a shot of penicillin. Another damn slut."*

"So, what do you think I should do Ms. Blake?"

"Go for it. I mean tell him hell I don't know."

"I really like him."

"Ok look Uma I really enjoyed lunch with you. It was interesting, but I have to get back to work."

"Oh yeah and thanks. Ms. Blake can we keep this between you and I please?"

"Oh yes you have my word on that. I guess that I will see you back at the office."

Yasmeen can't wait to get in her car to call Zada. All Yasmeen can think about is Mahmoud and how she too has feelings for him. Yasmeen thinks that maybe she's just fooling herself. She should just let go. When Uma gets back to the parking garage, she sees Mahmoud getting out of his black Jaguar. She rushes to get out of her BMW. Mahmoud is about to close his door when Uma calls out to him.

"Hey doctor so how was your lunch?"

"Well I haven't had lunch yet."

"Oh, and why not?"

"I had to get some work done, so I'm have a late lunch."

"Well you should let me take you out."

"Take me out!"

"Yes."

"Out where?"

"To dinner anywhere you'd like, and we can do anything that you like."

"No, I don't think so, but thanks for the offer."

"Come on Doc I just want to get to know the real you."

"There is not much to know."

"Well go out with me and let me find out for myself."

"No that's…"

"I won't take no for an answer, so I will see you tonight ok."

Uma runs off before Mahmoud can say no. Mahmoud has no interest in Uma, he knows that she and Aaron are seeing each other, so why would she want to take him out. Mahmoud shakes his head. He is about to walk inside when Yasmeen drives up. Mahmoud decides to wait for her. Mahmoud walks over to Yasmeen car. His heart is racing as she steps out with her long sexy chocolate legs.

I thought that was you.

"And you thought right. What are you doing out here?"

"Well I was on my way inside when I saw you drive up."

"Ok so you waited for me and why?"

"Well I was going to send you an email about the five o'clock meeting today after work."

"What? Are you kidding me?"

"No, I'm not."

"Come on doctor Shashivivek a meeting today!"

"Yes. Look it's not going to take long. I have somethings that we all need to go over before tomorrow morning."

Yasmeen rolls her eyes. *"You just wanted to ruin my lunch didn't you. Yasmeen walks ahead of Mahmoud. Send me an email because I might forget.*

"Yasmeen really!"

"What? You know that I'm a busy lady and I shut down after three."

As Mahmoud walks behind Yasmeen he bits his bottom lip.

Mahmoud reach for the door. *"Here let me get that for you."*

Thanks, I thought that I was going to have to ask. And don't be looking at my ass."

Mahmoud is taken by surprise. *"What?"*

"Just kidding I just wanted to see if you were paying attention."

As Yasmeen walks away Mahmoud can't take his eyes off her. He would like nothing more than to hold her in his arms again. It's five o'clock when Yasmeen, Ashton, Jacob, and Zada meets up with Maxwell, Rebecca, Brandon, and Mahmoud at the conference room. Zada is about to say good bye to Yasmeen and Ashton when Mahmoud opens the door to the conference room. Everyone is surprised to see Uma on her knees giving a blow job to the guy from the engineering department. Zada is standing behind Mahmoud and Yasmeen when Mahmoud opens the door everyone's mouth drops open. Rebecca smiles with delight. As the guy from engineering tries to pull his pants up but not before they all see his dick when he pulls it out of Uma's mouth.

Rebecca speaks out. *"Is that Uma? Yes, I do believe it is."* Pulling out her cell

"Girl she had her mouth on him like a suction cup. Yass Ms. Thang was gripping both of his ass cheeks to."

Zada laugh. *"Poor man looks like he was trying to get away."*

Rebecca joins in. And do y'all see how small it is Ashton?

"Hell, yeah look like she was trying to suck the life out of the poor man through that little thing… He was almost gone too."

Yasmeen laughs. *"Uma's the grim ripper. Y'all. I'm going to call her leach mouth. She was latched on to him and that little things. He couldn't beat her off with a stick. He must have promised to pay a bill or something Za!*

"I hope that she got the money first because he's not coming back."

"Can you blame him? But I must give it to her she was trying her best to work with what he had which wasn't much!"

Mahmoud tries to hold back his laugher as Uma rushes pass them in embarrassment. She is mortified to see her coworkers staring at her. Aaron walks up after Uma walks down the hall. Rebecca can't wait to tell Aaron.

"You just missed the show."

Aaron looking confused. *"What show."*

"Uma and the engineering *guy. She was cleaning his pipe."*

"What?"

"You heard me, she was sucking him off!"

"So, who's next? Doctor Shashivivek you and I need to talk."

"About what Yasmeen?"

"This meeting. You see I can't be apart, of this. No way. I did not sign up for this. This is not the meeting that I had in mind. Being a sarcastic. I have got to find me another job. Doctor Khalidah has his staff in here giving head. This place is a mad house!"

Mahmoud looks at Yasmeen. *"This was not…"*

"Yeah right."

"Come sit here in your seat Yasmeen."

"No, I don't think so. I have a new seat now thanks to Uma."

"But you have always sat next to me why change now!"

"I'm not going to sit there after that man had his ass on this table as a matter of fact, I'm not going to sit at this table anymore.

Aaron can't believe that Uma would do something so stupid. When Aaron gets home, Uma is waiting for him in his drive way. He takes a deep breath as he gets out of his Porsche. Uma runs over to Aaron and puts her arms around his neck. He pushes her away.

"Aaron I'm so sorry but will you let me explain?"

"Explain what? Explain how everyone saw you sucking the IT guy dick. That fucking loser"

"Aaron, it wasn't like that."

"Really, how was it? Was that not you, giving head to another man in the conference room today?"

"Yes but…"

"But my ass. Now get out of my way."

"Aaron please can I at least come in so that we can discuss this?"

"No, you can't come in and there's nothing to discuss! We're done, you need to leave, I have nothing more to say to you!"

"So, it's over just like that?"

"Yes!"

"So, I guess that you're going back to fucking that whore Rebecca!"

"No, I never stopped fucking that whore. I just included you whore!"

Aaron close the door in Uma's face. She gets back in her car and drive away. On her way down the street she passes Rebecca. Uma turns her car around and follows her back to Aarons house. Rebecca is knocking on Aaron's door when Uma runs up to confront her just as Aaron opens the door.

"So, bitch you got what you wanted. I hope that you are happy, you slut!"

"Who are you calling a slut with your nasty ass? You're the one who was sucking some random guys dick!"

"Aaron is my man remember that."

"No, you whore he has always been my man I just let you, borrow him, now I'm taking him back bitch!"

Aaron pulls Rebecca into his house and pushes Uma back as she tries to force her way in. Aaron slam the door leaving Uma standing on the porch crying. Uma can't believe how Aaron treated her. After all she only suck the guys dick, she didn't screw him like he's doing Rebecca.

The next day before Yasmeen can get in her office Uma is standing at her door waiting for her. Yasmeen takes a deep breath as she approaches Uma. Yasmeen says to herself. *"What in the hell! Please not again today. Trying to smile. Uma you're here early and may I ask why are you waiting at my door?"*

"Ms. Blake, I really needed to talk to you. It just couldn't wait please."

Yasmeen puts her briefcase down. *"Ok let's talk. What's on your mind."*

"Let's see. Where do I start. Ok I know that you and everyone else saw and knows about what happened on yesterday."

"Yes, pretty much everyone who was there knows."

"I'm so humiliated. I don't know what to say. I'm just so shamed. On top of everything Aaron broke up with me and he went back to that bitch Rebecca!"

Yasmeen rubs her head. *"Well I'm sorry to hear that. Maybe he just needs some time to think. I just don't know what you want from me. I mean if you and Aaron were supposed to be together why would you go give a head job to another guy? It just doesn't make sense."*

"Yes, I know, and I don't know why I did it. It just happened. We had been conversating in passing, and we made plan to meet. One thing leads to another and I don't know what happened after that."

"You sucked his dick."

"I know that, but I don't know why?"

"Well did he promise you or gave you something."

"Not yet but we did talk about a down pay on my house, but now he's not returning my call either. He really wasn't worth it.

"Yeah I have to agree with you on that. Uma why didn't you get the money first, I'm just saying."

"I was stupid, I guess. Why did I do that? I really cared about Aaron."

Yasmeen is confused as she looks at Uma. *"Ok… Umm yes Uma just give him some time like I said."*

"How much time?

"That I don't know.

"Well can you talk to him for me Ms. Blake?"

Yasmeen eyes widen. *"For now, I'm going to need you to call me Yasmeen and no I can't talk to him. Uma I'm not going to get in the middle of this mess. You, Aaron, and Rebecca can figure this this out on y'all own time just leave me out of it."*

"Ms. Blake… Yasmeen I just need help!"

"*Well I can't help you, not with that. All this that you all have going on is just over my head.*"

"*Well can you at least talk to doctor Shashivivek for me?*"

Yasmeen is surprised. "*Talk to doctor Shashivivek about what?*"

"*About me. You know after I got back from lunch with you, I asked him out to dinner.*"

"*And what did he say?*"

"*Well he said no at first, but I told him that I would not take no for an answer. Then I ran away before he could answer. Then this blow job thing happened. Now I don't know.*"

"*Uma do you really think that doctor Shashivivek would seriously go out with you after the incident that happened?*"

"*Why not? I mean it might take a little convincing and that's where you come in.*"

"*No that where I say are you out of your mind? You should really hear yourself right now.*"

"*Please.*"

"*Please… No. First you want Aaron, then you want doctor Shashivivek. Uma there is something seriously wrong with you. I suggest that you get professional counselling like last week counselling.*"

"*Yasmeen, you don't understand.*"

"*You're right, but I'm going to fix that.* Picking up her phone. *Hello doctor Khalidah, how are you? Listen I have Ms. Wells in my office and I really need you to come get her. Well no but she needs to talk to somebody and I'm sorry that I'm not the one that she needs to talk to.*"

Just as Rosetta enter Yasmeen office Jacob and Maxwell walks in behind her. Yasmeen lays her head on her desk as Uma exits her office with Maxwell and Jacob. Uma thanks Yasmeen as she leaves.

"*What was that all about?*"

"*Don't even ask Rosetta.*"

"*Yass what wrong with her?*"

"*Hell, if I know. I think that her cheese fell off her bread. That chick crazy.*"

"*I just know that she was in here talking about what happened yesterday.*"

"*Yes, that and her wanting to be with Aaron, doctor Shashivivek, and shit I don't know. Aaron must have it going on?*"

Rosetta Laughs. *"Well I heard that he was good in bed."*

"Well I wouldn't know and thank God that I will never find out!"

Yasmeen looks at Rosetta smiling to herself. Yasmeen has always known that she had a thing for Aaron. Yasmeen knows that it is just a matter of time before that nasty whore makes her move. It been three weeks and Uma's still on her mission to get Aaron back or Mahmoud. Uma don't know how much more of Mahmoud turning her down she can take but she will keep trying. As always it is Monday and Monday means meetings. Yasmeen and Ashton are sit at the table talking when Brandon who is still infatuated with Yasmeen walks in with Rebecca and Aaron. Just as Aaron is about to take his seat Uma storms in she runs up to Aaron. Aaron pushes her back after she takes a swing at him.

"What in the hell is your problem?"

"You're my problem. Aaron, I have been calling you and texting you for over a week now. Why haven't you returned any of my calls?"

Ashton turns to Yasmeen. *"There is nothing like some good entertainment to start your Monday morning off."*

"I wish that we had some popcorn. I think this show is going to be good."

"I have been busy Uma!"

"With who? Pointing to Rebecca. *I hope not that ugly bitch!"*

"As a matter of fact, he has been with me you whore!"

"Oh, really Aaron! Ok well since you don't know how to answer your phone. I guess I will deliver the message to you in person Mr. Aaron Sinclair, I'm pregnant with your baby! Uma looks over to Rebecca. *Yes, bitch I'm caring your man's baby!"*

"Yasmeen, I told you this was going to be good, but I was not expecting that!"

"Me neither. The wheel just came off and hit the fence."

Aaron and Rebecca are both bowled over. Aaron cannot believe him own ears. He looks over at Yasmeen who's smiling.

"What?"

"You heard me. I'm pregnant!"

Aaron feels nauseated "And you couldn't tell me this at home! You had to come to work and make a seen! How do you know if it even mine?"

"I did try to tell you, remember you didn't answer your phone, so I did what I had to do you bum and you know that this is your baby. We both do!"

"How would I know? Most important how would you know. If you are pregnant, anybody could be the father. Hell, that could be the IT guys baby, the milk man, or the guy who does your yard."

. *"Aaron this is your baby and you know it. You know that we never stop sleeping together, even after that incident."*

"Well I'll just wait on the blood test!"

That's right you no good bitch!"

Yasmeen gets up and gets between Uma and Rebecca shaking her head at Aaron. Aaron looks away.

"Ok... Ok that's enough. You both needs to stop. Aaron this is between you and Uma, so we're going to leave you two alone to discuss this. Come on y'all let's give them a minute. That mean you too Rebecca out!"

"He my man Yasmeen and I'm staying. What would you do?"

"Don't go there with me. Now get your ass out of here!"

Yasmeen closes the door after Rebecca walks out leaving Aaron and Uma to talk. After ten minutes Mahmoud, Jacob, and Maxwell show up. Mahmoud is surprised to see everyone standing outside of the conference room.

"Why are you all standing out here doctor Ward? What going on?"

"Well doctor Sinclair and Uma are talking over an issue that they are having and I'm sure that they are going to share it with you and doctor Khalidah.

"So, do you know what they are talking about?"

Well, we all do but I would rather they tell you, right Yasmeen?"

"Yeah... Yeah let them tell the both of you." Yasmeen points to Maxwell and Mahmoud.

Mahmoud narrows his eyes. *"Ok then shall we go inside."*

Jacob pull Yasmeen back. *"What's going on?"*

"Well I'm not at liberty to say. You know how everybody is always telling me to mind my business, well I'm going to do just that for the next hour."

Mahmoud walks into the conference room he immediately looks at Aaron who is sitting on the opposite side of the table. Uma is sitting with her hands over her face. Mahmoud takes his seat as he puts on his glasses. Yasmeen looks at Mahmoud she can see the anger in his eyes. Yasmeen is about to speak when Brandon bumps into her his hand rubs across her round firm ass. Brandon wishes that he could just grip Yasmeen ass without her knocking the shit out of him.

"Excuse me, oh by the way what that fragrance that you're wearing?"

Yasmeen smiles. *"So, you like it? It's called back up off my ass!"*

Mahmoud looks at Brandon. *"So, can we start this meeting or talk about what's going on with Uma and you doctor Sinclair?"*

Aaron take a deep breath before answering Mahmoud because he knows that his job is on the line. Aaron looks around the room he hopes that Yasmeen hasn't said anything. His heart is beating so fast that you can see his shirt moving. Sweat start to run down his face. Aaron looks around at Uma. *"I think that we should start the meeting Doctor."* After the meeting Uma goes to Maxwell's office where she tells him and Mahmoud everything. She discloses to them that she's pregnant with Aaron's baby and the fact that he doesn't think that the baby his. Maxwell and Mahmoud are disappointed in both Uma and Aaron. Later Jacob is talking to Yasmeen, Zada, Tia, and Ashton at the end of the hall.

Jacob to Ashton. *"So, Uma is having doctor Sinclair's baby."*

"That's what she said, in front of all of us this morning Jacob."

"Wait a minute now isn't he and Rebecca still doing whatever.

Zada jumps in. *"Yeah that's what I was thinking and wasn't Uma the one walking around saying she was not here to make friend and that she doesn't socialize with co-works."*

Tia laughs. *"Yeah that's what she said. She may not socialize with her coworkers, but she sure is giving that thang up like it's a free for all. I think Jacob got some."*

"Hell, no I didn't!"

"Are you sure?"

"Hell, yeah I'm sure. She never even talked to me."

"So, you wanted some?"

"No Yasmeen. My wife would kill me because you would tell on my ass. Anyway, that guy is a loose cannon, he is screwing everybody around here."

"No, he's not. He never screwed me!"

Tia and Zada speaks at the same time. *"Me either!"*

Jacob laughs." *I'm just saying that doctor Sinclair has been with a lot of women and lately he has been running them crazy. I need to ask him what's his secret."*

Tia reply. *"STD and a lot of crazy."*

It's has been a long day all Yasmeen wants to do is to go home slip into a hot bubble bath with a glass of wine. Yasmeen tells herself that it's going to be a long week. Yasmeen mind starts to wonder if Mahmoud and Uma got together, did she suck his dick too? Yasmeen shake that thought out of her head. She hopes that she's wrong, but then again who knows! When Yasmeen gets home her cell phone rings, it's Aaron. He has been calling her all day. Yasmeen turns her phone off. She grabs a bottle of wine and a glass. Yasmeen starts to undress as she makes her way to her bedroom for a much need bubble bath.

Chapter 7

Brace yourself here comes the Storm…

A month has passed Uma is still caring Aaron's baby and Rebecca is still in love with Aaron, who is still a sum-of, sum of everybody man. After lunch Yasmeen is sitting in her car contemplating on whether she should just go home for the rest of the day, because for a Thursday it feels like a long Monday. For Yasmeen, everything has gone wrong and she has no one to talk to. Zada's off and Ashton has been on call all week so he's at Oscar house sleep. *"Where are your friend when you need them? Home sleep!"* Yasmeen is about to get out of her car when she Mahmoud and Zoe pull up in her red Camaro. Yasmeen sits in her car and watch Mahmoud as he leans over and put his arm around Zoe. Yasmeen can't see if they are kissing or not because Mahmoud big ass head is obstructing her view, Yasmeen assumes that they are. Yasmeen feels as if she had just been punched in her stomach. She knew that Mahmoud and Zoe were friends and nothing more at least that's what Mahmoud told her. Who can she believe Mahmoud of her lying eyes? Yasmeen turns her head as Zoe drives away and Mahmoud enters the building. He doesn't see Yasmeen watching him. Yasmeen can feel her blood boiling and she doesn't know why after all Mahmoud is not her man. Before Yasmeen gets out of her car, she tells herself to forget about Mahmoud and to push away everything that she's feeling because she can't miss something that she never had, besides it was only a school girl crush. The more Yasmeen talks to herself the more stupid and foolish she feels for even entertaining the thought of her having a crush on a soon to be married man. Yasmeen laughs to herself. Yasmeen is walk through the lobby, she's feeling better that is until she sees Wallace and Mahmoud standing at the entrance door laughing and talking. Yasmeen wishes that she could just melt then she wouldn't have to speak. Yasmeen tries to sneak pass them in the hopes that they don't see her, wishful think because Wallace being Wallace, he sees everything.

"Well hello Ms. Blake I almost didn't she you. How are you?

Yasmeen to herself. *"Shit! Oh, hey Wallace. Yes, I'm just great, you have a blessed day!*

Yasmeen is walking so fast that it looks like she's run. She hears Mahmoud yell out. *Is Wallace the only one that you see standing here.* Yasmeen pretends not to hear Mahmoud as she continues to run walk to the elevator. As the elevator door's close Yasmeen leans back on the wall and close her eyes. Yasmeen opens her eyes when she hears the elevator doors open on the next floor. Yasmeen gasps when she sees Chase getting on the elevator. Yasmeen is about to get off when Chase grabs her by her arm.

"Yasmeen, I need to talk to you."

Yasmeen pulls away from Chase. *"I have nothing to say to you."*

"But Yasmeen I just wanted to tell you that…"

"Save it for somebody who cares."

Yasmeen, I really need to talk to you!"

"No what you need to do is to go take a long walk on a short bridge."

Yasmeen walks away as the door to the elevator closes. When Yasmeen gets back to her office Jacob is waiting by her office door with Rosetta. Yasmeen gets a sinking feeling in her stomach. She knows that something is going on but what and how much will it affect her. Yasmeen puts her war face on and prepare herself for what is to come.

"Hey, Yasmeen we need to talk."

"Ok and what do we need to talk about?"

"Can we go to my office?"

Yasmeen looks at Rosetta as she whispers, *I'm sorry.* They both follow Jacob back to his office. Yasmeen sits down beside Rosetta. Yasmeen tell herself *what has this slick bitch done?* Yasmeen looks over at Jacob he can see the anger and wonder on Yasmeen's face, so he tries not to make eye contact with her.

"Ok everyone's here so start talking Doc!"

Jacob takes a deep long breath. *"Yasmeen, I want you to know that you and…"*

Yasmeen butts in. *"You what?"*

"You and… Well you will be going out of town to the Life Seminar with Aaron and Rosetta will be taking your place at the Medical conference for the next two days with myself, doctor Shashivivek, and doctor Khalidah."

Yasmeen shaking her head. *"No… No, I'm not going anywhere with Aaron!"*

"Yasmeen I'm not asking you I'm telling you!"

Yasmeen stands up. *"And I'm telling you that I'm not going. By the way who's idea was this?"*

Jacob looks over at Rosetta. *"Well Yasmeen it was no one's idea. Rosetta just mentioned that she has never been to this conference, she said that she would love to go to this time that all. Yasmeen, you are always going."*

"So, Rosetta did you not go to this same conference last year or did the both of you forget? Oh, and did you not go to that two-week conference in Chicago five months ago? Yasmeen walks to the door. You know what I do care who goes to the conference I don't want to go anyway, and I will tell you this, I will not be going with Aaron either, so, you can do whatever you want! Now you two can discuss that!"

Rosetta gets up. *"Yasmeen wait…"*

"Don't you dare come near me! Your best bet is to stay the hell away from me both of you!"

Yasmeen leaves Jacob office and slams the door behind her. Yasmeen goes back to her office where she contemplates weather she should stay or go home. Jacob is still in his office talking to Rosetta. He's knows that he has made a big mistake Jacob thinks to himself how he can fix this before things get too out of hand. *"Rosetta, you can go back to your office and I'll go talk to Yasmeen."* Jacob leaves his office. Soon he's knocking on Yasmeen door. Without answering Yasmeen flings the door open. *"What?"* Jacob almost speechless. *"Yasmeen, we really need to talk about this."*

"You didn't talk to me before you and Rosetta made your decision so why do you want to talk to me now?"

"Look Yasmeen can I come in?"

"Do whatever you want!"

Jacob take a deep breath before he sits down. Jacob knows that Yasmeen is upset but he doesn't understand why she's making a big deal out of it. Jacob just wants to know where Yasmeen head is and what can he do.

"Yasmeen, I don't understand. I mean did you want to go to the conference?"

"Let's get one thing straight! I don't care about going to that conference. Hell, you can take Rosetta with you to all your conferences and meetings I don't care, but what I do care about is you and her going behind my back and you having the audacity to say that I never give her the chance to go anywhere! As her supervisor, I afford her all the opportunity that I possibly can, and you know it! I have always been fair with her and I have always courage Rosetta to attend medical conferences. I have even come, to you on many occasions asking if Rosetta could attend if not with me or instead of me have I not?"

"Well yes you have."

"Well I dare you say that I am the one who's always going! That's not what bothering me! what gets me is you telling, me that I'm going to this Life Seminar with Aaron, you most, be out of your mind! I will quit first before I go anywhere with Aaron!"

"Yasmeen it's only a seminar!"

"Yeah a seminar that I won't be attending!"

"Ok what if I can work something out where you and Aaron won't have to be or ride together, would that work for you?"

"You know I really don't care all I know is that Aaron and I are not going ...

"Yasmeen it's only one day and you will be fling on the same plane that's it. I will get your seat changed ok and I'm sorry that I interfered."

Yasmeen goes to the Life Seminar and to her surprise it went better than she had planned. Yes, Aaron did everything that he could think of to get Yasmeen's attention he even had their seat changed on the airplane. It didn't matter because Yasmeen had so much fun ignoring Aaron and Timothy the OR nurse who wouldn't stop hitting on her. Yes, Timothy is quite handsome, but he has a reputation like Aaron he likes the ladies. He must have asked Yasmeen out over a hundred time and her answer has always been no! He keeps asking with the hopes that Yasmeen will one day say yes. One thing for sure Yasmeen likes the chase if nothing more she loves to see Aaron face when he can't get what he wants. A week after the Life Seminar Timothy again ask Yasmeen out but this time, he ask her out to lunch. To Timothy surprise Yasmeen agree to meet him for lunch.

"You are so beautiful, and I'm so honored to be here with you."

"Really Tim?

"Yes, really Yasmeen you know that I have been trying to get with you from the first day that we met."

Yasmeen says to herself. *"What an asshole. I hope that he doesn't think that I like his whoring ass. So, Tim don't you have a girlfriend?"*

"Who me?"

"Yes you, do you see another Tim at this table?"

"No…No I do have friends but that's about it. I'm not in a relationship if that's what you're asking."

"You need to stop."

"Stop what? Yasmeen I'm trying to get to know you better."

"You're trying to get in my panties"

"No not really, but if it leads to that."

"You know what thanks for lunch, but I've got to get back to work."

"Ok look Yasmeen let me take you out this weekend and show you a good time."

"I don't think that would be a good idea."

"Why not?"

"I just don't think so, but thanks for the offer."

"Well think about it here my number call me beautiful.

Yasmeen take Timothy's number knowing that she has no intention on call him. Yasmeen drives away, and she lets Timothy number fly out of the window. Yasmeen call Zada to tell her about her going to lunch with Timothy they laugh. The next morning Mahmoud over hears Aaron talking to Timothy.

"Tim, I hear that you had lunch with Yasmeen."

"Yes, I did. What's it to you?"

"Well she and I use to date, so I didn't think that you should be going out with her."

"I don't care what you think! I can go out with whoever I want, I don't need your permission!"

"Yes, you are right you can go out with anybody that you want, just as long as it's not Yasmeen!"

"Look Doc you had your chance and you struck out."

Aaron walks away to keep from punching Timothy lights out. Mahmoud cannot believe his ears Yasmeen and Timothy. Mahmoud precedes to his office the whole time he can't stop thinking about Yasmeen. the more he thinks the madder he gets. Timothy is walking through the lobby when he sees Yasmeen, Tia, and Zada coming toward him, he smiles with delight he hopes that Aaron is somewhere watching.

"Well hello beautiful ladies. Yasmeen can I please get just a moment of you time."

"What is it Tim?"

"I just wanted to know if I could take you out this weekend?"

"No Tim." "Come on Yasmeen I promise to show you a great time. Dinner and a movie what do you say?"

"I still say no!"

"Come on Yasmeen don't be like that. Just go out with me."

"Why me? Why do you want to go out with me? Timothy I'm sure that there are plenty of other women who would love to accompany you out on a date."

"I'm sure there are, but they are not you."

"Tim will you please get out of our way we have to get back to work."

"If you go out with me."

"I said no! Now move."

"Well I'm going to follow you to your office."

"No, you're not."

"Yes I am."

Yasmeen thinks that she must get this idiot out of her face and keep him from following her. Yasmeen is desperate. She looks at Tia and Zada she winks her eye. *"Ok Tim I'll go out with you if I can pick the place and movie."*

"Ok that a deal, so I'll see you at eight. Oh, do you still have my number?"

"I do it's in my car, so I will call you."

"Can I pick you up from your house?"

"No!"

"Why?"

"Because... Ok fine!"

Timothy claps his hand. *"Ok text me your Address."*

Yasmeen gets on the elevator. *"Ok I will now let me get to my office Tim."*

"I know that you are not going out with that dog!"

"I know that's right Za! If you go out with him, you may as well start seeing Aaron again.

"Now you both know me better than that, I just told him that to shut him up! I know he Ain't about shit, beside we are going to Vegas for the weekend or did you both forget."

"Oh, hell yeah I've already picked my shit, as a matter of fact, I'm following you ass home Yass my shit in the car I'm ready!

When Yasmeen arrives at her office Rosetta is waiting on her with two cups in her hand. Yasmeen rolls her eyes, because she and Rosetta has not been talking much unless it was about work.

"Hey Yasmeen I brought you a peace offering."

"No thank you I've had my peace for the day."

"Come on Yasmeen I miss you. I'm sorry."

Yasmeen Rolls her eye as she enters her office with Rosetta following close behind. Yasmeen already knows that the trip was boring, and Rosetta couldn't get lucky. Yasmeen sits down at her desk and wait. She knows that Rosetta wants to be nosy about something with her slick ass.

"So, I hear that you and Timothy had lunch the other day."

"It was yesterday and no before you ask. I know that you fucked him. Did you hear that?"

"I was just asking."

"You were being nosy!"

Yasmeen tell Rosetta that she has to get ready to meet with a patient and they leave. As Yasmeen walks down the hall, she gets the feeling that something bad is about to happen. Yasmeen starts praying asking God to forgive her for lying to Timothy. Yasmeen tell herself that whatever it is that is about to transpire she hopes that she can deal with it. Timothy is on his cell phone talking when Mahmoud walks up behind him. Timothy is too busy talking so doesn't see Mahmoud.

Guess, what bro? Guess who I got a date with this weekend? Yasmeen, I have a date with Yasmeen Blake. Your boy is going to blow her back out. I'm going to have her backing that big ass up to me all weekend. I'm going to have her running around here like them other bitches. I'm going to have her ass begging for this dick. Oh, you already know I'm going to beat her back out. On my way home, I'm going to stop by the store to get a box of magnum. You know what's up. She is getting, all this dick. Oh yeah, I'm going to lick that pussy."

Timothy turns around to see Mahmoud staring at him. Mahmoud is furious, and Timothy can see it in his eyes as he hangs up his phone, he walks fast down the hall. Mahmoud doesn't want to believe that Yasmeen would consider going out with such a loser. Before lunch Mahmoud is standing at the nurse's station he is still fuming when Yasmeen walks up to him. *"Hey, I need to talk to you if you're not busy."* Mahmoud looks at Yasmeen, all he can see is red. Mahmoud and Yasmeen walks into the units' patient's conference room. By the time that they reach, the conference room Mahmoud is so angry he feels like smoke is coming out of his ears. As soon as Yasmeen opens her mouth all the anger that he's feeling comes pouring out. Soon Mahmoud and Yasmeen are yelling at each other.

"Who do you think that you are? You don't tell me what do Yasmeen!"

"Oh, I'm Yasmeen Blake and I' m not telling you what to do I was just asking you!"

"Well I'm the doctor!"

"Well you need to act like it and stop making poor decisions about the patients that are in your care Doctor!"

"Poor decisions! I don't make poor decisions! I decide what best for my patients at that time! Just because it's does meet your standers doesn't mean that...

"Yes, it does. All you do is make half ass decisions that works for you without thinking about what work on behalf of the patients, you are a selfish human being!"

"Yasmeen don't you interrupt me! I am a great doctor!"

"You're full of yourself that's what you are, and you make me sick!"

"I make you sick?... I make you sick?"

"Yes, you do! I don't know why I'm still standing here talking to you because you don't know how to listen all you know how to do is talk!"

"Don't you walk away from!"

"Who's going to stop me? It sure not you! I'm done you're not talking about nothing, you're just wasting my time!"

Yasmeen walks out of the conference room leave Mahmoud furious. He tries to control his anger, but he can't because the one thing that he despises is for anyone to turn their back to him and Yasmeen is going to pay for that. This is not the end. Thinking about Yasmeen in bed with Timothy doesn't help. Mahmoud explodes on the inside. When Mahmoud walks out into the hall, he sees Yasmeen and Zada talking. Yasmeen looks up at him and frowns up her face. She walks away to avoid Mahmoud. Yasmeen has had a great weekend despite the mishap's that happened between her and Mahmoud. Yasmeen blocked all that out of her mind. It's Monday back to reality and back to work. Yasmeen already knows that today is going to be hell, because Jacob called her at home. He wants to meet with her before the nine o'clock meeting. Yasmeen walks into Jacob's office. She is stunned to see Maxwell. She already expected to see Mahmoud, so she was not at all surprised to see him sitting in Jacob's office. Yasmeen can't figure out why is Maxwell there? Yasmeen looks at the empty chair next to Maxwell.

"What is this Jacob?"

"Yasmeen please come in and have a seat."

"Ok now what."

"Well Yasmeen I know that you already have an Idea of why I call this meeting."

"I have an idea but why don't you enlighten me."

"Yasmeen, we are here to talk about the incident that happened between you and doctor Shashivivek on Friday."

"Ok what about it?"

As Mahmoud looks at Yasmeen the only thing that he can picture is her and Timothy. The same anger that he felt before suddenly take hold of him as he looks at Yasmeen who is smiling."

"This is what I'm talking about that arrogant attitude! I will not tolerate this kind of behavior from her Jacob!"

"Arrogant attitude! Who are you referring to?"

"I'm referring to you!"

"Well you my name is Yasmeen, so use it when you talk to me… him!"

"Him!"

"Yeah him or He which do you prefer?"

"Yasmeen, you are rude!"

"So are you!"

"So, are you just going to let her talk to me like that?"

"*Yasmeen, you really should watch your tone and be mindful of how you talk to people!*"

"*Be mindful and watch how I talk to people! People need to be mindful of how they talk to me! No, I will not kiss* Yasmeen points her finger. *Yours, his, or his ass. The two of you can kiss up to him but I'm not. All I did was ask him a question! What was it too hard for you or did you not know how to answer it?*"

"*You need to have better control of you staff doctor Baldwin!*"

"*Control who? Nobody controls me not even you and this is your hospital!*"

"*Yasmeen sit down!*"

"*You don't tell me to sit down! You can ask me doctor Baldwin!*"

"*Yasmeen I'm warning you!*"

"*You're warning me!*"

"*Yes, I'm! Look Yasmeen I don't want to suspend you, but I will! Now will you please sit down!*"

All Yasmeen see is red. Yasmeen feels as if Jacob, Mahmoud, and Maxwell are trying to gang up on her which put her on defense.

"*No, I won't sit down, and you don't have to suspend me Jacob Baldwin this is my two-week notice!*"

"*What do you mean two-week notice!*"

"*You three put your heads together and y'all figure it out!*"

Yasmeen storms out of Jacob's office and out to her car. Maxwell never says a word he just looks at Mahmoud and Jacob. Who still has no idea as to what just happened. Yasmeen sits in her car she can't stop crying. She feels betray just because she stood up for her patient. Yasmeen speeds out of the parking garage. Mahmoud is walking through the lobby when Wallace catches up to him. Wallace is not aware of what happened at the meet, but he knows that Mahmoud is just hurt from the thought of Yasmeen being with another man.

"*Hey Doc.*"

"*Hey Wallace. Do you mind. I'm in a hurry.*"

"*I can see that. I just wanted to ask you did you hear about Ms. Blake?*"

Mahmoud stops walking. He looks at Wallace with so much angry and hurt in his eyes. Mahmoud assume that Wallace is talking about the meeting that they had with Yasmeen. Mahmoud prepares himself to tell Wallace that he needs to mind his business.

"What about her?"

"I don't know if you knew this, but Timothy asked her out. He was going around bragging about what he was going to do."

"Ok"

"Well now he's running around mad because she stood him up. I heard that she went to Vegas with her friends. That joker is mad."

"Really?"

"Yes really. I just thought that you should know that."

Mahmoud puts his hands up to his face. He feels like an, complete asshole for letting his emotions get the best of him. He knows that he must make it up to Yasmeen, but how when she won't even talk to him, especially after the way he acted towards her. When Mahmoud gets up to the patient floor her hears Zada and Timothy talking.

"Hey Za, where's your lying friend.

"Boy why?"

"Because I want to ask her why did she do me like that? Why she stood me up?

"You should have known better, you knew Yasmeen was not about to go out with you! For one thing, you talk too damn much, and you are full of shit now move and leave my friend along.

"Ok so it's like that Zada?"

"Yes! It's just like that!"

Mahmoud can feel himself smiling at the same time his heart breaks.

"Can I speak with you Zada."

"Yes, Doc Boy move! Doc can you tell him to get from up here this is not his floor."

Zada laughs as she and Mahmoud walk down the hall.

"Zada where is Yasmeen?"

"Doc I don't know. I have been calling her but she's not answering her phone."

"I assume that you know about what happened."

"Yes, she did tell me before she stopped answering her phone."

"Look can you please tell her to call me? I just want to apologize for the way that I acted. Please have Yasmeen call me I need to talk to her. I know that I'm the last person that she wants to talk to right now... Just have her call me ok."

"Ok I will tell her."

"Thank you."

After four days, no one has heard from Yasmeen. Jacob and Maxwell has been calling her cell and house phone, but their attempts are useless. Yasmeen is still unreachable. Mahmoud and Jacob has repeatedly asked Zada about Yasmeen where about. Zada tell them that like them she has not talk to Yasmeen, which is a lie. Zada and Ashton knows that Yasmeen is on vacation for the next two weeks and she made them promise not to tell that she went to visit her brother. Jacob knows that Yasmeen is out on vacation but he's not sure if she will be coming back, because he and Maxwell have been getting call from other companies that Yasmeen has applied to for jobs. The last thing that Jacob or Mahmoud wants is for Yasmeen to quit over a petty miss understanding. Yasmeen has been in many confrontations with him before so why is this one so different. Jacob wonders if there's something that Yasmeen is not telling him and if, so he need to get to the bottom of it. It's has been almost two weeks and still no word from Yasmeen. Jacob knows that Yasmeen can be unpredictable at times, but this takes the cake. No matter how mad she gets Yasmeen has never up and disappeared without saying a word. Jacob, Maxwell and Mahmoud get together, and they decide to go over to Yasmeen house after work. when they get to Yasmeen's house, they see her Mercedes parked in the driveway. Jacob knocks on the door. Yasmeen is on the phone talking to Zada. She just got back in town the day before. Yasmeen hears a knock on the door, she wonders who it could be. Yasmeen gets up. Jacob who is standing at the door with Mahmoud and Maxwell heart begins to pound in his chest as he hears, Yasmeen footsteps coming to the door. When Yasmeen opens the door, she is surprised to Jacob, Maxwell and Mahmoud standing outside of her door. Yasmeen reaction is to slam the door in their face but what good would that do. Yasmeen wants to know why are they at her house? Most importance how they know where she lived?

"What are you doing here?"

"Yasmeen, we came here to talk to you."

"We don't have anything to talk about and how did you know where I lived?"

"Well Yasmeen Maxwell and I did come to pick you up several times before, so I guess I remembered."

"Ok now why are y'all here."

"To talk to you now can we come in?"

"No and like I said we have nothing to talk about."

"Yasmeen, we have a lot to talk about."

"We do? Like what Jacob?"

"Like when are you coming back to work?"

"Don't I give you my two-week notice?"

"You did but Yasmeen you know that I'm not going to except that."

"Oh, so you want it in writing. Ok hold on."

"No Yasmeen you know that's not what I want!" Mahmoud stands back and observes Yasmeen. he knows that Yasmeen really don't want to quit but at the same time he can see the anger in her eyes. Mahmoud feels responsible for this conflict so it's up to him to make things right.

" Yasmeen all we want is to talk to you that's all please."

"You know that I really didn't have anything to say to you doctor Shashivivek!"

"Yes, Yasmeen I know but will you at least hear us out?

"Ok I'm listening."

"Well can we come in? I mean we don't want to talk out here please."

Yasmeen hesitate before she allows them to come into her house. Yasmeen remembers what happened the last time she allowed someone to come into her home. She was almost raped. Yasmeen takes a deep breath as she picks up a letter opener.

"Ok come in and make it quick because I have more pressing things to do!"

"Wow what a nice place you have."

"Well thank you. Now get to the point Jacob!"

"Ok, well Yasmeen you know that the last time that we talked things did end well."

"Yes, Yasmeen and I blame myself for that. I was having a bad day and I took it out on you, Yasmeen, I do apologize. I should have handle thing differently. I know that you were only look out for your patients. Will you forgive me and come back to work?"

Yasmeen doesn't know what to say. Yasmeen wasn't expecting this. Yasmeen looks into Mahmoud's beautiful blue eyes, she turns away as heart start to speed up. Yasmeen tells herself that she can't give in, but her emotions take over her mouth.

"Ok I will think about it."

"So, all is forgiven?"

"No… maybe I don't know!"

"So, we'll see you at work tomorrow?"

"No."

"Next week?"

"No Maxwell next year maybe I'll see! Now get out!"

After Jacob, Maxwell, and Mahmoud leaves Yasmeen stands with her back against the door, contemplating if she's really going to go back to work. Yasmeen knows that her patient's needs her and the last thing that she wants to do is turn her back on them just because of two assholes. Yasmeen closes her eyes. She's startled when she hears loud banging on the door and someone calling her name. The first thought that comes to her mind is that Jacob must have lost his fucking mind to be banging on her door like a crazy person. Yasmeen opens the door and before she can say a word Oscar comes rush in. He pushes past Yasmeen. Yasmeen can see the panic all over Oscars face and he is freaking out. Before Yasmeen can ask him what the matter he collapse onto the sofa and begins to fall apart. Yasmeen has never seen Oscar this way before, but as a friend Yasmeen knows that it's her job to find out what wrong. Yasmeen sits down beside Oscar. Yasmeen holds Oscar hand. *"Oscar what's going on?"*

"What going on? What going on? I will tell you what going on! Yasmeen where were you when I needed you, Yass, I really needed you!"

"'O' I was visiting my brother, you knew that, but I'm here now! What is it? You're really scaring me right now!"

Oscar holds Yasmeen hand tight. *"Yasmeen what I'm I going to do?"*

"Do about what? Oscar, you really need to pull yourself together and tell me what you're talking about, so I can help you!"

"Yasmeen this can't be happing! Not now!"

"What can't be happing? Calm down and talk to me!"

"Yasmeen my life is over!"

"Your life is not over, but it will be because I'm going to kill you if you don't tell me what you're talking about!"

"It's your so-called friend!"

"Who Ashton? What is he sick?"

"No Rosetta, but when Ashton finds out I know that he going to leave me!"

"Ashton is not going to leave you. Now what did Rosetta do?"

"She had me served with child support papers today at work!"

"What? Why? Oscar what are you not telling me?"

"Yass, I told about the threesome that we had about a year ago!"

"Yes, you told me about that, but I think that you may have left some parts out."

"I need a drink!"

Yasmeen gets up and fix two drinks. Yasmeen mind is still racing as she tries to figure out what Oscar is talking about. Yasmeen knows about the threesome that Oscar, Todd, and Rosetta had but that's all she knows. Yasmeen handing Oscar his drink. *"Now tell what's going on 'O'!"* Oscar takes a deep breath. *"Yass, you remember when I told you that Rosetta came over to the house one night talking about, she knew that you and I were fucking and how she had always wanted to fuck me."*

"Yeah I remember."

"Well I told her that you and I were only friends and that you were like a sister to me. Well you already know that we all ended up in the bed that night. Yass what you don't know is that she kept coming back. It was like she couldn't get enough."

"How many times did she come back?"

"Like, six or seven. She was on some shit. Talking about she was going to change Todd and I back. Which I don't know how the pussy wasn't all that."

"What? Ok now where does this child support come in at?"

"Well one night she came over and Todd wasn't home yet. We were talking. Then she asked if she could suck me off. Well I'm still a man so if a woman wants to give me head hell why not. Soon one thing leads to another and before I knew it, we were fucking. When we were finished, she told me that she was in love with me. I told he that I did not feel the same and that she was married and that we could not do this again. She got mad she left. I thought that was the end... well aren't you going to say something?"

"Ugh, Yuck. I mean didn't y'all use protection? Ugh!"

"No not that time we didn't!"

"So, there could be a possibility they her daughter is yours?"

"A possibility yes!"

Yasmeen hit Oscar on the head. *"How could you be so stupid. You know how that girl is! All she wants is for somebody like your ass to take care of her. I should punch you in your face."*

"*I sorry Yass!*"

"*Sorry my ass! You know what I can't even look at you right now and where is Todd? Does he know about this shit?*"

"*Yes, I told him and he's on his way over here to meet me. Yass, I know that you're angry...*"

"*Angry is not the word for what I am! Oscar I'm not angry that you slept with Rosetta! I'm pissed that you didn't protect yourself you, asshole!*"

"*Yass do you think that Ashton will leave me once he finds out?*"

"*I don't know. He shouldn't 'O' this happened before you and he got together right!*"

"*Yes. Yes, after that night I promise you that I didn't sleep with her again.*"

"*Well I suggest that you tell Ashton before he finds out from her.*"

"*But I don't know how to tell him.*"

"*Just tell him. If you care about him tell him. I'm sure that he will understand that you fucked up dumbass!*"

It's Monday Rosetta is sitting in the conference room talking to Rebecca and Aaron when Uma, Brandon, Maxwell and Mahmoud walks in. Uma rolls her eyes at Aaron as she sits down. Rebecca smiles as she whispers to Rosetta. They both look at Uma. Ashton walks in with Jacob they are both surprised to see Rosetta instead of Yasmeen. Jacob takes a deep breath, he looks at Mahmoud who has an uncertain look on his face. Mahmoud and Jacob look around the room without asking the million-dollar question. "*Where in the hell is Yasmeen?* "Mahmoud is just about to start the meeting when Yasmeen walk in wearing a blue wrap dress with a peek-a-boo front. The dress hugs Yasmeen ass and breast like a body pillow under silk sheets. Yasmeen is wearing a pair of blue and white heels that ties around her beautiful smooth legs. Her hair is pulled back in a bun. You can hear everyone gasp as Yasmeen sits down next to Ashton. Rosetta is about to get up to leave when Yasmeen motions for her to sit back down.

"*No sit back down don't leave I'm just here to listen if that's ok.* Yasmeen look around the room. *Oh, and good morning all!*"

"*Bitch you look good!*"

"*Ho, I know! make your mouth water don't I!*"

"*Welcome back Ms. Blake.*"

Yasmeen lock eyes with Mahmoud without saying a word she puts her glasses on and clears her throat. After the meeting is over Yasmeen rushes out the door before anyone can ask her anything, she is not yet ready to talk to Jacob or Mahmoud. Yasmeen is sitting in her office looking at the blue screen on her computer when she hears a knock at the door. Yasmeen knows that it's Jacob, so she prepares herself for what she has been dreading all weekend. Yasmeen forces herself to smile as she opens the door. Instead of Jacob standing at the door it's Uma. Yasmeen knows that whatever Uma wants it can't be good and why in the hell is she bring the bullshit to her. What is this bitch up to?

"Yes!"

"Good morning Yasmeen. Ms. Blake so good to have you back."

"Yeah whatever. Did you need something? I have a lot of work to do."

"Yes, I was wondering if I could have a word with you."

"Look Uma I don't have time for anybody foolishness I just got back, and I really don't want to be here. Now say what you have to say and Make it quick!"

"Ok, may I come in please?"

Yasmeen step to the side as she waves Uma in., they both have a seat. Yasmeen minds start to visit a hundred places as to why Uma wants to talk to her. It has been three weeks what does Uma have to say to her. They are not friend, and Yasmeen has no desire to be friends not with this chick. Yasmeen rubbers her forehead not wanting to ask Uma the question. What do you want? She hesitates before she speaks.

"So, what's on your brain? I know that whatever it is it has nothing to do with work.

"Why do you say that."

"Because I haven't been here and if you want to know anything about a patient, I suggest that you go ask Rosetta."

"You're right it's not work related. I want to ask you about you and Aaron."

Yasmeen looks unsure. *"About me and Aaron! What about me and Aaron?"*

"Well I found out that you and Aaron use to date. Uma puts her hand on her stomach. *I'm sure that you know that I'm carrying his baby."*

"Ok and what in the hell does that has to do with me? Look I don't know what your point is, and I really don't care, but it's no secret that Aaron and I briefly date. What I want to know is why are you concerned about me and Aaron? As far as me knowing about you carrying Aarons baby, I think that the

entire hospital knows. Look Uma I told you that I wasn't going to deal with your bullshit and that's what I meant."

"Yasmeen I'm not trying to cause a problem. I was just saying that I found out because I didn't know."

"Ok now you know."

"I guess what I want to know is…"

"Hell, fucking no before you say it! No, I do want Aaron in no way shape or form. What me and Aaron had was over long before you even got here. So, you and whoever can have Aaron, just leave me out of it!"

"Did you know that he still has…"

"I don't care what he has. He could have three dogs and a zoo I would not care. I don't want anything to do with Aaron Sinclair, you can keep that to yourself! I can promise you that you don't have to worry about me and Aaron, not now, not ever, that ship went down like the titanic! Look girl we are not even going to go there. As a matter of fact, you can leave now!"

"I care a lot for Aaron."

"Aww I'm sorry, but Aaron Ain't shit!"

"How did you get over him?

"I just did… I just did and I'm sure that you know that he cheated on me with Rebecca and I don't share so he had to go. I walked away, and I never looked back thank God."

"Don't you miss the sex?

"Nope I can't say that I do."

"Really?"

"Yes really. Look I can honestly say that I've had way better sex with the invisible man."

"What. I don't understand?

"I know but you will. Just think about it and get back to me when you figure it out."

"Wait, so you've had better than Aaron?"

"Oh yes! Look I really need to get back to work so if you don't mind."

"Oh ok. I just want to know how you got over him without going back?"

Yasmeen thinks to herself. "Easy I never slept with his. Not once and I never will. Look Uma just give it sometime. Now stop crying you're upsetting the baby. Thing will work themselves out."

"Thank you for putting my mind at ease. Uma hugs Yasmeen. Thank you."

157

As Uma walks out Rosetta and Jacob are standing at the door. Yasmeen takes a deep breath as she puts her hand up to her face. Seeing Rosetta and Jacob standing in the door makes her blood go cold. Yasmeen knows that all they want is to ask her questions that's none of their business. Yasmeen walks over to her desk without saying a word. Jacob closes the door behind him as he enters Yasmeen's office.

"Good morning, it's great to have you back."

"Yes, I was so happy to see you."

"I bet you were Rosetta, now what do I owe this unpleasant visit."

"We just wanted to welcome you back that's all."

"Welcome me back yeah right."

"Yasmeen do you think that we could talk later in my office?"

"You can talk, and I'll listen because I really don't have anything to say."

Jacob gets up and walks out leaving Rosetta. Before he opens the door, Jacob looks back at Yasmeen and smile. Yasmeen sits back and looks at Rosetta wanting to punch her in the face. Rosetta is itching to find out where Yasmeen has been. She sit's up in her seat.

"So where were you and why didn't you call or answer your phone Miss Lady?"

"So, you served Oscar with child support papers! I didn't know that you and by best friend were fucking."

Rosetta doesn't know what to say as she looks in Yasmeen eye. Yasmeen waits for an answer that she already knows the answer to, she just wants to hear it from Rosetta lying ass. At first Rosetta refuses to answer as she looks down at the floor, hoping that Yasmeen would just change the subject.

"So, Rosie your daughter is like six months now right."

"Yes, Yasmeen she's six months."

"What did Wendell have say about this mess and how did this baby thing come about?"

"He had a lot to say."

"Rosetta did you really think that my friendship with Todd and Oscar was more than a friendship? I mean you actually thought that I was sleeping with Oscar?"

Yes, I did."

"But why? I told you that they are like family to me. Hell, everybody knows that."

"I know Yasmeen I was just..."

Rosetta can't finish her sentence, she breaks down as she starts to tell Yasmeen everything. The whole nasty truth. She tells Yasmeen that she has always been attracted to Oscar and that him being gay was never a factor. Rosetta only wanted what Yasmeen had and she would do anything to get it. Rosetta tells Yasmeen that getting pregnant was never part of the plan and that it was a mistake, of course, Yasmeen know better. Yasmeen know that getting pregnant with Oscar child was more than Rosetta plan it was her goal. Rosetta tells Yasmeen how it was Wendell's family who put the idea in his head that their daughter wasn't his and that it was his bitch of a mother who pushed him to have a DNA test because their baby girl was too light, and she looked nothing like Wendell of Rosetta didn't help. From day one Wendell family has never cared for Rosetta and they let it be known. Wendell's mother has always said that Rosetta was a no-good whore and she was only after Wendell money. Wendell got a settlement for over two hundred thousand dollars just before they got married. Once and for all Rosetta wanted to shut Wendell's family mouth and to get them out of their business. Rosetta agreed to have their daughter tested and to her surprise his family was right. Not only was Wendell not the father he also moved in with is mother who is now pushing Wendell to have their son tested. Rosetta knows that her marriage maybe over after Wendell finds out that Oscar is the father of her beautiful little girl. But the one thing that she's sure of is that Wendell is the father of their son. Yasmeen don't know what to think. She could care less about what happens to Rosetta it's the innocent baby who caught in the middle of this trash. Yasmeen heart is saddened. A week later Oscar and Rosetta goes to court and Oscar finds out that he is the father. Oscar is crushed because the last thing that he wanted was to be the father of Rosetta child. Ashton decides that it would be best if he and Oscar not see each other for a while. Oscar is going out of his mind he never wanted to hurt Ashton because he really cared about him. Yasmeen knows that Oscar is sorry and that he doesn't deserve to loss Ashton. Yasmeen decide to pay Ashton a visit with the hope of fixing both Oscar and Ashton relationship. When Yasmeen gets to Ashton house, she can see that he has been crying. She tries her best to comfort him. For the first time Yasmeen doesn't know what to say. So, for the next thirty minutes Yasmeen just holds Ashton and they sit in silence.

"Ashton, I don't know what you're feeling right now, but you really need to talk about it."

"Yasmeen I'm so hurt!"

"Sweetie I know, but you need to talk to Oscar."

"Why so that he can lie."

"No, so that you can start the healing process."

"I don't what to talk to him. Yasmeen, he cheated on me.

"Well he didn't, really cheat on you Ashton."

Ashton push's away in anger. "So are you going to defend him after he had a baby with that bitch.!"

"No that's not what I'm trying to do. Ashton I'm not trying to defend Oscar, but the two of you were not together and he didn't know that Rosetta was pregnant."

"It doesn't matter!"

"Well it should. Look Ashton we all make mistakes good or bad but if you care about Oscar, which I know that you do, you need to try and forgive him. If you want to end the relationship fine but forgive him."

"I can't"

"Yes, you can."

"Yass, he cheated."

"Ash, he didn't. The baby had already been here months before you two got together. This happened before your time"

"But...

"But my ass. Yes, he fucked up, but he never cheated on you."

"Ok what if I slept with a woman how about that?"

"Then that would be cheating. But why in the hell are you looking at me? I hope that you are not thinking about you and I cause baby I don't want your ass and this pussy is not for you."

"I was just saying! Hell, I don't want you either so don't flatter yourself."

"Oh yes you want me so don't lie. You want this chocolate."

"You know what you're full of yourself."

"So are you, now call Oscar and talk to him."

"Yass, I don't know what to say."

"Say what you feel. Let him know that you're hurt. Tell him that you will forgive him but it's going to take you some time. Say anything just as long as you talk."

"I just can't"

"Ok don't talk to him, but you should know that Rosetta says that she still wants Oscar so if you want her to have him fine."

"She still wants him!"

"Yelp so I guess she can have him being that you don't care about him anymore. I'll just call Rosetta and tell her to go for it. Who knows it just might work.

"I wish you would call that whore. Let me tell your ass something Oscar is my man. Yasmeen don't make me fuck you up in here."

"You don't want him, anymore right? So, Rosetta can have him."

"I didn't say that!"

"Well call him and get in his ass Ashton, let him know what he almost lost by being stupid.! Let Oscar know that you will not tolerate him fucking up again no matter how big or small. Make your demand, Ashton stand up for yourself. I know that you love Oscar and hell he loves you but don't let him think that what he did is ok. Than fuck him like you never fucked him before!"

"Yass you're right."

"I know that I am, now call your man. Tell him that he has ten minutes to get his ass over here or it's over."

"What if he can't"

"Oh, he will. Now call him."

"Thank you, Yasmeen and thank you for being my friend."

"You're welcome. Ashton, I love Oscar and Todd like my brothers and I would never want to see them get hurt moreover I don't want them to hurt anybody. You know that I will always call them out on their bullshit. You have made Oscar so happy and he really cares about you. So, I say thank you but punish him a little. Let me get out of here because I don't want to see this shit."

"Yass bye and again thanks for being my friend."

Yasmeen kisses Ashton on the cheek and she leaves. It is Monday morning meeting Yasmeen is sitting quietly next to Jacob and Ashton. Since Yasmeen and Mahmoud blow up. Yasmeen has been reluctant to talk doing the meeting or to Mahmoud. With Yasmeen not talking the meetings are now long and boring. Yasmeen tries to keep her comments to a minimum for the most part. At the end of the meeting Mahmoud asked Yasmeen if she has anything that she would like to add. Yasmeen rolls her eyes as she pushes her chair away from the table then she walks out without saying a word. Mahmoud knows that Yasmeen is still vax with him. He has tried to make things better between them, but Yasmeen is stubborn, but Mahmoud is unyielding in getting Yasmeen to give him one more chance. Mahmoud still cares a lot about Yasmeen so he's not giving up because one day she will be his. Yasmeen and Ashton are in her office talking when Rosetta walks in. Rosetta don't know that Ashton and Oscar are a couple. For over a year Rosetta has been trying to get Ashton to notice her. Ashton can feel a surge of anger wash over him as Rosetta walks over to him.

"Hello doctor Ward don't you look delicious."

"Hi Rosetta bye Rosetta."

"Oh, you don't have to leave, you know that I like looking at you!"

"Well I don't like looking at you. What you need to be doing is looking at your husband! I will talk to you later Yasmeen."

"What about me."

Ashton walks out of Yasmeen office without saying another word. Yasmeen knows that Ashton is still angry that Rosetta is the mother of Oscar daughter even though he has forgiven Oscar he has much hate for Rosetta.

"Yass that man knows that he fine and one day he's going to give in to me. I bet that he's good in bed to! Do you think that he has a big dick?"

Yasmeen looks at Rosetta with disgust. *"I don't know, and I don't care to find out! You need to leave that man alone; don't you have enough problems to deal with? Girl believe me you don't need to add anymore, so, leave that man alone!"*

"Why so that you can have him. I have been watching the two of you."

"You know what that's why you're fucked up now! It's that same bullshit thinking that got you in the predicament that you're in, fucking somebody because you think that I am! Let me tell you this and I want you to listen close because I won't tell you this again. Rosetta if I was fucking doctor Ward or anybody else for that matter, you would know it and you wouldn't have to guess! Stop worrying about my pussy and stop giving yours up! See you're worrying about the wrong thing! What you should be worrying about is how you're going to save your marriage?"

"Yasmeen you're right and I'm sorry I should not have said that. I just assumed that…"

"Assumed what, that just because I talk to someone that means that we are sleeping together? Hell, if that's true I talk to you so does that mean that we're fucking?"

"Yasmeen I'm sorry."

. *"Don't be sorry be careful. Now if you don't mind, I have a lot of work to do!"*

Rosetta exits Yasmeen's office Yasmeen shakes her head. *"God help her."* After lunch Yasmeen walks into the lady's room and Uma is standing at the sink holding her stomach. Yasmeen can see that Uma is having some type of discomfort.

Are you ok?"

"Yes, I'm fine. I'm just having a little cramping that's all. I'll be ok."

"Uma if you're having cramps maybe you should go see your doctor. I mean with you being pregnant and all, you may need to go see if the baby is ok."

"Yasmeen do you have any children, or have you ever been pregnant?"

Yasmeen dry her hands off. *"No but what does that have to do with you having cramps.*

"Well how would you know what I need to do?"

"You know what you're right I wouldn't know. Whatever happens to you, you deserve it and don't come to my office again.

Yasmeen leaves Uma in the Lady's Room. As Uma walks into the hall she sees, Aaron coming towards her. Before Uma can say anything, blood starts running down her legs. Uma looks down, when she sees the blood she cries out to Aaron. Aaron rushes over to Uma. He looks at her and smiles because he knows that Uma has lost the baby, the baby that he never wanted. Aaron gets a wheelchair and rolls Uma down to the Emergency room. By the time that they get there it's too late, the baby is gone. Uma cry's out not that she has lost the baby but because she knows that without the baby there will be no Aaron, she realizes her risk of losing him forever. Her heart aches for Aaron's love that he has withheld from her for months. The anticipation of her baby was the only thing that was keeping Aaron in her life and now that it's gone so is Aaron. Aaron kisses Uma on the head and tells her that it's going to be ok and that he will be there for her. Rebecca walks in just as Aaron releases Uma's hand. Aaron puts his arm around Rebecca as they leave Uma alone crying.

Chapter 8

Stand up and never be too proud to admit when you're wrong.
Pride can sometimes be an ugly thing…

It has been a week since Uma lost her baby and Aaron has been calling Yasmeen every day, he still cares a great deal for her, but Yasmeen is very stern that she wants nothing to do with him. Yasmeen gets out of her car, she sees Aaron walking towards her. Yasmeen heart starts to beat fast as she put her key between her finger. All Yasmeen can think about is the day that Aaron attacked her. This time she will be prepared for his ass. Mahmoud gets out of his car and he watches Aaron and Yasmeen.

Yasmeen, I need to talk to you!"

"I have nothing to say to you Aaron, now leave me alone."

Aaron grabs Yasmeen arm. *"Will you talk to me!"*

Yasmeen pulls away. *"Get your fucking hands off me! Don't you dare touch me. We have nothing to discuss especially in this garage. Now move Aaron before I scream!"*

"Not until you talk to me!"

Yasmeen looks up she see Mahmoud walking toward them. Yasmeen runs over to him.

"Will you please keep him away from! This man is crazy!"

"What's going on here?"

"Nothing I just what to talk to her, that's all."

"I don't want to talk to you, go away and leave me alone!"

Yasmeen runs to the elevator leaving Aaron and Mahmoud outside. She can't stop shaking. When Yasmeen gets to her office, she locks the door and sits the dark crying. After nine-thirty Yasmeen walks to the file room and Aaron walks up behind her.

"*Yasmeen will you talk to me please!*"

"*Aaron! What are you doing?*"

"*I just want to talk. Will you please give me a minute of your time?*"

"*Ok Aaron you have one minute.* Looking at her watch. *Start talking.*"

"*What you want me to talk out here?*"

"*Yes, I want you to talk out here!*"

"*Can we at least go in your office?*"

"*Look either we can talk out here or we can't talk at all. It's up to you!*"

"*Ok have it your way. You know you look lovely today as always.*"

"*Really Aaron your time is running out so get to the point!*"

"*Ok well as you may or may not have heard that Uma lost the baby.*"

"*Yes, I heard. Sorry for your loss now if you would excuse me, I have work to do.*"

"*Yasmeen, you know that I miss you.*"

"*What, are you kidding me? Your girlfriend just lost your baby and you're standing here telling me that you miss me. Aaron, you need help.*"

No, I need you."

"*That will never happen.*"

Aaron walks up to Yasmeen and whisper in her ear. *I Know that you miss me Yasmeen. I was the last one to taste that sweet wet pussy remembers that day in your office, how wet you get, I did that. That's my pussy and I love you. No matter what you will be mine again so stop pushing me away.*"

Yasmeen whispering to Aaron. "*Yes, I remember. I also remember you trying to rape me in my home. Do you remember pulling out a gun and threating to kill me Aaron? Do you remember me begging you not to hurt me, because I do!*"

Aaron takes a step back he can still see the hurt in Yasmeen's eyes. That's the one thing that Aaron wish's that he could take back. Yasmeen walks away with tears in her eyes. Yasmeen tells herself that Aaron is just a selfish bastard who only cares about getting his rocks off. The only reason that he can't get over her is because he didn't get to fuck her, and he never will. The best decision that she made was letting Aaron go. When Yasmeen gets back to her office, she sees Mahmoud waiting by her door. Yasmeen first though is to turn and run back down the hall, but he sees her. Yasmeen takes a deep breath and tosses her hair back as she thinks *"What in the hell does he want?"* Yasmeen walks pass Mahmoud as if she didn't see him stand at her door. Mahmoud follows Yasmeen into her office.

"Ms. Blake, I would like to have a word with you."

"About!"

"About the incident this morning with you and doctor Sinclair."

Yasmeen sits back in her chair with her arms folded staring at Mahmoud. Yasmeen can feel herself getting angry and her eyes starting to burn with tears. Yasmeen holds her head down to compose herself because the last thing that she wants is for Mahmoud to see her cry again. When Yasmeen looks, she looks right into Mahmoud eyes which send chills down her spine. For a minute, she loses her train of thought.

"And what do you what to know!"

"I want to know what happened."

"That I don't know! When I got here, he was waiting on me. Why I don't know! You will have to ask him that, all I know is that it's not what you think!"

"And what do I think?"

"Why don't you tell me because I would hate to make you mad and end up in a group meeting!"

Mahmoud put one finger on the side of his head. *"Ok are you and doctor Sinclair seeing each other?"*

Yasmeen is flushed with anger. She sits forward in her seat. This is the one thing that she never wants anyone to think. Aaron is the only man that Yasmeen will never want. The relationship that she had with Aaron is completely over. Yasmeen thinks that Mahmoud must be out of his fucking mind to even ask her some shit like that.

"Look doctor Shashivivek let me set you straight so that you won't ever in your life ask me that question again. Clearing her throat. *I'm one hundred percent sure that you have heard that doctor Sinclair and I use to date. Understand that was before you got here. Listen to me now, I said use to. Now when you got here what we had was long over with and you know why. So, to answer your question is hell no I'm not seeing doctor Sinclair! I don't want anything to do with Aaron Sinclair with his nasty ass. And I don't know why he was wanting in the parking lot! Do you understand what I'm telling you? There is nothing going on between him and I!"*

Mahmud breathe a sigh of relief. His heart is now at peace, just to hear that Yasmeen is over Aaron makes Mahmoud so happy. Mahmoud can feel a smile spreading across his face as he looks in Yasmeen beautiful brown eyes.

"*Yes Ms. Blake I do understand. I just thought you. Well you know how things have been around here with him.*"

"*Yes, I know but I can promise you that I'm not apart of it.*"

"*Well thank you for your time and I didn't mean to upset you. I just wanted to know what was going on and I will see to it that doctor Sinclair not both you again if that's what you want.*"

"*Oh yes that's what I want!*"

"*Consider it done.*"

After Mahmoud leaves Yasmeen can't stop thinking about him. The last thing on her mind is work. Yasmeen can still smell his cologne throughout her office. She can still see his face smiling at her. Yasmeen puts her hand up to her face and tries to get Mahmoud out of her head. Yasmeen can feel her nipples starting to get hard and her clit start to throb. Yasmeen jumps up from her desk she can't allow herself to have these feelings for a man whom she has never had relation with. Yasmeen grabs her purse, briefcase and runs out of her office. Three days has passed it's Friday the last day of the work week and all Yasmeen can think about from her car on her way to her office is getting this day over with without any unnecessary drama. Yasmeen sings to herself as see gets off the elevator. Yasmeen proceeds to her office, she stops singing when she sees Uma waiting at her door. Yasmeen starts talking to herself. *I hope that witch, is not waiting on me not after I told her ass not to come to my office again?* Yasmeen takes a long deep breath. *Ok Yasmeen it's going to be a good day. Now you just walk pass this bitch like the wind. Keep your ass moving because there is no way in hell that she's waiting on you.* When Yasmeen gets to her office door, she doesn't even look at Uma. She unlocks her door and closes it behind her before Uma can say one word. Yasmeen can hear Uma knocking on the door, but she refuses to answer. After five minutes Uma is still at the door. Yasmeen is frustrated by Uma persistent knocking, Yasmeen flings the door open.

"*What in the hell do you want?*" "*I wanted to talk to you.*"

"*No, you don't. Didn't I tell you not to bring your ass to my office anymore. Did you think that I was playing with you?*"

"Yasmeen, I just needed someone to talk to."

"Well you don't need to talk to me!"

Uma puts her hand up to her face. *"Well you know that I lost the baby."*

"I'm sorry to hear that. I hope that you ok. Yasmeen attempts to closing the door. *Now have a good day."*

"Yasmeen wait!"

"Wait for what?"

"I still need to talk to you."

"No, you don't. Do you remember when I tried to talk to you? It was the same day that you lost your baby. Do you remember the shit that you said to me, because I do? I told you not to come to back to my office.

"I know what you said, and Yasmeen I do apologize for what I said. I just need to talk to you."

"Well that's not going to happen now good bye!"

Yasmeen slams the door close. Uma walks away. She knew Yasmeen would be upset but she thought that she would have at least talk to her, Uma was wrong. Yasmeen says what she means, and she means what she says. At twelve o'clock Wallace is on his way to lunch when Mahmoud approaches him.

"Hey, Wallace do you have a minute?"

"For you Doc always."

"Well I need to ask you something about Yasmeen."

"Ok well I don't know a lot about Ms. Blake, but what did you want to know? Depending on what it is you need to know, I might be able to help."

"Well do you know if Yasmeen and Aaron are seeing each other again?"

Wallace is caught off guard. *"What... No...I mean that's something that I know for sure is not happing. Doctor Sinclair might be seeing somebody but it's not Ms. Blake. He doesn't have a chance not with her! Doc when I tell you that it's over between them it's over. Ms. Blake is nothing like the other two, but of course you already know that."*

"So why is he still going after her?"

"Your guess is as good as mine on that. I think that he just can't except the fact that she doesn't want him. He knows that he lost a great woman and he don't know how to get her back, Doc it's too late for him but for you time is running out too! Have you made you move yet?"

"No... What... what move? You're insane."

"What are you waiting for?"

"Wallace, I don't know. Look I don't know what you're talking about!"

"Ok, ok you know what I'm talking about, but you keep waiting. You are going to miss out then you'll be running around here like Aaron. You remember what happened when you thought that she was going out with what's his name right!"

"Wallace I'm not going to… Wallace come have lunch with me.

"Ok, just as long as you're paying."

Mahmoud laughs as he and Wallace walk to Mahmoud's car. Two weeks later and everything in Yasmeen life seems to be going smooth like butter. Yasmeen is at her favorite bar waiting on Oscar, Todd, Ashton, Zada and Angelina to arrive. Yasmeen is early, she decides to have a drink while she wants. As she is about to pick up her drink, she hears a familiar voice behind her. Chills runs down her spine as she turns around.

"Hello beautiful!"

"Aaron what…what are you doing here?"

"Well I'm meeting someone here and you?"

"Well I'm meeting some friends."

"No please don't leave Yasmeen, please sit back down I really need to talk to you."

"Aaron, I told you that I don't have anything to say to you!"

"Well you don't have to talk, you can just listen."

Yasmeen pushes Aaron's arm away as she sits back down. Yasmeen wants to leave but at the same time she needs to hear what Aaron has to say. Is he sorry or just stupid? Yasmeen is having mixed emotion and none of them are good. Yasmeen hates Aaron and he knows it. Yasmeen takes a drink from her glass.

"Ok what do you want to talk to me about Aaron."

"Yasmeen, you know that I really miss you." *"How many times are you going to tell me that? Aaron, I don't have time for your bullshit!* Yasmeen push's Aaron away. *Now get out of my way!"*

"Ok…ok Yass sit back down please!"

"Aaron say what you have to say!"

Aaron looks in Yasmeen eyes he smiles as he touches the side of Yasmeen's face with the back of his hand. Yasmeen turns away.

"Yasmeen, you are so beautiful and I'm so sorry for hurting you. I hope that one day you will forgive me. Yasmeen, you may not believe me, but I still love you."

"Yeah I bet you do! You love me and all the rest of them."

"Yasmeen, I don't love them."

"Aaron do you hear yourself?"

"Yes, I do, and I wish that you would give me another chance. Yass, I made a mistake. I'm not perfect."

"Aaron no one is. Aaron, I did care for you, but you wounded me so bad and I hated you for, so long. Aaron not only did you cheat on me, it's like you rubbed it in my face."

Yasmeen takes a long pause to hold back her hurtful tears. This is the conversation that she has always wanted to have with Aaron for months. Yasmeen hopes that Aaron will see her disappointment with him and he will go away for good.

"Yasmeen, it was not my intention to rub anything in your face."

"Well you did! Not only did you rub your affairs in my face you even got Uma pregnant. So, I couldn't take you back even if I wanted to. It's over between us but I forgive you because I've got to move forward with my life.

"Yasmeen I'm truly sorry. But I really need to tell you this."

"What do you have to tell me Aaron."

"Your friend has been calling me."

"Who Zada?"

"Hell, no Zada hates my guts! I'm talking about Rosetta. She has been calling me for the past two weeks. Aaron looks at his cell phone. *She's calling, me now.*

"Calling you for what?"

"Why do you think?"

"I don't think anything. Now why is she calling you Aaron? Are you fucking her too?"

"No Yasmeen I'm not fucking her, but she wants me to. She invited me over to her house."

"Did you go?"

"No!'

"You haven't gone yet but you will. Have fun!"

"Look Yasmeen I don't what to fuck your friend!"

"But you will and she's not my friend!"

"So now you're mad at me for telling you?"

"No, I'm not mad at all. Thanks for telling me Aaron and you can fuck whoever you want to, remember we're not together!"

"I want to fuck you."

"That will never happen. I don't fuck!"

"Well one day I will make love to you beautiful. One day I will lick your pussy until you cum. I love you Yass remember that."

Aaron put a hundred-dollar bill on the bar before he kisses Yasmeen on the cheek and walks away before Yasmeen can react. Yasmeen wipes the side of her face. She is disgusted when she thinks about where Aaron's mouth has been. As the bartender hands Yasmeen, the changes she tips him as she thinks to herself hell, we're going to have a round of drinks on Aaron nasty ass. Yasmeen smiles when she looks up to see Zada and the rest of the gang walk in. Yasmeen can't wait to tell them about Rosetta's slutty ass. It's not long before Mahmoud, Jacob, and Maxwell walk in. Yasmeen and Mahmoud eyes lock on each other. Yasmeen looks away she can feel a lump starting to form in her throat. Jacob walks over to Yasmeen and ask if they could join them. Before Yasmeen can say no Ashton and Zada welcome them all. Wouldn't you know it out of all the seat Mahmoud could have sat in he, pick the one next to Yasmeen. Yasmeen wished that she could have vanished into thin air. After an hour and three rounds of drinks Yasmeen is really enjoying the company of Mahmoud. Everyone is talking, eating, and having an amazing time until Aaron and Rebecca decide to invite themselves to the table. Yasmeen feels unease as Rebecca continues to stare at her not to mention the fact that every time Yasmeen looks in Aarons direction, he's either licking his ashy ass lips or sticking his long disgusting tongue between his fingers at her. Mahmoud leans over and whisper in Yasmeen's ear. They both laugh and for the rest of the night Mahmoud and Yasmeen whispers back and forth to each other. As Aaron watches them the more irritated, he gets. Soon Oscar is whispering to Yasmeen and Mahmoud. Mahmoud puts his arm around Yasmeen shoulder and pulls her close to him. Yasmeen doesn't resist, and Aaron explodes in anger and he jumps up from the table. He wonders if Yasmeen is only trying to hurt him by flirting with Mahmoud. Aaron tells himself that there is no way that Yasmeen or Mahmoud can be interested in each other. When Aaron returns to the table Yasmeen and her friends are gone so is Mahmoud. Aaron grabs Rebecca and they leave. When Yasmeen gets home, she can't sleep because all she can think about is Mahmoud and how good he felt when he put his arms around her. Unlike before Yasmeen didn't want him to let her go. Mahmoud embrace seemed so familiar and Yasmeen doesn't know why. Yasmeen can still smell Mahmoud's breath as he whispered in her ear. She can feel the warmth on her neck like the wind. After two AM Yasmeen finally falls asleep but all she dreams about is Mahmoud. The next morning when Yasmeen walks outside Aaron is standing beside her car. Fear runs all though her body. Yasmeen wants to run but her feet won't move, and her keys falls to the ground as she panics. Yasmeen puts her hand inside of her purse hope to find her pepper spray.

"Aaron what…what on earth are you doing here?"

"And good morning to you too!"

"Why are you here Aaron? You need to leave now!"

"Relax sweetheart I just want to ask you one question."

Yasmeen reach for her car door. *"I don't have anything to say to you and I would appreciate it if you would stay the hell away from me and my home."*

"I have been up all-night thinking about you."

"Well that's your stupidity because I didn't think about you at all Aaron!"

"I was thinking about you and doctor Shashivivek!"

"Me and doctor Shashivivek! Why would you be think about us?"

"Because I want to know are you sleeping with him!"

"That's none of your business! Who the hell are you to question me anyway? For your information no, I'm not sleeping with doctor Shashivivek, but if I was what's it to you? You don't own me!"

"Well last night you two seem to have a lot to talk about."

"Yes, we did, and if you must know we were talking about you!"

"You were talking about me? What about me?"

Yasmeen laughs uncontrollably. *"We were trying to figure out who you were doing* that *little tongue thing for me or him. Did you want to lick him ass or what?"*

"Yasmeen don't you fucking play with me! You know that…"

Yasmeen cuts Aaron off. She knows that he's mad and she's enjoying herself. Yasmeen continue making fun of Aaron. At the same time Yasmeen is still on guard she's not about to let Aaron get close to her. Yasmeen gets in her car.

"I didn't hell, you were looking at him more than me. Who knows you might want to try something new."

"Fuck you Yasmeen!"

"No thank you but ask doctor Shashivivek he might fuck you. Now got that shit out of my driveway!"

Yasmeen drives away laughing leaving Aaron standing in the driveway fuming. Zada meets Yasmeen in the parking garage. They laugh as Yasmeen tells Zada about her encounter with Aaron. Zada tells Yasmeen that she should have made a speed bump out of Aaron. Yasmeen is laughing when her thoughts go back to Mahmoud. She tries to play it off with a smile, but she can no longer hear Zada talking because Yasmeen can only hear Mahmoud's voice in her ear. Yasmeen is sitting in her office with the door open when Rosetta walks in. Yasmeen immediately is overwhelmed with anger. Yasmeen fights to control herself from telling Rosetta that she knows about her wanting to fuck Aaron. The last thing that Yasmeen wants is to give Aaron the satisfaction of thinking that she's jealous.

"Good morning boss lady."

"What's good about it?"

"Don't you sound happy to see me!"

"Not at all! Now what do you want?"

"I don't want anything, but I heard that y'all were at the bar last night."

"Yes, we were, and we had a great time."

"I wish that I would have known that you all were going."

"We didn't plan to meet up there it just happened. I guess we all needed a release. You know I was surprised to see Jacob, Maxwell and Mahmoud out on a Wednesday night. Oh, and Aaron was there to with Rebecca."

Yasmeen smiles as she watches Rosetta's facial expression transformation from happy to disappointment. Yasmeen knows that she has Rosetta right where she wants her, but Yasmeen isn't finished with her no-good ass. Hell, no not yet!

"Oh, really so they are still together?"

Yasmeen crosses her legs. *"Girl yeah, but you know how Aaron is. He was with Rebecca, but he was still telling me how much he still wanted to be with me and that he still loves me with his tired ass. Oh, and that's not the half of it. How about his cell was just going off it was some dumb bitch!"*

"Oh, for real? Who was it?"

"Girl I don't even know. He kept hitting the ignore button on her ass. I told him to answer his phone... Aaron looked at his phone and said it's that bitch again I wish that she would stop calling me because I didn't want her ass, fuck her Yass I want you. You know Aaron not shit, his trifling ass with one bitch and he got another bitch blowing his phone up!"

Rosetta uneasy. *"So, he didn't answer his cell?"*

"Girl no! That ass turned his phone off and bought us some more drinks. Oh yeah how about when I came outside this morning his ass was waiting on me."

"No, he wasn't"

"Yes, he was. I started to mace his ass."

"Oh, I better let you get back to work."

"Oh no you're good sit down."

"You know I really have to do my report, but I'll come back later."

Yasmeen to herself. *"Yeah you have to report to Aaron with your slick ass.*
After Rosetta leaves Yasmeen calls Todd at work to discuss Rosetta. Yasmeen knows that Rosetta is going to run to Aaron because one thing she hates is rejection. Yasmeen made sure that she hit Rosetta where it hurts. Aaron has just gotten out of the shower when he hears his doorbell ring. Aaron looks at his cell phone for a missed call. He gets dressed as he wonders who in the hell could be at his door. Aaron knows that it's not Rebecca or Uma because they know better than to show up without calling first. Aaron thinks to himself that maybe Yasmeen finally came to her senses and now she wants him back. Aaron laughs because he knows that will never happen. Aaron runs downstairs and opens the door. Aaron is surprised to see Rosetta standing on his porch smiling at him. All Aaron can say is what the fuck! Rosetta is the last person that Aaron wanted to see in fact he didn't want to see her at all.

"Girl what in the hell are you doing here?"

"I came to see you, so are you going to invite me in or leave me standing out here?"

Aaron rubs his hand over his face. He knows that if he lets Rosetta in, he without a doubt will fuck her. This is one person that Aaron must

174

resist, no matter how good she looks in that short green dress. All Aaron wants is for her to suck his dick.

"*No, I can't let you in.*"

Rosetta pushes Aaron back with one finger. "*Oh yes you can!*" Rosetta walks in and Aaron steps back without a fight. He watches Rosetta as she walks into his Living room. She takes a seat on the sofa with her legs open. Aaron can feel a bulge starting to form in his pants as he sits down beside Rosetta.

"*Rosetta what do you want?*"

"*I told you. I want to talk to you.*"

Aaron rub Rosetta thigh. "*You want to talk with your legs open like that and you're not wearing any underwear.*"

Rosetta push's Aarons hand away. "*Oh, I talked to Yasmeen and she told me what you said.*"

Aaron lays him head back and laughs. "*You did huh. Wow!*"

"*So, I was blowing your phone up?*"

Aaron looks at Rosetta as he continues laughing. "*So, she told you. Well you did hell. You just kept calling me.*"

"*Really and what did you do Aaron?*"

"*Hell, I turned my phone off.*"

"*You could have answered my call. Instead of ignoring me. Better yet you should have let Yasmeen answer it!*"

"*Why would I do that?*"

"*So, she would have known who the bitch was on the other end.*"

"*What?*"

"*Well you said that I was a bitch right!*"

"*No, I didn't say that. Is that what Yasmeen told you? No, I didn't say that.*"

"*Well why didn't you tell her it was me?*"

Aaron stops laughing as he stares in Rosetta's eyes. Aaron realized that Yasmeen never told Rosetta that she knew about her being interested in him.

"*So, is that what you wanted, for me to tell Yasmeen knowing that you're a married woman?*"

"*Aaron, I don't fucking, care if she knows! But I do care that you didn't tell me about you and Rebecca!*"

"*Ok what about Rebeca? You know that I am still fucking around with her. Why do I have to tell you anything?*"

"*Oh yeah I forgot, you don't want me. You're still waiting on Yasmeen. Aaron, you know what you're stupid! Yasmeen doesn't want you so stop wasting your time and energy!*"

Aaron temper rises when he hears Rosetta say that Yasmeen doesn't want him. Aaron is infuriated as he jumps to his feet.

"*You need to fucking leave Rosetta! Get your ass out of my house!*"

"*Why? What did I do Aaron?* Pulling Aaron back down on the sofa. *Aaron I'm sorry I should not have said that. Let me make it up to you.*"

"*No, you need to leave!*"

"*I said that I was sorry.* Pulling her dress up. *I guess I was just mad.*"

"*Rosetta don't do this.*"

"*Why not?*"

Rosetta climbs on Aaron's lap and kisses him. Aaron gives in as he kisses Rosetta back. Aaron pushes Rosetta down on the sofa as he pulls her dress over her head. Aaron sucks on her caramel breast. Rosetta bits her lip and smiles with pleasure. Rosetta moans as Aaron inserts his manly fingers in to her hot pussy. Aaron push his fingers in and out of Rosetta pussy. He can feel Rosetta's uterus as he pushes two fingers deep inside her. She screams out in satisfaction. Rosetta can feel Aarons big hard dick and she can't wait to have him inside of her. Rosetta reaches down and grabs Aarons dick as he pushes her leg up in the air. Rosetta looks at Aaron and smiles because she knows that he's about to fuck her right. Rosetta has been waiting for this for, so long. Rosetta calls out Aarons name. Aaron looks down at Rosette and gets up. When he think about the last time, he had an unannounced woman at his house he lost Yasmeen who meant so much to him. Aaron shakes him head as he think "*What if Yasmeen walked in now!*"

"*I can't do this.*"

"*What's wrong baby why did you stop?*"

"*We shouldn't be doing this. It's wrong.*"

"*Come on don't do this to me. Aaron, I want to feel you inside of me.*"

"*No, we already went to, far!*"

"*I need you Aaron! Baby please!*"

Aaron pushes Rosetta away and throws her dress in her face. "*Here put your dress back on and get out.*"

"*Why is it because you're feeling guilty or are you thinking about your precious Yasmeen?*"

"*Both Rosetta! No matter what you or anybody else do, you will never compare to Yass. We both should be ashamed of ourselves! You should feel guilty too, after all you're supposed to be her friend and look at you lying here about to fuck her ex. Yasmeen said that I ain't shit and she's right. You know what you ain't shit either. Aaron smells his finger. And your pussy stank!*"

Rosetta put her dress back on. "*To hell with you. How about this, how about my ain't shit ass tell Yasmeen that you tried to fuck me!*"

Aaron walks over to Rosetta. "*How about this, how about I call your husband and tell him how I had my hand shoved in his wife pussy, and how I had her screaming out my name begging me to fuck the dog shit out of her!*"

"*Aaron don't you dare!*"

"*No, you want to tell and so do I.*"

"*I see why Yasmeen wants nothing to do with you and I hope that she never takes you back!*"

Aaron grabs Rosetta by her arm and pushes her out the door. "*You fucking whore! Get the fuck out of my house bitch with that, stank ass pussy!*"

Aaron slams the door and he throws his phone. All he can think about is Yasmeen finding out about him and her so called friend fucking around. Aaron tells himself that he should just give up on getting Yasmeen back because he knows that there is no coming back after this. He has destroyed any chance that he may have had left. Aaron thinks back to the night at the bar when he ran his hand across Yasmeen soft smooth chocolate face and he remembers how sweet she smelled when he kissed, her cheek. Aaron pours himself a drink as his phone rings. Aaron knows that it's Uma because she too wants to fuck, but the only woman that Aaron wants at that moment is Yasmeen. The one that he can't have. Aaron takes his drink and goes upstairs. When Rosetta gets home, she breaks down as she looks around at her empty house. Her husband is gone, and he may not be coming back, but all she can think about is Aaron and how bad she wants him. Rosetta sobs uncontrollably. She wonders what is this hold that Yasmeen has on Aaron that he can't let her go. What does Yasmeen have that she doesn't. Rosetta screams *I hate you Yasmeen! I hate you!*

Chapter 9

A journey of a thousand miles begins with a single step…

After a week Rosetta's hate for Yasmeen has grown and so has her lust for Aaron. Rosetta can't stop thinking about Aaron. Rosetta wants to tell Yasmeen about her and Aaron encounter just to hurt her, but she knows that if she does Aaron will never forgive her. Rosetta hates going to work seeing Yasmeen's face and having to pretend to be her friend. When, will this end? Yasmeen walks to her office and Rosetta is walking behind her. Aaron stops Yasmeen and gives her a box. Rosetta blood boils as Yasmeen looks back at her and smiles. Yasmeen knows that Rosetta envy's her and she loves it. Yasmeen put the box on the desk.

. *"I don't know why he keeps buying me things Rosie. He's knows that it's over, but he insists on giving me gifts."*

"Must be nice."

"No not really because I don't want to lead him on. I know that he's in love with all this chocolate."

"You know Yass I think that you're getting a kick out of this."

"You might be right. Do you think that I should just give him another chance? I have been thinking about it."

"Hell no! Why would you do something so stupid? For crying out loud Yass he cheated on you or did you forget!"

"No, I haven't forgot, but we all make mistakes."

Yasmeen knows that Rosetta is about to lose her mind thinking that she wants Aaron. Yasmeen laughs inside as she plays her game with Rosetta.

Yasmeen will never have Aaron. Yasmeen is just playing mind games with Rosetta when Maxwell enters her office.

"*Good day ladies. Yasmeen are you busy?*"

"*No not at all.*"

"*Well may I have a word with you please. Rosetta would you mind?*"

"*No not at all. As a matter of fact, I was just leaving. Bye Yasmeen*! To herself. *Bitch*!"

"*Bye sweetie... How may I help you?*"

"*Yasmeen, we need to talk! This has gone on far too long!*"

"*What has gone on too long. I'm not following you.*"

"*This thing between you and I. Yasmeen I know that you are mad with me, but I had nothing to do with what happened that day.*"

"*What are you talking about?*"

"*I'm talking about the altercation that you had with doctor Shashivivek.*"

"*Ok*"

"*Ok why are you taking it out on me?*"

"*What do you mean? I'm not taking anything out on you.*"

"*Well why didn't you talk to me anymore?*"

"*I do take to you. Look I'm over that.*"

"*Well why didn't you come to my dinner party this past weekend?*"

Yasmeen puts her hand over her mouth. "*Your dinner party. Oh, my goodness it was this past weekend? I'm so sorry I thought it was this coming weekend! You know that I would have come. I wasn't thinking!*"

"*Well I just wanted to say that my wife she's was very hurt. She was looking forward to seeing you.*"

"*Come on don't do this to me Maxwell. You know how I feel about Saidah. I'm going to call her right now and tell her that it was your fault.*"

"*It wasn't my fault!*"

"*Yes, it was! Remember you hurt my feelings and you didn't tell me.*"

"*Are you serious? She already blames me.*"

"*Good. Hey, Saidah I'm sorry that I miss the dinner. You know your husband didn't tell.* Yasmeen winks at Maxwell. *He really hurt my feelings. Yes, ok I will see you at six. You're going to get it.*"

"*Yasmeen why would you do that.*"

"*Pay back. Now we're even.*"

It's Monday morning Yasmeen gets to work at eight thirty when she usually gets there before seven thirty or no later than eight o'clock. Yasmeen walks to her office to retrieve her report for the week. Yasmeen is frantically looking through her files when she remembers that she left her report at home. Yasmeen puts her hand on her forehead as her purse falls to the floor and all the contents inside spill out on to the floor. Yasmeen is on the verge of screaming. For Yasmeen this is not a typical Monday because everything is going wrong.

Yasmeen talking to herself. *"Shit I can't believe this. Now I got to go all the way back home! To top it off my head is killing me, and I feel like crap. Today is not my day.* Yasmeen picks up her desk phone. *Rosetta good morning can you come to my office? No just come here please."*

Yasmeen grabs her purse and rushing to the door just as Rosetta walks in. Yasmeen's head is pounding and spinning. Again Yasmeen purse falls to the floor and Yasmeen put her hand on the wall to keep from falling.

"Yass are you ok?"

"Yes…yes I'm fine I just lost my balance. Away I need to run back to my place so if doctor Baldwin or anyone comes looking for me can you tell them that I'll be right back."

"Ok not a problem."

"Thanks a bunch."

Yasmeen runs down the hall all the way to her car. It's after nine and the meeting has already started when Yasmeen rushes in. Mahmoud and Brandon watches Yasmeen until she takes her seat next to Uma and Jacob. Yasmeen rubs both of her temple as her head continues to hurt.

"It's nice of you to join us."

Yasmeen looks at Uma with her teeth clinched tight. *"Not today hoe-bag!"*

"I was just kidding."

"I said not today hoe-bag!"

Jacob whispering to Yasmeen. *"Are you ok?"*

"No, my head is killing me."

"Have you taken anything?"

"Not yet but I will when I get back to my office."

After the meeting Ashton and Yasmeen are about to walk out of the conference room when Uma calls out to her.

"Hey can we talk?"

Yasmeen closes her eyes to stop the room from spinning. *"No, we can't not right now."*

"I just wanted to…"

Ashton cuts Uma off. *"Didn't she say not right now, or do you not understand English.* Ashton puts his hand on Yasmeen back. *Now get out of our way!"*

Ashton walks with Yasmeen back to her office. Ashton makes sure that Yasmeen takes her medication before he leaves. Yasmeen is sitting at her desk with her eyes closed her head feels like it's about to explode. Yasmeen dozes off when Rosetta enters her office.

"Hey, are you ready to go?"

Yasmeen looks at Rosetta with one eye open. *"Go where?"*

"To lunch. Did you not get the email that doctor Shashivivek sent out that he's taking all his medical staff out to lunch? I hear that it's one of those high-end restaurants too.

Yasmeen looking through her email. *"Is that today?"*

"Yes, it's today now come on. Who's driving me or you?"

"You know what Rosetta why don't you go ahead and I'll meet you there. I really need a minute ok."

"Are you sure? I mean I don't mind waiting for you."

"Yes, I'm sure. Go on ahead I'll be along I just need to get myself together. You go on I don't want you to be late."

"Ok, I'll save you a seat."

"Great. Now go on I'm coming."

Yasmeen stomach starts to turn. She can feel herself about to toss her cookie. Yasmeen gets to the restroom just in time. Yasmeen washes her mouth out as she looks in the mirror. Her eyes are now red and puffy. Yasmeen can feel her body shaking as sweat runs down her face. Yasmeen manages to make it back to her office where she calls Zada. Everyone has arrived at the restaurant. Everybody but Yasmeen Mahmoud looks around and he is crushed for he knows that Yasmeen is not coming.

"Jacob where's Yasmeen?"

"I'm not sure. I do know that she had a head ache this morning. Let me call her.

Jacob continues to call Yasmeen, but his calls go unanswered, at the same time Ashton and Rosetta to are calling Yasmeen. The only thing that's running through Jacobs mind other than Yasmeen having a head ache is that she's still has not forgiven him and Mahmoud.

"Rosetta where's Yasmeen? she does know that she's supposed to be here!"

"Yes, Jacob she said that she would be here, and I've called her but she's not answering her phone."

Lunch is quiet, Aaron is sitting between Uma and Rebecca. Rosetta can't keep her eyes off Aaron who refuses to look in her direction. After lunch Mahmoud, Maxwell, Ashton, and Jacob are on their way to Yasmeen office to find out why she missed the luncheon. Before they can make it through the door Zada meets them coming in. Jacob can tell by the look on Zada's face that something is wrong.

"Hey Zada, where is Yasmeen?"

Zada puts her hand on her chest. *"Doctor Baldwin we had to rush Yasmeen to the emergency room!"*

"What...when... why didn't somebody call me?"

"We did! Check your phone!"

Jacob looking at his phone. *"I did get a call for the ER. Zada is she ok?*

"I think that she's going to be ok but she's really sick."

They all rush to the ER. Yasmeen is out cold with an IV bag hooked up to her arm. Jacob rubs Yasmeen hand, but she doesn't respond. Mahmoud heart drops as he stands their looking at Yasmeen knowing that there is nothing that he can do for her. Zada rubs Yasmeen head as she calls her name. Yasmeen tries to eye's her eyes, but she is too sedated. Yasmeen body shakes from her hundred and five-degree fever.

"Can you stay with her and keep us informed? You don't have to worry about going back to work Zada I will handle that. I just need you to stay with Yasmeen and if you need me for anything don't hesitate on calling me. I will... we will be back as soon as we can."

Everyone leaves but Zada and Ashton. Jacob is beside himself he knew that Yasmeen wasn't feeling well but he had no idea that it was this serious. The next day Mahmoud and Maxwell are talking to Jacob when Rosetta walks up. "So how is Yasmeen doing Jacob?"

"She is doing, better Maxwell and she's at home now, right Rosetta!"

"Oh, I think so."

"*So, you haven't gone to check on her?*"

"*No why would I?*"

Mahmoud is disappointed with Rosetta answer. "*Well she is your friend and friends are supposed to take care of each other.*"

"*Well not me! I am not about to go over to her house and get sick. Not me huh I will see her when she gets back.*"

"*Some friend you are Rosetta!*"

Mahmoud walks away to go find Zada. Yasmeen has been on his mind all night. He needs to be sure that she's alright. Mahmoud gets off the elevator he sees Zada and Tia at the nurse's station he runs over to Zada with urgency.

"*Hey, Zada I have been looking for you.*"

"*Yeah I know I just got to work. I was just about to call you.*"

"*So how is Yasmeen?*"

"*She's better than she was on yesterday but not much. She has a bad case of the flu. I just hate seeing my friend like that you know. I stayed with her last night and I didn't get any sleep because I was so worried about her. Doc I was so scared I have never seen her like that. I'm so use to her… running around here pissing everybody off.*"

"*Yeah me too. I Can tell that she's not here.*"

"*You know that I had to fight with her before I left. She wouldn't take her meds. I hate that I have to work tonight but Oscar and Todd are going to go check on her when they get off, of course I will be calling her every chance that I get.*"

"*Great and I'm relieved to hear that she's going to be ok. Can you tell her that I said hello and to get well soon?*"

"*Doc you can call her you know or go over to her house. Do you know where she lives?*"

"No, I can't do that."

"*Why you can't! Doc here let me give you here address and phone number. If nothing else, you can call her, and I'll tell her that I gave you her information when I talk to her in a little while.*"

Mahmoud takes the paper from Zada and puts it in his pocket as he walks away. Mahmoud goes back to his office and contemplate on calling Yasmeen. There is nothing that Mahmoud would like more than to hear Yasmeen's voice but knowing that she's sick, the last thing that he wants to do is to upset her by calling. When Zada exit her patients' room she's surprised to see Aaron waiting for her. Zada has never forgiven Aaron for cheating on Yasmeen so she tries to keep her distance whenever possible. Zada looks at Aaron and rolls her eye as she attempts to walk pass him.

"*Hey, Zada I just found out about Yasmeen. Is she ok?*"

"*She's going to be just fine.*"

"*Is there anything that I can do?*"

"*Yeah leave her alone!*"

"*Now Zada you know that I still care a lot about Yasmeen. You may not believe me, but I am concerned about her wellbeing. I just want to know how she's doing that's all.*"

"*Look Aron I don't doubt that you are concerned about her, but like I said she going to be ok. She has the flu!*"

"*Well should I go…*"

"*Don't you dare take your ass over there! Yasmeen is very sick and weak, she has no time for your shit! Now get out of my way!*"

"*Why can't I go see her?*"

. "*Because she's at Oscar's house and you know that there're not going to let you come over! We're taking care of her and she don't need you! Go find one of your hoes!*"

Zada walks away leaving Aaron standing in the hall with his mouth open. Zada goes on break so that she can call Yasmeen to make sure that she's ok and to let her know that Mahmoud might call her. Yasmeen is still so weak, it takes her a while to answer her phone.

"*Hey sweetie, I just wanted to make sure that you we're ok. Oscar and Todd should be on their way. Oh, did doctor Shashivivek call you?*"

"*No and why would he be calling me?*"

"*Because I gave him your number and told him to.*"

"*Za why would you do that? You know that I don't like that man.*"

"*Yass he's very worried about you we all are. He just wants to make sure that you're ok but if you don't want him to call, I will tell him not to ok.*"

Yasmeen closes her eyes. "*No don't do that he can call, but Za I feel, look, and sound like crap so if he calls and I don't answer tell him to leave a message. Za thank you for everything.*"

"Don't thank me yet. You know I got your account number. Yasmeen try to laugh. *I'm just kidding. I just wanted to make you smile. So, is it ok for doctor Shashivivek to call?"*

"Yes, it's ok."

"Alright then you take your meds and get some rest. I'll see you in the morning when I get off. I love chick."

"And I love you back sis."

Oscar, Todd, and Ashton just left Yasmeen's house. Yasmeen gets back in bed. Her body aches and fever has taken over her. The only thing that she wants to do is sleep until she feels better. Yasmeen pulls the cover up over her aching fever body. She tries to get comfortable but just the touch of her sheets mades her skin hurt. Just as Yasmeen lays her aching head on the pillow and close her aching eyes the doorbell rings. Yasmeen knows that it's Oscar maybe he forgot something. Yasmeen lies in bed without moving she hopes that he would just use his key. Yasmeen kick the covers off her when she remembers that she put the slide lock on the door. Yasmeen grabs a blanket and throws it cross her shoulder as she forces herself to the door. Every step that she takes causes her so much pain. Yasmeen's body is weak, and the door seems so far away. Yasmeen is about to give up when the doorbell rings again. Yasmeen is almost in tears as she makes her way to the door. Yasmeen opens the door and to her astonishment it's not Oscar or Todd. Yasmeen in a Weak voice. *"Doctor Shashivivek what… what are you doing here?"*

"I… I just wanted to see how you were doing. I sorry I should have call first."

Yasmeen resting her head on the door. *"No, I mean why are you here I'm sick with the flu and I really don't want you to get sick."*

"I'll be fine don't worry about me. May I come in?"

Yasmeen is just about to say no, but her head starts spinning, she's on the verge of passing out. Before Yasmeen can fall to the floor Mahmoud catches her and carry's her to the couch. Mahmoud sits down beside Yasmeen and rest his hand on her head.

Mahmoud rubs Yasmeen face. *"Yasmeen you're burning up."*

"Please give me that blanket I'm so cold."

"I know you are. Mahmoud lay the blanket across Yasmeen. *I need to take your temperature ok."*

"No… *No, it hurts!*"

"What hurts?"

"*Everything hurts! My skin hurts! My eyes hurt! Everything hurt!*" Tears start to run down Yasmeen cheeks.

Mahmoud wipes the tears from Yasmeen cheeks. "*I know it does. Now here.* Putting the thermometer in Yasmeen's mouth. *let me take your temperature.*"

Mahmoud looks at the thermometer, Yasmeen's temperature reads hundred and four. "*Yasmeen will you let me take care of you?*" Yasmeen nods her head yes as Mahmoud place a cool compress on her forehead and lays Yasmeen head on his chest. Mahmoud pulls the blanket up over her shoulder. Yasmeen falls asleep in Mahmoud's arms. Mahmoud watches Yasmeen as she sleeps. All he can think about is how beautiful she is as he strokes her hair. Mahmoud can feel the heat of the fever being released from Yasmeen's body. He embraces her in his arms as he smiles because never in a million year did Mahmoud think that one day Yasmeen would be in his arms sleeping. Mahmoud falls asleep with Yasmeen's hand on his chest. It's three o'clock in the morning Yasmeen is jolted up from her sleep all she can see is Mahmoud looking at her. They both try to adjust their eyes. Yasmeen sits up as she looks around not knowing where she is.

"*What's the matter Yasmeen?*"

Yasmeen rubs her eyes. "*I'm sorry.*"

"*Sorry for what?*"

"*Falling asleep on you.*"

Mahmoud pulls Yasmeen back close to him. "*It's ok. Here let me check your temperature. It feels like your fever has gone down, but you still feel a little warm.*"

"*What time is it?*"   .

Mahmoud looks down at his Rolex. "*Wait that can't be right. It's three in the morning!*"

Yasmeen quickly jumps to her feet and falls back down she grabs her head, as the room spins. Mahmoud puts his arms around Yasmeen as she lay back on his chest Yasmeen can hear his heart beating she closes her eyes.Yasmeen fever may have gone down, but the pain is still there. Yasmeen skin feel like hot pins poking her all over. Yasmeen can feel herself about to throw up. Again, she jumps up and run to her bathroom with

Mahmoud close behind. After Yasmeen is done, she sits on the floor and sobs. Yasmeen is not crying because she feels bad. She's crying because Mahmoud is seeing her at her worst. Mahmoud wipes Yasmeen face with a wet hand towel.

Mahmoud holds onto Yasmeen face. *"Sweetheart why are you crying?"*

"Look at me! Yasmeen puts her hand up to her face. I know that you most think the worst of me right now Mahmoud!"

Mahmoud looks in Yasmeen eyes with so much understanding as he wipes her tears with his thumb and helps her to her feet. *"Yasmeen why would you think that. I know that you are sick and I'm here to help you not judge you ok."*

"Ok. But I need to take a shower."

"So, you want me to give you a shower?"

"No of course not I was just saying!"

"Oh…ok well let me go get your medication ok, I'll be right back."

Mahmoud returns with Yasmeen medication than he leaves her alone before she starts to undress. Mahmoud is sitting in the living room when Yasmeen stumbles over to him. Mahmoud takes Yasmeen by the hand and leads her back to her bedroom. He guides Yasmeen to the bed.

"Yasmeen, you need to rest, and I need to get home, but I will stop by on my way to work I promise and I will call you when I'm on my way. Oh, I will show myself out."

Yasmeen tries to get up. *"But I have to lock the door and turn the heat on it's cold in here."*

Mahmoud gently pushes Yasmeen back on the pillow. *"No, I will take care of that you need to rest.* Pulling the covers up. *And no need to turn on the heat it just your fever is starting to come back."*

Before Mahmoud can leave Yasmeen's bedroom, she is fast asleep. Mahmoud kisses her on her forehead. Mahmoud makes sure that the door is lock before he leaves. The next morning just as Mahmoud promised he stops by to check on Yasmeen who still has a high fever. Mahmoud gives her meds and puts her back to bed. When Zada get off she goes straight to Yasmeen house. Yasmeen tells her that Mahmoud came over and that he took good care of her. The only thing that she didn't tell her was that he stayed most of the night, maybe he will tell her. Yasmeen head starts to pound and Zada can see that she's not feeling well. Zada tells Yasmeen to rest and they can talk later. Just before she passes out on Yasmeen's couch. A week has passed since Yasmeen has had the flu. Without fail Zada, Oscar, Todd, and Ashton have made it their mission to take care of Yasmeen. They have been by Yasmeen side day and night whenever possible. Mahmoud too has been coming over twice a day to make sure that Yasmeen's every need is met. He has not missed a day. Even Wallace as come by to check on Yasmeen. Yes, somedays with Yasmeen are better than others, Mahmoud has had to fight with Yasmeen to get her to eat. Like Yasmeen Mahmoud can be stubborn when it comes to getting what he wants and right now he wants Yasmeen to get better. With each day Mahmoud can see that Yasmeen is getting stronger and her health is improving. After a week and a half Yasmeen is feeling much better so she decides to get dressed. Nothing to fancy just a pair of gray gym shorts with Pink across the back. The shorts shows a little of her ass cheek when she walks, with a matching tank top. The tank top shows off her well-defined abs when she raises her arms. Yasmeen pulls her hair back into a ponytail. Yasmeen looks at herself in the mirror she touches her smooth chocolate brown skin, she can tell that she has lost some weight from being sick. Yasmeen turns around to check out her ass. She smiles as she tells herself that she looks good and that her weight loss is in all the right places. Yasmeen is cleaning her room after putting a load of clothes in the washer when her head starts spinning. Yasmeen knows that she most likely has exerted herself and she needs to slow down. Yasmeen is about to climb back into bed when the doorbell rings. Yasmeen takes her time in getting to the door. The last thing that she wants is to pass out then Oscar will know that she has been doing everything that he told her not to do. Yasmeen rubs her face before opening the door.

"Hey what are you doing here Mahmoud?"

"What do you mean"

"I just mean that it's like one o'clock, so I wasn't expecting you to come until later I guess."

"Well I had a later lunch... Is it ok if I came in? I won't stay long."

"Ok yes... Sure come in."

Yasmeen walks ahead of Mahmoud and sits down. Mahmoud can't help himself. He can't take his eyes off Yasmeen. The thoughts that he's having he tries to run them out of his head.

188

"Well you're looking great today! What have you been up to?"

"What do you mean?"

Mahmoud putting his hand on Yasmeen forehead. *"I mean that you are looking a little flushed. Now what have you been doing Yasmeen don't you say nothing?"*

"Well I got dressed."

"I can see that you look wonderful, but you know that that's not what I'm talking about. Yasmeen what have you been doing besides getting dressed?"

"Well I... I washed a load of cloths and I did a little cleaning, not much."

"Yasmeen didn't we talk about this yesterday. Yasmeen, I know that you may feel better but you're not a hundred percent yet. Yasmeen, you should be resting not trying to clean. I told you that I would take care of that didn't I?"

"Yes, you did, but I was feeling ok. I just wanted to do something."

"You can rest and don't give me that sad face Yasmeen it's not going to work, you have to listen."

Yasmeen puts her hands over her face. Mahmoud feels bad, so he put his arms around Yasmeen and rest his chin on her head.

"Yasmeen, I'm sorry please don't cry I just want you to get better. I know that you are used to doing things your way and you hate depending on others, but I'm here for you so let me help you please... I've got to get back to the office, but I will see you when I get off."

Yasmeen walks Mahmoud to the door. *"Ok and thanks for checking in on me."*

"You are welcome Yasmeen, by the way did you wear that for me?"

"No... Laughing. No, I wore them for me doctor."

"Just kidding but when I come back those cloths that you have in the washer better still be in there unless Oscar or someone other than you put them in the dryer. As a matter of fact, I'm going to let Zada know..."

Yasmeen cuts Mahmoud off. *"No, you don't have to do that. Why would you tell Zada?"*

"Because I'm sure she told you to rest."

"Well she may have said something like that, but can we keep this between us?

"No because you don't listen. Now I will see you after five now you go get some rest."

After another week Yasmeen is over the flu and she's feeling much better, thanks to all the care and help that she received. As Yasmeen walks down the hall to her office she smiles as she thanks God for his mercy. Yasmeen promised herself that she would be or at least try to be nicer to Mahmoud because after all he did take care of her. Yasmeen knows that it's not going to be an easy fight and she's got to fight with herself, but she's willing to give her all. Yasmeen steps off the elevator. She's wearing a beige two-piece suit, that compliments her sexy frame. The suit jacket is unbuttoned to show off her white blouse. No one sees Yasmeen as she approaches in her matching beige and white high heels. Mahmoud, Maxwell, Jacob, Aaron, Rosetta, and Uma are standing at the Nurses station talking to Tia, Zada, Ashton, and Cindy. They are not at all aware of Yasmeen walking up behind them. Wallace is the first one to see her. He's so excited as he yells out her name. *Ms. Yasmeen welcome back!* In an instant everybody turns around. Yasmeen smiles as she greets Wallace with a firm hand shake. Without thinking Mahmoud runs over and embraces Yasmeen in his arms. He holds Yasmeen so tight she can feel his rock-hard abs. His body feels so good, Yasmeen closes her eyes. She can smell Mahmoud cologne as he spins her around. Aaron stands back and observe Mahmoud. His heart almost stops because Mahmoud is holding on to Yasmeen the way he would love to. As everyone gathers around Yasmeen welcoming her back. Rosetta, Uma, and Rebecca watches with envy.

Jacob hugs Yasmeen. "*Why didn't you tell me that you were coming back today? Are you feeling ok?*

"*Yes, I'm feeling much better thank you. I didn't tell you because...*"

"*Come here baby! I missed you so much Hun. Cindy* Looks Yasmeen over. *Don't you look good. Hell, I need to catch the flu, so I can come back looking like you. Yasmeen are you sure that you were sick. Sick people don't look this good!*"

"*Oh, I'm sure right Zada.*"

"*Yes, she was sick, but my friend back now, and don't you ever get sick like that on me again!*"

After the greeting is over Mahmoud goes back to his office. He's surprised to find a floral arrangement setting on his desk. He is about to read the card when he gets a knock on the door. Mahmoud reply *come in* and in walks Yasmeen. Mahmoud can feel his heart smiling.

"Wow you got flowers! I wonder who they are from!"

"So, do I. Reading the card. *You are welcome. You know no one has ever sent me flowers before."*

"Yeah right Doctor Shashivivek…

"Call me Mahmoud."

"Ok Mahmoud, I just want to say thank you and I really appreciate everything that you did for me. The flowers are my way of saying thank you."

"Yasmeen, you really didn't have to because what I did for you was for the kindness of my heart."

"I know that, but I still wanted to say thank you because you didn't have to help me, but you did."

"Yasmeen, you're welcome."

"So, does that mean we can go back to how we used to be?"

"Oh no I don't want things to go back to how they used to be between us. Yasmeen, I think that we should move past any differences that we've had. I don't want to fight with you anymore. Yasmeen whenever we have a disagreement, I think that we are at a place now where that we can talk about it so, no let us not go back to the way things used to be between us. Mahmoud extends his hand out to Yasmeen. *"Do you agree!"*

"I agree."

"Really Yasmeen, I'm happy that you're feeling better."

"Me too. Well I better get to work. Guess I'll see you around."

"Yes, you will. Oh, by the way Yasmeen you look amazing.

Yasmeen turns around and smiles before she exits Mahmoud's office. Yasmeen and Jacob just finished talking when Rosetta enters her office. Out of all the people in this world Rosetta is the one person that Yasmeen doesn't want to see. Not now! Not ever.

"Yasmeen welcome back and don't forget to come see me before you leave."

"Why didn't you tell me that you were coming back today?

"For the same reason that you didn't call to check on me!"

"Yass, I know that you ain't tripping on that. I was going to…"

"You were going to tell a lie. Save it because I don't want to hear it Rosetta. You showed me just who you are! You are not a friend, at least not a friend of mine! So why would I be tripping? I wasn't expecting you to call or come by!"

"Yasmeen, I am your friend!"

"Like hell you are! Even Aaron called and sent me flowers."

"He did!"

"Yes, he did just about every day."

"Yasmeen, you know that I really do care about you and I am your friend. Your best friend."

"Like I said, like hell you are! Rosetta the only thing that you care about is fu… Rosetta, I really didn't want to talk to you right now. I'm not feeling good!"

"Can I get you anything?"

"No just leave please."

Rosetta leaves Yasmeen's office she's heated. Yasmeen shakes her head as she close her eyes. Yasmeen already knows that whatever so call friendship that they had is over. Not because of Aaron, but because Rosetta can't be trusted. She is and has always been a shady bitch. Rosetta is known for cutthroat tactics, but they don't work on Yasmeen. After lunch Yasmeen is sitting in her office when she gets a knock on the door. Yasmeen gets up to answer the door because she is expecting, a patient family member at any moment. When Yasmeen opens the door her first instinct is to slam the door when she sees, Aaron standing at the door smiling like he just finished jacking his dick.

"What is it that you want?"

"Well I'm happy to see you as well Yasmeen. May I come in?"

"Sure, Aaron why not, but make it quick!"

"I just wanted to welcome you back and to let you know that I'm glad to see that you are doing better."

"Thank you for caring."

"Yasmeen, you know that I will always care for you. Looking Yasmeen over. *Damn you look good shit…"*

"Aaron what do you want? I don't feel like this today."

"Well I came to check on you, but I see that you are just as fine now as you were then. I can see that you lost a little weight but shit baby you still looking good. I can't believe that I fucked up with you!"

"Well you did and it's ok."

"Yasmeen come on give me one more chance! You know that you still want me!"

"Aaron, we are finished? I can never have you back so let's not go there."

Aaron holds Yasmeen hand. *"Do you remember the last time that we were in here like this? I can still taste you."*

Yasmeen pulls her hand away. *"Do you remember what I did to you the last time you tried to touch me."*

Aaron takes a step back. *"Yes, Yasmeen you could have really hurt me you know!"*

"That was my intent."

"You know what Yasmeen I'm going to get you back. Oh, *and by the way you're going to give me some good dreams tonight."*

It has now been two-weeks Yasmeen is sitting at home watching lifetime alone on a Friday night. She is sitting on the couch eating popcorn in a pair of shorts and a tank-top. Todd is out of town visiting his family. Oscar and Ashton are at the beach for the weekend and Zada had to work over-time. So, it's just Yasmeen she didn't want to go out, she just wants to stay in and curl up with her body pillow. Yasmeen reaches up and pulls her hair tie out. Her hair falls and frames her face Yasmeen pulls her blanket up over her long chocolate smooth legs. Yasmeen can hear her cell phone ring from her bedroom. She tries to ignore it because she's just too lazy to get up. She hopes that it will stop ringing, but it doesn't. Yasmeen thinks that it may be Oscar or Todd, so she runs to answer it. Yasmeen looks at her phone. *"Shit what does he want? Hello Mahmoud. How are you?*

"I'm good and yourself? What are you getting into?"

"Nothing much just sitting here watching TV."

"Why aren't you out with your friends?" *"Oh, they are out of town and Zada's at work… Wait a minute you're asking me all these questions. Why are you not out with your friends?"*

Mahmoud chuckle. *"Well Maxwell is at home with his family and I had no desire to go out."*

"So, where's your girlfriend?"

"I don't know, because I don't have one."

"Oh, I forgot you're engaged."

"What does that have to do with anything. She's there and I'm here."

"So, you're bored?"

"I guess you could say that."

"I see, so you call me when you're bored."

"No Yasmeen I called you to call if that makes sense to you."

Yasmeen cross her long legs. *"No not really. I think that you're bored."*

"You must be bored too, home on a Friday night watching chick flicks alone."

"Who said that I was alone!"

Mahmoud gets testy. *"So, you got company!"*

"No but I do have my pillow."

"Would you like…"

Yasmeen interrupts Mahmoud. *"Would I like for you to come over!"*

"Well if you what me to I can."

Yasmeen bits her lower lip. *"That's up to you. I mean if you want to watch lifetime you are welcome to come over."*

"I'm on my way.!"

Mahmoud arrives at Yasmeen townhouse at eight-thirty. He hugs Yasmeen and kisses her on the cheek. Yasmeen and Mahmoud sit on the couch with the lights out watching TV eating popcorn. Soon they forget about TV as they start talking Yasmeen jokes with Mahmoud about Uma and Rebecca. Mahmoud massages Yasmeen feet as they talk. Not once does Yasmeen pull away or ask what is he doing? Yasmeen gets that familiar feeling deep inside of her like he's an old friend. Soon Yasmeen is laying in Mahmoud's arms and they are talking non-stop. Yasmeen wishes that she could tell him everything about her, but she can't not yet so, she shuts down. Before they know it's two o'clock in the morning. I guess time does fly when you're having fun. The last thing that Mahmoud wants to do is leave. Yasmeen walks Mahmoud to the door. Mahmoud wishes that he could kiss Yasmeen, but he doesn't want to push her away, so he settles for a hug instead. Yasmeen and Mahmoud spent the rest of the week-end together getting to know each other. This is just the first of many week-ends that they will share. Yasmeen can't wait to tell Oscar and Todd. At work Yasmeen and Mahmoud share the occasional smiles that only they know about. Yasmeen has a secret and she's not telling nobody but Oscar and Todd. It's another Saturday night. Aaron is sitting at home drinking. He has been calling Yasmeen since he got home. Her phone keeps going to voice mail on the first ring. The more Aaron calls Yasmeen the more he drinks. The only thing that he wants is to hear her voice. Aaron saw Zada and the others at the bar. Zada told him that Yasmeen had a date. All Aaron can think about is with who?" Aaron is sitting on his sofa drinking and calling Yasmeen hoping that she will answer. Someone knocks on the door Aaron runs to the door. He's not happy to see Rosetta but he's drunk and mad, so she will have to do. Before Rosetta can get a word out of her mouth Aaron pulls her inside and kisses her. As Aaron pulls her shirt over her head Rosetta reaches down and unbuttons Aaron pants. Aaron unhooks Rosetta bra and she smiles as Aaron puts a mouthful of her breast in his mouth. She can feel Aaron's nail in her back. Rosetta wipes her legs around Aaron as he carriers her upstairs to his bedroom. Aaron can't get his clothes off before Rosetta has his hard dick in her mouth. Aaron grabs her head as he angrily pushes his big dick deep in her mouth. Rosetta gags. Aaron pulls his dick out of Rosetta's mouth and slaps her across the face with his long hard dick. Aaron pushes Rosetta back onto the bed and he puts her legs on his shoulders and thrust his hard dick inside of her. This is the moment that Rosetta has been waiting for. She screams as Aaron fucks her. Aaron pounds Rosetta pussy like a drum. Rosetta is about to cum when Aaron flips her over and rams his dick up her ass. She cries out in pain as Aaron storks get faster and harder. He is on the verge of his climax. They both scream. Aaron pulls out, Rosetta can feel his warm juices running down her back and down the crack of her ass. Aaron stands in front of Rosetta smiling as he tells her *Suck this dick bitch!* Then he pushes his dick back into Rosetta's mouth. After Aaron ejaculates all over Rosetta face and mouth he pushes her away and walks back down stairs naked. Aaron picks up his cell phone and he sees that he has a missed call from Yasmeen.

Aaron listening to his message. *"Hey, Aaron this is Yasmeen it's about twelve mid-night. I see that you have called many times... Well I going to assume that you are asleep, so I want call back... Anyway, have a good night and I will talk to you later bye."*

Aaron calls Yasmeen back but Yasmeen doesn't answer. Her phone continues to ring. Rosetta walks behind Aaron and puts her arms around Aarons waist and calls his name at the same time Yasmeen answers her phone. To keep Yasmeen from hearing Rosetta Aaron hangs up and pushes her away. When Aaron calls Yasmeen back his call goes straight to voice once again. This infuriates him, because he knows that Yasmeen heard Rosetta.

"Why in the fuck would you do that? You saw me on the fucking phone!"

"Was that Yasmeen?"

"That's not any of your business who it was! You know what get the fuck out! You wanted her to hear you didn't you. Grabbing Rosetta by her arm. *Get the fuck out! You got what you wanted now you can leave! You want Yasmeen to know that I fucked you now take you ass over to her house and tell her*! Aaron pushes Rosetta out the door. *When I want to fuck you again, I'll call you!"*

It's Monday Yasmeen and Ashton are sitting in the conference room conversating when Aaron walks in. Uma and Rebeca are not too far behind. All weekend Aaron has been unable to figure out who Yasmeen was with. Aaron has made up his mind that he must know who Yasmeen spent her weekend with and not to mention that Yasmeen would not take any of his calls after he hung up on her. Aaron stands on the opposite side of the table.

"Excuse me but Yasmeen can we talk?"

"Ok go ahead I'm listening."

"Not here. In private… Out in the hall."

"Ok but I don't know why! What does he want to talk to me about Ash?"

"I don't know! do you need me to come with?"

"No but I'll yell if I need you."

Yasmeen walks out into the hall. Aaron has his back to her. Yasmeen can see that somethings bothering him, but what? Yasmeen mind starts to race. Is he sick? If so, why is he telling her? Yasmeen approaches Aaron with her hand on her hip.

"Ok Aaron what did you want to talk to me about?"

"About Saturday night. You know that I had some one over. I'm quite sure that you heard her."

Yasmeen putting her hands up. *"Wait, wait hold on. Aaron, I did not know that you had company. I was just returning your call after you had called my phone like fifty times. I thought that something was wrong that's the only reason I returned your call. Tell her that I don't mean any harm. "*

"Yasmeen that's not it. I just don't want you to be mad at me."

"Why would I be mad? Aaron there is nothing between us anymore. You can see whoever you want. Hell, I am!"

"I know! That's what I wanted to talk to you about. Yasmeen who were you with?"

"You don't need to know that!"

"Oh yes I do!"

"Well I'm not telling you. Oh, and by the way who did you have over? Was it Rosetta? You don't have to answer that, I won't tell Uma and Rebecca."

"Why would you say that Yasmeen?"

Yasmeen snickers as she walks away. Aaron rubs his hand across his face. Yasmeen returns to the conference room and takes her seat next to Ashton. She and Ashton are still taking when Jacob, Maxwell, Brandon, and Mahmoud walks in. Mahmoud looks at Yasmeen and smile. Before Mahmoud starts his discussion, he looks around the room as he clears his throat.

"Look I know that what I'm about to say is not going to sit well with some of you. So, I ask that you let me finish Ms. Blake ok."

"Why are you calling me out?"

"I'm not, I was just saying, and I would like to talk to you after the meeting."

"Yeah ok uh huh. We can do that. We sure can doctor Shashivivek!"

"Yasmeen be nice and hear him out before you blow up."

Yasmeen whispers to Jacob. *"Jacob who are you talking to?"*

"I guess nobody. Yasmeen please don't!"

Don't what?"

"Yasmeen just wait until after the meeting."

"So, you know what he's about to say."

"No, I don't but I do know how you are."

"Oh, do you really doctor?"

"Yasmeen please for me please!'

"Ok, you don't have to beg me."

After the meeting Yasmeen and Mahmoud remain seated. Yasmeen can see Aaron pacing back and forth. He still wants to know who Yasmeen was with Yasmeen smiles as Jacob closes the door. When Yasmeen turns round Mahmoud is looking at her. Yasmeen sits back as she crosses her long legs.

"So, what do we have to talk about doctor…"

"Ok first thing first. I missed talking to you last night Yasmeen."

"And I missed talking to you. I was over at Oscars place. When I got back it was late and I wasn't sure if you were still up."

"Yes, I was up waiting on you to call."

"Why didn't you call me"

"I wanted to, but I knew that you had mention that you were going to be over there. I didn't want to be a bother."

"You could have come with me."

"Next time I will. Yasmeen what I wanted to ask you was will you have lunch with me today?"

"Who me?"

"Yes you! I don't see anybody else in here."

"Ok where do you want me to meet you?"

"You don't want to ride with me?"

"Sure, I can ride with you. I don't see why not. Wait I 'm not going to have somebody waiting for at my car when I get off am I?"

"Yeah Aaron."

Yasmeen bumps Mahmoud shoulder. *"Oh, you're funny."*

When Yasmeen gets back from lunch with Mahmoud, she sees Rosetta at the end of the hall. Rosetta has been avoiding her all day. Yasmeen dare to ask why. Yasmeen smiles because the only thing on her mind is Mahmoud. Yasmeen is not sure how she should be feeling about Mahmoud because he is engaged, and she don't want to get hurt. Yasmeen tells herself that Mahmoud is just a friend. Yasmeen lies to guard her heart. Two weeks has passed Yasmeen and Mahmoud are still enjoying each other's company. Yasmeen is sitting at her desk singing when Rosetta walks in.

"Who got you so happy?"

Yasmeen looks up from computer. *"Well we both know that it's not Aaron!"*

Rosetta can feel that Yasmeen knows about her and Aaron so she in a haste leaves Yasmeen office without saying a word. Aaron is sitting alone with his hands over his face when Mahmoud walks in his office. Mahmoud can see the frustration on Aaron's face when he looks up.

"Hey, may I come in?"

"Oh...oh yes sure Doc. Please...please come in, have a seat."

Mahmoud studies Aaron. *"Doctor Sinclair are you ok?"*

"No not really."

"Well do you want to talk about it?"

Aaron shakes his head no, because he doesn't want anyone to know that he's still in love with Yasmeen. After all the things that he's done he still can't get over her. Aaron needs to get it all out and who's better to tell than Mahmoud. He's the one person that understands him.

"You know I don't know what it is Mahmoud. I can't get over her."

"Get over who?"

"Yasmeen! I don't know why, I just can't. I know that she would never have anything more to do with me! Yes, I know that I cheated, and I hurt her, I know that and I 've told her that I was sorry. You Know Yasmeen she's not trying to hear it!"

Mahmoud doesn't know what to say as he searches for words. *"Well what did you expect from her?"*

"I expected her to understand, Doc I'm a man with needs! Needs that she wasn't fulfilling!"

"What do you mean. Mahmoud has an unsure look on his face. *Was she not good in bed?"*

"Oh, I'm sure she's amazing in bed but I never got the chance to find out. Aaron push himself away from his desk. *Because I fucked up! If I would have just waited thirty more fucking minutes. I waited six months and I couldn't wait thirty minutes that's all.* Flustered. *Why didn't I wait?'*

"Well you said that you had needs... I don't know. Mahmoud clears his throat. *So, you waited six months?"*

"Yes, I did! Six long months. Oh, but we had fun. You know the more I waited the more I wanted Yasmeen. there's just something about her that I can't get over Doc what would you have done?"

"I would have waited. I mean if you cared for her like you said you should have waited until she was ready. No matter if it was six months or six year."

"I tried! I really did… You know Doc you're right. I didn't plan to cheat on Yasmeen it just happened. I wasn't thinking. Rebecca came over, she started sucking me off, one thing leads to another, Yasmeen walked in, and my life was over that day! She should've given me a second chance! She wouldn't even let me explain."

"Explant what? You know what Aaron you have a lot going on."

"I know with Uma, Rebecca, and all the other ones. Hell, I don't want them! They mean nothing to me. I want Yasmeen and now I think that she's seeing someone. She won't even take my calls and it's driving me insane!"

"Why?"

"Because Doc…look you may not see it, but Yasmeen is a good woman with a heart of gold. I know that she comes off as being a hard ass but once you get to know her you can't help but love her. She's an amazing woman."

"Yes, I know."

"What? How do you know?"

Mahmoud thinks fast. *"Well I see how she is with the patients. They are always telling me how caring she is."*

"Doc. What should I do?"

"You should get yourself together. I mean you made your choice now live with it. Aaron, you do want her to be happy right!"

"Yeah with me!"

"Look I have to get back to work. I just wanted to remind you of the two o'clock meeting."

"Oh yeah I forgot. Doctor Shashivivek thanks for listening. I just needed to get that off my chest."

Mahmoud leaves Aaron office as he thinks to himself. *"She made him wait six months and she still didn't give herself to him, Wow!"*

When Mahmoud gets home, he can't stop thinking about Yasmeen and the conversation that he had with Aaron. Mahmoud thinks could Yasmeen have been playing a game or did she really care about Aaron. He just has to find out. Mahmoud knows in his heart that what he feels for Yasmeen is more than just a friendship. The more time that he spends with her the stronger his love for her grows. Mahmoud wonders is Yasmeen's capable of caring for him the way that he cares for her or is he just fooling himself. Mahmoud is eager to find out if he can break down this wall that she has up around her heart. Mahmoud knows that he has reports to complete, but he can't get his mind off Yasmeen. Mahmoud cell phone rings it's Rebecca. She just won't give up. Mahmoud pushes the ignore button. Mahmoud cell continues to ring he is about to turn his phone off when he looks down and sees that it's Yasmeen. Mahmoud smiles as he answers. A week has passed Mahmoud and Wallace are at the end of the hall talking.

"So, are you ready for the dinner Mahmoud?"

"What dinner?"

"*You know the dinner at Ms. Blake house Wednesday. Didn't she invite you?*"

"*No, she didn't invite me! She invited you?*"

"*Well yeah… I mean Mrs. Zada told me about it.*"

Mahmoud can feel his emotion of anger surging through his body. Mahmoud is about to walk away when Yasmeen walks you smiling.

"*Well good morning. I went by your office looking for you.*"

"*Oh, may I ask why?*"

"*Well let me get back to work. I will talk to you later Doc and I'll see you Ms. Blake.*"

"*What did I tell you Wallace?*"

"*I mean Yasmeen.*"

"*Ok Wallace. Well to answer your question, I'm having a get together at my house on Wednesday and I wanted to personally invite you. I mean if you're not busy I would like for you to come… Zada didn't tell you, already has she?*" "*No, she didn't tell me and yes I would love to come. Thanks for the invite Ms. Blake.*"

"Ok Doctor Shashivivek, anyway, I'm just having a few people over for… Do you like seafood?"

"Yes, Yasmeen I love seafood."

Yasmeen breathe a sigh of relief. "*Oh good, I wasn't sure! So, I'll see you Wednesday.*"

"*Wait what time should I be there?*"

"*Oh, seven o'clock, at my house.*"

"*Should I bring anything?*"

"*No just you, I got this.*"

Mahmoud to himself. "*Yes, you do.* Oh, Yasmeen *how about I bring me and some wine?*"

"*That'll work.*"

It is the Thursday after Yasmeen seafood dinner. Mahmoud, Maxwell, Ashton, Wallace, and Jacob are in the hospital lobby talking. Rosetta, Anne-Marie, and Rebecca over hears them talking. So, they walk over to join in on the conversation.

Jacob rubbing his stomach. "*That was the best seafood that I've had in a long time Maxwell!*"

"I did not know that she could cook like that! I mean I have heard that she could cook but I had no idea that she..."

"What is this? Who cooked what Jacob?"

"Oh, we're talking about Yasmeen. She invited us over last night for seafood. Licking his lips. *She cooked crab legs, fish, shrimp hum what was it? oh gumbo!"*

"Don't forget the oysters. You couldn't stop eating them you and Wallace."

"Because they were so good Ashton. You know I brought me some for lunch."

Ashton hold his bag up. *"Me too. Wallace, I think that we all did. Mahmoud how about you?"*

"Yes, and you can't have any!"

"Wait a minute what all do you have in there?"

"You don't need to know that. Maxwell, but I will be eating good for lunch!"

"I didn't know about Yasmeen having a seafood dinner.

Jacob puts his hand on Rosetta's back. *"Well I'm sorry to say that you missed out on a good one!"*

"Yes, she did. Ms. Blake showed out. Doc we had fun, didn't we?"

Mahmoud agrees as they all start to walk away leaving Rosetta in the lobby wondering why she wasn't invited. Rosetta runs to the elevator and rushes to Yasmeen's office. Yasmeen is on the phone when Rosetta enters her office. Yasmeen looks at the clock on the wall as she continues her conversation.

"Yes, may I help you?"

"Yes, you may! Yasmeen why wasn't I invited to your little dinner?"

"Well first of all I don't do little anything, and second I didn't want you there!"

"And Why not?"

"Why would I? Rosetta, you don't talk to me. I don't know the last time that you and I had a conversation if it wasn't about work."

"Well you still could have invited me."

"Well I didn't want to."

"Why Yass?"

Yasmeen rubs her temple. *"Look Rosetta I had an appreciation dinner for everyone who was there for me when I was sick, and you were not on my list."*

"Yass you're not right, but that's ok."

"What so you're mad now? I got it! Rosetta why don't you have a dinner and not invite me, you could invite Aaron, Rebecca, Anne-Marie, and all your little buddy's. You could have a fuck Yasmeen dinner, how about that."

"Yasmeen why would I do that? We're friends"

"Now you know that's not at all true."

"Yass why do you keep saying that?"

"Because it's true so let's cut the bullshit!"

"So, you don't think of me as a friend?"

"Rosetta do you actually think of yourself as a friend? I mean really Rosetta!"

"What Yasmeen is this about me not coming to see you?"

"Rosetta, I really could have cared less if you came to see me, but you who calls yourself a friend, you didn't even call not once!"

"Yass, you had the flu and I have two children! I didn't want to take a chance on getting them sick. That's why I didn't come over!"

"I understand, and you are right, but I had no idea that the flu could be contracted though the phone. I guess you do learn something new every day."

"Yass, you know what I'm trying to say!"

"No, I don't.! Look Rosetta let's stop beating this dead horse! I have a meeting to get ready for."

"So, can I get a hug?"

"No, I might still be contagious."

Rosetta try to hug Yasmeen. *"I'm still your friend no matter what you may think."* Yasmeen push Rosetta away. *"The touch of death girl get-off of me... I must look like Aaron to you."*

"Yasmeen whatever! I know the next time that you have something I better be on the list!"

"I promise you will be on the list of people who are not invited."

After two months Aaron is still fucking Rebecca, Uma, and Rosetta. The more Aaron fucks Rosetta the more she resents Yasmeen. Every time Aaron is in bed with Rosetta, he reminds her of his love for Yasmeen by calling out her name. Rosetta knows that no matter what she does she will never measure up to Yasmeen in Aarons eyes. Rosetta wishes that she could just tell Yasmeen about her and Aaron, just to hurt her because she knows that Yasmeen is still in love with Aaron, but she won't admit it with her lying ass. Rosetta has made up her mind up that Aaron is going to be with her and she's willing to destroy anyone who gets in her way, especially Yasmeen Blake. She is the first one on Rosetta's list. That bitch has got to go!" Unlike Aaron and Rosetta. Yasmeen and Mahmoud's friendship has grown. The more time that Yasmeen spends with Mahmoud the more she longs to be with him. He is all that she thinks about. Yasmeen want to distance herself but she can't! Yasmeen knows that Mahmoud will never be hers but still she is drawn to him. Yasmeen can't explain why she feels that Mahmoud is supposed to be in her life. It's Saturday night Mahmoud and Yasmeen have just finished dinner at Mahmoud's house. They are sitting together in the Livingroom drinking wine.

"Thanks for dinner."

"You are more than welcome. I hope that you enjoyed it."

"Yes, I did Mahmoud. I must say you have some skills in the kitchen."

"Well I'm glad that you noticed."

"Oh, I noticed. You know that I pick up on everything."

"Yes, you do… Yasmeen would you say that you and I are friends?"

"Yes…yes I would consider you as a friend."

Mahmoud puts his glass down. *"Well as friend we can talk about anything right."*

"Yes, but that depends on what you ask."

"Yasmeen, I just don't want to say something that might cause you to get angry with me.

Yasmeen takes a sip from her glass. *"I'm not this anger bitter woman Mahmoud. I'm capable of having a conversation. Now what do you want to ask me?"*

Mahmoud rubs his hands together. *"Yasmeen what did I do to make you hate me?"*

"I never hated you. I may have disliked you, but I wouldn't say that I hated you."

"Ok why did you dislike me when we first met?"

"No, you had this attitude like I'm better than you."

"No, I did not!"

"Yes, you did! Mahmoud when I spoke to you, you looked at me like I know she's not talking to me and you didn't even say a word to me!"

Mahmoud laughs. *"Yeah that's because you didn't give me a chance Yasmeen. All I could hear you saying was…Well I must be the only one in the room or did he leave his voice at home!"*

Yasmeen can't stop laughing as she thinks back to that day. she can still see the look on Mahmoud and Maxwell's face. *"Well you could have said good morning. That's all I'm saying!"*

"Well I'm sorry if I came off that way. I didn't mean to and I'm sorry!"

"Well it's too late now!"

"What?"

"I'm just playing."

"I glad that you find it funny. Mahmoud sips on his wine as he watches Yasmeen. *Yasmeen is there something going on with you and doctor Ward?"*

Yasmeen looks at Mahmoud and bust out laughing as she puts her hand on her chest. She can't control herself. Mahmoud narrows his eyes as he tries to figure out why Yasmeen is laughing instead of answering his question. *"Why are you laughing?"*

Yasmeen tries to compose herself. *"Mahmoud, you do know that Ashton is gay!"*

"No, I didn't know that."

"Yeah and he's dating my best friend."

"Oh, I had no idea. Yasmeen please don't tell him that I asked…"

Yasmeen cuts Mahmoud off. *"Don't worry I'll keep it between us."*

"So, Ashton is dating Todd or Oscar?"

"Oscar. Since we're talking about dating. Where is your girlfriend what's her name?"

Her name is Zoe and she's not my girlfriend."

"Come on now I saw you and her. You didn't see me, but I saw you in the parking garage one day and I think that the two of you were kissing in her car."

"I think that I know what day you are referring to, but we were not kissing. What you saw was me hugging her. She told me that she was engaged. That's what you saw."

"So, you never kissed her?"

"When we dated yes, I kissed her, but not after our relationship ended."

Yasmeen must find out all the details about Mahmoud even if it takes all night. Yasmeen intends to drill him like he's on trial.

"So why did you two break up? Was it because you're engaged?"

Mahmoud pours another a glass of wine. *"No, me being engaged had nothing to do with it. We decided that we were better off as friends."*

"Why? "

"I guess that it wasn't meant to be."

"Yeah when did you come to that conclusion after you had slept with her?"

"No, we never had sex if that's what you're getting at."

"I can believe that, but may I ask why? I'm sorry you don't have to answer that!"

Mahmoud pours wine into Yasmeen's Glass. *"No, it's ok. I'll answer that. I guess that I was too much man for her."*

"Yeah if you say so."

"Well Yasmeen I have some question for you, and I want you to honest with me."

"Ok that's fair. What do you want to know?"

"I want to know do you plan on getting back together with Aaron?"

"Hell no!"

"Why not? Did he not satisfy you?"

Yasmeen clears her throat. *"What do you mean sexually?"*

"I mean satisfy all of your needs."

"Well he brought me gifts, but we never had sex not once."

"And why not Yasmeen?"

"I don't know there was just something about him that I didn't trust. Don't get me wrong now I wanted to, but something inside of me told me that he didn't deserve me, and it was right. Thank God for little voices."

"Will you ever forgive him?"

"Oh, I have forgiven him for cheating on me a long time ago. Anger takes over. *But I will never forgive him for what he did to me! I hate him!"*

"What did he do to you? Yasmeen why do you hate him?"

Yasmeen puts her glass down. *"Wow… you know what it's…it's getting late I need to be getting home."*

Mahmoud put his hand on Yasmeen knee. *"Yasmeen what did he do?"*

"I don't want to talk about this anymore."

Yasmeen turns her head away from Mahmoud as tears start to burn her eyes. Yasmeen try to suppress her tear by redirecting her thoughts, but Yasmeen can feel tears rolling down her face like rain and her heart hurts with anger. Mahmoud kneels in front of Yasmeen as he cups her face in him hands. He looks in her eyes with such conviction. Mahmoud can feel Yasmeen's pain. His Heart aches from seeing Yasmeen crying.

Mahmoud wiping Yasmeen tears and in a soft whisper he ask. *"Yasmeen please tell me what Aaron did to you."*

"He tried to rape me…He came to my home and he tried to rape me. He pulled out a gun on me and said that he was going to kill me!"

"He did what? Yasmeen what did you do about it?"

"Nothing…I did nothing!"

"Why not?"

"Because I was ashamed."

"Why? You didn't do anything wrong?"

"Please don't tell anybody…please."

"I promise. I also promise you that he will never hurt you again I give you my word Yasmeen."

Mahmoud is overwhelmed with anger. This is not what he expected to hear from Yasmeen. As he holds her in him arms, he wishes that he could kiss her pain away. Mahmoud can feel Yasmeen warm tears on his neck. Yasmeen looks up at Mahmoud as he kisses her on the forehead. Mahmoud wipes Yasmeen tears as he kisses her soft lips. Yasmeen pulls herself away. Mahmoud pulls her back to him and he kisses her with such passion that Yasmeen melts in his arms. Yasmeen wants to push Mahmoud away, but she can't. She can feel his tongue in her mouth as she grabs the back of his head to receive his kiss. Mahmoud gently bites Yasmeen 's bottom lip softly as he pushes her back on the sofa. Mahmoud welcomes Yasmeen warm wet kisses on his neck as he grips her ass. Yasmeen not wanting to push Mahmoud away, but she does.

"I better go."

"Yeah ok but not before you kiss me again."

Yasmeen kisses Mahmoud so deep and passionate that she can feel his dick starting to harden. Yasmeen wants Mahmoud, her mind is telling her no, but her body is screaming yes. For the past week Yasmeen has been avoiding Mahmoud and she don't know why! She hopes he will forget about everything that she told him and most of all she hopes that he will forget about the kiss that they shared because she damn sure can't! No matter what she does Yasmeen can still feel Mahmoud's soft lips and his strong hands touching her body. Yasmeen is sitting in her office, she can't concentrate on anything, her thoughts are flooded with Mahmoud. This is not like Yasmeen to be consumed by her own thoughts. What is this obsession she has for a man that she can't have? Yasmeen shakes her head as she tells herself that she needs to get out of her office and get some fresh air so that she can focus on her work. Yasmeen gets up from her desk and walks out into the hallway Mahmoud and Jacob are standing five feet away from her door. Yasmeen first impulse is to run back into her office, but it is to late Mahmoud sees her. Mahmoud quickly walk towards her. He ushers her back into her office.

"Why have you been avoiding me?"

"I've been busy."

"Too busy to take my calls?"

"Mahmoud, I think that this is a mistake."

"So, kissing me was a mistake?"

"Yes...No Mahmoud I...I'm afraid."

"Afraid of what? Are you afraid of me Yasmeen?"

As Yasmeen stands before Mahmoud, she cannot lie so her heart speaks the truth. *"I am afraid of what you may think of me. I'm ashamed of myself."*

Mahmoud pulls Yasmeen to him. *"I think that you are an amazing woman. Yasmeen, you have nothing to be ashamed of.* Putting his arms around Yasmeen Waist. *I missed you."*

"I missed you too."

Yasmeen wraps her arms around Mahmoud's neck as he kisses her. Yasmeen, kisses Mahmoud she feels like she has kissed him before that night at his house. Yasmeen thinks that maybe in a past life. Yasmeen holds Mahmoud tight. Yasmeen just can't shake the familiar feeling that she gets when she's with Mahmoud. Yasmeen heart tells her that with Mahmoud is where she belongs, but her mind tells her that he will never be hers. Yasmeen wants to push Mahmoud away, but she can't. Yasmeen gives in to her passion as Mahmoud hands move from her waist to her round ass, he grips both of her ass cheeks before they both releases their embrace. They just stand there looking in each other's eyes. Neither of them wants to leave. Yasmeen puts her hand on the side of Mahmoud's face she smiles as she walks him to the door. Another two weeks has past Aaron is walking through the lobby when Rosetta runs over to him smiling.

"Good morning Aaron, I just wanted to tell you that I had a wonderful time last night."

"At least one of us did!"

"What do you mean? I thought that I..."

Aaron cuts Rosetta off. *"Look I told you that if you want me to continue fucking with you need to learn how to suck my dick the right way! I don't need to feel your fucking teeth and when I tell you to lick my ass you need to lick my ass immediately and not sit on your ass like you forgot how to do it!"*

"Aaron I'm sorry. I will do better."

"I will not tell you again. Now get out of my way before somebody see's us! Oh, and stop sucking on my neck I'm not you man. Nobody needs to know that I'm fucking you!"

Uma walks up just as Rosetta walks away. Her heart breaks when she hears Uma telling Aaron how much she missed him last night. Rage takes over Rosetta when she hears Aaron telling Uma that he missed her too and that he can't wait to see her tonight. Rosetta runs to the restroom with tears in her eyes. Why is Aaron doing this to her? Why is he rejecting her and why does he treat her like shit? Rosetta must make Aaron see that they belong together no matter what it takes because she knows that she can be the woman that Aaron wants her to be. Mahmoud, Maxwell, Brandon, and Ashton are all on the elevator when Yasmeen and Jacob get on at the next floor. Yasmeen and Mahmoud are standing face to face. Yasmeen does everything in her power to keep from looking at Mahmoud. Not wanting to lock eyes with Mahmoud Yasmeen looks down at the floor, but she can feel him staring at her. Yasmeen smiles to herself as she raises her knee up just enough to show her shapely thigh through the split of her shirt. Yasmeen inhale and puts both of her hand on her hips as she thrust her breast forward. She can see Mahmoud from the corner of her eye as he runs his hand over his mouth, but little does Yasmeen know that Mahmoud is not the only one watching her. Brandon is standing behind Maxwell trying to control himself. Trying to control his erection that is growing in his pants as he longs to suck on Yasmeen perky breast. When the elevator doors open to the lobby Yasmeen is the first one off with a big grin across her face. Mahmoud shakes his head. Three days later Yasmeen and Mahmoud have just returned from having dinner. They are at Yasmeen's house enjoying each other's company. Yasmeen looks at

Mahmoud she's hesitant about asking him the question that has been on her mind for weeks. The last thing that she wants is to come off as be nosey, but she must get some answers.

"So, can I ask you something? You know what forget it I…"

"No Yasmeen go head and ask your question."

"No, it's none of my business."

"I'll be the judge of that. Now what is it that you want to know?"

Yasmeen turns to face Mahmoud. *"What about your fiancé?"*

"What about her?"

Yasmeen takes a deep breath. *"I mean you… You and her… The two of you will be getting married soon right."*

"Well I don't know what you mean by soon, but we should be getting married in a little over a year from now."

Yasmeen gets a sinking feeling in her stomach this is not what she wanted to hear. She can feel the hairs on her arms tingling as she looks at Mahmoud.

"Mahmoud why are you here?"

"Because I want to be. Yasmeen do you want me to leave?"

"No…no I don't want you to leave but if you want to."

"Yasmeen I'm where I want to be, and you can ask me anything I promise to be honest."

"Ok tell what's your fiancé like?"

"I don't know, your guess is as good as mine."

Yasmeen looks at Mahmoud with a skeptical look on her face. She thinks he's dicking with her or is he just avoiding her question by being an asshole.

"Mahmoud she's your fiancé how can you not know what she's like…forget it! You don't have to tell me!"

"Yasmeen, I would tell you, but I don't know. We have never met or at least I don't remember."

"Are you kidding me right now? "

"No Yasmeen I'm not."

"So, you want me to believe that you are about to marry a woman that you have never met!"

"You can believe what you want, but I'm telling you the truth."

"So why are you marring her if you never met her?"

"Because she was promised to me by her parents when we were young. My parent decided that it was ok for her to be my wife."

"So, you agree with it?"

"No not really. I guess that why I've been putting it off. We were supposed to get married three years ago, but I told my parent no because I wasn't ready. Now they are really pushing us to get married."

"How does that make you feel?"

"I don't feel anything."

"Mahmoud do you love her?"

"In time I guess that I will."

"I'm happy for you, but I couldn't see myself marring someone that I didn't love. Not to mention someone who I didn't know."

"Well some people in my culture they still believe in arranged marriages and my parents are two of those people"

"So, you're ok with your parent choosing the person that you're to spend your life with?"

"I didn't say that I was ok with it."

"You didn't say that you weren't"

Mahmoud pulls Yasmeen back down on the sofa. *"You're right. I don't know how I feel about it. I just try not to think about it."*

"You're good because I would be out of my mind. Anyway, I'm happy for you. Oh, am I invited to the wedding?"

"I don't know we'll see about that."

"What?"

"I'm just kidding of course you're invited."

"Thank you."

Mahmoud holds Yasmeen's hand. *"Now it's time for you to answer some questions for me."*

Yasmeen looks uncertain. *"Ok what do you want to know. I think that I'm going to need a drink."*

Mahmoud holds Yasmeen hand tight. *"No, you don't need a drink to answer my questions."*

"Ok. What is it that you want to know?"

"Why is that you're not married?"

Yasmeen body trembles all over just to hear Mahmoud asking the question of why she's not married. Yasmeen tells herself that she can answer any question with ease without hesitation because she's quick on her feet. Yasmeen has an answer for everything, but she's speechless. Yasmeen feels like all the air had been sucked out of her and she can't breathe. Yasmeen sits in silence for what seems like hours without so much as blinking her eyes. She doesn't even feel Mahmoud as he puts his hand on her back. She can no longer hear his voice. All Yasmeen can see is Gregory's face before her and his beautiful bright smile. She can smell his cologne. As Yasmeen sits motionless, she can hear Gregory voice. The love that Yasmeen has for him is still the same as it was more than three years ago. Yasmeen's heart pounds in her chest. It's not until Mahmoud touches Yasmeen knee that brings her back.

"So, are you going to answer my question?"

"What… What question… I'm sorry what was your question?"

"Why are you not married?"

Yasmeen know damn well what the question was. She was hoping that he wouldn't ask it again. Why is Mahmoud so fucking intrusive, can't he see that she's hurting. Yasmeen pulls a gold chain from her shirt that she keeps around her neck. The chain holds her engagement ring along with Gregory's wedding band that she had made for his. Yasmeen holds them tightly in her hand before kissing them. Before Yasmeen can gather her thoughts, she starts to speak.

"I was engaged to my best friend the love of my life. The only man who understood me and loved me unconditionally. We set a date…We were so happy. I truly loved him. I know that God made him just for me. I remember it was two months before we were to be married and a drunk driver took him away from me. Tears start to form. *It was a drunk driver who destroyed my life in an instant. Gregory was my rock and I couldn't wait to be his wife. All I wanted was to live the rest of my life with him, making him as happy as he had made me. I loved him from my soul. It has been over three years and I still miss him like it was yesterday. You know I still talk to him. I know That he's looking down at me smiling.* Tears roll from Yasmeen eyes. *Oh God I love that man. I love him so much. God why did you have to take him away from me so soon. Why… please tell me why. God, I don't understand.*

Mahmoud looks at Yasmeen with so much compassion. He wishes that he could take away all the hurt that Yasmeen has inside. Mahmoud moves closer to Yasmeen as he tries to comfort her.

"*Yasmeen, I sorry! I didn't know. Had I known I would have never asked. Please forgive me.*"

Yasmeen pushes Mahmoud away. "*No, I'm sorry. It's like every time we're together I turn into this bag of emotion and I don't know why. I think that you should leave!*"

"*No Yasmeen I won't leave! I'm not going anywhere. I'm here for you. Yasmeen don't push me away. I promise that you will never be lonely again if you would just trust me.*"

"*Mahmoud, I can't! Would you just leave!*"

Mahmoud pull's Yasmeen to him. "*No! I'm going to stay here with you tonight. I'm not going anywhere!*"

"*No!*"

"*Yes...Yes I am!*"

Mahmoud puts his arms around Yasmeen and holds her tight. Yasmeen closes her eyes as she holds on to Mahmoud not wanting him to let her go. Yasmeen can feel a sense of peace that washes over her. Yasmeen heart tells her that everything is going to be ok and that she will never have to cry any more. Mahmoud stayed with Yasmeen all night assuring her that she's safe. He showered her in his kisses until the morning. Mahmoud is sitting in his office when Aaron knocks on the door. Mahmoud looks at Aaron without greeting him as he thinks about what Yasmeen told him.

"*Hey Doc, do you have a minute? I really need to talk.*"

"*Sure, have a seat...*"

"*Doc I wanted to run something by you.*"

"*Ok what is it?*"

"*Doc it's about Yasmeen.*"

Mahmoud try to contain himself. "*Yasmeen! What about Yasmeen?*"

"*Well Doc I told you the last time that I think she's seeing someone.*"

"*Ok and why is that a cause for you to be concerned? Aren't you seeing other people as well?*"

"*Yes but, she won't answer my calls or texts.Doc I keep trying to talk to her and she just pushes me away. When I go to her office, she won't answer the door, and I know that she's in there because most of the time I see her go in. Then when I see her in the hall and try to have a conversation with her, she threatens, to kick me in the nuts again.*"

"*Again!*"

Sabrina Jones

"*Yes! Do you remember that day when you found me on the floor in the conference room? Well Yasmeen kneed me in the nuts and she just walked out!*"

"*Wow. I had no Idea... Aaron I'm curious in knowing why you won't leave her alone?*"

"*Because I love her Doc!*"

"*What about Rebecca?*"

"*I don't want her or Uma. Doc I want Yasmeen back, that's why I'm going over to her house today! She won't talk to me so I'm going to her. I'm going to get her to talk to me and I will find out who this asshole is!*"

Mahmoud wants to jump across his desk and choke the hell out of Aaron. Mahmoud slams his fist down on the desk.

"*Don't you dare go over to her house!*"

"*Why not!*"

"*Because if she wanted you to come to her home, she would have invited you. Aaron I'm warning you don't take your ass over to Yasmeen's.*"

"*But Doc!*"

"*But Doc my ass! You need to get your shit together! I'm telling you if Yasmeen comes in here on tomorrow and tells me that you came to her home you're out of a job. Do I make myself clear!*"

Aaron is puzzled by Mahmoud reaction. This is not at all what he had expected. Why is he on Yasmeen side and not his. Aaron shakes his head before he speaks. He just wants Mahmoud to say that he should go to Yasmeen house and try to win her back.

"*I hear what you're saying, but I just want Yasmeen to talk to me and explain why she won't at least try to work things out. Doc I can change I really can.*"

Mahmoud is about to boil over with anger as he tries to get Aaron to understand that Yasmeen belongs to someone else. "*Aaron do you really think that Yasmeen wants to work on a relationship with you after you cheated on her? Not only did you cheat on her, but you're still sleeping with the woman that you cheated on her with... Aaron what are you trying to do. I mean I saw you out with Uma last night, and I saw you come in with Rebecca this morning. I've also observed you and Rosetta together on more than one occasion... Are, you sleeping with her too?* Aaron looks away. *So, what you just want to keep hurting her? Is that it Aaron? How many times are you going to throw your affairs in her face? If you care for her as much as you say that you*"

*do you would not be putting her through this trash! Yasmeen is a good woman
and she deserves a good man who will respect and love her.*"

Aaron walks out of Mahmoud's office without saying another word.
When Aaron leaves Mahmoud picks up the phone and calls Yasmeen. He's
still upset when Yasmeen answers.

"*Yasmeen, I need you to come to my office now!*"

"*Come to your office! Mahmoud I'm in the middle of something I can't
come now!*"

"*Well I'm on my way to your office so don't leave until I get there! I need
to talk to you!*"

"*Talk to me about what?*"

"*I will tell you when I get there!*"

"*Do I need to get security*" "*What... No, you need to just wait for me!*"

Yasmeen puts the phone down on its base. She wonders why would,
Mahmoud need to talk to her and why was there such urgency in his voice.
What's going on? Did his fiancé come to town? Yasmeen heart drops as
she question's herself. The door to Yasmeen open and in rushes Mahmoud.
Yasmeen walks over to greet Mahmoud as her heart starts to beat out of
control. Before Yasmeen can speak Mahmoud pulls her in and kisses her.

"*Hello to you to. Mahmoud is this about our little dispute that we had
this morning?*"

"*No Yasmeen I'm use to you by now.*"

"*Then what? Did I do something wrong? I mean I don't care I just what
to know.*"

"*You did nothing wrong. Yasmeen have you thought about moving?*"

"*Moving! Why would I be thinking about moving. I mean I was going to
buy a house but that was when Gregory and I you know... Mahmoud what's
going on with you?*"

"*Yasmeen Aaron came to see me. He's planning on coming to your house.*"

"*Come to my house! Why would Aaron come to my house? Mahmoud, he
had better not come to my house. I swear to you that I will kill him!*"

Mahmoud can see that Yasmeen is upset. Mahmoud holds Yasmeen
in his arms he can feel her body shaking with anger.

"*He says that he wants you back. He said that he has he been calling you?*"

"*Yes, but I haven't been taking his calls, Mahmoud you know that!*"

"*I know.*"

"I don't want him. I just want him to leave me alone. That's all I want.. I'm so sick of this! I can't do this anymore, I'm tired! My soul is tired! I'm tired of running!"

Mahmoud grabs Yasmeen hands. *"Yasmeen you don't have to run anymore, I will handle this! You don't have to worry now stop crying! Didn't I tell you that I would always be here for you! Stop crying Yasmeen and look at me. When you get off, I want you to go to my house."*

"I can't do that!"

"You can, and you will! Yasmeen, I will see you at my house."

Mahmoud kisses Yasmeen and leaves. For the past week Yasmeen has been staying at Mahmoud's or Oscar and Todd house., but mostly at Mahmoud's in his guest room. Aaron kept his word, he had been going over to Yasmeen house everyday sometime twice a day. Aaron has been unable to reach Yasmeen which only infuriates him. Aaron tell himself that this time he's going to get what he wants from Yasmeen no matter what. This time he won't stop. Aaron and Rosetta are lying in his bed. They have just finished fucking. Aaron can't stop thinking about Yasmeen, he picks up his cell phone and calls her. Rosetta over hears Yasmeen voice mail which causes her much Anger, when she hears Aaron message *"Yasmeen where are you sweetheart? Please call me."*

"Why do you insist on calling her?"

"Because I can. Why do you care?"

"Aaron, I just don't like seeing you so mad. I'm sorry."

"You're right. You know what I think that doctor Shashivivek is gay."

"Who Mahmoud? Aaron what would make you say that? You do know that he's engaged!"

"Yeah but to who? Doctor Khalidah! Really have you ever seen this fiancé? He doesn't even talk about her. Rosetta, you know that I went to his office about a week ago. I was telling him that I want to get back with Yasmeen…

"Get back with Yasmeen!"

"Yes, get back with Yasmeen! Now shut the fuck up and listen! I was talking to him about Yasmeen and he got so mad. That mother fucker threatened to fire me. I think that he has a thing for me. He wants some of this good dick too."

"Yeah he wants you or Yasmeen!"

Aaron push's Rosetta off him. *"Yasmeen!"*

Rosetta smiles to herself. "*Yeah maybe he likes Yasmeen! That would be something.*"

"*No, the fuck it wouldn't! I bet you would like that. Get the fuck out of my bed! Aaron pulls Rosetta up by her arm. Let me find out that you are trying to set Mahmoud up with Yasmeen bitch and I will tear your world apart! Get your shit and go!*"

"*Aaron, I'm sorry! I shouldn't have said that. I was just mad. I know that Mahmoud is not interested in Yasmeen. They can't stand the sight of each other. I'm sorry baby don't be mad at me.*

Rosetta gets down on her knees and starts giving Aaron head. Aaron puts his hand on top of Rosetta's head, but he can't stop thinking about Yasmeen and who she's with. Aaron wonders is she fucking him? Is she sucking his dick? Aaron can't imagine Yasmeen being with anyone but him. Aaron can feel Yasmeen tight pussy and how wet she gets. Aaron releases in Rosetta mouth. Mahmoud, Jacob, Maxwell, Ashton, and Aaron have been out of town for a week at a medical convention. Yasmeen is missing Mahmoud like crazy. She tells herself that she needs to get over him and that it's wrong for her to feel the way that she does about a soon to be married man. Yasmeen can't help it. She knows that it's wrong, but it feels so right. Yasmeen has told Oscar and Todd about all the times that she and Mahmoud have been spending together but she has yet to tell Zada. Oscar and Todd are at Yasmeen house waiting on Zada and Tia.

"*So, has your sweetheart called you yet?*"

"*My sweetheart! I don't know what you're talking about 'O'!*"

"*Cut the shit Yass, you know that you want that man!*"

"*Hell, Yes, she does Todd! I bet you be thinking about climbing his tall ass like a monkey climbing a tree. Todd, she didn't want to fuck Aaron, but I know that she wants that dick... Yasmeen does he have a big one?*"

Yasmeen can't stop laughing but she knows that Mahmoud is blessed. Not that she has personally seen Mahmoud's dick she has felt his bulge many times.

"*You two are just nasty! I've told you that we are just friends.*"

"*Yeah friend fuck right O!*"

" *All the time. I think that you would call it fuck friends or Yass and Mahmoud. Yass do you let him hit you from the back or do you ride him like a cowgirl?*"

"No, we're not fucking and you two are sick. He's engaged."

"Yeah to your pussy!"

"Todd that's not True. Why are we even talking about this and how did we get on this subject?"

"Yass stop lying to yourself! We both know that you're wet just thinking about all that man and as much time that y'all spend together I know that y'all ain't talking. Now tell us everything!"

"There is nothing to tell. We just kissed a few times that's it! Y'all need to be ashamed of yourselves."

"Yass you're right. We shouldn't be teasing you. Now give me a hug. Now tell the truth you want to fuck Mahmoud don't You."

Yasmeen laughs as she pushes Todd away. The doorbell rings. On the way to the door Yasmeen can't stop thinking about Mahmoud. Yes, Todd and Oscar are right Yasmeen does have feelings for Mahmoud but she's not ready to admit it to anyone but herself. Yasmeen must be sure that Mahmoud feels the same because a kiss is just a kiss.

Chapter 10

The body Wants what the heart desire...

When Mahmoud gets back in town he goes on call for a week, and oh what a busy week it has been. Mahmoud has spent most of his time in the operating room. Both day and night. Yasmeen has only seen Mahmoud twice and that has been in passing. He calls when he can just to say hi, Yasmeen is starting to feel rejected. She knew that there would be days like this. Yasmeen understand that Mahmoud has a job to do and she would never ask him to choose, but after two weeks Yasmeen has had time to think and she has come, to the conclusion that she and Mahmoud would be better off as friends. She tells herself that in time her feelings will subside and she will be ok. It not going to be easy getting over Mahmoud yes, they a ball but all good things must come to an end. Two days later Yasmeen hasn't heard from Mahmoud. She has been calling him and he hasn't returned any of her calls. Yasmeen is sitting alone at her dining room table drink wine. She starts to think that this is how Aaron must feel. Yasmeen laughs as she shakes her head. Yasmeen push's herself away from the table. *"This is some BS. Why in the hell am I setting her comparing myself to Aaron. Fuck this I am in no way like that shit bag. You know what Yass you need something a little stronger chick.* Yasmeen picks up a bottle of Patron from her mini bar. *I don't know what I'm doing, and I don't give a fuck.* Yasmeen is in her feelings. *Who said that you need a man to put you to sleep.* She pours herself a drink. *Hell, two shoots of you I know will knock me on my ass. Here's to me with my sad lonely ass!"* Yasmeen takes a shoot and it burns like hell. *"Damn this shit's too strong for my weak ass. I'm going to need a chaser with this!"* It's ten o'clock on a Friday night and Yasmeen has had three shoots of Patron. Yasmeen is setting on the floor in her living room with a pair of boy shorts with no underwear on and a tank top with the lights down low listening to old slow jams. Yasmeen head is spinning so fast. Her cell phone has been ringing, for the past forty minutes but Yasmeen can't move. Yasmeen lays her head back on the sofa and closes her eyes. *"Yasmeen what in the hell have you done?"* Yasmeen pulls herself up onto the sofa hopping that her head will stop spinning. She tries to go to sleep. As soon as Yasmeen dozes off someone starts banging on the door none stop. Yasmeen puts her hand over her ears, but the banging gets louder. *"Who in the hell could that be at this hour? Maybe if I sit quietly, they will go away!* But the banging continues. *Go away and stop banding on my door!"*

"*Yasmeen opens the door!"*

"No now go away!"

"Yasmeen open this fucking door now!"

"Shit that sounds like Mahmoud. Yasmeen stumbles to the door. Who is it?"

"It's me Mahmoud! Yasmeen let me in!"

"Mahmoud it's late and I don't feel like talking. Can't you come back another time?"

"No, I can't now open the door!"

"Oh, shit I can't let him see me like this. Yasmeen smooths her tank top and retie her hair and trying to act normal. *Just a minute."*

"Yasmeen don't you play with me!"

Yasmeen take a deep breath before opening the door. *"Oh, Mahmoud what are you doing here? Shouldn't you be at work?"*

Mahmoud push past Yasmeen. *"What have you been doing? I have been calling you for almost an hour!"*

Yasmeen try to hold herself up. *"Oh, I was just in here relaxing. You know I was about to call it a night."*

Mahmoud looks around. *"So, you have been drinking?"*

"I may have had a glass or two."

"Yasmeen why are you drinking?"

Yasmeen try to make her way to the sofa. *"Let me see. Why I'm I drinking?* Mocking Mahmoud. *I'm drinking because I'm grown and because I want to. Now why are you here?"*

"I'm here because I was worried about you when you didn't answer my call."

"Well as you can see, I'm fine."

Yasmeen gets up and trips over her coffee table, hitting her toe. She cries out in pain. Yasmeen falls to the floor. Mahmoud rushes over to Yasmeen side and helps her onto the chair.

"Yasmeen what's wrong?"

Yasmeen holds her foot. *"I hit my toe!"*

Mahmoud rubs Yasmeen foot. *"No, I mean why are you sitting here drinking? Is there something that you want to tell me?"*

"Yes, I think that we should not see each other anymore not like this."

"You don't mean that."

"Oh, but I do!"

"Where is this coming from?"

"From me."

"Why?'

"Mahmoud, I have been thinking."

"Is that why you're drinking? Yasmeen this is not you. Let me help you to bed and we will talk in the morning ok." Mahmoud tries to kiss Yasmeen, but she pulls away. *"So, you don't want to kiss me?"* Mahmoud picks Yasmeen up and carries her into the bedroom where he kisses her passionately. Mahmoud kisses Yasmeen breast through her tank top before he pulls her shirt over her head revealing her beautiful brown mounds sitting straight up on her on her chest. Mahmoud rubs his face across Yasmeen breast and runs his long tongue down her six-pack abs.

"I want you but not like this Yasmeen. I want you to give yourself to me when you are ready. Are you ready?"

"No...No not yet. I'm sorry."

"Yasmeen it's ok. I can wait."

"Are you mad?"

"No, but I do have to get back to the hospital I have patients waiting on me."

"Ok."

Yasmeen is about to put her shirt back on Mahmoud stops her. *"Don't put that on.* Mahmoud sucks on Yasmeen nipples and it feel so good that Yasmeen can't help but call Mahmoud's name. Maybe it's the Patron but

Yasmeen wants Mahmoud. She's just moments away from giving herself to him when his pager goes off. The next morning Yasmeen wakes up to Oscar and Todd standing over her calling her name. Yasmeen rolls over and pull the covers up over her head. Oscar shakes Yasmeen. *"Yass get your ass up! Got me calling you like I'm crazy!"* Todd pulls the covers off Yasmeen. *"Yeah... why in the hell didn't you answer your phone!"* Yasmeen holding her head. *"Go away!"* Oscar pulls Yasmeen leg. *"Go away my ass! Yass get your ass up now! I was worried about you!"* Yasmeen turning back over. *"I'm fine 'O' now leave me alone!"*

"Oh, ok I'll leave you alone! Come on Todd let's leave her alone! I don't have time for her shit! Oscar walks out of the bedroom. *Got me out of my bed over here worrying about your ass!* Yasmeen sits up in her bed still holding her head which is pounding. Oscar walks back into the room holing the bottle of patron. *"And who in the fuck did you have over here! Look Todd she's been in here drink Patron and talking about leave her alone. Oscar* Pulls Yasmeen out of bed. *Yasmeen get up now! Girl I should...you know what get out of my face!"*

"I'm sorry you know that I didn't mean it 'O', but my fucking head is killing me!"

"Good I hope that it explodes! Yasmeen, I thought that something had happened to you!"

"Who did you have over here Mahmoud?"

Yasmeen close her eyes. *"No, nobody was here Todd."*

Yasmeen starts to cry not because she's sad but because she's sick as hell and her head feels like somebody beating a base drum.

"Nobody was here. I just had two or three shoots alone, that's it. Now I got you and Oscar over here mad and yelling at me. I said that I was sorry! Please stop yelling!

"Whatever I'm gone."

"So, you're just going to leave me? Just like that!"

Yasmeen head is really pounding. Oscar returns to the room he hands Yasmeen two Tylenol and a glass of water.

"Here take this!"

Yasmeen looks up at Oscar. *"Are you still mad with me?"*

"Yes, I am! And why in the hell were you drinking alone? Yass that's not like you! What's wrong?"

"*I guess that I was just in my feelings. I started think about my life. Oscar, you know that my four-year anniversary just passed!*"

"*I know Yass. So, what are you going to do just sit here and get drunk?*"

"*Yes!*"

"*No, you're not!*"

"*You don't understand Todd! I'm supposed to be married to the love of my life and I'm sitting here alone! Oscar, I miss Gregg so much! I miss him!*"

"*We know that you do, but do you think that Gregg wants you down her drinking? No Yass he wouldn't! You can't drink your pain away.*"

"*I don't know want else to do. 'O' tell me what to do!*"

"*Yass, you have to celebrate his life. Remember all the good times that you both shared and then you got to live your life.* With tears in his eyes. *Yasmeen I'm not telling you to forget about Gregg I'm just telling you that it's time for you to move on and stop doing this to yourself. Gregory is not happy knowing that you are here on earth miserable. He knows that you love him, and he would want you to be happy with someone who could take care of you in a way that he can't!*"

"*Oscar I'm scared, and I feel as if I'm cheating on him.*"

Todd turn to Yasmeen with understanding in his eyes. "*Oh, sweetheart you're not cheating on Gregg and you have nothing to be afraid of. Yass, you know that Oscar and I will always be here for you. Yass your happiness is important to us. We only want the best for you.*"

"*I know but I can't!*"

"*You have to try.*"

"*Todd, I can't.*"

"*Would you just try for Oscar and myself.*"

"*Ok...ok but I'm going to take my time.*"

Oscar kisses Yasmeen on the head. "*Ok now get your ass up. I'm glad that you're hung over!*"

Yasmeen falls back on the bed. A week has passed its Thursday Yasmeen is walking to her car not paying attention, so she doesn't see Aaron when running up behind her. Yasmeen opens her car door Aaron pushes her inside and he falls on top of her. Yasmeen hits her face on the steering wheel. At first Yasmeen is not sure of what has just happened until she looks up and see Aaron on top of her. Yasmeen mind flash back to the day that Aaron tried to rape her. Yasmeen starts to scream. "*Get off me Aaron!*

Stop it! Get off…" Aaron holding Yasmeen hands. *"Not until you talk to me! Now stop fighting, I'm not going to hurt you. I just want to talk!"* Yasmeen stop fighting. Yasmeen hopes that Aaron would let her go. *"Ok…ok…ok Aaron what…what do you want to talk about?"*

"About us. And why won't you give us a chance?"

"Aaron, you have somebody. Please let me go. Aaron you're hurting me!"

"Yasmeen, I love you! I miss what we had!"

"Aaron what we had is over you messed it up. Aaron you're really hurting me!"

"I sorry, Yasmeen kiss me! Aaron tries to kiss Yasmeen. *Stop moving and kiss me!"*

"No Aaron I don't want to kiss you, now stop!"

"Why is it because you're seeing someone else?"

"I'm not seeing anyone! Get off me. Somebody, help me!"

"Kiss me Yasmeen!"

"Ok…ok I'll kiss you but you're hurting my arm baby. Let my arm go sweetie."

Aaron smiles as he releases Yasmeen arm. Yasmeen is about to kiss Aaron she closes her eyes and knees Aaron in the nuts. Yasmeen pushes Aaron off of her and he falls to the ground. Yasmeen takes off running through the parking garage back to the hospital lobby. As Yasmeen runs down the hall, she sees Jacob, Maxwell, and Zada coming towards her. She runs to Zada crying, blood from Yasmeen lip is dripping onto her shirt. Zada screams when she sees Yasmeen bleeding." *"Yasmeen what happened to you!"*

"Help me! Please help me!"

Jacob and Maxwell gather around Yasmeen trying to get her to calm down so that she can tell them what happened.

Jacob holds on to Yasmeen. *'Yasmeen what happened! Yasmeen talk to me!"*

"Aaron…Aaron did this to me!"

"Aaron what did that son-of-a-bitch do! Where the fuck is, he!"

"He's down there! Yasmeen points to the garage. *He's down there!"*

Zada drops her bags. *"I'm going to kill him!"*

Maxwell pulls Zada back. *"No, you stay here with Yasmeen!"*

Both Jacob and Maxwell takes off run down the hall to the garage where they find Aaron on the ground outside of Yasmeen car with his hands between his legs. Maxwell knows how much Mahmoud cares about Yasmeen, so he calls Mahmoud to inform him of what had just happened. By the time Mahmoud gets to the garage Zada has already taken Yasmeen to the ER. Jacob and Maxwell escorts Aaron to Jacobs office to wait for Mahmoud. When Mahmoud gets to the ER examine room Yasmeen is still upset. She holds a bag of ice to her face as Zada holds her hand.

"Hey Zada, is she ok?"

"She going to be fine, her lip has stop bleeding."

"Zada can you leave us alone? I need to talk to Yasmeen if it's ok."

"Oh yeah sure. Yasmeen I'll be right outside if you need me."

Zada walks out and Yasmeen puts her hand over her face. She doesn't want Mahmoud to see her face. Mahmoud walks over to Yasmeen and lefts her chin so that he can examine her face. Mahmoud fights to control his anger.

"Did he hit you?"

"No. I hit my face on the steering wheel when he pushed me in my car!"

"Yasmeen what happened?"

"I don't know. I was just walking to my car next thing I know Aaron was on top of me trying to kiss me. Tears rolls down Yasmeen face. *It's my fault! I wasn't paying attention. I should have…"*

Mahmoud puts his hand on Yasmeen shoulders. *"Stop it! It's not your fault! Aaron was wrong for what he did! Do you hear me? Look at me Yasmeen!"*

"I just feel so stupid! I should have been paying attention! Mahmoud I'm just so mad!" Yasmeen rest her head on Mahmoud's chest.

"I know you're upset, so am I. Yasmeen it's going to be ok. I'm going to go back to my office. Mahmoud kiss Yasmeen on her forehead. *I'll see you later."*

Mahmoud walks out into the hall where Zada Oscar and Todd are waiting. Mahmoud rushes back to his office. He's fuming. Mahmoud can't wait to see Aaron. All Mahmoud can see is Yasmeen crying. Mahmoud is sitting at his desk when Jacob, Maxwell, and Aaron walks in, before they can sit down, Mahmoud confronts Aaron.

"Doctor Sinclair what were you thinking? You know what? You wasn't thinking because if you were you would not have assaulted Yasmeen!"

"I didn't mean for any of this to happen I just wanted to talk to her."

"So, you were going to force her to talk to you? I told you to stay the hell away from Yasmeen! Now she in the ER for something that you did!"

"I just wanted to talk! I love Yasmeen!"

Mahmoud gets in Aaron face. *"Know what you are is reckless! You are a loose cannon! You are suspended until further notice doctor Sinclair!"*

"What! "

"You heard me now get out of my office and stay the hell away from Yasmeen! I'm done with you, now not get out! The both of you walk him out of here!"

Aaron cannot believe that Mahmoud suspended him but he's glad that he didn't fire him for being stupid. Mahmoud can't stop thinking about Yasmeen. He rushes over to her house not caring who's there. He just wants to see her. When Yasmeen opens the door Mahmoud grabs Yasmeen and kisses her repeatedly.

"Are you ok?"

"Yes, I'm ok."

"Get your things you're coming with me."

"What? I can't go with you!"

"Why not?"

"Because I'm going over to Todd and Oscar."

"No, you're going with me, so call them and let them know that you're going with me Yasmeen. I'm not leaving without you!"

For two weeks Yasmeen and Mahmoud have been staying at each other's house. Aaron has not contacted Yasmeen and he's still on suspension. Uma and Rebecca have been avoiding Yasmeen. Rosetta wants to ask Yasmeen what happened but she's afraid to hear the answer. Rosetta knows that Aaron is in love with Yasmeen but why? She's determined to make Aaron fall in love with her and forget all about Yasmeen Blake. Yasmeen has just finished cooking when Mahmoud comes over with flowers. They embrace each other as they set down to dinner. Mahmoud holds Yasmeen hand. *"Yasmeen, we need to talk."*

"We do!"

"Yes, we do."

Yasmeen puts her fork down. *"Ok what do we need to talk about?'*

"About us."

Yasmeen can hear her voice in side of her head. *"I know this man is not about to tell me that he doesn't want to see me anymore!* Yasmeen looks up at Mahmoud. *Ok what about us?"*

"Well Yasmeen we have been seeing a lot of each other and I do care for you a lot, but...

Yasmeen cuts Mahmoud off. *"But you want to see other people."*

"No...no that's not what I was going to say. Do you want to see other people, because I don't?"

"No, me either. Go ahead finish what you were saying."

"Yasmeen what I wanted to know is would you like to date me?"

Yasmeen is in shock. *"No Mahmoud! Mahmoud, I like you, but we can't be a couple. You're engaged to be married. I just don't want to get hurt Again, I'm sorry!"*

Yasmeen runs to her room and Mahmoud runs behind her. When he catches up to her, he pulls her back. Yasmeen remembers what she promised Oscar and Todd, but she cannot take a chance on getting her heart broken. Just thinking about being in a relationship terrifies Yasmeen.

"Yasmeen, I know what my situation is. Yasmeen, I would never hurt you, I promise. Mahmoud pulls Yasmeen down on her bed. *I understand, I just thought that I would ask. I do care for you and I have for a long time."*

Yasmeen tear up. *"I care about you to, but I'm afraid of getting my heart broken again."*

"Yasmeen, I would never hurt your heart. I just want you to give me a chance to make you happy. I want to be with you."

"What about your fiancé?"

"You don't need to worry about that. Now will you give us a chance?'

"Yes!"

"Yes!"

Yasmeen shakes her head. *"Yes, Mahmoud I will give you a chance."*

Before Yasmeen can say another word, she and Mahmoud are on the bed kissing. For the first time everything feels right. Yasmeen rolls on top of Mahmoud as he removes her shirt and bra. Yasmeen unbuttons Mahmoud's shirt for the first time Yasmeen kisses Mahmoud smooth muscular caramel chest. Yasmeen runs her finger along his rock-hard abs. Yasmeen straddles Mahmoud as he kisses her breast. Yasmeen can feel Mahmoud warm mouth and his wet tongue as he sucks on her hard nipples

Mahmoud pulls Yasmeen to him and they are skin to skin. Yasmeen gently bites Mahmoud bottom lip.

"*Do you have protection?*"

Mahmoud staring lovely into Yasmeen eyes. "*No, I don't. Sweetheart there is no rush, we have nothing but time. All I want is you Yasmeen.*"

"*Mahmoud will you hold me?*"

Mahmoud puts his arms around Yasmeen and he holds her tight. Yasmeen can feel that little door in her heart opens and it feels wonderful. This is the first time that Yasmeen has not dreamed about Gregory. Yasmeen feels safe in Mahmoud's arms. She can think of no other place that she would rather be. It's Monday and for the first time in a long time Mahmoud and Yasmeen are on the same page. After the meeting Mahmoud pulls Yasmeen to the side and kisses her not caring who sees them.

"*Good morning beautiful!*"

Yasmeen smiling with delight. "*Good morning doctor Shashivivek!*" Mahmoud exchanges another kiss with Yasmeen. "*So, will you be joining me for lunch Ms. Blake?*" Yasmeen walks away. "*I don't know you will just have to wait and see.*" Yasmeen exits the conference room leaving Mahmoud with a big smile on his face. When Yasmeen gets back to her office Rosetta is standing at her door holding the biggest bunch of beautiful red, white, and yellow roses. Yasmeen heart sinks because she knows that they are from Aaron. Yasmeen loves roses but not from Aaron. Yasmeen fills her lungs with air as she prepares to discard the roses.

"*It's about time boss lady! I have been waiting for you.* Handing Yasmeen, the roses. *Here these came for you! I was just about to read the card!*"

Yasmeen removes the card. "*You can throw them out!*"

Rosetta following behind Yasmeen. "*What are you sure? Hell, I wish that somebody would send me flowers.*" "*Well you can have those.* Reading the card. *Wait a minute give me those back!*"

Yasmeen face brighten up when she sees that the roses are from Mahmoud. she can't stop smiling as she put her nose to the roses and sniff them. Yasmeen bites her lip as she thinks about Mahmoud kissing her which makes her blush.

"*Well I know from that big ass smile on your face they can't be from Aaron!*"

"No…no there not from Aaron."

"Well who are they from? Rosetta reaches for the card. *Let me see!"*

Yasmeen putting the card in her purse. *"They are from my special friend.* Yasmeen beams from ear to ear. *This card is for my eyes only. Rosetta do you mind I have a call to make.* Rosetta takes a seat. *"Go ahead I'm not going anywhere until you show me that card!"*

Yasmeen rolls her eyes as she removes the card from her purse and exits her office to call Mahmoud. Leaving Rosetta questioning who sent Yasmeen the roses and why in the hell is she being so secretive. What is Yasmeen up to is she trying to make her mad and who is that bitch calling? Yasmeen calls Mahmoud. *"Thanks for the roses. They are beautiful and yes, I would be honored to have lunch with you. Ok I will see you then."* When Yasmeen walks back in her office Rosetta is still sitting there mad as fuck. Yasmeen smiles because she knows that Rosetta is pissed, but she doesn't care. *"So, when is doctor Shashivivek going let Aaron come back to work?"*

"I don't know but you can go ask him yourself!"

"I was just asking!"

"And I was just answering your question! I don't care about when Aaron comes back, but it obvious that you do!"

"Yass yes I do care! I care about everybody. Aaron is a good man and he doesn't deserve this!"

"Oh, and I do? I deserved to be assaulted is that what you're saying?"

Rosetta tries to explain. *"No, you didn't deserve to be assaulted nobody does. That's not what I'm saying at all. Yass, you know that Aaron cares a lot about you! Hell, he's in love with you!"*

"Rosetta do you hear yourself! You don't even know Aaron so don't sit here telling me about how he loves and cares for me! You don't hurt the people that you care for! You don't assault the people that you love in a parking garage for no reason!"

"Yasmeen I'm not saying that you should get back with him, but you should at least forgive him."

Just to hear Rosetta defending Aaron send Yasmeen into a rage. *"Forgive him! Rosetta, I forgave him when he cheated on me! I forgave him for breaking my heart, but I will not forgive him for assaulting me! Do you know what Aaron did to me?"*

"No. What did he do to you?" "Ask him! Get your ass up and go ask him!"

"All I'm saying is Aaron needs his job. For crying out loud Yasmeen have a heart!"

"I have a heart bitch!"

"I'm just saying. Yasmeen, you are the one leading him on. He brought you a car and you keep accepting him gifts"

"Rosetta who in the hell are you supposed to be Aarons protector! What are you fucking him too, is that it? You're fuck Aaron with your nasty ass! Yasmeen shakes her head. *You have some nerve to bring your ignorant ass up in my office confronting me about another man when you're married. Then you have the audacity to tell me to have a heart after you cheated on your husband and had a baby with another man! You're the one who should have a heart! I have more heart than anybody that you will ever know with your slick and slimy ass. And for the record I got rid of that fucking car and I never asked Aaron for damn thing! You're damn right if he wants to send me expensive gifts after I've told him to stop, oh well that's on him, his money, don't impress me! I make my own money! I told Aaron that I'm done with him, so he's leading himself on! Now when you go see Mr. Aaron tell him to leave me the fuck alone!"*

Rosetta can't say a word as tears run down her face. Jacob and Ashton come rushing in Yasmeen's office as Yasmeen is walking over to Rosetta.

"What going on in here? We can hear you out in the hall!"

"Get her ass out of my office Ashton!"

"What happened?"

"She's in here telling me that that I need to forgive Aaron and that I'm led him on! That bitch crazy!" Rosetta raise her voice. *"Yasmeen Aaron doesn't deserve this that's all I'm trying to get you to understand! Why would you jeopardize his job! Yasmeen if you weren't so mean you would go to Doctor Shashivivek and talk to him!"*

"Do you hear this girl? Get her out of here before I stomp the dog shit out of her!"

"Do you not understand what Aaron did? Rosetta, you need to come with me. Yasmeen, I need you to calm down ok and let me handle this."

"Jacob just get her out of here!"

Ashton stay with Yasmeen as Jacob escorts Rosetta crying to his office. Yasmeen is sitting at her desk still fuming. *"Ash I was having a great morning until that bitch brought her ass in here talking about Aaron. He attacked me and she's blaming me for it!"*

"Yass, I told you that something is off about the bitch."

"I know what it is, she's fucking him! Ash I know it! She's mad because I got these roses and I wouldn't tell her who they were from. That stupid hoe thinks they're from Aaron. Bitch please!"

Yass don't let that slut bad get to you with her trifling ass!"

"I give you my word if she comes back in, here I'm going to fuck her life up! I'm going to beat her ass today!"

"Yass she's not worth it! Now who sent those flowers!"

"My man. My new boo!"

"Who Mahmoud?"

"What? You're tripping. I don't know what you're talking about."

"Oh, you know. I told you that Mahmoud had a thing for your chocolate ass. So, have you let him hit it yet?"

"What? Ash no! You're supposed to be calming me down not talking about Mahmoud."

"Hell give him some and that will calm both of you down."

"Whatever! I can't with you."

Yasmeen meets Mahmoud for lunch. She tells him about her encounter with Rosetta. Mahmoud assures her that everything is going to be ok and not to worry. Yasmeen kisses Mahmoud and she thanks him again for the flowers. When Yasmeen returns back to work, she's happy once again that is until she sees Rosetta waiting at her door. *"Oh, I'm fixing to beat this bitch ass!* Yasmeen rush down the hall. *This stupid mother fucker must have a death wish! Bitch I know that you're not waiting for me!"*

"Yasmeen, I just wanted to apologize for how I acted this morning. I'm sorry."

"Ok now move!"

"Yasmeen please. I shouldn't have said the things that I said. I just have so much going on and I don't have anyone to vent to. Yasmeen, I know that I was completely out of place for defending Aaron the way that I did. Please forgive me."

"Whatever. I've got work to do."

"Can we talk?"

"No, I'm still mad at you! I should punch you in your face!"

"Ok go ahead just as long as you talk to me when you're done."

Yasmeen draws back her fist and punch's Rosetta in her nose. "Now get your stupid ass out of my face!" It has been a month Aaron is back at work and he's still fucking Rebecca, Uma, and Rosetta. No matter who Aaron fucks his mind is still on Yasmeen. He just won't give up on Yasmeen. Yasmeen and Mahmoud are keeping their relationship under wrap. They just want to avoid the drama for now. Only Maxwell, Todd, Oscar, and Ashton know about them. Yasmeen is in the lobby talking to Wallace when Uma interrupts them. Since Uma, miscarried she and Yasmeen have had little to say to each other which is fine with Yasmeen. The one thing that Yasmeen doesn't have time for is Uma and Aarons crap. Uma addresses Wallace. *"Excuse me but don't you have work to do? I need to have a word with Ms. Blake!"* Fire runs all through Yasmeen when she hears Uma disrespectful rude ass. Yasmeen can feel her horns coming out like spikes. Yasmeen puts her arm out to stop Wallace. *"No Wallace don't You leave! Heifer I don't know who you think you are, but don't you ever in your life approach anybody I'm talking to like that. You are just rude!"* Uma's at a lost for words. *"Well I need to talk to you!"* Yasmeen is beyond irritated. *"Well I suggest that you wait your turn! Better yet go make an appointment! I might see you but don't count on it!"*

"Are you serious?"

"Dead ass! I've told you that I don't like you because you're rude and you're full of shit! Now run your happy ass up out our face!"

"But Ms. Blake!"

"Bye chick! Be gone! Now what were we talking about?"

"I'm sorry I didn't mean to come off as rude Mr. Wallace!"

Yasmeen interjects. *"Well you did! Go on now before you make me act like you out here in this lobby!"* Uma walks away in a haste. Wallace looks at Yasmeen and laughs as he shakes his head in amazement. *"Ms. Yasmeen, you are one of a kind! What am I going to do with you? You had that woman shaking in her heels!"*

"I don't care! Wallace that was uncalled for and you know it! She knows that I don't care for her with her big head!"

"Ms. Yasmeen that's why I like you. You just don't care what you say or how you say it. You don't hold back for nobody!"

"And I'm not supposed to!"

"*Well tell me this when are you and doctor Shashivivek going to go out? I think that you two would look good together.*"

Yasmeen shakes her head. "*What Wallace? You know what bye Wallace., now you got me running! Bye Wallace have a nice day!*"

"*No come back I'm not finished!*"

Yasmeen gets on the elevator. "*Well I am!*"

Mahmoud has been in London for two weeks visiting his family for the holiday. Even though he has been calling Yasmeen everyday sometimes two or three times a day, Yasmeen has been going out of her mind thinking about Mahmoud over in London. The only thing that she keeps obsessing about is Mahmoud fiancé. Yasmeen's mind is in a million places. She questions herself that maybe Mahmoud went back home to get married or maybe his fiancé wants to spend Christmas with her soon to be husband. The burning question in Yasmeen's head is will he be coming back? Yasmeen knew Mahmoud's situation when she got involved with him. Hell, it wasn't a secret, Yasmeen only has herself to blame. Yes, Mahmoud did buy Yasmeen a gift that she has yet to open. Oscar and Todd have been encouraging Yasmeen to be positive and stop trying to create her own story. Yasmeen has made up her mind that she's not going to wait around for Mahmoud and end up getting hurt! No matter what her heart says she will not be made a fool of. Yasmeen thinking is not rational she has even thought about returning Aaron's many calls, but that thought went back to hell where it came from. Yasmeen has not talked to Mahmoud all day and it's two days before New Year's. Yasmeen has decided to go out with Todd, Oscar, and Ashton to have a little fun. Maybe she'll get lucky! Whatever that means. No matter what Yasmeen will not be sitting at home this year. Yasmeen has just returned from the gym. Before Yasmeen can get out of her car Rosetta is standing at her car door smiling. *All Yasmeen can think is Why in the hell is this bitch in my driveway.* Yasmeen rolls her eyes as she gets out of her car reluctantly. "*What are you doing here?*"

"*Well I came to see you.*"

Yasmeen walks away. "*And why would you come see me.* Unlocking her door. *Out of all your friends you came to see me Yasmeen!*"

"*Yes, I came to see you. Why are you surprised?*"

"*Rosetta let's face it you and I are not friends and we haven't been for a long time.*"

"Yasmeen, we are friends. I mean yes we don't talk as much and we've had some disagreements but we're still friends."

"Girl who in the hell have you been talking to? They must be an asshole!"

"Yasmeen, I know that I fucked up, but I missed you. Now can I come in?"

Yasmeen puts her keys down. "You can come in, but the feeling is not mutual! No, I did not miss talking to you so don't ask!"

"That's a yes you did!"

"That's a hell no I didn't!"

"Anyway, what have you been up to?"

"Umm working, paying bills, minding my business, you know same shit different day!"

"No, I mean what have you been doing?"

"Well I just came from the gym and I'm about to go wash my ass. Yasmeen looks down at Rosetta's wrist. *Where did you get that? You know Aaron sent me a bracelet just like this and I sent it back to him."*

Rosette pulls her hand away. *"Oh, this old thing! My husband... well my soon to be ex-husband brought this for me."*

Yasmeen smile to herself. *"This lying bitch! She knows that Aaron gave her that shit! It looks just like the one Aaron... Never mind Rosetta what do you really want?"*

"Why are you so suspicious?"

"Because you came to see me!"

"Yass, I just want us to be like we use to. Please give me another chance. Yass, I really miss you!"

Yasmeen speaks to herself. *"This deceitful bitch is up to no good... We will just have to see about that."* Rosetta hugs Yasmeen but, Yasmeen pushes her away. *"Ok I didn't see that coming Judas!"*

"Whatever! Yasmeen what do you have planned for New Years? Wait let me guess you're going out with your new man!"

"No, I don't have a man and if you must know I'm going out with Oscar, Todd, Zada you know the usual gang my friends! We're going to our favorite place."

"Oh really! That great you know I'm going to be there too. You know what Yass I've got some one that I would like you to meet. How about I bring him with me!"

"How about no!"

"Yass come on! Why not?"

Yasmeen walks away. *"Because I'm not interested bitch!"*

"But Yass he's a nice guy and you haven't met him!"

"Rosetta I said no!"

"Yasmeen ok how about I invite him, and I'll introduce you two and we can go from there."

"Rosetta, you can do whatever you want to but I'm not promising you anything because I'm not interested. Now if you don't mind, I need to take a shower."

"Ok but will you at least talk to him?"

"Let me think about it and I'll let you know."

"Well I'm going to invite him and I'm going to tell him about you Yass."

Yasmeen push's Rosetta out the door. *"Yeah, yeah you do that. I've got to go now you have a good day. Next time call before you come bye!"*

Yasmeen slams the door and stand with her back to the door shaking her head. Yasmeen is about to get in the shower when the doorbell rings. *"Oh, come on! Talk about determination!"* Yasmeen bolt to the door and angrily flings the door open. *"What?"*

"Well damn that's how you answer the door!"

"I thought that you were Rosetta."

"Rosetta! Why would you think that we were Rosetta?"

Yasmeen hugs Zada. *"She was waiting on me when I got home. Y'all come in."*

"And why was she here?'

"Yeah and what did she want?"

Yasmeen retie her bathrobe. *"Oh, she said that she wants us to be friends."* Zada laughs. *"That sounds like some bullshit Yass!"*

"Yeah I know right. How about she said that she has some guy that she wants me to meet."

"Yeah she's trying to get your ass away from Aaron by pushing you off on somebody that she fucked with her loose pussy!"

"Todd I was thinking the same thing. Oh, but here the kicker. You remember that gold diamond bracelet that Aaron sent me for Christmas. How about she had it on. I asked her about it' Za you know that my name is on it. Miss thang said that her husband gave it to her!"

"You should have snatched it off her arm and said bitch why would your husband give you a bracelet with my name on it!"

"Yasmeen you had better stay away from the snake. You see what her ass did to me! Got me taking care of her ass for the next eighteen years. Every time I think about that it pisses me the fuck off!"

"You should have kept your dick in your pants or did like Todd and wrapped it up."

Both Todd and Oscar laughs. *"Fuck you Zada!"*

After Todd, Zada, and Oscar leaves Yasmeen is in the shower, she closed her eyes and lets the hot water falls all over her smooth chocolate skin as she leathers with shower gel her mind starts to wonder. She thinks about the last time she and Gregory took a shower together. Yasmeen feels guilty because this is the first time in months that she has thought about Gregg. As Yasmeen rubs soap all over her body she smiles as she leathers her breast with soap. Yasmeen can feel Gregg hands caressing her between her legs as she runs her fingers across her wet pussy. The soap leather runs down Yasmeen soft round ass, she bites her lip as the water beats down on her perky D cup breast. Yasmeen pinch her nipples and opens her mouth as the water rolls down her face. Her body shakes as she screams out Gregory name in ecstasy. When Yasmeen gets out of the shower, she feels rejuvenated as she sings to R. Kelly your body's calling playing in the background when the doorbell rings. *"Shit who in the hell is that at this hour. That had better not be Rosetta."* Yasmeen skin is still wet as she pulls her tank-top over her head her nipples are still hard. Yasmeen runs to the door pulling her yoga pants up. *"I'm coming stop ring my doorbell and give me time to get to the door!"*

Yasmeen opens the door and before she can get the words out of her mouth Mahmoud grabs Yasmeen up in his arms lifting her off her feet as he kisses her. Yasmeen feels like he never left. Yasmeen knows that she's angry with Mahmoud, but she forgets how to show it. she wants to push Mahmoud away, but she can't. After kissing Mahmoud Yasmeen gets up the strength to push him away. So many questions run's through Yasmeen mind as she stands before Mahmoud not knowing how to feel. She wants to run into his arms, but she hesitates.

"Mahmoud what are you doing here?"

"I came to see you!"

Mahmoud reaches out to touch Yasmeen, but she backs away. *"Mahmoud why are you here!"*

"Do you want me to leave?"

"Yes, I do!"

Before Yasmeen can run away Mahmoud grabs her and holds her tight but gently in his strong masculine arms. He holds her face in his hands. He kisses her so passionately as he whispers, *"You don't mean that."* Yasmeen can feel her body relax as she gives into Mahmoud soft sweet kisses. The last thing that Yasmeen wants is for Mahmoud to leave. *"Sweetheart I'm sorry for not calling you, but I wanted to surprise you. Please don't be mad."*

"Mahmoud..."

Mahmoud interrupts Yasmeen. "I'm sorry. I had a long flight. Yasmeen, I just wanted to see you face to face. I missed you so much." Yasmeen takes a seat on the sofa. *"So, did you see your fiancé?"*

"Yes, Yasmeen I did. We had dinner with our families, we set around the table and we all talked, but not about the wedding. Just general conversation. Mahmoud holds Yasmeen's hand. *At no time were we ever alone.* Kissing Yasmeen hand. *Yasmeen every free moment that I had I called you. Yasmeen, you were all that I thought about. You have no reason to be mad and you have nothing to worry about. Do you trust me?"*

"Yes, I trust you."

"Well kiss me like you missed me!"

Without saying another word Yasmeen pulls Mahmoud over to her and she kisses him with all the breath in her body. Mahmoud welcomes Yasmeen soft lips and tongue into his waiting mouth. He softly sucks on Yasmeen bottom lip. "I Missed you and I don't want you to leave."

"I'm not going anywhere."

Mahmoud picks Yasmeen up and carries her to the bedroom. Mahmoud removes Yasmeen's tank-top he commences to kisses every part of Yasmeen's body leaving nothing out. Mahmoud kisses Yasmeen feet and suck on her toe's. Unlike with Aaron there is not one part of Yasmeen that wants Mahmoud to stop. Yasmeen's mind, heart, and body are on the same page they all want Mahmoud. Mahmoud can't keep his hands-off Yasmeen. He devours her kisses. Mahmoud tells himself that this is the woman that he want's and he will do everything in his power to make sure that this is the woman that he gets. The next morning

Mahmoud is in the shower and Yasmeen is looking at her reflection in the mirror, when she looks down at the Christmas gift from Mahmoud that she never opened. As Yasmeen rips it open, she hopes that Mahmoud doesn't hear her. Yasmeen heart skips a beat, for this is the most beautiful diamond neckless that she has ever seen and for the first time Yasmeen is torn between the man she wants and the man that she lost. Yasmeen cuffs her rings that she has always worn around her neck. When Yasmeen hears Mahmoud coming out of the bathroom, she tucks the remnants of the gift in her dresser draw and she holds the neckless from Mahmoud in her hand.

"Do you like it?"

"What… Oh yes! Yes, I love it. Mahmoud it's beautiful, but I…"

Mahmoud puts his arms around Yasmeen waist. *"Yasmeen, you don't have to wear it. I just wanted you to have something almost as beautiful as you."* Yasmeen kissing Mahmoud. *"Mahmoud this is beautiful, and I will wear it but not now."*

"When you're ready it will be here for you. Yasmeen, I do understand there is no need to explain."

"Mahmoud, I need to tell you something."

. *"Ok what is it?"*

"Well I didn't know that you're coming back and I kind of made plans to go out for New Year's Eve with Todd and Oscar."

"Ok… ok. You're right you didn't know that I was coming back. Look have fun."

Yasmeen can see that Mahmoud is disappointed, but she still decides to tell him about Rosetta just to see how he would react. *"Mahmoud, you know Rosetta came over on yesterday."*

"Oh really! What did she want?"

"Well she said that she wants to fix me up with this guy."

"Yasmeen are you trying to piss me off? If you are, it's working!"

Yasmeen laughs as she puts her arms around Mahmoud neck. *"No why would I do that?"*

Mahmoud push Yasmeen down onto the bed. *"Because you're Yasmeen and you know just how to push my buttons. Look I don't mind you going out just as long as you have dinner with me before you go out."*

"Now you know that I have to get dressed!"

"Well you can get dressed at my place. Oh, and that Rosetta thing we're not even going to talk about."

"And why not?"

"There is no need. Now kiss me!"

Yasmeen kisses Mahmoud she rolls over on top of him. It's New Year's Eve and Yasmeen is getting ready to go over to Mahmoud's house when her cell phone rings. Yasmeen knows that it's not Oscar because she told him that she would meet him at the club. She knows just who it is! Rosetta, she had been calling all day. Yasmeen looks at her phone and turns it off. When Yasmeen gets to Mahmoud house, he greets her at the door. In his hand he's holding a beautiful red single rose and a glass of wine. After dinner Yasmeen is upstairs getting dressed. She's wearing a short gold sequence off the shoulder dress that hugs every curve that Yasmeen has. Yasmeen pins her hair to one side and slips on her stilettos. She runs her hand down the back of her dress and smiles. Yasmeen looks over at the clock. It's eleven forty-five. Yasmeen grabs her purse and runs down stairs. When Yasmeen gets down stairs she stops dead in her tracks when she sees candles lite throughout the house. On the coffee table there are chocolate cover strawberries and wine. The floor is covered with rose petals. Yasmeen puts her hands over her mouth and her eyes tear up. Mahmoud is standing in the entrance to the living room. He's smiles with delight as he admires Yasmeen's beauty. Mahmoud takes Yasmeen by the hand and leads her into the living room. *"You're not going to make it to the club on time, so why don't you bring the New Year in with me and then you can go meet your friends."* The only thing that Yasmeen can do is agree with Mahmoud's suggestion by shaking her head. She's speechless anyway how can she tell him no. Mahmoud hands Yasmeen a glass of wine as they stand face to face and count down to a new year. *"Happy New Year Mahmoud!"* Mahmoud kisses Yasmeen. *"Happy New Years to you beautiful and I'm so happy that you're here."* Mahmoud takes the wine glass from Yasmeen hand and he kisses her like he has never kissed her before. There is nothing inside of Yasmeen that's saying no as Mahmoud picks her up and carries her upstairs back to his bedroom. Yasmeen and Mahmoud are in Mahmoud's king size bed kissing; Yasmeen soul thirst for Mahmoud. Yasmeen craving for Mahmoud is so strong. It has been a long time since she has felt this yearning for a man. Yasmeen can see that Mahmoud wants her just as much as she wants him. Mahmoud whispers to Yasmeen. *"I want you! Are you ready to give yourself to me?* Yasmeen willingly says, "Yes do you have protection?"* Mahmoud reaches over and push's out a box of magnums three pack. *"Yes, I do."* Yasmeen thinks to herself. *"Magnums Yeah right!"* Mahmoud continue to kiss Yasmeen's beautiful frame as they undress each other. Mahmoud traces Yasmeen breast with his long tongue. Mahmoud works his way down to Yasmeen belly button. Yasmeen can feel Mahmoud's breath as he kisses the inside of her thigh. For the first time Mahmoud kisses Yasmeen where it counts. Yasmeen grips the side of the bed. Mahmoud puts both of Yasmeen's legs up on his shoulders and licks her clit. Yasmeen lets out a moan as Mahmoud darts his long tongue in and out of her now wet pussy. Yasmeen opens her legs wide as Mahmoud spreads her pussy lips apart and buries his face in her pussy juice. Mahmoud pushes Yasmeen legs back to her shoulder and inserts his middle finger deep inside of her as he sucks on her clit. Yasmeen's body starts to shake. Mahmoud smiles because he knows that he has found her G-spot. Yasmeen grabs the back of Mahmoud's head as she screams out in ecstasy. Mahmoud comes up for air. Yasmeen looks at Mahmoud as he removes a condom from the box. Yasmeen can't wait to see what Mahmoud is really working with. Yasmeen watches Mahmoud as he puts the condom on. When Mahmoud pulls his dick out Yasmeen gasp and her eye widens! Yasmeen says to herself. *What the fuck have I gotten myself into*! *Mahmoud, I don't think that's going to fit!* Mahmoud is disappointed. *"We don't have to do this if you don't want to."* It's not that she doesn't want to. Yasmeen was not expecting Mahmoud dick to be so big. She can see the disappointment on his face. Yasmeen pulls Mahmoud close and whispers in his ear. *"Please don't hurt me."*

"I'll be gentle."

Mahmoud climbs on top of Yasmeen and rubs the tip of him large dick on the entrance of Yasmeen tight pussy. Mahmoud slowly pushes his dick inside of Yasmeen. She arches her back as he penetrates her completely. They both scream. Yasmeen tries to push herself away, but Mahmoud grips her shoulders and pushes his way inside. Their bodies connect. Mahmoud looks down at Yasmeen as her body moves like a snake in water. He can no longer control himself as he cries out in satisfaction *"Shit!... Damn!... Oh, shit Yasmeen!"* Soon both Mahmoud and Yasmeen rapture in extreme pleasure. Yasmeen legs feels like jelly. Mahmoud carry's her to the shower. Mahmoud picks Yasmeen up and pins her to the shower wall. With Yasmeen legs around his waist Mahmoud thrust his manhood deep inside of her. The water cascade over their body like rain. Yasmeen squeezes her pelvis. Mahmoud screams out Yasmeen's name. He can no longer contain himself. Mahmoud is on the verge of launching his rocket. His body tenses up and his rhythm quickens, he's seconds away from exploding in sheer pleasure. Yasmeen holds on to Mahmoud like her life depends on it. Mahmoud kisses Yasmeen as he lowers her to her feet. Yasmeen and Mahmoud make their way back to the Mahmoud's bed where she falls asleep in his arms. Mahmoud smiles as he watches Yasmeen sleep. He runs his hand down one side of her cheek and kisses the tip of her nose. Mahmoud holds on to Yasmeen and soon he falls asleep with Yasmeen in his arms. The, next morning Yasmeen wakes up to breakfast in bed. Mahmoud looks at Yasmeen, he's in awe.

"What? Why are you staring at me like that?"

Mahmoud moves closer. *"Because you are so beautiful, and I'm delighted that you are here with me my Queen."*

Yasmeen heart drops as she feels a wave of peace. She looks into Mahmoud's eyes lustfully. *"What did you call me?"* Mahmoud sit the breakfast tray on the floor. *"I called you my Queen. You are my Nubian Queen and I'm going to make you so happy!"* Yasmeen search her mind. She can't comprehend what's going on. The last time anyone called her a Nubian Queen was Gregory. Yasmeen wonders is she hearing things or did Mahmoud sound just like Gregg. Yasmeen body starts to tingle all over. *"Kiss me my Queen!"* Mahmoud kiss Yasmeen before he licks her pussy. Mahmoud looks up at Yasmeen. *"I want you... I need you now."* Yasmeen runs her finger through Mahmoud silky black hair. *"And I want you to!"* Mahmoud Kisses Yasmeen stomach. *"We 're out of condoms. Do you trust me?"*

"Yes, I do. Do you trust me?"

"With my whole heart."

Yasmeen pulls Mahmoud up to her and once again he pushes his big beautiful caramel dick into her sweet wet pussy. This time Yasmeen surrenders herself to Mahmoud completely. She gives him everything that she didn't give him last night. Yasmeen rolls Mahmoud over onto his back.

She climbs on top of him and lower herself down onto his rock hard twelve-inch dick. Mahmoud watches in amazement as Yasmeen rolls her hips like a slow-moving fan. Yasmeen jerks her ass back and forth as Mahmoud pushes his dick deeper inside of her. He can feel Yasmeen contracting her pussy walls, he can feel her Cuming. Mahmoud flips Yasmeen over so that he can inter her from behind. Mahmoud screams as Yasmeen rotates and pops her ass. He collapses in passion. Mahmoud is out of breath as he kisses Yasmeen on her ass. When Yasmeen gets home, she is fucked out and she's still smiling as she thinks about Mahmoud. Yasmeen pulls her cellphone from her purse, she knows that she has a lot of missed calls. Yasmeen looks down at Phone. "*Shit!*" She remembers that she forgot to turn her phone back on. Yasmeen calls Oscar immediately. She knows that he's going to be pissed about last night. Yasmeen is in her bed when Todd, and Oscar comes busting in the room pulling the covers off her.

"*Get your ass up!*" Oscar pulling Yasmeen foot. "*Yeah get your hot ass up and tell us everything!*" Yasmeen can't stop laughing. "*There is nothing to tell. He cooked dinner, we ate, we had wine, we shared a New Year's kiss… And I came home.* Yasmeen walking to the bathroom. *That's it.*

"*Wait one minute! Why in the hell are you walking like that? Bitch… Bitch! Hell, no you didn't! Yass tell me that Mahmoud tore that ass up! Todd, she can't walk! Look at her.*

Todd yells out in excitement. "*No, you didn't! Yass was it good as I think it was?*

Yasmeen stops in her tracks. The last thing that she wanted was for Oscar and Todd to know the she slept with Mahmoud. Her heart races as she tries to think of a lie. Lying is not something that Yasmeen is good at, but she doesn't want them to think bad of her. "*What…? My walk… Oh I pulled a muscle in my leg.*" Todd laugh. *Yeah on Mahmoud's shoulder. The only muscle you pulled was the one between Mahmoud's legs.* Todd runs over to Yasmeen. *You had sex with him didn't you and don't lie, because you're not good at it! Yass, we know when you're lying so don't even try it! Now did you give it up?* Yasmeen close her eyes tight. "*Yes, we did it.*" Both Oscar and Todd fall back on the bed laughing and kicking their legs in the air. They are so happy for Yasmeen her four-year drought is over. Todd make room on the bed for Yasmeen. He and Oscar want details. "*Is he good in bed?*"

Yasmeen smiles with tears in her eyes. *"Yes, he was amazing!.. So y'all are not mad and y'all don't think that I cheated on Gregg Todd?"*

"No Yass why would we be mad? We are so happy for you! Yass, you didn't cheat on Gregg. As a matter of fact, I bet that he's looking down on you saying it's about time!"

"Yass, you deserve to be happy and from the look on your face you're, damn happy! Aaron is the one who's mad! Let me tell you about last night. First all three of Aaron women were there. Yass how about he come strolling in with a new chick on his arm. Uma and Rebecca looked like they wanted to kill his ass, but oh girl tried to play the shit off. I overheard her telling him that you were coming. Yass when I tell you that his ass was in my face every five-minute's asking about you. I was like get your ass back over to your date and stop worrying about Yasmeen.

"He ain't shit."

"Oscar tell me about it!"

"But he was just as piss- as his three sluts when your ass didn't show up. Zada with her crazy self didn't help. She going to say oh Yasmeen's new man got her legs in the air by now, she not coming at least not coming here and she was right! Girl Aaron was so mad right O?"

"You should have saw him. Oscar demonstrates. *He grabbed that chick by the arm and damn near dragged her ass out of there. Yass, he probably dropped her ass off and came straight over here looking for you.* Yasmeen, Oscar, and Todd continues talking about Aaron and the New Year's party Zada and Ashton arrives. Yasmeen tries to engage in the conversation she can't stop thinking about Mahmoud. After three hours everyone leave's and Yasmeen finally go to bed. Yasmeen is still asleep when the doorbell rings. Yasmeen slowly makes her way to the door hoping that it's not Aaron or Rosetta. Yasmeen opens the door with her eyes half open. Her eyes pop open when she sees that it's Mahmoud and he looks good in his brown button-down polo shirt and black dress pants. Mahmoud Walks in and kisses Yasmeen on the head.

"Good evening my Queen! How are you?"

"I'm good just sleepy. How are you?"

"I'm better now. Why didn't you call me?"

"I said that I was going to call you when I got up."

"Yeah that was yesterday. Today is Sunday."

"What are you kidding me? Today is not Sunday Mahmoud!"

Mahmoud shows Yasmeen his cellphone. *"No, I'm not kidding you."*

"You mean to tell me that I slept all day!"

"Yeah so did I. I guess that we were tired!"

"I guess we were."

"Well would you like to go out to dinner? It's almost eight o'clock and I know that you haven't eaten."

"Ok just let me go take a shower and get dressed."

"May I come with you?"

Yasmeen looking back over her shoulder. *"Only if you promise to be good!"*

Mahmoud follows Yasmeen into her bedroom. *"Oh, I'll be good!* Mahmoud kiss Yasmeen neck. *I'll be better than good.*

After dinner Mahmoud and Yasmeen spend the rest of the night in a passionate embrace. It's Monday morning Yasmeen has been avoiding eye contact or talking to Mahmoud. After the meeting Yasmeen is about to run out when Mahmoud pulls her back.

"What are you ignoring me?"

"Yes...No... I don't know!"

"Did I do something wrong this morning?"

"No, you didn't. I just..."

"So, you just want to keep our relationship a secret?"

Yasmeen is unsure what she wants. *"Yes.... I'm not sure. What do you want?"*

I want you! So, if you don't want anyone to know about us, I'm ok with it. I just want you to be happy."

Yasmeen throws her arms around Mahmoud's neck and kisses him. Yasmeen knows that she wants to be with Mahmoud. Yasmeen gazes into Mahmoud eyes. *"Mahmoud, I am happy, and I don't mean to ignore you. You know that I despise people being in my business."*

"Yasmeen, you don't have to explain! When the time is right, we'll let everyone know."

Yasmeen rub Mahmoud's chest. *"I don't want to smother you, so I will try to resist you at work.*

"So, I'm irresistible?"

Yasmeen walks away. "I'm not going to answer that!"

Mahmoud pulls Yasmeen back. *"No don't run away! Do you find me irresistible?"*

"Yes, I do."

"Show me!"

"What?"

"You heard me! Show me!"

"Here? Right here?... No!"

"Why not?"

"No and I have to get back to my office."

Yasmeen kisses Mahmoud and she retreats to her office. Yasmeen is sitting at her computer when she gets a knock on the door. It's Rosetta. Yasmeen looks up and shakes her head. Rosetta is not who Yasmeen wanted to walk in her office. *"Good morning and happy New Year's to you."*

"Same to you."

"What happened to you New Year's Eve?"

"Something better came up."

"Like?"

"Like none of your business!"

"Yasmeen why want you tell me who you're seeing? Is it doctor Ward? No, he was at the party. Yass who is it?"

"You mean that I didn't tell you?"

"Yass no you didn't!"

"Well it must not be any of your business!"

"Really? Anyway, I know that you heard that Aaron has a new boo."

Yasmeen clap her hands. *"Good for him.* "Yasmeen can see the disappointment on Rosetta's face, which makes her smile. Yasmeen decides to push Rosetta buttons. *"I hope that it's not anyone from here!"*

"No, she's not from here.'

"Good. I do hope she the one for him you know, I hope that he marries her."

"What? Are you out of your mind?"

"No, I'm not and why are you getting so testy?

I'm not... You know how Aaron is."

Yeah, he'll fuck anything what a pussy. I do hope that this new woman changes him. You know what? I'm going to encourage Aaron to be a one woman's man and you're going to help me!'

Rosetta sit up in her seat. *"Yasmeen no I'm not!"*

"Why not? You do want him to be happy and to get over me, don't you?"

Rosetta jumps to her feet. *"Yasmeen, I don't want any part of this. I've got to get back to work anyway."*

Rosetta storms out and Yasmeen can't stop laughing. She knows that Rosetta has a thing for Aaron and like Uma and Rebecca Aaron is fucking her over too. Yasmeen loves to see Rosetta squirm. After lunch Yasmeen is walking through the lobby when Aaron approaches her. As Aaron stands before Yasmeen everything in him wants to kiss her full beautiful glossy lips. *"Hey Yass, I just wanted to tell you happy New Year's since I didn't see you at the party."* Yasmeen almost speechless. *"Aaron… Same… same to you. Thank you, now have a nice day."* Aaron stepping in front of Yasmeen. *"Yasmeen give me a minute please. I just wanted to tell you that I'm sorry for everything and I won't bother you anymore. I'm sure that your friends told you that I'm seeing someone new. Yass, I really like her."* Yasmeen smiles she's happy that Aaron is seeing someone and that he won't be bothering her. Everything in Yasmeen knows that he's lying. Aaron is a no good, snake. Yasmeen knows that he's up to something. Yasmeen decides to play along. *"Yes, they did, and I can't tell you how happy I am for you. Aaron, I wish you the best of luck. Who knows maybe the two of you will make it official and one day get married."* Aaron steps back. *"Wait a minute! Hold on I didn't say all that. I just said that I was seeing someone!"*

"Aaron I'm just saying that maybe it's time that you settled down."

"You mean like you?"

"Like me! What do you mean?"

"Come off it Yass, Zada told me that you're seeing someone too! I take it that you were with him and that's why you didn't come out New Year's Eve?"

Well yes, I am seeing someone, and I was with him."

"So how long have you been seeing this jerk and who is he?"

Yasmeen walks away. *"Aaron why would you say that you don't know him like that and I'm not going to tell you who he is because it's not any of your business!"*

"Do you care for him?"

"Aaron yes I do!"

"Have you slept with him?"

"I'm not going to answer that! Good-bye Aaron!"

"So that's a yes! How could you Yasmeen? Why?"

"Good-bye Aaron"

Yasmeen walks away. Aaron is so angry that he kicks the trashcan over. All Aaron can think about is how he dated Yasmeen for six months and he never even seen her pussy Aaron is determined to find out who this man is. After a month Mahmoud and Yasmeen are still seeing each other and their relationship is getting stronger. Mahmoud finds himself thinking about Yasmeen and missing her when they are apart. Yasmeen herself longs for Mahmoud, she knows that things between her and Mahmoud has gone too far. She knows that he's going to break her heart even though Mahmoud has promised her that he would never hurt her. Yasmeen and Mahmoud are in Yasmeen's bed kissing when Yasmeen pushes Mahmoud away.

"What is it Yasmeen? Don't tell me nothing, because you have been distancing yourself. Tell me what's wrong."

Yasmeen heart hurts. *"We need to end this."*

"Why?"

"Because you and I both know that we are just fooling ourselves and Mahmoud...

Mahmoud puts one finger up to Yasmeen's lip and kiss her. He can see the hurt in Yasmeen's eyes. Mahmoud rolls on top of Yasmeen. *"Is this about me getting married? Yasmeen I've told you that you don't have to worry about that. Let me handle this my Queen. I know that you care about me and I care about you. Yasmeen please trust me."*

"Mahmoud, I want to trust you, but I'm scared... I'm so scared."

Mahmoud kisses Yasmeen tears. *You have nothing to fear."*

Yasmeen heart tells her to let go as Mahmoud kisses her neck. He gently licks, kiss, and suck Yasmeen nipples as they start to harden in his mouth. Mahmoud massages Yasmeen breast as he runs ice down her stomach. Yasmeen body quivers. Mahmoud kisses Yasmeen's inner thighs. He pulls Yasmeen closer to him as he strokes the top of her clitoris with the tip of his long cold tongue. He darts the ice in and out of Yasmeen's pussy with his tongue. Mahmoud squeezes Yasmeen's firm ass as she lifts her hips and fucks Mahmoud's mouth. Yasmeen screams out Mahmoud's name as she releases her pussy juice. Yasmeen must show Mahmoud how much he means to her. Yasmeen flips Mahmoud over onto his back.

Yasmeen inserts ice into her mouth and she gently nibble on Mahmoud's ear. Yasmeen lets the ice run down Mahmoud neck. Mahmoud closes his eyes he's in ecstasy as Yasmeen licks his smooth chest working her way down to his twelve-inch dick. Yasmeen kisses Mahmoud inner thigh. He grabs the bed sheets as Yasmeen encircles his dick with both of her hands. Yasmeen kisses and lick the head of Mahmoud dick before she guides his dick in her wet cold mouth. Yasmeen lubricants Mahmoud erected dick with her wet mouth. She licks down both side of his big Carmel dick like an ice-cream cone. Yasmeen holds the base of Mahmoud dick as she gently rotates her hand back and forth as she slowly sucks and blow cool air onto the head of his dick. Mahmoud can feel Yasmeen soft lips as she pulls his dick in and out of her mouth. Mahmoud rolls his eyes up and moans with extreme delight. Mahmoud looks down at Yasmeen. His dick is so wet from Yasmeen's mouth, Mahmoud can no longer control himself as he screams *"Shit please don't stop. Fuck...oooh Yasmeen yes! Yasmeen Please I'm Cumming!"* Yasmeen looks up at Mahmoud and smile. Mahmoud grabs Yasmeen hands and pulls her up into a squatting position and lowers her onto his waiting dick. Yasmeen straddles Mahmoud as he grinds his pelvis in a circular motion. Yasmeen rocks back and forth as she rides Mahmoud like a cowgirl. Mahmoud holds Yasmeen hips and she squeezes her breast. Yasmeen can feel Mahmoud pushing against her walls as he thrust himself inside of her. Yasmeen screams. *Oh God I'm Cumming!* Mahmoud rolls Yasmeen over onto her back. Mahmoud stands at the end of the bed and push Yasmeen legs to her chest. He grabs Yasmeen ankle's, as he enters her. Mahmoud slowly and gently grinds his hip as he penetrates Yasmeen. With both of Yasmeen heels on his shoulders, Mahmoud enjoys the view of his dick thrusting in and out of Yasmeen soaking wet tight pussy. Mahmoud strokes quicken. Yasmeen wraps her long chocolate legs around Mahmoud's waist as they both reach their climax. Mahmoud collapses on top of Yasmeen. With sweat dripping from their body, Mahmoud tries to catch his breath. He kisses Yasmeen and they fall asleep in each other's arms after a long sexual shower.

Chapter 11

What done in the dark....

For the past two weeks Aaron has been keeping his distance from Yasmeen. Not once has he called or texted her. He can see that Yasmeen is happy with her new life. Yasmeen has yet to tell Aaron that she's in a relationship with Mahmoud. Yes, she has told Zada and Tia, but Aaron and Rosetta are still guessing. Every time Aaron sees or hears Yasmeen name anger take over him. He's wants to hate Yasmeen, but he can't. Aaron can't hate Yasmeen and he can't stop fucking Rosetta, Uma, Rebecca, or his new girlfriend. Aaron is walking through the parking garage when Brandon runs up behind him with a big smile on his face.

"*Good Morning Aaron!*"

Aaron looking back. "*Good morning to you and, how are you?*"

"*I'm good, but I've been meaning to talk to you.*"

Aaron stops walking and faces Brandon. "*Talk to me about what?*"

"*About Yasmeen.*"

Aaron eyes narrow. "*What about Yasmeen?*"

Brandon looks around. "*Look Aaron I know that you and Yasmeen dated, things didn't work out... Aaron I... I was wondering if you would mind if I asked her out?*"

"*What? What did you say?*"

Brandon runs his hand cross his mouth. "*Look I think that Yasmeen is a wonderful person and I would like to get to know her, so do you think that I have a chance?*"

Aaron pushs Brandon. *"Fuck no I don't think that you have a chance you Son-of-A-bitch. Why don't you ask your fucking wife!"*

"Aaron I'm not trying to piss you off. Hell, you've moved on. Look man I just wanted to let you know. I'm not asking for your permission."

"You don't have to ask me shit, but I'm telling you that you had better stay the hell away from her. If I even, see you talking to her I'll beat the fuck out of you! I will break your fucking-neck you prick! Aaron punch's Brandon in the stomach. *Do I make myself clear? Oh, and I'm going to call your wife and let her know about your little crush asshole!"*

Brandon shakes his head as he holds his stomach. Aaron still has feelings for Yasmeen. As Aaron walks through the lobby tears run down his face because like Brandon Aaron knows that Yasmeen is an amazing woman who he lost. Yasmeen is in her office talking to Rosetta who's hell bent on finding out who Yasmeen new man is.

"Yass why won't you tell me?"

"Tell you what?"

"Who you're seeing!"

"Because it's none of your business! Now stop asking you will find out one day, but not today."

"Yass we're friends why won't you tell me!"

"There's nothing to tell!"

"Ok so you brought yourself that new Jag?"

Yasmeen laugh. *"No, I didn't! He did."*

Just tell me who he is damn. Why are you keeping him a secret? I bet Zada and Tia knows who he is, and I know that you told Oscar and Todd. Yass, you told everyone but me!"

"Well since you're all up in my business! There is something that I want to know! Yasmeen folds her hands. *Rosetta are you sleeping with Aaron?"*

Rosetta can feel her underarms starting to sweat. Her heart beating in her throat. Rosetta knows that Yasmeen is looking at her. Rosetta looks away. *"What? No! Sleeping with Aaron...No...no! Why...why would you think that. I mean yes, I do talk to him when every I see him. Yasmeen, I mean just because you broke up with him doesn't mean that I have to stop talking to him. He's a nice guy.*

Yasmeen knows that Rosetta is lying. Yasmeen doesn't care really, she just want's Rosetta to come clean with her lying ass. *"Ok calm down and breathe before you blow a gasket over there!. You got sweat running all down your lying ass face."*

Rosetta wiping her face. *"No, it's hot in here!"*

"It's not hot to me. So, are you going to tell me are you fucking Aaron or not?"

Rosetta walks to the door. *No! No Yasmeen and I don't know where that is coming from Me and my husband are working things out and I am not cheating! Now let me get back to work!"*

"Ok if you say so!"

"Oh, I say so! Have a nice day Yasmeen."

Rosetta rushes out of Yasmeen office and she runs right into Aaron as he's about to knock on Yasmeen office door. Rosetta pushes pass Aaron as they lock eyes. Aaron closes the door in Rosetta face. Rosetta's heart pounds and her mind races. What does Aaron want with Yasmeen? Rosetta ask herself is Aaron the one who brought her the new Jaguar that's parked outside. Rosetta minds gets the best of her and anger takes over. Rosetta reminds herself why she despises Yasmeen. What is it that Aaron sees in her? Rosetta thinks about all the times that she has been fucking Aaron and the only thing that he's ever paid was one car note, gave her five hundred dollars, and a bracelet with Yasmeen name on it. As Aaron steps into Yasmeen office she walks around her desk with urgency.

"What are you doing here and why did you close that door?

"Yasmeen, I need to talk to you!"

Yasmeen walking over to the door. *"No, you need to open this door and leave Aaron!"*

"I just need to talk to you that's all! Just hear me out please."

"Aaron, we can talk out in the hall! Now open this door!"

"Ok have your way."

When Aaron opens the door, Rosetta is standing on the other side with her ear pressed to the door.

"What in the hell are you doing? Get your ass out of here!"

Both Aaron and Yasmeen are surprised to see Rosetta at the door. Rosetta runs back to her office. Inside Yasmeen is laughing her ass off. At the same time, she's trying to figure out what Aaron wants. She can't call Mahmoud because he, Jacob, Ashton, And Maxwell are at a meeting on the other side of town.

"Ok Yasmeen the door is open now will you listen to me?"

"Ok what is?"

"Yasmeen is there something that you want to tell me?"

"Yeah get the hell out of my office!""

Aaron walks over to Yasmeen. *"You know what I'm talking about! Don't lie to me! Let's be honest with each other! Yasmeen are you seeing Brandon? Is he your new man?'*

Yasmeen eyes wide. *"What? Have you lost whatever mind that you had left?. Why would you ever say something so stupid?"*

"Well he asked me if he had a chance with you! Obviously, he has a thing for you!"

"Well Obviously you and Brandon are idiots! Aaron, I don't even like Brandon's bitch ass, so why would I want to date him? Not to mention the fact that he's married! I don't want you and I sure as hell don't want Brandon! Yasmeen walks back to her desk. *You know what get out!*

"Yasmeen, I think that I have a right to know who you are seeing!"

"You don't have the right to know a damn thing about me! I'm a grown ass woman and I can do what I damn well please! The only thing that you need to know is that I am not seeing Brandon and I want you to leave me the hell alone. Take your little ass down the hall to your girlfriend!"

"Who Uma?"

Yasmeen smiles. *"No Rosetta Mr. honest!"*

Aaron is not at all shocked. *"What?"*

"Let's not lie to each other ok Aaron, are, you fuck Rosetta?"

Aaron knows that he can't tell Yasmeen the truth. He looks around the room in a panic. His mouth starts to dry out. It feels like he has a mouth full of cotton. Aaron looks in Yasmeen beautiful chestnut brown eyes.

"No Yasmeen no! I would never lie to you!"

"You just did! Now leave Aaron."

"Yasmeen I'm not lying to you."

"Ok Aaron but what's done in the dark will come to the light."

Aaron walks out without saying a word. Yasmeen smiles she knows that Aaron and Rosetta are both liars, which doesn't matter because Yasmeen heart is with Mahmoud. A week later Rosetta and Aaron are in bed at Rosetta's house. Rosetta has just finished giving Aaron a blow job. Aarons mind is still on Yasmeen. Rosetta can see that Aaron mind is occupied and she knows with who.

Rosetta kissesAaron chest. *"What's on your mind?"*

Aaron push's Rosetta away. *"Nothing, I'm just not feeling you. I need to go!"*

"Where? "

"Away from here! Away from you!'

Rosetta pulls Aaron back onto the bed. *"Why Aaron? I need you! Aaron make love to me."*

"No, I don't love you!"

"What if I were Yasmeen?"

"But you're not."

"I can be. Aaron show me how you would make love to Yasmeen. Aaron, I can make you happy just let me try."

"What about your husband?"

"He moved out, so we don't have to worry about him. Aaron make love to me."

"How about I fucked you like the slut you are!"

Aaron pushes Rosetta down on the bed. He guides his dick into her pussy. She screams as Aaron fucks her. Rosetta grips Aaron's ass as he pushes his hard dick deep inside of her. Aaron pulls his dick out and slaps Rosetta on her pussy with his big hard dick. She cries out in ecstasy. *Fuck me harder daddy! Fuck me!* Rosetta's pussy hungers for Aaron's dick. Aaron has Rosetta legs up on his shoulders when the bedroom door flies open all Aaron hears is *What the fuck*! Before he's hit in the back of his head. Rosetta screams. Aaron falls to the floor where he is kicked repeatedly in the ribs. Aaron looks up as he is punched in the face. He tries to fight back as blood pours from his nose and lip. Aaron doesn't know what to think as he hears Rosetta shouting *Baby, I'm sorry please*! Aaron soon realizes that it's Rosetta husband Wendell who is beating his ass. Aaron scrambles to his feet where he and Wendell continue to fight. Aaron thinks to himself as he runs for the bedroom door. *This has got to be a fucking dream*! Aaron grabs his clothes and makes a dash for the stair when he feels a kick to his ass which sends his tumbling down the stairs. Aaron gets up and runs out the door. Later that same night Yasmeen, Zada, Angelina and Tia join Oscar, Todd, Joshua, and Ashton at their favorite bar. A smile spreads over Yasmeen face when she sees Mahmoud waving her over. He's sitting with Maxwell and Jacob. Yasmeen takes a seat next to Mahmoud who immediately whispers in her ear. *You are so beautiful.* Everyone is laughing, eating and drinking when Rebecca and Rosetta walk in together. Yasmeen looks at Rosetta she can tell that she's been crying.

"Hey lady I wasn't expecting you to come out! Are you ok your eyes..."?

Rosetta cuts Yasmeen off. *"It's nothing! I'm fine."*

Zada looks over at Rosetta. *"Girl it looks like you have been crying right Ash."*

"It sure dose Za."

Rosetta is about to speak when she sees Wendell walk in behind Uma. Rosetta heart damn near stops as he walks over to the table. All she can think is why in the hell is he here. Rosetta can see the anger in Wendell's eyes as he approaches.

"Hey man I didn't know that you were coming!"

Wendell shakes Joshua hand. *"I didn't plan to. I just needed a drink."* Wendell looks at Rosetta. *What is this bitch doing here?"*

Rosetta pled with Wendell. *"Wendell please don't do this."*

"Wendell please my fucking ass. Rosetta, you ain't shit. Why are you sitting here in Yasmeen's face like you are her friend? Yasmeen she is not your friend! Yasmeen, you are too good for this slut!"

"Wendell what are you talking about?"

"Oh, you mean that you haven't told her Rosetta?"

Zada speaks up. *"Told Yasmeen what?"*

Rosetta is on the verge of tears. *"Wendell please!"*

"Oh, so y'all don't know about me catching Rosetta in my house, in my bed fuck Aaron tonight! Rosetta you don't tell them that not only was our daughter not mine, but our three-year-old son also is not mine. Wendell gets in Rosetta's face. Tell Yasmeen how you have been grinning in her face, pretending to be her friend and all the while you have been fucking her ex you nasty foul whore! Rosie tell them how I beat your man's ass! I should have killed the both of you in our bed!"

Joshua takes Wendell outside. "Come on man this is not the place."

"You don't know how much she hurt me!"

"I know man, but this is not how you should be handling this."

Joshua takes Wendell outside. Everyone's looks at Rosetta in disbelief.

Rebecca throws her drink in Rosetta face. *"You have been sleeping with Aaron? Rosetta, how could you?"*

Rebecca runs out of the bar crying. Rosetta looks at Yasmeen she whispers *I'm sorry.* Yasmeen is not at all surprised, but she's still hurt. Rosetta leaves. Yasmeen looks around and all eyes are on her. Mahmoud puts his arms around Yasmeen.

Are you ok?"

"Yes, I'm just great, but I must say this has been a night to remember."

"Are you ready to go?"

"Yes please!"

Yasmeen follows Mahmoud back to his house. Yasmeen turns her cell phone off because it keeps ring and the last thing that she wants to do is talk about what transpired. Yasmeen can feel her body shaking. Mahmoud can see that Yasmeen is still upset. Mahmoud walks up behind Yasmeen. He wrap's his arms around her not knowing what to say. He wonders if Yasmeen still has feelings for Aaron.

"Are you ok Yasmeen?"

Yasmeen turns around without mumbling a word. She throws her arm around Mahmoud's neck and squeeze him so tight. Mahmoud can feel Yasmeen body shaking.

"Sweetheart why are you shaking."

"I was so afraid!"

"Yasmeen afraid of what?"

Yasmeen with tears in her eyes. *"I was afraid that Wendell was going to say your name."*

"My name! Why did you think that?"

"I don't know. All I heard him say was my name and in bed. My mind went blink, so I didn't hear him say Aaron's name at first. I thought that my heart was going to jump out of my chest!"

"Yasmeen, you have nothing to worry about. I would never betray you like that. I need to know are you going to be ok knowing that Aaron…."

Yasmeen cuts Mahmoud off. *"I'm just find. I'm so happy and I don't care about Aaron or Rosetta. I don't want to talk about them. All I care about is you. I mean I feel bad for Wendell, but I'm so happy.* Pushing Mahmoud down to the sofa. *And I'm about to show you how happy I am!"*

Yasmeen pulls her dress up to her waist as she mounts Mahmoud, she delivers soft passionate kisses that devour Mahmoud mouth. Both Mahmoud and Yasmeen fight to unbutton his pants. Mahmoud rips Yasmeen black lace panties off as he guides his hard dick into to Yasmeen moist pussy. As she straddles his waist. Yasmeen lower herself onto Mahmoud dick. She rides ten-inches of Mahmoud's twelve-inch dick with satisfaction. He grabs her buttocks as he bounces her up and down. Yasmeen grinds her pelvis like a washing machine. Mahmoud kisses Yasmeen neck, Yasmeen bites her lip. She wraps her arms around Mahmoud's neck as she welcomes every inch of him inside of her. Mahmoud close his eyes and savor's Yasmeen warm wet tight pussy. Mahmoud grabs Yasmeen shoulders and she holds him tight as she screams. *Oh yes, yes give it to me*! Mahmoud suck and lick Yasmeen nipples.

Mahmoud looking up at Yasmeen. *"You feel so good. Yasmeen my Queen you're amazing."*

Mahmoud carries Yasmeen upstairs for a night filled with pleasure beyond her wildest dreams. Aaron in sitting at his dining room table when the doorbell rings. He makes his way to the door. Just as he opens it Rebecca slaps the shit out of him bruised face.

"How could you do this to me again! Aaron tell me why?

Aaron holds his face as he tells Rebecca. *I'm sorry.* Rebecca falls into Aaron arms sobbing Aaron can see that she's hurting, but all he can think about is Yasmeen. Aaron is about to kiss Rebecca when Uma walks up. Aaron walks upstairs leaving Rebecca and Uma outside. The last thing that he wants is to explain anything to anybody. The next morning Yasmeen is still at Mahmoud's. Yasmeen is getting ready for work when Mahmoud walks up behind her and kisses her on the neck. She smiles as she kisses him lovingly on the cheek. Mahmoud embraces Yasmeen in his arms as he enquires if she's going to be ok going into work knowing that Rosetta and Aaron will be there. Mahmoud is concerned about Yasmeen's emotional state. Yasmeen turns to Mahmoud and puts her arms around his neck. She smiles and ensures him that she's not in the least bit mad at Rosetta or Aaron. She just disappointed in their actions. She tells Mahmoud that Aaron means nothing to her and that she and Rosetta had not been friends for a long time. Yasmeen looks deep into Mahmoud's eye and she tells him that the only thing that would have hurt her is if Mahmoud was the one the Rosetta was sleeping with. Yasmeen jokes as she asks Mahmoud if he has any interest in Rosetta, Rebecca, or Uma. Mahmoud laughs as he whispers in Yasmeen ear. *"How about we get back in bed and discuss this further."* Yasmeen contemplates on taking Mahmoud up on his offer, but she knows that she must go to work. When Yasmeen gets to work Jacob informs her that Rosetta called in. Yasmeen is not at all surprised for she knew that Rosetta didn't want to face her. To Yasmeen surprise Aaron has also called in and Yasmeen is crushed because she really wanted to see what he looked like after getting his ass cut by Wendell. When Yasmeen gets off work she's at all happy to see Rosetta is in her driveway waiting for her. Yasmeen's blood runs cold and all she wants to do is rip Rosetta's face off. She thinks about putting her car in drive and running Rosetta ass over, but why give everybody the satisfaction of seeing her drag that bitch down the street and back for what? Aaron Sinclair! Hell, no he's not worth a bucket with a big ass hole in the bottom. Yasmeen gets out her Jag and strolls to the door. She walks pass Rosetta like she's invisible. Rosetta continues to talk but Yasmeen doesn't hear a damn thing that she's saying because she doesn't give five fucks. Yasmeen opens her house door and slams it close in Rosetta's face. For the next three days Rosetta has been calling and texting Yasmeen nonstop. Yasmeen is getting tired of avoiding Rosetta. For the fourth time Rosetta has showed up at her house like she has something to prove. It's no longer about Aaron shit has just gotten personal. Yasmeen gets out of her car and she confronts Rosetta.

"Why are you in my driveway? Did I tell you to come to my house?"

"No Yasmeen you didn't. I just think that we need to talk."

"There is nothing that you and I need to discuss!"

"Oh, but there is. Yasmeen, you need to know that I'm sorry and I never intended for this to happen."

"Save your bullshit lies, I've heard them all before. You intended for this to happen you just didn't intend for me to find out at least not like this. Rosetta all I want, is to know is why did you push Aaron off on me? Why did you beg me to go out with Aaron knowing that you wanted him? Why didn't you just fuck him without involving me? I had no interest in Aaron and for months it was you who constantly beg me to go out with him! Why did you do that? Did you think that this was a game? Answer me!"

"Yasmeen I'm sorry. "

"Like hell you are!. Do you know what you are? You are a conniving, deceitful bitch who I never want to see again! You have been scheming against me for year's why? What did I ever do to you other then try to be a friend, that would make you so envious of me? First you fucked Oscar and had a baby with him why? Because you thought that I was sleeping with him! I have always told your nasty ass that Oscar, Todd, and I are friends' good friends I would never cross that line! Then you go fuck Aaron, you had the audacity to stand in my face and boldly lie to me after Aaron himself told me that you were calling him! Yeah that night when we all were at the bar your fuck buddy showed me his phone. I knew that you were fucking Aaron! Yasmeen pulls Rosetta arm. *And this Bracelet that he gave you, he brought it for me bitch it has my name on it! Now tell me what the fuck we need to talk about. You Cheated on your husband not once but three times that he knows of! Now you want to play victim. I'll tell you who the victim is! Your husband is a victim for trusting you and your kids are innocent victims who are tangled up in your bullshit! Rosetta do you even know who your son's father is?"*

"Yes! Yes, Yasmeen I do know who my sons' father is!"

"Well unburden yourself and tell me who his father is!"

Rosetta body quakes as tears roll down her face. *"Chase is my sons father Yasmeen! Chase is his father!"*

Yasmeen feels like she had just been punched in the gut. Yasmeen pushes Rosetta onto the hood her car and puts her hands around Rosetta's neck.

"Tell me that you're lying! Rosetta how could you be so low?

"I'm sorry Yasmeen please don't tell Anne-Marie!"

"Rosetta I'm not going to tell her anything, but you are! Does he know?"

"No he doesn't."

"Why? Why would you? Rosetta she's your friend. How could you betray her?"

"It just happened. Yasmeen did you and chase…"

Yasmeen is beyond furious. *"Hell, no I would never do that to Anne-Marie! We were friends no matter what happened between us I would never do something so foul! I guess that's the difference between you and me. I'm a friend until the end!"*

Rosetta calling out to Yasmeen. *"Are you still my friend? Yasmeen please I need you now more than ever. Yasmeen please!*

Yasmeen makes her way into her house where she collapses on the floor sobbing. All she can think about is Oscar and that there's a chance that he may be infected with HIV. Yasmeen calls Mahmoud and he rushes to her side. Yasmeen tells Mahmoud everything. Mahmoud holds Yasmeen, he assures her that everything will be ok. Yasmeen wants to believe him but, in her mind, all she can think about is how is she going to tell Oscar that there is a chance that he may be infected. The next morning Yasmeen can't wait to get to work. Yasmeen is damn near running through the lobby when she sees Aaron walking towards her. Both of his eyes are still black and blue. He looks like the shit that he is. Yasmeen can see that he's waiting on her and she would love nothing more than to ask him about his fight with Wendell but she on a mission. Without breaking her stride Yasmeen walks pass Aaron pushing him to the side. *"Not right now!"* Yasmeen gets on the elevator her heart is pounding she can feel her anger growing as she enters Chase office he is sitting at his computer.

"We need to talk, and we need to talk now!"

Chase looks up at Yasmeen. *"Good morning to you too!"*

Yasmeen walks over to Chase. *"Don't fuck with me! Chase, you know good and hell well why I'm here!"*

Chase can see the anger in Yasmeen eyes. His mind flashes back to the last time that he saw Yasmeen this upset thing, did not go so well. Chase has no idea as to what Yasmeen is talking about and he doesn't want to find out, because he knows that it can't be good for Yasmeen to come barging in his office like a mad woman. He contemplates on kicking her out like she did him, but he recants that thought before it develops fully in him head.

"Yasmeen, you are the one who came busting in my office!"

"Ok and your point is?"

"Yasmeen I'm just saying that I don't know what's going on. By no means I'm I trying to fight with you, but I don't know what you're talking about. Can you please tell me, please?"

"Chase I'm sure that you have an idea!. Chase did you tell your wife about your situation?"

Chase take a deep breath. *"No Yasmeen I didn't, but I did get checked and I convinced Anne-Marie to get checked as well and we both are negative. Yes, what's her name is positive but I'm not. Look Yasmeen I know that you and I are nowhere near friends but thanks for not saying anything."*

"Oh, I wasn't about to do your dirty work! Since we're on the subject of dirty work are you going to tell Anne about you and her other best friend?"

Chase look at Yasmeen with uncertainty. In his mind he questions what in the hell is Yasmeen talking about and he dare to ask as his heart races. Chase mouth starts to dry out and beads of sweat forms on his forehead. Chase rubs his face, because he knows that he's about to regret asking Yasmeen what friend? *"Other friend? She doesn't have another best friend."*

"So, I guess that you have amnesia now. Well let me help you out! Let me see if I can help you remember Your wife's other best friend. What's her name? Oh yeah Rosetta. You do remember Rosetta don't you, because she too was in your wedding!"

Chase falls back in his seat and close his eyes tight. Again, this is not what he wanted to hear. Chase wonders is Yasmeen out to get him for breaking up she and Anne-Marie's friendship or maybe she wants him? Hell no! Chase dismisses that thought because he knows better. Yasmeen has always hated him with her smart mouth, and he never cared much for her because she has always been so out spoken. That the one thing that Chase despised most of all and the fact that she always knows other people's fucking business.

"Rosetta!"

"Chase don't lie to me, because she already told me about you and her! Now you are going to do the same! All I want to know is why? That's all!"

"Ok Rosetta and I messed around for a little while before Anne and I got married. I ended things with her after we got married. Yasmeen that's why I didn't want you and Anne to be friends because I didn't want to take the chance on her finding out."

"So, you and Rosetta are no longer fucking? Is that the lie you want me to believe?"

Chase exhales. *"Yasmeen ok we have been together off and on but it's not like that! I mean yes, we fuck from time to time. Yasmeen, I know that it's wrong and you were right about me I'm a dog, but I love my wife. Yasmeen please don't tell her. I promise you that I haven't fucked with her in over five months. I think that that's why she started sleeping with Aaron.* Chase smiles. *Your Aaron or should I say your use to be Aaron*

"Well that might be one reason, but she has always wanted Aaron, but that just water under the bridge. I've been over Aaron, but let me wipe that smirk off your pathetic face by saying congratulations You know Rosetta son?"

"Yes."

"Well he's yours. Yasmeen turn and walk out. *Oh, I suggest that you tell Anne-Marie because things are about to get real ugly, real, quick for you. So, keep smiling and have a nice day!"*

Chase runs behind Yasmeen. *"What? Yasmeen wait what do you mean her son is mine! Please tell me that you're fucking kidding me!"*

Yasmeen spitefully smile. *"Oh now Mr. Brice you know that kidding is the one thing that I don't do when it come to you. Oh, I see that you are no longer smiling what did that mean lady tell you some unpleasant news? Don't worry it's going to be ok your wife will understand. Who's smiling now you bastard!"*

Chase tries to get Yasmeen to come back and tell him that she's just joking. Chase runs back in his office where he paces the floor. Chase thinks that this can't be happening. There is no way that Rosetta's son is his. What will he tell Anne-Marie, his wife who just found out that she's pregnant with their second child? Yasmeen walks down the hall smiling to herself after she thanks God. Yasmeen knows that she still has to tell Oscar just so that he knows. Yasmeen is about to leave to meet Oscar for lunch when she gets a knock at the door. She hopes that it' not Rosetta again. Yasmeen yells out come in and in walks Uma. Yasmeen rolls her eyes as she sits her Louis Vuitton bag down on her desk and mumbles to herself *"Not this bitch!"* Yasmeen can only imagine what she wanted, and Yasmeen is in no mood for Uma's shit.

"What do you want?"

"Yasmeen did you know?"

"Know what?"

"Know about Aaron and Rosetta!"

Yasmeen picks up her bag. *"I didn't know, and I don't care! They are not my concern. Now if you would excuse me, I'm on my way to lunch."*

Uma hold back tears. *"Look Yasmeen I know that you don't care for me."*

"And you would be right!"

"Yasmeen, I just want to know why Aaron did this?"

"Uma you're asking the wrong person! Rosetta office is out there and I'm sure that you know where to find Aaron. All I can tell you is that I have a bag full of fucks and I don't give one!"

Uma breaks down. *"Yasmeen please help me!"*

"Uma what do you want from me? What can I do besides walk you down to Rosetta's office? I've told you I don't give a fuck. You should be having this conversation with your man not me!"

"But you dated him too!"

"Ok and?"

"Yasmeen tell me want I should do!"

"Move on, get over it!"

"But I love him, and I know that you loved him too!"

Yasmeen walk over to Uma. *"Now that's where you're wrong! I never loved him! Yes, I did care for him like you care for a pair of cheap shoes. You buy them, you wear them a couple times. They hurt your feet, so you throw them in the trash and you buy a better pair."*

"So, you don't have any feeling for Aaron?"

"Sweetie I've moved onto, much bigger and better things and I suggest that you do the same! Uma, I don't have to tell you that Aaron's full of shit. Why would you want to be with someone who you know is cheating on you with multiple women? Uma, you should care more about yourself. Now I really have to go."

Yasmeen and Uma exit's her office. Uma watches Yasmeen as she disappears down the hall, she wishes that she had Yasmeen attitude and strength. Uma's heart is broken all she can do is cry. Why can't she let go? What is it about Aaron that makes her love him when he treats her like shit? After work Yasmeen is on her way to her car when she sees Rebecca. Rebecca heart drops as Yasmeen walks pass her smiling without so much as a hello. Rebecca really wants to talk to Yasmeen, but she knows that Yasmeen will only tear her down. Rebecca knows how Yasmeen must have felt when Aaron cheated on her. She can't say sorry enough because she feels the same hurt if not more. Rebecca thought that Rosetta was her friend. She confided in that bitch and all the while she was fucking her man right under her nose. Yasmeen, rush's home to get ready for her date with Mahmoud. Yasmeen get out of her car and runs to the door she doesn't see Aaron walking up behind her.

"Well it's about time you got home!"

Yasmeen turns around and all the color drains from her face when she sees Aaron standing behind her smiling.

"Aron what are you doing here? You need to leave now!"

Aaron pulls Yasmeen by her arm. *"No, we need to talk!"*

"Aaron there is nothing that you and I need to talk about, now leave!"

"Yasmeen, I just wanted to tell you that I'm sorry."

"Aaron, you don't have to apologize to me about anything. You and I are finished!"

"Yasmeen no we're not so don't say that we are!"

Yasmeen fear turns to rage. *"Aaron we're done! You disgust me, and I can't believe that I ever dated you!"*

"Yasmeen please!"

"Please what Aaron? Please listen to you lie to me again!"

"Yasmeen, I made a mistake by sleeping with your friend. Yass, I was wrong!"

Yasmeen shakes her head. *"Aaron how many times are we going to have this conversation about you and your cheating ways? Aaron, you are a grown ass man, you know what the hell you're doing, so don't come to my home with you made a mistake, you deliberately lied to me, watch I already knew! Now put your big boy trousers on and own up to your shit! Aaron, you have hurt some many people."*

"Including you."

"No not this time. You stop hurting me a long time ago. I am talking about Uma, Rebecca, Wendell, and only God know who else."

"Yasmeen that was something that just happened!"

"No Wendell beating the hell out of you is something that just happened. You fucking Rosetta is a nasty habit of yours!"

"Yasmeen, I need help and I need you!"

"No what you need to do is leave me alone!"

"Yasmeen answer one question for me and I'll leave."

"Ok Aaron what is it?"

"Yasmeen are you seeing someone?"

"I've told you that yes I am and he makes me happy."

"Are you sleeping with him?"

Yasmeen walking away. "You said one question that's two!"

"Who is he? Do I know him Yass?"

Yasmeen unlocking the door. "Good bye Aaron!"

"Yasmeen who is he? Are you fucking Maxwell or Ashton?"

"Are you out of your fucking mind! I'm not you!"

Yasmeen slam the door in Aarons face. At dinner Yasmeen tells Mahmoud about Aaron. Mahmoud is furious. He has told Yasmeen many times that she should move, but Yasmeen has refused. Mahmoud starts to question why Yasmeen continues to stay in a place where she's not happy.

"Why want you move? Do you like Aaron popping up at your place unannounced anytime he wants?"

"No, I don't like it!"

Mahmoud tries not to yell. *"Well move damn it!"*

"Move where! Mahmoud it's not like I can just up and move!"

"Yass yes you can! Let me help you."

"I can't!"

"You can if you wanted to! I need to leave!"

"Mahmoud please! I do want to move, and I have been looking but…"

"But what? Is it about money? If so, I'll pay it. You don't have to worry about anything just tell me where. Let me help you gorgeous. You are my Queen and I want to make you happy."

"Ok."

"Ok and in the mean time you're going to stay with me!"

"Mahmoud, I can't!'

"You can, and you will. Yasmeen I'm not going to take a chance on you getting hurt!"

Yasmeen knows that Mahmoud means well so she decides not to resist his offer and to allow Mahmoud to help her. Yasmeen smiles as she kisses Mahmoud. Mahmoud holds Yasmeen in his arms as he whispers. *"My Queen there is nothing that I wouldn't do for you.* Yasmeen heart pounds with passion but is soon replaced with despair when reality hits her in the face. Mahmoud is not hers to keep. He's already promised to someone else. How can she let Mahmoud go after all the heart wants what the heart wants, but she will never hurt anybody like Aaron hurt her? Yasmeen Smile because in her mind she tells herself *"Well who says that I can't have fun in the meantime."* Yasmeen just hopes that when the time comes, she can let Mahmoud go.

Chapter 12

When it comes back around and lands on you...

After the Monday meeting Yasmeen and Ashton are conversating when Uma walks up, she needs to talk to Ashton. Yasmeen walks away because she really doesn't want to hear what Uma has to say. Yasmeen arrives at Mahmoud's office, she greets Nancy Lockhart Mahmoud's secretary. Nancy is an older Hispanic lady with long salt and pepper hair that she keeps braided up in a bun. She has olive skin tone, brown eyes, and thin red lips with a beautiful smile. When Nancy looks up and see Yasmeen she runs around her desk. She is happy to see Yasmeen she thinks of Yasmeen as her daughter and Yasmeen look at her as a mother figure.

"*It's about time that you came to see me!*"

"*You know that I had to come see my favorite lady.*"

Nancy Kiss Yasmeen on her cheek. "*You better. You are so beautiful Yasmeen and it's just makes my day to see you. Oh, and I made you some cookies.*"

"*Thank you. You know how I love your cookies. Is doctor Shashivivek in?*"

Nancy looks over her glasses. "*Yes, he is.*"

"*Do you know if he's with a patient? I need to see him.*"

"*No, he's not. He just went in his office.*"

"*Good!*"

"*Be nice Yasmeen he's a good man, you need to stop giving him such a hard time. As a matter of fact, I think that he likes you.*"

Yasmeen smiles to herself. "*Really well I hope that he likes me enough to sign these orders or we're going to have a problem!*"

"Yasmeen be nice!"

Yasmeen looks back over her shoulder. *"What I'm always nice."*

As Yasmeen walks away a big smile spreads across her face as she thinks. *"If only you knew!"* Before Yasmeen knocks on Mahmoud's door she adjusts her dress so that her beautiful brown cleavage shows. Yasmeen is wearing a dark purple dress that wraps around her waist and is secured by a square shaper button. Yasmeen licks her soft lips when she hears Mahmoud's voice telling her to come in. Yasmeen opens the door just enough to peek her head in. When Mahmoud looks up and see Yasmeen standing in the door he gets up from his desk and rush over to her. Mahmoud pulls Yasmeen inside and quickly close the door.

"You know that you didn't have to knock. My door is always open to you."

"Well I didn't want to disturb you."

"Too late, you've put an end to my work for the day."

"I sorry maybe I should let you get back to work?"

Mahmoud pulls Yasmeen back to him. He grabs her ass as he kisses her neck. Yasmeen holds her head back and close her eyes. Mahmoud kisses feels so good Yasmeen doesn't want him to stop. Just feeling Mahmoud's breath on her ear sends shivers down Yasmeen's spine. Mahmoud whispers in Yasmeen's ear. *"I want you now!"* Mahmoud, picks Yasmeen up and sits. her down on his desk, with Yasmeen long legs around his waist. Mahmoud rip Yasmeen panties off and insert his long finger inside of Yasmeen wet pussy.

"We can't do this here!"

"Why not? Yasmeen don't you want me?"

"You know that I do, but what it someone walks in?"

"Don't worry about that I lock the door. You're so beautiful and you feel so good."

"What about these papers that I need you to sign Doctor?"

Mahmoud undo Yasmeen dress. "Oh, those papers can wait!"

Yasmeen unzip Mahmoud's pants. *"Are you sure that you want me?"*

"Oh, I'm sure and I'm about to show you!"

Mahmoud stands between Yasmeen parted legs he pulls her close So that her ass is hanging slightly off the edge of his desk. Yasmeen wraps her long legs tightly around Mahmoud's waist as he put his hands on her hips and introduce his hard dick to her wet pussy. Yasmeen leans back on her elbows and enjoy Mahmoud as he sucks on her nipples. Mahmoud thrust his big dick in and out of Yasmeen tight pussy. Mahmoud moans, he can feel Yasmeen clenching down on his dick. He can no longer control himself. Mahmoud cums so hard that Yasmeen can feel his dick pulsing inside of her. They both scream. "Shhh…" Yasmeen grinds her hip as Mahmoud looks down at his dick covered in his and Yasmeen juices. Yasmeen puts her legs down and Mahmoud bends Yasmeen over his desk where he enters her from behind. Theirs a knock at the door. Mahmoud thrust slows down, but he doesn't stop. The last thing that Mahmoud wants is for Yasmeen to leave, he could careless who's at the door.

The voice at the door calls out. "Doctor Shashivivek!"

Mahmoud out of breath. *"Go away I'm busy!"*

Without another work Mahmoud thrust his dick deep inside Yasmeen. With Mahmoud hand over her mouth Yasmeen tries to hold in her scream Yasmeen explodes in ecstasy. Mahmoud gently bites Yasmeen on her ass.

"Don't leave!"

"I have to get back to work and clean myself up."

"Well I do have a restroom in here, so allow me to help you."

Mahmoud picks Yasmeen up and carries her to the restroom in his office. He sits her on the sink. Mahmoud dick starts to harden as he kisses Yasmeen. With Yasmeen legs around his waist Mahmoud thrust his big hard dick inside Yasmeen sweet wet pussy. After another thirty minutes Yasmeen is on her way back to her office. She smiles as she thinks about what just happened and the fact that she has a good three hours to go with no panties on. Yasmeen text Mahmoud. *"Where are my panties?"* He texts back *"In my pocket!"* Yasmeen can't stop smiling as she texts back "Why?" Mahmoud answers *"Because they are mine and so are you!"* with a smiley face. Yasmeen smiles as she walks to her office door when she looks up, she sees Rosetta watching her. They lock eyes as Yasmeen enters her office. Yasmeen is in her office watching the clock she can't wait until lunch so that she can go back to Mahmoud's house take a shower and put on some panties. Yasmeen laughs to herself at the thought of her sitting in her office bare ass. Yasmeen looks down at her phone when she realizes that it has been a week and she has not heard from Aaron not once. Yasmeen smile as she looks up at the ceiling and thank God. Yasmeen returns to her office after lunch and She's really feeling herself, but not for long. As Yasmeen walks down the hall she can see Anne-Marie pacing nervously in front of her door. Yasmeen steps slows as she approaches. Before Yasmeen can get a word out of her mouth Anne-Marie speaks.

"Hey, Yasmeen it's been a long time."

"Yes, it has."

Anne-Marie smile nervously as she searches for her words. *"Yasmeen I'm sorry for coming to your office like this, but I really need to talk to you."*

Yasmeen can only imagine what Anne-Marie has to say. Thoughts start to run thought Yasmeen's head. Why does Anne-Marie want to talk to her, they're no longer friend and they haven't spoken to each other in years. Why now? Yasmeen hesitates before she speaks. "Talk to me, about what?"

"Yasmeen, you are the only one that I… look Yasmeen I just need to talk to you please."

"Ok talk I'm listening!"

"Can we talk in your office? I really don't want to talk out here in the opening."

Yasmeen takes a deep breath she and Anne-Marie enters her office. Yasmeen takes her seat behind her desk with anticipation.

"You may have a seat Anne-Marie."

"Oh, thank you. So how have you been?"

"That enough small talk! Now what do you want to talk to me about?"

"You're right. Let me start by saying that I'm sorry about everything. I wish that I could go back in time where we were friends, but I can't. Yasmeen even though we are no longer friends you are the one person that I know I can confide in."

"Well if we were friends you could confided in me. I mean Rosetta is down the hall!"

"Yeah about her! I guess that you haven't heard!"

"Heard what?"

Anne-Marie fight to hold back her tears. *"That she and I are no longer friends and my husband, and I are no longer together!"*

"Oh, I'm sorry to hear that, but may I ask why?"

"Well Rosetta had Chase served with child support papers and we found out that my husband is the father of her son. Tears start to roll down Anne-Marie face. I found out that they have been having an affair before and after we were married. Oh, but that's not the kicker. My husband who promised

me that he would never cheat or hurt me has also been sleeping with my other ex-best friend and she's HIV positive."

Yasmeen trying to act surprised, because she already knew about everything but the child support papers. Yasmeen heart breaks. She goes over to Anne-Marie and tries to console her. *"I'm so sorry. Anne, you don't deserve this."*

"Yasmeen, I don't know what I'm going to do. I trusted them, and they betrayed me. What I'm I going to do?"

"I'll tell you what you're going to do. You're going to wipe your tears, hold your head up and go back to work. When you get off, you are going to go talk to Oscar and you're going to ask him what you need to do. Now what you're not going to do is sit here and feel sorry for yourself. Yes, I know that it hurts but it's going to be ok. Anne-Marie I'm not telling you not to cry. What I'm telling you is don't cry here don't give them the pleasure of seeing you break down. Don't let them win. Let them see how strong you are even though you're weak."

"But I still love my husband."

"And that ok but you make him pay for what he's done. You know why he's doing this to you? Well I'll tell you. It's because he can! He knows that you're not going anywhere because he has all the money and you depend on him. It's time that you stood on your own two feet. Girl you have a good job, you're educated…"

"But he has all my money to. We have a joint account, and everything is in his name."

"Your dumb ass! I mean why would you do that? What in the hell is wrong with you?"

"It was his idea."

"You know what you're sitting here when you should be at the bank withdrawing your money!"

"You're right. Should I go now?"

"You should have gone, when you first found out."

"You're right! Thank you, Yasmeen. Thank you for everything!"

"Anne-Marie just because you love someone doesn't give them the right to mistreat you. He should love you as much as you love him. If you're give him a hundred percent, then he should be giving you the same and nothing less. I'm not telling you to end your marriage. I'm telling you to stand up for yourself."

"I promise you that I will. Can I call you later?"

"Sure, you can, but not too late."

It has been a week and Anna-Marie has been calling Yasmeen every day. Yasmeen knows that she's hurting, and Yasmeen can only imagine how she feels. After hearing Anna-Marie crying night after night Yasmeen doesn't have the heart to tell her that they can never be friends and to stop calling her. Yasmeen does her best to console her. The last thing that Yasmeen wants is for Anna-Marie to think that they are friends because friends they will never be after Anna-Marie turned her back on Yasmeen for three years for a no, good cheating ass man. Yasmeen has been living with Mahmoud for a month and they are having the time of their life. Yasmeen knows that their arrangement is only temporary until her house is ready which will be in two weeks. Yasmeen knows that Mahmoud doesn't want her to go and she don't want to but they both know that it's for the best at least that's the story that Yasmeen keeps telling herself. After an hour of having sex with Mahmoud he looks into Yasmeen eye with so much passion, before he whispers "I love you!" Yasmeen heart stops and she can't find the words. Yasmeen looks at Mahmoud like he just called her a bitch. She can see that he is waiting for her to respond, but she can't. Yasmeen pushes Mahmoud away as she tells him *"It's getting last and I'm sleepy."* Yasmeen can see the hurt in Mahmoud eyes as he rolls over to his side of the bed without saying another word. The next morning Mahmoud leave before Yasmeen gets up. For two days Mahmoud avoids Yasmeen. Yasmeen knows that she must make things right with Mahmoud before she moves out, because the last thing that she wants to do is hurt Mahmoud. Yasmeen question herself how can Mahmoud be in love her when he belongs to someone else? Yasmeen is on her way to Mahmoud office, she knows that he has just finished surgery and he has an hour before his next one. Yasmeen refuse to spend her last days have Mahmoud not talking to her or holding her at night. As Yasmeen rushes to Mahmoud office she passes Aaron whom she has not talked to in weeks.

"And good morning to you Yasmeen!"

"Hey Aaron! Bye Aaron!"

"Hey Aaron! Bye Aaron! What kind of shit is that! Yasmeen what is your problem?"

Yasmeen looks back. *"Right now, you're my problem!"*

Aaron stepping in front of Yasmeen. "*I haven't talked to you in weeks and that's how you address me? Oh, I get it! You miss me.*"

"*No as a matter of fact I'm over the moon that you haven't been talking to me, please keep up the good work!*"

"*You know what Yasmeen I'm so glad that I'm over you.*"

"*That makes two of us. It would be better if you also forget my name and not speak to me. Aaron pretend that I'm in visible and you don't see me!*"

"*You know what Yasmeen you think that you're God's gift to men! I mean you walk around here with your, don't care attitude and that your big ass. I know your kind. You want some attention!*"

"*Not from you and my man loves my big ass. Aaron, I don't think that I'm God's gift to men, I'm only a gift to him and he likes it when I give him my gift, especially when I give him his gift in the morning.*"

"*Go to hell Yasmeen!*"

"*I went, but they sent me back. Satin said that he only had one spot for you, now move you have wasted enough of my time!*"

"*Oh, so I'm a waste of time?*"

"*You have always been a waste of time to me!*"

"*So, Yasmeen you don't miss me?*"

"*Who are you?*"

Yasmeen walks away smiling as Aaron kicks over a trashcan. Yasmeen rushes to Mahmoud office just as he is about to leave. Her heart is pounding, and she can feel her knees shaking as Mahmoud looks up at her. Yasmeen can still see that he's hurt.

"*Mahmoud, I need to talk to you…I have something to tell you.*"

"*Can it wait? I have to be in surgery in thirty minutes.*"

"*No, it can't wait.*"

Mahmoud walks over to Yasmeen.

"What is it that you want to tell me? That your house is ready? Is that it?"

"*Yes, the house is ready, but that's not what I wanted to talk to you about. Mahmoud… Mahmoud do you hate me?*"

Mahmoud pulls Yasmeen over to him. He looks in her beautiful brown eyes. "*Yasmeen, I don't hate you! Why would you say that?*"

"*Well you haven't talked to me or touched me in two days.*"

"*Yasmeen I'm sorry but…*"

"*Mahmoud will you forgive me?*"

"Forgive you for what Yasmeen?"

Yasmeen inhale with tears in her eyes. *"I wanted tell you, but I was afraid."*

"Tell me what Yasmeen?"

"That I love you. Mahmoud, I love you." Before Yasmeen can get another, I love you out Mahmoud kisses her. *"Yasmeen, I love you my Queen!"*

"I love you my king. I had better let you get to surgery."

Mahmoud holds Yasmeen in his arms. *"You're not going anywhere until you tell me that you love me again.*

"Mahmoud Shashivivek, I love you."

"Why do you love me?"

"There is so reason for my love for you. I love you because of who you are. I love you for being you. There is not condition for my love. I don't have a reason why just know that I love you. Now why do you love me?"

Mahmoud kiss Yasmeen. *"I don't need a reason like you I love you because I do. I love you Yasmeen Blake."*

Yasmeen walks back to her office she can't stop smiling and she can't wait to tell Oscar and Todd. Yasmeen body feels light as she catches herself twirling down the hall like a child. Yasmeen looks at her cellphone and smile as she reads *"I LOVE YOU."* After work Yasmeen rush's out of her office she can wait to get home to Mahmoud. when Yasmeen gets to her car, Rosetta is wait for her. With her car remote in hand Yasmeen walks over to Rosetta. Yasmeen mind starts to race. Why is she still here and what does she want? For days Rosetta has been evading Yasmeen at all cost.

"Can you move away from my car?"

"Yasmeen, we need to talk."

"Is it about work?"

"No!"

Yasmeen unlocks her car door. *"Well there's nothing that we need to talk about!"*

"Yasmeen please talk to me! I've gone by your house but you're never there at least when I come by."

Yasmeen walk over to Rosetta. *"Rosetta you dodge me all day and now you want to talk. We don't have anything to talk about and stop coming by my house!"*

"Yasmeen, we have a lot to talk about!"

"Oh yeah like what?"

"Like Aaron!"

"Bitch we don't need to talk about Aaron. Fuck you and Aaron!"

"Yasmeen please!"

"Please my ass! Girl I don't want to talk to you about and Aaron, he's your problem!"

"Yasmeen, I fucked up… My life, my marriage, our friendship, everything is over."

"And who's fault is that?"

"Mine Yasmeen it's my fault. Look I know that you have heard about Chase being the father of my son."

"Yes, I did."

"You know that Anne-Marie is not talking to me."

"Do you blame her. Rosetta You and her, were supposed to be best friends and you were sleeping with her husband all this time! Oh, and not to mention the fact that you had his baby. How low down is that?"

"I made a mistake! Nobody's perfect!"

"And you're, right nobody's perfect, but to say that you made a mistake is an understatement. A mistake is putting salt in your tea instead of sugar, not fucking your best friend husband. Oh, wait you didn't know that he was her husband because you were only a bride's maid in her wedding! You know what Rosetta save the bullshit!"

"You're right like always Yasmeen you're right!"

"Look bitch don't patronize!"

"I'm not. I'm sorry, I just need someone to talk to"

"Go talk to Aaron because I have to go!"

Yasmeen gets in her car and drive off. Rosetta falls to the ground sobbing. As Yasmeen drive home, she can't help but to think about how fucked up things are all around her. Yasmeen takes a long deep breath and thank God for opening her eyes before it was too late. Yasmeen rush into Mahmoud house she runs upstairs undress and jump in the shower. Yasmeen is standing in the middle of the bedroom floor rubbing lotion all over her smooth chocolate skin she is about to put on one of Mahmoud button-down dress shirts when she hears a voice behind her. *"No need to put that on!"* Yasmeen spins round only to see Mahmoud standing in the door with two glasses of wine in his hand. Mahmoud walks over to Yasmeen and kisses her on the nape of her neck. *"It took you long enough I was about to come in after you."* Yasmeen wraps her arms around Mahmoud neck very seductively. *"And why didn't you?"* Mahmoud kisses Yasmeen soft lips. *"Oh, I am!"* Mahmoud lifts Yasmeen up and carries her back in to the bathroom naked. Yasmeen can feel Mahmoud dick hardening and she can't wait to have him inside of her. Yasmeen and Mahmoud are standing face to face as the water runs over their bodies. Mahmoud cups both of Yasmeen perky breast in him hands before sucks on her nipples. Yasmeen grippes Mahmoud's ass, she can feel the tip of his long tongue as it traces up and down her breast. Yasmeen wraps her legs around Mahmoud neck as he buries, his face between Yasmeen legs. Mahmoud hold Yasmeen up on his shoulders as he licks her wet pussy. Yasmeen body shakes. Soon Mahmoud has Yasmeen bent over the sinks with his big hard dick inside of her wet tight pussy. Mahmoud moans he can feel the walls of Yasmeen warm pussy squeezing his dick and sucking him deep inside of her. Yasmeen scream as Mahmoud rhythm starts to quicken as he thrust his dick in and out of her. Yasmeen legs weaken as she Cum. Mahmoud holds Yasmeen wet body in his arms and he whispers. *"Are you ready for round two?"* It has been two weeks and Yasmeen's is finally moving in to her new house with the help of her friend's and four professional movers. Yasmeen pull one of her many handbags down from the closet shelf a picture of Gregory falls to the floor. When Yasmeen see's the picture she falls to the floor sobbing. Oscar and Todd walks in to find Yasmeen on the floor.

"Yass what's wrong?"

"I can't do this! Oscar I can't…"

"You can't do what Yass?"

"I can't leave! This was me and Greg's home. I can't leave him here!"

Oscar taking the picture from Yasmeen. *"Yass you're not leaving Gregory, he's gone, and you will always carry him in your heart, you have to move on., we have talked about this. You know Greg would want you to be happy and he's not at peace knowing that you are here on earth miserable and alone thinking about him."*

"But I still love him."

"I know you do, and you are also in love with Mahmoud right."

"Yes but…"

Todd takes the picture out of Oscar hand. *"No butts! I tell you what I'm going to take this and you're going to stop crying because we still have work to do!"*

"Todd wait you can't throw Greg's picture away!"

"I'm not I'm just going to hang on to it for you ok."

After four hours everything in Yasmeen townhouse is gone so is everyone else. Yasmeen looks around for the last time and smile as she thinks about Gregory. Yasmeen walks to the door she looks back. *"Come on sweetheart it's time for us to go. Greg, I want you to know that I'm happy and I will never forget you. I love you."* Yasmeen locks the door her phone rings it's Mahmoud. Yasmeen smiles with delight as she walks to her car. Yasmeen looks up in surprise.

"Aaron what are you going here?"

"Well it's good to see you too my love!"

"Mahmoud how far away are you? Aaron is here!"

"What? Yasmeen I'll be there in a minute!"

Aaron walks over to Yasmeen. *"You have been avoiding me Yasmeen!"*

"I don't know what you're talking about, but you need to leave!"

"Yass, I have been come over here every night for three weeks and you're never here. Why Yasmeen? Is it that your new man is fucking the shit out of you nightly or are you just trying to piss me off?"

"I don't care about you being pissed! Now get out of my way shit bag!"

Aaron push's Yasmeen onto her car. *"Don't you dare walk away from me! Now we going to go back inside and you're going to fuck me too!"*

"Aaron get off me! Stop it!"

"You know what? Aaron pins Yasmeen hand down. *I'm going to fuck you right here!"*

Yasmeen is still fighting to get Aaron off her when Mahmoud pulls up. Mahmoud runs over to Aaron and hits him in the back of the head. Aaron falls to the ground in pain. Mahmoud picks Aaron up by his neck and tosses him over the hood of Yasmeen car. Mahmoud takes Yasmeen into his arms.

"Are you ok sweetheart? Mahmoud looks Yasmeen over. I'm here now!"

Aaron can't believe his eyes as he picks himself up. *"Sweetheart! What in the hell do you mean Sweetheart! Yasmeen please don't tell me that you two are together!"*

"I'll tell you! Yes, we're together and don't you ever touch my woman again or you will be sorry!"

"Are you serious. Please tell me that you're kidding!"

"This is not a joke Aaron! Yasmeen and I are a couple and we have been for a while now. Mahmoud helps Yasmeen in her car. *Are you sure that you're ok?"*

"Yasmeen, how could you? He doesn't want you! He's just using you. Yasmeen this man is engaged! You don't mean shit to him!"

Aaron can feel his warm tears running down his face as he watches Mahmoud kiss Yasmeen. It's at that moment Aaron knows that Mahmoud and Yasmeen are lovers. His heart aches.

"I wonder what your father has to say about this!"

Mahmoud pulls his cell phone out and hands it to Aaron. *"I don't know why you don't call him and find out!"*

Mahmoud push's Aaron to the ground. Both Mahmoud and Yasmeen drive away leaving Aaron behind screaming obscenities. Aaron can't control his anger, so he picks up a brick and hurl it through the window where he discovers that the townhouse is empty, and Yasmeen is gone. *"That Bitch!"* Aaron runs to his car. His face is wet with his tears as rage takes over him. Aaron contemplate going over to Mahmoud's house and confronting him, but he knows that he's no match for Mahmoud. As Aaron drives down the highway all he can think about is Yasmeen and how she has hurt him. Aaron feels like he has been driving for hours thinks to himself *"I should have killed her when I had the chance!"* Aaron weeps because he knows that Yasmeen is never coming back. Aaron pulls up in the driveway and jumps out of his car. Leaping up to the front door Aaron bangs on the door. The door open and Aaron push his way in.

"You knew about this didn't you Rosette!"

"Knew about what? And what happened to you?"

Aaron grab Rosetta by her face. *"About Yasmeen and Mahmoud and don't worry about what happened to me! Just answer my fucking question!"*

"I don't know what you're talking about Aaron! Aaron you're hurting me!"

"Rosetta, I know that you knew about them and don't you lie to me! Rosetta tell me the truth!"

"I am telling you the truth! I don't know anything about Yasmeen and Mahmoud!"

Aaron push Rosetta onto the sofa. *"Oh, so you didn't know that Yasmeen was seeing Mahmoud? Is that what you want me to believe you stupid bitch?"*

"Aaron, I didn't know sweetheart. This is the first time that I've heard of this…Aaron are you sure…I mean who told you this Uma?

"Am I sure? Hell, yeah, I'm sure and nobody told me shit I saw them with my own eyes! I don't need Uma to tell me a damn thing. I was at Yasmeen house…"

"You were at Yasmeen's house? Why Aaron? Why were you at Yasmeen's house?"

"Because I wanted to! Don't you ever question me about where I go! Who in the hell do you think you are!"

"You're right Aaron and I'm sorry. So, did Mahmoud do this to you?"

"No, I did this to myself! What the hell do you think? You know what I blame you for this and I can't be here with you right now!"

"You blame me? What did I do Aaron? I didn't tell you to go fuck Rebecca! You did that on your own! So, if you want to blame someone, I suggest you go look in the mirror!"

"Who in the fuck do you think you're talking to? Bitch I'll knock your head off your fucking shoulder!"

"I sorry Aaron! You promised me that you would never hit me again."

"Well I lied!" Aaron grabs Rosetta by the back of her head and shoves her to the floor. Aaron is about to leave when Rosetta grabs him by the leg begging. *"Aaron please don't leave I said that I was sorry! Please don't go!* Aaron push Rosetta away and walk out the door. The last thing that Aaron want is for Rosetta to see him cry. Aaron can still hear Rosetta calling his name as he drives away. When Aaron get to Rebecca house, she is outside waiting for him with open arms. Aaron tells Rebecca everything as he holds back his tears. Rebecca kisses Aaron she knows just what he needs, and she will do anything to get Aaron's mind off Yasmeen even if it's only for three hours. As Rebecca suck on Aaron hard dick he still can't stop thinking about Yasmeen and if she's making love to Mahmoud the way she should have make love to him. It Monday morning Mahmoud is about to step out of his Black Maserati when he sees Aaron walking towards him. A wicked smile spread across him face for he knows just what Aaron wants. Mahmoud is standing outside his car with his briefcase in hand when Aaron approaches. Aaron takes a deep breath to suppress the anger that he feels inside.

"Why? Just tell me why?"

Mahmoud smiles at Aaron showing his perfectly even white teeth. *"What I don't get a good morning?"*

Aaron bites his lip. *"Good morning! Now tell me why?"*

"Why what?"

"Why did you go after Yasmeen?"

"Well she is a woman, a very beautiful woman might I add, and I am a man."

"Yeah you're an engaged man or did you forget."

Mahmoud smiles. *"No, I didn't forget and that's not something you need to worry about."*

"So, what are you just using her? I mean what's your plan? Is it to hurt her?"

"My plan is to make Yasmeen feel like the queen she is, and I will never hurt her. You've already done that. My plan is to kiss her, hold her, keep a smile across her beautiful soft lips, and do whatever she desires."

"So, are you fucking Yasmeen?"

"Fucking! I am a grown man I don't fuck anymore. I haven't fucked since I was in high school! Fucking is for boy and want a be men who don't know what they're doing! I know what I'm doing!"

Aaron can feel a lump growing in his throat as he speaks. *"So, are you making love to her?"*

Mahmoud laughs as he looks up. *"I'm not going to tell you that, but I will tell you whatever I'm doing makes her very happy."*

"Mahmoud, I thought that you were my friend! I came to you! I told you everything and all the time you wanted Yasmeen for yourself! Mahmoud you know how much Yasmeen means to me. She and I are made for each other."

"What about Uma, Rebecca, and Rosetta are they made for you as well?"

Aaron blood starts to boil it takes everything in him to keep from punching Mahmoud in his face. Aaron feels as if Mahmoud has betrayed him. All Aaron want are answers.

"Mahmoud, I know what you're doing. You and Yasmeen are playing some kind of sick twisted game and you both are just trying to hurt me, is that it? You don't want Yasmeen! I mean you two can't stand each other!"

"That was then this is now, and I don't play games with people emotions!"

"Oh, so she's ok with you getting married in less than six months?"

"You seem to have all the answer why you don't tell me doctor Sinclair!"

"I don't know everything because if I did, I would have never opened up to you about Yasmeen!. But I will tell you this Mahmoud Shashivivek by the end of the day everybody and I do mean everybody will know about you and Yasmeen! I will see to that!"

Mahmoud puts his briefcase down. *"That fine with me and while you're telling everybody about me and Yasmeen you had better tell yourself not to ever put your hands on my woman again because if you do, I will fucking kill you! Do I make myself clear? I will not have this discussion with you again. Now get out of my way, some of us have work to do. Oh, does in bother you that I moved her away and I have a key to our new house? Of course, not you have other, woman just not Yasmeen.*

Mahmoud walks away Aaron hurl his jacket across the parking lot. Anger takes over Aaron and he kick's the tire of Mahmoud car setting off the alarm. Aaron runs away. By the time Aaron reaches the lobby anger and fear surge through his veins like hot wax igniting an inferno of emotion that takes over Aaron and all he can see is Yasmeen face the night that she caught him in bed with Rebecca. Aaron can still see the hurt in her eyes as it plays like a movie in his head. Aaron cellphone rings bring his thoughts back to him he looks down to see Rebecca number and he hits the reject button as he remembers it's Monday. Aaron runs his hands over his face as he walks to the elevator. Aaron takes in a long deep breath knowing that Yasmeen face will be the first face that he sees so he prepares himself. Aaron bites his lower lip as he walks into the conference room and to his surprise Yasmeen is not present, but Mahmoud, Maxwell, and Jacob are sitting together talking. Mahmoud and Aaron make eye contact as Jacob beckon for Aaron to sit next to him. Aaron can feel the sweat run down his back as he looks at the empty seat between Jacob and Mahmoud.

Aaron search for an excuse. *"No that's Yasmeen seat I can sit here. Thanks anyway."*

Mahmoud push the chair away from the table. *"No Yasmeen can sit there I want you to sit here my friend. I'm sure Yasmeen won't mind.*

Aaron hesitate before he takes his seat between Jacob and Mahmoud. Anger wash over Aaron like an eclipse. He closes his eyes. when he opens his eyes the first thing that he sees is Yasmeen with Ashton walk thought the door. Yasmeen is wearing a floral sleeveless blue dress that hugs her body like a glove and accentuates her shapely round ass. Yasmeen long black hair frame her face with flowing curls. Aaron can smell her sweet perfume lingering in the air. Aaron can't take his eyes off her as she continues talking to Ashton not once did Yasmeen look in Aaron direction. Aaron is about to lick his lips when Mahmoud leans over to him and whisper in his ear. *"See the big smile! I did that this morning and that walk, I did that too! Mahmoud put his hand on Aarons arm. Oh, and by the way if you ever kick my car again, I'll rip your leg off and shove it up your ass!"* Aaron head snaps back as he studies Mahmoud face not knowing what to say, he sits back in his seat. Mahmoud looks around the room before he speaks.

"Before we start does anyone have anything that they want to address? *Doctor Sinclair how about you?"*

"Huh what?"

"Do you have anything that to say to us?"

"No...no I don't!"

"Are you sure?"

Aaron looks away without saying another word. Aaron look over at Uma he can see the question in her eyes. Aron tunes everything out, he hears nothing. When Aaron tunes back in he is sitting at the table alone. Aaron looks around the room thinking where did everyone go, but more important where is Yasmeen as he runs out of the room. Yasmeen is sitting at her desk when there a knock at the door. Yasmeen reluctantly reply come in and like a dark cloud in walks Rosetta with a cup of tea in one hand and a full of shit smile on her face. Yasmeen rolls her eyes and shaking her head as she thinks to herself *"I know what this cow wants!"* Yasmeen looks at Rosetta standing in the door.

"And what do you want?"

"I thought that you might want some tea."

"Why would you think that I would want you to bring me anything?"

"Look Yasmeen I know that things between us has been strain's so I'm here to made amends with a peace offering."

"No, you came to be nosey! I don't won't your tea I have my own!"

"Yass, I missed you and..."

Yasmeen cut Rosetta off. *"You see me all day when you're not avoiding me, and not once have you even looked my way, so lets just jump over the BS and tell me what do you want? What are you fishing for? Did Aaron tell you to come in here?"*

"What?... No ...No why would Aaron tell me to do that?"

"Because he ain't shit just like you! Now what do you want?"

"Ok... Yasmeen I just wanted to talk to you, you know like we use to."

"Are you kidding me? You know good and hell well that I don't want to talk to you!"

"I just want to know what's being doing on with you?"

"Ok I'll play your game. Well girl you know me. I'm just a home body. Oh, did I tell you that my ex-friend is fucking my ex? She's a nasty hoe!"

"Yasmeen I just want to know how come you didn't tell me about you and doctor Shashivivek?"

"For the same reason you didn't tell me about you and Aaron, it not any of you damn business!"

"So, you are dating Mahmoud?"

"Is that what Aaron told you?"

"No...No Aaron didn't..."

"So, you're going to sit in my face and lie!"

"You're right and I'm sorry. Yes, Aaron told me about you and Mahmoud. So, is it true?"

"Yes, it is. Now if you don't mind, I have work to do."

"Wait Yass how long?"

"Long enough."

"Do you want to have lunch?"

"Hell, no I want you to get out of my office."

"Yasmeen You do know that he's engaged?"

"Yes, I do, and you knew that Chase was Anne-Marie husband, yet you fucked him anyway and had a baby with him and Oscar. Do you want to talk about that?

Without saying another word Rosetta gets up and walks out. Yasmeen put her hand over her face as she sinks deep in her chair. Yasmeen can still her Rosetta's words *"You do know that he's engaged?"* Yasmeen heart begin to pound as her head spins, she can feel the wall closing in around her. Yasmeen jumps and runs to the door her handshakes as she reaches for the handle. *"I have to get out of here"* Yasmeen flings the door open only to be pushed back with such force that she stubbles to keep from falling. Yasmeen looks up as she hears the metallic lock on the door click. Yasmeen panic turn to immediate anger when she look up to the one person that turns her blood ice cold Aaron! Yasmeen instantly run for the phone as Aaron rips it from her hands. *"Give me that!"* Yasmeen bite Aaron hand and push him away from her." *Aaron get the hell out of here or I'll scream, you son-of-a-bitch!"*

"And I'll break your fucking neck!"

"Well I guess you're going to have to break my neck, but I can promise you the it's not going to be easy! Yasmeen picks up the base of the telephone and throws if at Aarons face. *Come on bitch I'm ready for your sorry ass this time! Aaron this is the last time that you're going to assault me!"*

Aaron grabs Yasmeen hands as she claws as his face *"Yasmeen stop it I just want to talk to you, that's all!"*

"How many times do I have to tell you that there is nothing for us to talk about now leave me alone! Get your nasty ass hands off me!"

"Yasmeen there a lot that we need to talk about, like you and Mahmoud! Yass what in the hell is that all about? Is this your way of getting back at me?"

"Getting back at you! Aaron, I don't give ten fucks about you, how many times do I have to tell you! Aaron nothing that I do has anything to do with you, you need to get that through your head! I need you to listen and listen with both ears, You and I are finished, over, complete! We don't exist anymore!"

"Yass you don't mean that."

"Like hell I don't!

"No, you don't! Mahmoud got you talking crazy Yass he doesn't want you! That basted is engaged, he's just using you! Yass why can't you see that!"

"Are you done?"

"No, I'm not Yasmeen I love you, why are you doing this to me? To us!"

"Aaron there is no us and I know that Mahmoud is engaged... And I love him."

Aaron feels as if heart was been snatched out of his chest. Tears runs down his face. *"Please Yasmeen, please don't do this! Why would you hurt me like this? You can't be in love with another woman's man."*

"But I am."

"No! Aaron wiped his tears. *No, we can work this out! I said that I was sorry what else do you want me to do? Just tell me and I'll do it!"*

"Aaron you're sleeping with my friend, well my ex-friend. Before that you cheated on me. Do you honestly think that I would take you back after all of that? No...no Aaron I will never be with you again so please move on and leave me alone. I'm happy for however long that maybe."

"I guess that you're fucking him right… We were together for six months and not once did you fuck me! I guess I didn't have enough money for you!"

"I guess you didn't now get out!"

"Ok I'll leave but not before you tell me how long have, you been fucking that asshole!"

"Long enough."

"How long?"

"Good bye Aaron."

"No not until you tell me. Yass you owe me that much."

"I don't owe you shit! What I do is my business! Now get out before I call my man!"

"Ok I'll leave. Yass he's going to hurt you and when he does, I'll be waiting! You'll be back and when you do, I'm going to fuck you really good then treat you like the rest of my bitch's."

"I would rather die before I come back to you, and you will never fuck me from what I hear you like to be flipped and fucked yourself that's what your girl told me and that your little dick gives out rather quick."

"Who told you that lie?"

"I'll never tell quicky-mart, but I will tell you this. Your girl said that your head game was weak, and that she stays because her bills has to get paid."

"Fuck you, nobody told you that shit! You're trying to piss me off"

"No, I'm trying to help little man. You need to look into getting some Viagra."

"Yasmeen you're making a big mistake by getting involved with Mahmoud! You say that I need to look into getting Viagra well you need to look into who you're sharing your bed with! I thought that you're smarter than this."

"I thought that you we're a man!"

"Oh, you know that I'm a man!"

"No Aaron I don't."

"Yasmeen there is time for you to find out!"

"That's ok I'll pass!

"You should have passed on Mahmoud! Yasmeen this man has a whole another woman waiting on him, a woman who he going to marry might I add! Come on Yass this is not at all like you!"

"Aaron you don't know me!"

"Well I know that you don't like to share you partners and that's just what you're doing or was this part of your plan?"

"What plan?"

"The plan where you act like you hated doctor Shashivivek. Yasmeen I must say that you had everybody fooled. You had me sold. Tell me what what did you get out of the deal, a new house, a car, money tell me what was in it for you? You can't really be love him!"

"What do you take me for? There is no deal and yes, I know that Mahmoud is engaged so you can stop pushing that in my face! I knew what I was getting into we both did, so for you to insinuate that I had alternative motives is nothing but bullshit! You know what I don't have to explain myself to you, why don't you go do what you think that you do best go fuck one of your many women!"

"Yasmeen I'm just looking out for you!"

"I don't need you to look out for me, you can't even handle your own relationships. You are the last person that I would want to look out for me!"

"So, you really love this guy?"

"Aaron get out of my office!"

"Yasmeen what are you going to do when he marries this other woman?"

"I'm going to go on with my life like you need to do."

"It's not that easy when you love someone to just move on unless you never loved them!"

"I didn't say that it would be easy, but you have to learn to let go."

"Did you ever love me?"

"I cared for you but that's way in the past."

"But did you love me?"

"How could I you never gave me a chance!"

"Well I loved you and I still do."

"That just lust that you're confusing with love there's a difference!"

"Yeah you would know. Yasmeen I'll keep a spot in my bed warm for you sweetheart."

"Mahmoud already has one for me in our bed!"

Aaron storms out. Aaron is sitting at his desk when Rebecca walks in. Aaron wipes away his tears as he tries to hide his hurt. *"What do you want?"* Rebecca can see that Aaron is hurt. *"Are you ok?"* Aaron closes his eyes as he thinks about Yasmeen and how much he still wants her even if it's only for sex. *"Rebecca what is it that you want? I have a lot of work to do!"* Rebecca sits down. *"Aaron, we need to talk!"* Aaron can sense the urgency in her voice. *"About what Rebecca? What do we need to talk about, me fucking you?"* Rebecca smiles as she pulls out a pregnancy test and hands it to Aaron. *"What's this?"* Aaron shakes his head. *"Aaron I'm pregnant!"* Aaron puts his hands over his face and thinks can his day get any worst. Anger takes over This is the icing on the cake. *"Of course, you are! Rebecca, I don't want a baby with you, as a matter of fact I don't want you!"* Rebecca knew that Aaron would react this way, but she had hoped that he would still want her. *"Aaron you don't mean that!"* Aaron explodes with anger. *"Yes, the hell I do Rebecca you're going to get ride to this baby do you understand me?* Warm tears run down Rebecca's face.

" No Aaron I'm going to keep our baby."

"Well you're going to lose me for good. You know what get out of my office. Your sister and I will see you in court when the baby gets here!

"My sister Aaron please tell me that you're lying!"

"Rebecca why would I lie to you, I don't give a fuck about you! I have been sleeping with your sister for weeks now didn't she tell you?"

"Aaron please no!"

Aaron laugh and Rebecca charges at him in rage. Aaron push's her to the floor. Aaron walks out leaving Rebecca on the floor sobbing. Just as Aaron promised by the end of the week everybody knows about Yasmeen and Mahmoud's affair. Time is run out for Yasmeen because in three weeks Mahmoud will be leaving to get married and there is nothing that Yasmeen can do about it even if she wanted to. Yasmeen has been trying to distant herself from Mahmoud but it's hard when you're in love. Aaron has given up on Yasmeen he has been avoiding her no calls, no gifts, or surprise visits. Life couldn't be better. Yasmeen and Mahmoud are at dinner when they see Aaron out with a new woman Yasmeen is over joyed, Yasmeen tells herself that Aaron has moved on.

Chapter 13

When the time comes hold your head up and keep going....

Yasmeen is laying in Mahmoud's arms after lovemaking. Yasmeen kisses Mahmoud as he holds her, she can feel her warm tear running down her cheeks. Yasmeen thinks about how happy Mahmoud has made her and how much she loves him. Mahmoud whispers I love you as tears roll down his face. Mahmoud and Yasmeen both know that this is the end. The time has come this is Mahmoud last day. Yasmeen has not been to work for days she just can stand to say good-bye. Yasmeen hopes that Mahmoud would just leave and spare her heart anymore pain. Yasmeen is sitting alone in the dark her phones has been ringing for hours but she refuses to talk to anyone especially Mahmoud. Yasmeen is in bed when she hears someone call her name. *"Yasmeen why have you not been answering my calls?"* Yasmeen sits up her heart skips when she sees Mahmoud standing over her.

"Mahmoud how did you get in?"

"I used my key. Yasmeen I was worried about you! You were supposed to come over last night?'

"I couldn't! Mahmoud why are you here shouldn't you be on your way to the airport?"

"Yes, but I just had to see you my Queen." Mahmoud sit on the bed beside Yasmeen and pulls her close to him. *Yasmeen you know that I love you and we both knew that this day was coming but we promised that we would always remain... Yasmeen do you really love me?"*

"Yes, Mahmoud I do, and I want the best for you. I'm sorry but this is just so hard for me!"

"This is hard for me too! Yasmeen do think that you and my wife could really be friends one day?"

Yasmeen want to say hell no, but she remembers what she promised Mahmoud. *"Yes, we can one day. Mahmoud, I said that we would."*

"I will never forget what we had… Yasmeen will you wait for me?"

"I can't Mahmoud you're getting married!"

"Will you wait for me?"

"How long?"

"For as long as it takes."

"Mahmoud!"

Mahmoud kisses Yasmeen. She wants to push him away, but she cannot! Mahmoud climbs in bed with Yasmeen. *"Make love to me my Queen!"* Yasmeen can't deny her heart. As Mahmoud enters Yasmeen her body erupts with passion, she can't control her emotions and her love for Mahmoud. Yasmeen cry out *"Mahmoud I love you and I will wait for you!"* Mahmoud makes love to Yasmeen like it is there first time. He kisses every inch of her chocolate frame. It has been a month since Mahmoud's has been gone. Even though he facetimes Yasmeen everyday no matter how many times they facetime each other Yasmeen misses him deeply. Yasmeen wants to move on, but she can't her heart is with Mahmoud and that is where it will stay. Yasmeen has just returned from lunch when Uma approaches her. *"Hello, Yasmeen it has been a long time since we talked."* Yasmeen continue on her way as not to see Uma. *"Yasmeen I just want to know if you're ok?"* Yasmeen stop, in her track. *"Uma why wouldn't I be?"*

"Well I know that you must be hurting knowing that Mahmoud…"

"No, I' just fine but I know that you are, I mean with Aaron and Rebecca's baby on the way after losing yours. You have to be crushed."

"Ouch! Yasmeen that was not at all called for!"

"Yes, it was."

"I was just being nice."

"Well don't! As a matter of fact, don't talk to me, don't speak to me, don't even look at me!"

"Yasmeen, I mean you knew that he was engaged, or did you actually think that he would be with you?"

"You're right I knew that he was engaged. Just like you, I mean did you think that Aaron would stay with you after you suck the I.T. guys dick bitch?"

"I can see where this is going so you have a nice day."

Yasmeen and Uma part ways. Yasmeen heads back to her office Rosetta is waiting in the hall. *"Hi Yass."* Yasmeen walk pass Rosetta without looking back. *"Hi, bye Rosetta, don't come to my office Rosie, I don't want to talk to you!"* Yasmeen enters her office, she locks the door as her tear rolls down her face. After work Maxwell is on his way to his car when Aaron catches up to him. "Hey doctor Khalidah do you have a minute?" Maxwell instantly stops his thoughts races why would Aaron want to talk to him. *"For you yes! Is there a problem?"*

"No not really I just want to know have you talked to doctor Shashivivek since he has been gone?"

"Yes, I have, he called me last night, why do you ask?"

"Good so he hasn't gotten married yet?"

"No not yet."

"Well can you give him a message for me the next time that you talk to him?"

"Sure, he's supposed to call me tonight, what's the message?"

"Great! Can you tell him that he doesn't have to worry about Yasmeen, I'll take care of her and congratulations! Who knows Yasmeen and I might be next and maybe he can bring his new wife, to our wedding!"

Maxwell knows that Aaron is being an ass. *"Aaron why would I tell Mahmoud such foolishness? How about you tell him when he gets back!"*

"Oh, he is coming back?"

"I'm sure that he is after all he's still your boss! Now if you're done, I have better thing to do"

"Ok just give him that message for me, will you?"

"I will not, and I suggest that you stay away from Yasmeen or you'll be sorry."

"Don't tell me that you're dating her now"

"I'm not going to stoop to your childish level! Good day doctor Sinclair!"

Maxwell drives off. Aaron smiles he can only hope that Maxwell tells Mahmoud. Another week has passed Yasmeen is at Todd and Oscar house along with Ashton and Zada. This is the first time that they all have been together since Mahmoud left. Yasmeen can only hope that she will get the answers that she need so that she can move on without Mahmoud. Yasmeen spends most of her days thinking about what she and Mahmoud had. Everyone around Yasmeen is conversating but her mind is a million miles away, wondering has Mahmoud gotten married and is he kissing her, touching her, making love to her, and why hasn't he called her in two days? Oscar calls Yasmeen's name which beings her back. *"Earth to Yasmeen! Come in Yasmeen!"* Oscar shakes Yasmeen. *"Yass are you ok?"*

"What? Yes…yes I'm just fine!"

"Are you sure?"

"Oscar, I said that I'm fine"

"No, you're not, your body here but your mind in out in space. Can we assume that you're thinking about Mahmoud?"

Yasmeen knows that she can't lie to Oscar because he knows her so well, how can she let them know that she's in love with a man who left her to get married and to start a whole new life without her? Before Yasmeen can think of a good lie her emotions pour out like someone opened the floodgate to her heart! *"Oscar I'm so confused and I don't know what to do! Why can't I let go?"*

"Because you love him. Yass it's going to take some time you can't get over someone you love overnight."

"Yeah sweetie it's going to take time and we will be right here to help you get thought this ok Yass. You don't have to go thought this along."

"Zada I just feel like my life is over!'

"Stop it! Don't say that! You know that Mahmoud loved you and the last thing that he would want is for you to talk like that!"

"I just want my life back the way it way before Mahmoud! Why did I ever get involved with him? Za I hate myself for loving him! I just want my life back and I want this hurt to go away! Yasmeen can no longer fight back her tears. *I want people at work to stop staring at me! I know what they are all thinking, that I'm a fool, that I'm stupid to get involved with a man like him! Damn it what was I thinking. This wasn't supposed to happen!"*

Todd puts his arms around Yasmeen to comfort her. *"Yass you're not a fool and to hell with them! They all can't go to hell!"*

"Todd I'm no better that Rosetta and the rest them running behind Aaron knowing that he will never belong to any of them no matter what they do!"

"Yass I'm not going to listen to this because you are not like them, not ever a little bit! What you and Mahmoud had was special! Yass you knew that this day would come, but the heart wants what the heart want's! Yass you know

that Mahmoud wanted you just as much as you wanted him! So, stop feeling sorry for yourself and remember all the good time that the two of you shared."

"What should I do?"

"You should live your life as only you know how."

"Todd I'm not ready to date not right now!"

"We don't expect you to not right now! That's not what I'm saying! Yass I'm just saying that you have to move forward and take time for you."

"But I promised him that I would want for him."

"Yass why would you say that?"

"Because I love him. I guess that I was just in the moment and I wasn't thinking."

"Are you really going to wait him?"

"No Za I'm not! I'm going to put my big girl panties on and go on with my life. The old Yasmeen Blake is back starting now!"

"Hold on wait one minute! Back that train up I don't want the old Yasmeen back!"

"Why not?"

"Because the old Yasmeen was hell! Oscar you don't know how much shit the old Yasmeen put me through! You should have heard some of the thing that she used to say to me in the morning meetings! I don't want the old Yasmeen back ever!"

"Ok how about the new me with some old habits?"

"Ok just as long as I get to keep the new Yasmeen after Mahmoud got hold of her!"

They all laugh and for the first time Yasmeen feels peace in her heart with the help of her friends." *"Yass can I ask you something personal?"*

"Of course, you can just as long as it's not about how Mahmoud was in bed!'

"Hell, I already know that man was great. What I want to know is how much money did he put into your account, six or seven figures?"

"What I'm not telling you that O?"

"Why not? Ok you can tell me later!"

"Hell, I want to know too, hell we all do! Shit he bought you a new house and car, so I know that he made sure that you were set!"

"How about we change the subject Za and O!"

"Ok enough take about Yasmeen and her money we will go back to that later! Let's talk about Aaron, Rebecca, and that baby Yass!"

"Yes, now you're talking Ash! You know that he has been staying clear of her!"

"It's to later for that Yass!"

"I know, but that not the kicker how about he's fucking her sister!"

"I know you're lying!"

"Oh no she's not. Miss thang drops him off and picks him up every day!"

"Za you better shut your mouth and keep on talking! Aaron is a nasty ass person, Yass I'm sure glad that you ended thing with him when you did!"

"So, am I, God is good!"

"Hold on Y'all we need some more wine this is about to be a long night!"

It's now after ten o'clock and the conversion is still going. Mahmoud has not crossed Yasmeen mind for hours. Yasmeen can feel her cell phone vibrating when she looks down to see that it's Mahmoud. Yasmeen hesitates before pressing the ignore button. Yasmeen is having to much fun and the last thing that she wants is for Mahmoud to interfere with what left of her night. Yasmeen can see that he has call three other times. Yasmeen continues laughing as she turns her phone off. It's Monday the beginning of another week. Yasmeen pulls into her parking space. Before exiting her car, Yasmeen check the mirror and blows herself an air kiss. For the first time in weeks Yasmeen feels great and there nothing that can bring her down. Yasmeen walks into the conferences room everyone stop talking all eyes are fixed on her. Yasmeen is wearing black dress pants that complement her shapely hips and a dark brown wrap low cut sweater with the diamond neckless that Mahmoud gave her for Christmas. Yasmeen hair is straight, and it hugs her face like a silk black scarf. Yasmeen flashes her bright beautiful smile as she takes her seat next to Ashton. Aaron can't take his eyes off Yasmeen long legs coming up out off a pair of black leather red bottom pumps. Aaron wonders *"Can she be wearing a thong?"* He smiles at the thought. After the meeting Yasmeen and doctor Baldwin are walking back to the office.

"Yasmeen have you talked to Mahmoud?"

"Yes, he calls me this morning why do you ask?"

"I was just wondering, I mean…"

"No, he's not married yet at lease to my knowledge."

"How have you been?"

"I've been good."

Yasmeen assures Jacob before they part ways. Yasmeen has been on the phone with patient's all day. Rosetta has been dying to talk to her, but she knows that she not on Yasmeen people to talk to list. Rosetta get up the nerve to go to Yasmeen office, when she gets to the door Yasmeen opens it and runs right in to Rosetta. *"Yasmeen I'm so sorry I was just about to knock!"* Yasmeen can see that Rosetta is shaking like a leaf on a tree. *"Did you need something?"* Rosetta can't bring herself to ask Yasmeen about Mahmoud, so she takes that low road. *"I wanted to know if you wanted to go to lunch with me?"* Yasmeen can see though Rosetta bullshit. *"No not today maybe some other time I already have plans."* Yasmeen makes her way down the hall. *Yasmeen can see Aaron making his way to her.* Yasmeen take a long deep breath she looks back over her shoulder to see Rosetta still standing at her door. Yasmeen thinks that maybe Aaron is not coming to see her after all, she smiles as she continues down the hall. *"Yasmeen I was on my way to see you!"* Yasmeen stops in mid stride. For one Aaron hasn't talked to her in weeks so why now!

"You were...Why?"

"First I wanted to tell you how breath takingly beautiful you are. Yasmeen you made my day."

"Thank you and I'm glad that I could help but if you keep walk Rosetta will make your day even better! Now if you would excuse me..."

"Yasmeen wait I came to ask you if you would have dinner with me tonight?"

"No Aaron I will not?"

"Why not?'

"Why not, I'll tell you why not! Aaron you have a baby on the way and you're dating your baby mama sister!"

"Yass its not like that besides you and I are friends."

"Aaron as your friend I am not having dinner with you."

"Come on Yass I just need someone to talk to that all."

"Aaron I can't and I'm not trying to get in the middle of your situation!"

"Please will you at lease think about, please?"

"Aaron no."

"Please!"

"Ok I'll think about it, but I can't make you any promises."

"Ok can I call you later?"

"No!"

"Well how will I know if you're coming?"

"Oh yeah well text me or whatever, Aaron I've got to go!"

Yasmeen disappear down the hall. Without giving a second thought to Aaron dinner invitation. Yasmeen tells herself that there no way in hell that she will take a chance on being seen with him. It's after four when Yasmeen walks out of her office, her long work day has come to an end. Down the hall Yasmeen can see Jacob and Maxwell talking, Yasmeen has no plan to stop. As she approaches Maxwell greets her with a smile. *"Hello, Yasmeen I didn't know that you were still here!"* Yasmeen pulls her long black hair to one side. *"Yes, doctor Khalidah I'm still here but I'm on my way out now, so I will see you both in the morning."* Yasmeen continues on her way when he hear Maxwell calling out her name. Yasmeen hesitates before turning around. *"Yasmeen would you mind if I walked you out? I have something that I want to discuss with you."* Yasmeen can see that Maxwell has something on his mind and Yasmeen knows just what it is, Mahmoud has gotten married. Yasmeen heart pounds in her chest. Yasmeen can feel sweat running down her back. *"Yes, I would like that."* It's a long walk to that parking garage. A ten-minute walk seems like an hour. "So, Yasmeen how have you been?" Yasmeen fight back her tears. *"I'm good now. It has been a long couple of months, but I'm ok."* The last thing that Yasmeen needs is for Maxwell to see her cry.

"Do you need anything?"

"No, I'm fine, really I am."

"Would you tell if you did? Mahmoud asked me to take care of you, so if you need anything and I do mean anything please let me know!"

"I promise I will and thank you."

"I know that Mahmoud has been keeping in touch with you"

"Yes, he has. Yasmeen screams in her head enough with the small talk and answer the million-dollar question. Yasmeen mouth takes over and there's nothing that she can do. *Maxwell have they gotten married yet?"*

Maxwell can see that Yasmeen is waiting for to answer. As quick as Yasmeen ask Maxwell answers *"No not yet and I'm not sure when, but when they decide my wife and I plan to attend the ceremony… I'm sorry…"*

"Why would you be sorry?"

"Because I know how you feel about Mahmoud."

"Yes I still have feeling for him, but you and he are friends, so I would expect you to be at his wedding. I'm going to be ok, just take a lot of pictures for me."

Maxwell hugs Yasmeen and kisses her on the cheek. *"Oh, I forgot to tell you how breath takingly gorgeous you look today.* "Yasmeen thanks Maxwell as they continue on their way to the garage. When Yasmeen and Maxwell arrive at the parking garage, they hear shouting. *I have been waiting her for thirty minutes Aaron what took you so long my bitch of a sister? Are you still fucking her?"* Aaron looks up to see Yasmeen and Maxwell gawking at them. *"No, I was working, now get your ass in the passage seat or get out of my fucking car! I don't have time for this shit!"* Aaron speeds away. Yasmeen and Maxwell say their goodbyes. After lunch Yasmeen is siting at her desk when she hears a light knock at the door. Before Yasmeen can get up Aaron walks in caring a vase full of red and yellow roses. Yasmeen is surprised not by the roses but by Aaron who is down on one knee. *"Aaron what in the hell are you doing? Get your ass up now!* "Rosetta is standing at the door, Aaron slams the door in her face.

"Yasmeen just hear me out please. Yasmeen, I know why you didn't go out with me last night, it was because of the incident I know! Just let me explain!"

"Aaron you don't have to explain anything to me."

"But I want to! Yasmeen, I know that you know about the baby..."

"Your baby."

"Yeah whatever. You know about me and Rebecca's sister, but it over between us. I end everything last night and I'm not sleeping or dating anybody. Yasmeen, I know that I've done a lot of fucked up things to you and I'm sorry. I love you, I want you back and I will speed the rest of my life proving it to you if you would just give us another chance please."

"Aaron that was so sweet how long did you practice that?"

"Yasmeen I'm pouring my heart out to you!"

"Let's not do this again."

"Why not? Yass I'm not the same Aaron and my life is not worth anything without you in it, I realize that now!"

"What kind of fool do you take me for? Aaron you have a baby on the way."

"And you slept with Mahmoud and I forgave you!"

"*I don't need you to forgive me! How dare you compare what you did to me and Mahmoud! Get out!*"

"*Ok again I'm sorry, but I'm going out of my mind, I can't sleep…*"

"*That's because you can't keep you dick in your pants! Maybe if you stop sleeping around with so many women you could get some sleep.*"

"*That not it, Yasmeen I miss you, I need you…*"

"*No, you need to get out of my office! Aaron, I have too much work to do. I have to get ready for this meeting in less than an hour… Aaron I can't do this with you right now!*"

"*Yasmeen I'm going to get you back if it's the last thing that I do!*"

"*You are something else. I don't know what but you're something else! Look on the other side of that door Rosetta is wanting for you, go get her as a matter of fact give her these lovely roses.*"

"*Fuck her these are for you and I'm not leaving until you except them!*"

Ok sit them down. Thank you, thank you Aaron now leave!

For the next two-week Aaron has been sending Yasmeen flowers, candy, fruits, and jewelry. Yasmeen except them only to piss Rosetta off. As the weeks pass on Yasmeen can feel herself pulling away from Mahmoud but she still loves him. Aaron pulls up in his drive way and Rebecca pulls in be hide him Rebecca runs over to Aarons BMW and snatch the door open. "*Get out of the car you bastard!*" Rebecca is not the person that Aaron wants to see in his drive way. For three months Aaron has had no contact with Rebecca. "*Why in the hell are you here? You need to leave!*" Rebecca slaps Aaron in the face, he grabs her hands and pulls her away. "*Don't you fucking hit me again, because if you do I will snap you neck! Now get the fuck away from me, crazy bitch!*" Aaron walks to his door and Rebecca runs up be hide him.

"*Why are you doing this to me Aaron?*"

"*Doing what?*"

"*Treating me like you shit! Aaron I'm caring our baby!*"

"*You're caring your baby! Rebecca, I told you that it's me or the baby and you chose to keep the baby, so as far as I'm concern it's over between us and I don't want anything to do with you or your baby!*"

"*So, is that why you're going after Yasmeen again or are you two back together?*"

"*I'm not going to answer that, you'll find out soon enough, now leave!*"

"No not until you talk to me!"

"What do you want to talk about or do you want me to fuck your brains out?" *"Aaron I miss you!"*

"You miss me or this dick?"

"Both!"

"That's too bad because you will never suck on this dick again!"

"Aaron please you know that you want me!"

"I don't want you or your sister! I have Yasmeen!"

"So, you are back with her? I hope that she's ready to take care of our baby!"

"She is actually because we're going to take it from you. Rebecca you are unfit, and I have the video to prove it!"

"Do you think that I'm going to let you take my baby?"

"No, I do think anything, it a fact!"

Aaron takes his phone out and shows Rebecca a video of her in bed with two men. *"Look at you sweetheart, smile for the camera!"* Rebecca tries to grab Aaron phone.

"You recorded that? Aaron you lied to me!"

"You need to leave before Yasmeen gets her?"

"Yasmeen is coming here? Aaron I'm not leaving!"

"Yes, the fuck you are! Rebecca, I don't want to call the cops on you, but I will!"

"Aaron, I don't give a fuck what you do but I'm not going anywhere!"

Rebecca jumps on Aaron hitting him in the face. Rebecca is still hit Aaron when the cops pull up, Aaron tries to get away. The police put Rebecca in handcuffs.

"How could you do this to me Aaron"

"You did this to yourself!"

Aaron tries to plea with the officer. The police tell Aaron that his neighbor call and that Rebecca is going to jail for CDV. This is the last thing that Aron wants. Aaron informs the officer that Rebeca is pregnant and that he doesn't want to press charges. After thirty minute the office lets Rebecca go with a warning. Rebecca and Aaron enter Aaron house. Aaron grabs Rebecca around her neck and pins her to the wall. *"I told you not to put your fucking hands on me now get the fuck out!"* Aaron pushes Rebecca out the door. *"Rebecca it's over between us and I don't want you to ever come to my house again!"* Rebecca bangs on the door but Aaron refuse to let her in. It has been a week Yasmeen is doing everything she can to keep her mind off of Mahmoud but it's hard to do when he continues to call her and with Aaron constant unwanted advances is driving her insane, Aaron is wearing Yasmeen down, so not only is Mahmoud running around in Yasmeen's thoughts Aaron has joined him. Yasmeen walk into the hotel balls room with Oscar and Todd on each arm Todd whispers to Yasmeen. *"It's your night Yass and we're so proud of you. You deserve this and more!"* Yasmeen kiss Todd on the cheek, she can feel all eyes on her as she enters the room wearing a silver sequence off the shoulder Fitted gown with matching stilettos. Yasmeen smiles as she thinks *"This is all for me!"* Yasmeen wishes that Mahmoud could see her, he would be proud of her hard work. At the end of the night Yasmeen thank everyone for her award. Yasmeen is talking to Maxwell and Jacob when Aaron pulls her to him and kisses her on the cheek. *"Congratulations Yasmeen!"* Aaron runs his hand down Yasmeen back. Yasmeen wants to push him away, but he smells so good and his touch on her skin feels even better. Yasmeen can feel Aaron hand on her ass he is about to kiss her neck when Yasmeen pushes him away. *"Thank you, Aaron!"* Yasmeen looks over at Maxwell she knows that he saw Aaron. Yasmeen tries to smile and makes her way to the other side of the room. The rest of the night Yasmeen avoids Aaron not because she's mad at him but because she wants him. It has been so long since Yasmeen has felt a man's touch and she longs for a good fucking! When Yasmeen gets home her cell phone hasn't stop ringing, it's Aaron. Yasmeen knows that if she answers Aaron will be in her bed with his dick inside her. Yasmeen fights with everything that she has, but her wet pussy wants to be licked. Yasmeen picks up her cell. *"Hello, Todd I'm on my way over I can't stay here tonight!"* Yasmeen puts her phone down and runs out the door. It's Monday when Yasmeen walks into work. She feels like a celebrity as she walks down the hall. Everyone is still congratulating her on her award not to mention the twenty thousand dollars that came along with it. Down the hall Yasmeen can see Rosetta waiting at her door. Yasmeen unlocks her door with Rosetta standing behind her with a big smile on her face. *"Again, congratulation Yasmeen."*

"Thank you."

"Yasmeen can we talk please?"

"About what? You know that I have to get ready for this meeting."

"I know but it won't take long."

"Ok I guess that I have a minute or two to spare. What is it you want to talk about? I know that it's not patient related."

"No, it's not. Yasmeen I miss talking to you, I miss our friendship, and most of all I miss you!"

"Well I'm sorry but I can't say the same!"

"Yass, I know that I fucked thing up and I sorry for that! Please forgive me, I know that I shouldn't have slept with Aaron!"

"I don't care about you going to bed with Aaron, hell I knew that you have always had a thing for him, I don't understand why you lied about it! You could have just told me. I mean yes I would have felt some type of away but hey what's done is done right!"

"I wanted to tell you but..."

"But you knew that it was wrong and nasty! Rosetta I would never go after someone you date weather you slept with him or not. My friend or whatever you want to call it man or ex is off limit!"

"I'm sorry!"

"Rosetta you could never be a friend to anyone because you're not designed to be that way. I know that you're talking behind my back, I don't care!"

"I have never talked about you."

"So, you're going to stand in my face like you do when I asked you about Aaron and lie!"

Rosetta can feel her warm tears rolling down her face. *"I had no right to talk about you. Yasmeen you have always been there for me and I let you down. I was stupid to think that I could go behind your back and you wouldn't find out. Forgive me! Yasmeen I've lost everything, and I have no one to blame but me!"*

"Look I forgave you along, time ago!"

"So, can we be friends?"

"No, we can never be friends!"

"Well can we at least try to build some type to relationship?"

"I don't know! I'm just not ready to let you back into my life right now. Rosie, I don't trust you."

"Just give me a chance please!"

"Rosie, I have to get ready for this meeting. I don't have time for this!"

"Ok I understand, but will you have lunch with me today?"

"I can't."

"Please have lunch with me, please! My treat!"

"Ok, ok, ok I'll have lunch with you now you have to go or I'm going to be late!"

For the past three days Uma has been trying to get Yasmeen to talk to her with no luck, Uma is unyielding, she has to know if Yasmeen and Aaron are back together. The more Yasmeen dismisses her the more desperate Uma gets. Uma wouldn't dare ask Aaron for fear of what he might do. Uma would rather take her chance on being slapped in the face by Yasmeen than to anger Aaron. Uma knowns how Aaron feels about Yasmeen and all she has to do is snap her fingers and Aaron is gone. Uma is on the elevator with her back to the wall when the door open and in steps Rosetta she and Uma lock eyes. Uma knows that this bitch has been fucking Aaron and Uma wants to scratch her eyes out. Without saying a word Uma looks Rosetta up and down with disgust. Rosetta takes in a deep breath just as the door open on the next floor and in walks Aaron the door is about to close when a hand pushes the elevator door back open. *"Hold the elevator please!"* Just like a sack of unwanted shit Rebecca enters the elevator not knowing that Uma and Rosetta are waiting inside. Rebecca is about to back out just as the door closes and the elevator take off to the next floor. Instead of going down the elevator goes all the way to the ninth floor. Aaron clears his throat he can feel Rosetta and Rebecca eyes locked on to him like leasers when Uma pulls him over to her and rest her head on his broad shoulder, just as the elevator doors open up and all Aaron can see are Yasmeen big bright smile. Aaron push's Uma back on the wall as Yasmeen, Jacob, and Maxwell enter. Yasmeen smile spreads across her lips and her eyes beams with delight. Aaron heart drops when he hears Yasmeen voice. *"What do we have here a four way?"* Jacob taps Yasmeen. But Yasmeen can't resist. *"Hello, Aaron how are you all? Oh, Rebecca how are you and the baby?"* Rebecca rubs her hand over her abdomen. *"Good thanks for asking."* Maxwell looks around as he waits. *"Do you know what you're having Yet?* Rebecca looks over at Aaron. *"No not yet."* Yasmeen can almost hear Aaron heart beating. *"Aaron, I beat that you're hoping for a son, you know little AJ, Aaron junior."* Aaron bites his lip and shakes his head in anger without saying a word. He wishes that Yasmeen would just shut her mouth. Aaron smiles. *"So, Yasmeen has Mahmoud gotten married yet?"* Yasmeen looks as Rosetta, Uma, and Rebecca smile slides across their lips like butter on hotcakes. Yasmeen know just how to fix a hot smile by turning it upside down. Yasmeen smile like the cat that swallowed the canary. *"I don't know but I will ask him when he calls me tonight. By the way when are you and Rebecca's sister getting married so that she can be the step- mom auntie. I mean you two are living together right?"* Aaron can feel sweat running down his face. Uma eyes burns with tears as she look's away. Aaron can feel everyone waiting for his answer, but he stands in silent. Yasmeen smiles. *"Why is everyone so quit somebody say something or I will Rosetta!"* Before Yasmeen can say another word the elevator door open and Maxwell and Jacob escort Yasmeen off the elevator. Yasmeen try to push back. *"What the hell this is not my floor!"* Jacob pulls Yasmeen by her arm. *"Yes, it is!"* The next morning when Yasmeen get to work Aaron is wait and she knows that he's waiting on her. Yasmeen gather her things as she exits her new Mercedes SUV she reaches over and picks up her I don't have time for the bullshit, not today attitude. When Yasmeen step out of her SUV, she runs her hand down her sharply sexy frame. All Aaron can see is Yasmeen long chocolate leg beneath her red skirt. Before Aaron can say a word, he explodes. *"Why in the hell would you say that!"* Yasmeen eyes narrows as she studies Aaron for she knows just what he's referring to but why make it easy for him.

"What are you talking about?"

"Don't play dumb with me Yasmeen, you know what am talking about!"

"No, I really don't Doctor. All I know is that I pepper sprayed you because I felt threaten.

Yasmeen pulls out a leather black case and holds it up she points it at Arron's face. He yells. *"Yasmeen don't! I just want to talk to you damn it! Arron shields his face. Please don't! please!"* Yasmeen can see the dread in Aaron face. Yasmeen lowers her arm. Aaron let s out a breath of relief. *"Get out of my way!"*

"Just tell me why?"

"Why what?"

"Why did you say that yesterday?"

"I said a lot on yesterday. Are you referring to the meeting?"

"You know good in hell well that I'm not talking about no damn meeting! I'm talking about what you said on the elevator!"

"Oh, is that what you talking about? Silly me, that just slipped my mind Doctor. Yasmeen puts her hand on her chest innocently. *Did I say something wrong?"*

"Really! Yasmeen why did you have to go there?"

"Go where?"

"Overboard and that little wise crack about the baby and me living with Rebecca's sister was…"

"Right! What you didn't want them to know, was it a secret?" Aaron looks away. *So, they didn't know about you and your boo thang, shame on you Aaron."*

"How did you even know?"

"Well I didn't until you just told me. It was just a lucky guess."

"Are you fucking kidding me?"

"You know me better than that, Kidding with you I don't do

"We don't live together she just stay over and no it wasn't a secret I just didn't tell anybody."

"Oh well I helped you out."

"You didn't help me, all you did was cause more problems!'

"With who Uma and Rosetta? Please don't worry about them they're still doing to fuck you, maybe more now."

"Yasmeen, I don't like fighting with you."

"I don't like seeing you."

"You don't mean that."

"Like hell I don't!"

"Well after today you won't have to worry about me anymore."

Yasmeen smiles so big that her face hurts. *Really you promise, Aaron? Don't play with me! You don't know how long I've waited for this day! Man, if you're serious… I'm about to pull my skirt up and do cartwheels all over this parking lot. Aaron tell me the truth you're leaving and getting married. I'm so happy… Look me in my eye and tell me the truth."*

"Yasmeen I'm leaving, I'm leaving to go to my office. Aaron laughs so loud that it echoes. *But please feel free to do cartwheels I would love to see it. I'm not going way where but with you.* Aaron smacks Yasmeen on the ass. *You will always be mine.*

"Fuck you Aaron! You really hurt me!"

"How, because I fucked Rosetta?"

"No because you lied. Aaron can just leave for about a year. I mean if you cared anything about me you would."

"Ok I'll leave if you make love to me."

"Well I guess you're staying.

Anger escapes Yasmeen. She has been dreaming of the day that Aaron goes away and out of her life. Yasmeen walks away her heart hurts with disappointment. *"Yass did you talk to Mahmoud last night?* Yasmeen turns around she can feel her heart lighten. *Yes, and I told him that you asked about his. He said go to hell. Oh, he said do you remember the last conversation that you two had, it still stands.* Aaron mind starts to play every word that Mahmoud said to him. When Aaron looks around Yasmeen is gone and Aaron is standing alone. Two days later Aaron is sitting at his desk when he door flies open. Yasmeen rush over to him pushing her cell phone up to his face. From the look in Yasmeen eye Aaron knows that this is serious. All he can hear is. "Do you know this *number?"* Aaron can't get a word out. *"Do you know who this is?"* Aaron tries to zero in on the number, but he can't his mind is racing.

"Yasmeen please calm down and tell me what's going on. How can I tell you who number that is when I can't even see it with your phone that close to my face!"

Yasmeen hands Aaron her phone. *"Can you see it now and I know you know who number this is! It's your bitch Rebecca's sister!"*

Aaron looks at Yasmeen's phone dumbfounded. *"Why is she calling you?"*

"That what I want to know and how did she get my number?"

"Yasmeen, I don't know but I will get to the bottom of this! When did she call you?"

"This morning after she left this message last night. Yasmeen play the message for Aaron. *I'm going to tell you the same thing that I told her, if she call's my phone again I will kick a file goal with her ass. Aaron you and your bitch better not ever..."*

"Yass, I don't know how she got your number! She must have gotten it off my phone while I was asleep, I didn't give it to her!"

"Bullshit!"

"It's not bullshit! Yass why would I do something so stupid, you know me better than that!"

"No, I don't! Your whore has no reason to call me about you with her trifling ass talking about we need to talk! She's calling the wrong one! What she needs, to do is lose my number!" Anger surge thought Yasmeen like lighting

"Yasmeen please! I didn't have anything to do with this. I would never do this to you sweetheart."

"Get your hands off me!"

"Please Yass I'm sorry that this happened, please believe me. I know that I've done some fucked of shit but not this."

Yasmeen can see the disappointment in Aaron face and the hurt in his voice. She push him away. *"Stay away from and I mean it!"* Yasmeen runs out of Aaron office she can hear him calling out to her. Aaron grabs his keys and dash out of his office. Aaron knows that he has to get Yasmeen to believe him but how? A week pass and Yasmeen hasn't heard from Aaron or his chick. Yasmeen is over- joyed her only wish is for the peace that she feels will continue, no Aaron no drama. Yasmeen and Zada pass Uma in the hall, she as happy as a fly on shit. *"Good morning Miss Blake how are you on this wonderful day?"* Yasmeen has the urge to be a big rain cloud, but she decides to be nice, because she knows that Aaron is responsible for Uma's temporary happiness. *"Good and you?"* Zada looks at Yasmeen as she holds back her laughter. *"Oh, I'm just fabulous!"* Yasmeen and Zada continue walking. Zada can no longer hold back her laughter. *"Aaron put it on her ass last night, he must have learned some new shit to have her ass around her walking on air!"* Both Yasmeen and Zada laugh. Yasmeen is still laughing when she gets to her office her laugher doesn't last long when she sees Aaron waiting for her. Yasmeen tosses her hair back she takes a long deep breath as she prepares for what is to come. *"And he's back, Why?"* Yasmeen steps quicken and her heart pounds with anger the closer she gets to her office. Before Aaron can utter a word Yasmeen cuts him off. *"Why are you here?"* Yasmeen maneuvers around Aaron to open her office door.

"And good morning to you!"

"Cut the shit! What is that you want?"

"Well I wanted to let you know that I'm no longer seeing Rebecca sister. It's really over this time!"

Yasmeen puts her hand on her chest as she frantically begins to look around her office. *"Oh, my goodness where is it? I know that I had one left*! Yasmeen begins to look through her purse. *Have you seen it? I just had it!"*

Aaron looks around. *"Seen what sweetheart?"*

"The fuck I give. I had one left!"

"Really Yass?"

"Yes, I was going to give it to you, but I can't find it, so I don't give a fuck about who you're seeing!"

"Yasmeen, I miss you and I felt bad about what happened that's all, no need to be an ass!"

"Aaron you know what you just made my day and you can make it better if you would just leave!"

"Kiss me first!"

"How about I pepper spray you!"

"Put that away Yass don't even play like that! Aaron walks to the door. *By the way I like that dress with your sexy ass!"* Yasmeen rolls her eyes not wanting to let on that she really appreciates the complement. Two weeks has passed when Yasmeen runs into Wallace on her way back to her office. Yasmeen knows that he has been dying to talk to her for over a week now. She knows just what he wants and the last thing that she needs is a lecture, so she has been avoiding Wallace but now she has nowhere to hide. Yasmeen takes a long deep breath as Wallace runs over to her. *"Hey Miss Yasmeen, you know that you are a hard person to catch up with. Did you get my message?"* Yasmeen hesitates as she, search for words. *"Yes, and I intended to get back with you, but I have been so busy with this upcoming event. Please forgive me!"*

"It's ok you know that I for one understand, but I did want to talk to you, that's if you have time."

"Sure, I have time right now, Wallace what is it that you wanted to talk about?" Wallace clears his throat. Yasmeen observe his face as he search, for the right words, *"I know that it's not my business, but I do know that you and Doctor Sinclair have been…"* Yasmeen cuts Wallace off because this is not at all what she wanted to hear. *"Been what having lunch!"*

"I just don't want you to get hurt that's all. You know that he's no good for you."

"*No good for me! Wallace what are you talking about? We just had lunch and I met him for dinner!* "

"*Miss Yasmeen I was just trying to look out for you.*"

"*I don't need anybody to look out for me and I don't need a bodyguard!*"

"*You're right. I didn't mean to upset you and I wasn't trying to be your bodyguard. I'm sorry Miss Yasmeen you have a nice day.*" Yasmeen can see the disappointment on Wallace face as he's about to walk away Yasmeen grabs him by the arm. "*Wallace I'm sorry I know that you're just been a friend and I really appreciate that. Wallace I can ensure that there is nothing going on between Aaron and me. We had lunch twice and I met him for dinner, which I should not have, I promise you that it won't happen again.*"

"*Miss Yasmeen I just don't want you…*"

"*I know and I won't because you and I both know that Aaron is not the one for me. Thank you for being my friend.* Yasmeen flashes Wallace a smile. *Now can you walk me to my office so that we can finish this conversation.* Yasmeen breathe a sigh of relief as she and Wallace walk down the hall. Thanks to Wallace who has kept her from making yet another mistake, because loneliness was taking over and Yasmeen was on the verge of giving in to Aaron. As Yasmeen and Wallace approaches, the cleaning closet door they can hear the unmistaken sound of passion coming from inside. "*Yasmeen what's that sound?*"

"*I don't know but there is someone in there.*" Yasmeen pushes the door open. Yasmeen and Wallace are shocked to find Rosetta and Aaron going at it like two dogs in heat. "*What in the hell is going on in here you two nasty asses? Come on now Aaron you could have taken her to your office or the back seat of your car, but the cleaning closet is just low not to mention disgusting!*" Aaron can't say a word. He pushes Rosetta aside as he puts his now limp dick away. Yasmeen rush down the hall to her office, to keep from exploding with laughter. Wallace is two steps behind her. "*Are you ok?*"

Yasmeen can no longer contain her laughter. "*Yes, I'm just fine, how about you?*"

"*I'm still shocked. I really wasn't expecting to see that.*"

"*You and I both.*"

"*I mean out of all the places they chose the mop closet why?*"

"*Because that's just how much he cares about her.*"

"*You know that a man will only go as far as you let him.*"

"Yeah and as a woman if we don't respect ourselves neither will anybody else. You know Wallace if a man would have sex with you next to a dirty mop shows that you mean nothing to him because if he did care just a little he would have taken you to the stairway or hell why not get a room at a cheap motel." Yasmeen is setting at her desk warm tears starts to run down her face as her thoughts takes her back to Mahmoud. She wonders what he's doing better yet is he enjoying it! It has been days seen since she has heard from him. The burning question enters Yasmeen mind. Has he gotten married? Could this be the reason for him not calling? Anger creep over her like cool air. At that moment there's a knock at the door. Yasmeen wipes her tears with the back of her hand. Yasmeen makes her way to the door. Yasmeen eyes narrows to see Rebecca standing in the door. The only thing that she can say is *"Yes may I help you!"* Which was the opposite of what she was thinking. Rebecca tries to speak but fear rend her speechless because it's been weeks since she's spoken a word to Yasmeen and now here, she in standing face to face. *"Are you lost?"*

"No, no I wanted to… I mean I need to… can we talk? If…if… if you're not busy. I can come back."

Yasmeen steps to the side. *"No come in.* Yasmeen sits on the end of her desk. *What do you want to talk to me about?"*

"Well, how are you? You look great as always."

"Thank you. Now cut the BS and tell me what you want!"

"Ok. Well you know that I'm carrying Aaron's baby."

"Congratulations!"

"Thank you…"

"Look I don't have all day. Everybody knows that you pregnant with Aaron baby, so I'm sure that you didn't come here to tell me that because if you did you can leave now!"

"You're right. What I came to say is that I'm sorry for everything, but I do love Aaron. Tears start to roll down Rebecca's face. *And I know that he will always love you, I have to live with that. Yasmeen I know that you and Aaron are back together. I just… I just love him. No matter what he does. I guess I'm stupid."*

Well you're right about one thing. Yasmeen can see the hurt in Rebecca's eyes and Yasmeen knows how it feels to be in love with a man that you can't have. *But you're wrong about me and Aaron.* Yasmeen sits down next to Rebecca. *Look for the hundredth time I don't want Aaron. Yes, we went out to dinner and had lunch once or twice but that's it. I don't know what he's telling you, but I don't want him, so you don't have to worry about that. It was stupid for me to go out with him it won't happen again, so you can stop it with the water works you're upsetting the baby. I don't want Aaron ok my hearts miles away."*

"Thank you… Thank you Yasmeen. I should let you get back to work. Oh, have you heard from Mahmoud?"

"Everyday! As a matter of fact he should be calling in the next ten minutes so if you don't mind letting yourself out." "Yasmeen sits back in her chair she covers her face as warm moistened tear run down her face she gives into the thought that Mahmoud is gone, At this point a simple goodbye would have suffice nothing more and nothing less than a goodbye. nothing less than a goodbye. Two day has pass and Yasmeen is on her way to her car when she spots Rosetta waiting eagerly beside her car. Yasmeen can only imagine what she has to say the thought makes her blood run hot. Yasmeen step quicken as she makes her way to her car. *"Yasmeen, we need to talk!"* Yasmeen Eyes narrow almost close. *"Why is it always we need to talk damnit we have nothing to talk about!"* Yasmeen fights with the urge to push Rosetta to the ground.

"Oh, but we do!"

"Is about a patient?"

"No, its about Aaron!"

"Aaron what do you and I have to talk about Aaron for? He's the last person I want to talk about especially with you!"

"Yasmeen, we need to talk about where you and I stand as far as our relationship with Aaron."

"Well I can tell you where you stand, at the back of the line picking up the leftovers. Rosetta you're not even in the same class with me!"

"Look I know that you want Aaron no matter what you say."

"If that's what you know than you don't know shit! What you need to know is how to stay out of other women's bed and keeping your nasty ass out of the cleaning closet fucking. I mean how can you know anything about me when you didn't know who the father of two of you children were."

"What about you and Mahmoud?"

"What about me and Mahmoud?"

"He belonged to someone else but that didn't stop you."

"Yes, to someone who he never met! Now what about you fucking your best friend husband for years not to mention having his baby, so don't worry about me, you're worrying about the wrong thing. You should be worried about what I'm going to say about your nasty ass when we go to family court."

"What? Yasmeen pleases tell me that Oscar is not trying to take my child!"

"In case you've forgot Oscar's not your only baby daddy turn style."

Yasmeen drives away leaving Rosetta behind wondering who's trying to take her kids. Yasmeen smiles as she adjusts her mirror.

Chapter 14

Even when we depart you will be forever in my heart......

Yasmeen returns home from yet another blind date. Every date that she has been on has ended with an over sexed, shit for brains, cornball, lying ass man trying to get in her silky draws or wanting her to sit on their face at the end of the night. Half of the night is spent on Yasmeen saying no and the other half is spent on Yasmeen say hell no, but tonight this guy was attentive he seem to care about Yasmeen he listened and not once did try to grab her ass not ever when he hugged her. For the first time Yasmeen contemplated dating this guy that Todd had set her up with. They seem to have a connection that is until his live-in girlfriend slash baby mamma called his cell phone and tracked his cheating ass down. Yasmeen can't wait to tell Todd about her perfect date hopeful he and Oscar will stop play match maker and let her find love on her own. Two day later Yasmeen is on the elevator of the Ritz Carlton. On her ride up Yasmeen ask herself, why are you here? Yasmeen knows that she is about to make the biggest mistake of her life one that she will live to regret a thousand times over. Yasmeen can feel her legs shaking with the passing of each floor. Before she knowns it, Yasmeen standing in front of a hotel room door. Her head begins to spin as she contemplates running back down the hall like a little girl. Yasmeen mind tells her that this is wrong, but her body tells her that it's been too long and that its time. Yasmeen closes her eye just as the door open, Yasmeen is rendered speechless. *"I thought I heard someone out here. I was beginning to think that you changed your mind."* All Yasmeen can do is shake her head and smile. *"Oh, and by the way you look magnificent as always sweetheart.*" Yasmeen comes back to reality just as she feels a pair of soft lips on her neck which causes her to melt right into Aarons arms. Aaron lifts Yasmeen up and carries her into the bedroom he whispers in her ear. *"I've dreamed of this moment for so long."* Aaron kisses Yasmeen ever so tenderly as he climbs on top her in his blue silk boxers. Yasmeen wraps her long legs around Aaron waist and hold on for the ride. Aaron rips Yasmeen pants off and thrust his long tongue deep inside of her wet pussy. Aaron pushes Yasmeen legs back over her head, he spread her ass cheeks as he licks Yasmeen from her juicy pussy to her asshole. *"Damn you taste good baby."* Aaron sucks on Yasmeen clit. Just as Yasmeen is about to cum Aaron push's his finger deep inside of her as he gently bites on her clit. Yasmeen pussy juices runs down Aarons chin like water. Yasmeen moans as Aaron plunge his long, hard dick into to her tight pussy. Aaron yells out Yasmeen name in pure pleasure. *"Yasmeen, I love you will you marry me?"* Yasmeen explodes in ecstasy as she screams. *"Yes, Aaron I will marry you!"* Yasmeen jolts up in bed in shear panic her face is wet with sweat she can't stop shaking what has she done? Her alarm clock buzzes in her ear. Yasmeen runs her fingers though her hair. *"Thank God that was only a dream one that I hope to never have again."* Yasmeen jumps out of bed and into the shower. The next day Yasmeen goes out of her way to avoid Aaron at all cost. Yasmeen can't get the thought of her fucking Aaron out of her head and it makes her stomach turns. Yasmeen is on her way to lunch when Aaron runs up to her. *"Yasmeen, we need to talk."* Yasmeen mouth runs hot just the sound of Aaron voice sickens her. *"No, we don't!"* Yasmeen runs into the restroom she makes it to the trashcan just in time. Yasmeen in setting in front her vanity getting ready for yet another blind date that she for once agreed to just to get her mind off her recurring dream that seems to be hunting her. Yasmeen takes a long deep breath as she unpins her hair. It falls and frames her smooth brown skin. Yasmeen licks her full lips before apply lip gloss. Yasmeen is about to apply her favorite Mac eyeshade when a vision of Gregory smiling back at her flashes before her and a calmness surrounds her. Yasmeen closes her eyes and smiles. The sound of the doorbell and banging on the door interrupts the moment. Yasmeen looks over at the clock. *"What the hell I still have two hours why is Za here already?"* Yasmeen slips on her robe and runs to the repeated rings of the doorbell. *"Hold your horse Za I'm coming!"* Yasmeen flings the door open. *"Where the fire? I still have …"* Not another word can escape Yasmeen mouth, her eyes bug out just as the blood and air drain from her body. Yasmeen want to slam the door and run but she's frozen in place. *"Hey sweetheart,"* Yasmeen takes a step back. *"What are you doing here? No why are you here?"*

"I had to see you my Queen."

"Mahmoud why? Why?"

"I know that you have many questions."

"And you know right! Why are you here?"

"I will answer you if would allow me to come inside please."

Mahmoud walks pass Yasmeen he takes a seat at one end of the sofa with his long flowing natural curled black hair. His smooth caramel skin that looks as if it has been lightly kiss by the sun and his rose-pink lip's. Mahmoud can't take his eyes off Yasmeen sitting at the other end clinching her robe tight. With so much emotion brewing inside, Yasmeen wants to hate Mahmoud, but she can't. *"So how have you been Yasmeen? I've missed you."* Yasmeen lash out in anger. *"How have I been? I was doing fine until you showed you! I haven't heard from you, then you show up on my doorstep asking how I'm doing talking about you missed me! You can just go to straight to hell!"*

"Yasmeen, I know that you are anger and I'm sorry for not call but I had so much going on…"

"Yeah I know! Look why are you here, shouldn't you be home with your wife?"

"No, I shouldn't"

"Well you sure as hell shouldn't be here!"

"And why is that?"

"Because I don't want you here so leave!"

"You don't mean that."

"Like hell I don't Mahmoud I want you out of my home and out of my life! Mahmoud reaches out for Yasmeen hand. *Don't you dare touch me!"*

"Do you really want me to leave?"

"Yes! I have a date to get ready for!"

"So, you're seeing someone?"

"Don't question me!"

"Do you care about him?"

*"Yes, I love him! What else do you want to know? Did I fuck him? Yes, in my bed, in the shower, on the kitchen table, on the floor…*Yasmeen can

no longer hold back her hurt with tears run down her face she erupts in uncontrolled emotions. Yasmeen realizes that she's still in love with Mahmoud even if he belongs to someone else, but no matter how much she loves Mahmoud she would never pursue him out of respect for his wife. *"Is that what you wanted to hear now get the fuck out!"* Mahmoud grabs Yasmeen and holds her in his arms. *"Please forgive me my Queen."* After Mahmoud leaves Yasmeen can't help but to think how she made a complete fool of herself at her own expanse. After her out burst how can she face him on top of everything else she let Zada down by backing out at the last minute. Before Yasmeen can get to her office her phones is ringing like a 911 hot line. Everyone knows that Mahmoud is back. Yasmeen has no desire to face anyone asking is she ok. Who would be ok after this? Yasmeen hides out in her officed and turns her phone off. Yasmeen as gone for two days without so much as a it going to be ok from anyone that is until she runs into Uma on her way to her car. Yasmeen pretend to be look for her car remote as Uma runs up behind her. *"Hey Yasmeen mind if I walked with you."* Yasmeen rolls her eyes."

"I don't know how I can stop you after all there're your legs and being that you've never walked with me before."

"I just wanted to talk to you to see how you've been. I mean I haven't seen you all week,"

"Maybe you haven't seen me because this week is not over with. "

"No really how are you holding up? You know I saw Doctor Shashivivek up here today."

"Yeah you and everybody else after all this is his hospital."

"Yasmeen have you even seen or met his wife yet? I haven't."

"Not yet but I'm sure if you take your mess ass over to his house you will!"

"I'm just concerned."

"Don't be!"

"I just want to know how you're doing."

"I'll be doing great if you stop interrogating me and let me get to my car. Uma we never conversed before so let's not start now!" Yasmeen push pass Uma and makes her way to her car before she has a mental break down but not before she spots Rebecca another one of Aaron's jump off's. *"Hey, Yasmeen I was worried about you."*

"Don't worry about me worry about your baby, now have a good Day!"
Yasmeen gets in her car and drives away without looking back. The next
day Yasmeen get to work she rush to her office only to find Mahmoud in
the hall waiting for her. Yasmeen lets her purse fall from her shoulder her
heart is beating so hard that she can hear every beat pounding in her ear.
Before Yasmeen can dare run Mahmoud pulls her into her office. Yasmeen
finds it hard to composes herself. She has not one question in her head not
even why is he here? *"Good morning Yasmeen, I know that you have been
avoiding."*

"With good reason."

"And what reason is that?"

"Well for one I've been busy, and you should be home with your wife not..."

*"Stop it Yasmeen we talked about this and we agreed that no matter what
we would remain friend."*

*"I know I just don't need all the unnecessary attention! I remember what
we both said."*

*"What changed? Yasmeen I still love you and I always will. I need you to
be honest. Yasmeen do you still love me. Please tell me the truth. Do you still
love me?"*

Without hesitating the word no comes to Yasmeen's mind and she
blurts out *"Yes...Yes I love you!"* Mahmoud kisses Yasmeen forehead and
holds her in his arms for the next ten minutes before he kisses Yasmeen soft
lips. *"Yasmeen I'm having a gathering on Friday and I need you to be there."*

"Gathering for what?"

"To introduce everyone to my wife."

*"I'm...I'm sorry but I have plan for Friday as a matter of fact I have plans
all weekend."*

*"You're lying. Yasmeen you promised me that you would be cordial, and
our relationship would not have any bearings between the two of you."*

"I know what I said and I'm a woman of my word but..."

*"No buts I'll see you on Friday at seven-thirty everyone will be there
so don't be late."* Mahmoud leaves Yasmeen alone conflicted with her
thoughts. How can she be happy for him and his new wife when she's still
in love with him? All Yasmeen can think about is what everyone will say.
Yasmeen takes a deep breath.*" Who in the fuck cares I'm Yasmeen Blake!"* It's
Friday and like Mahmoud said everyone is there even Aaron and his new

side chick. It's seven-forty-five everyone is seated everyone but Yasmeen. Todd, Oscar, Zada, Tia even chase are there ready to meet Mrs. Mahmoud Shashivivek. Everyone is there but Yasmeen. Todd, Oscar, Zada, and Ashton repeatedly calls Yasmeen cell which goes straight to voice mail. Mahmoud repeatedly ask Oscar. *"Where's Yasmeen? Have you heard from her?* Oscar nervously replies. *"Not yet but I'm sure she's coming."* If only he believed that because he knows how stubborn Yasmeen can be. At seven fifty-five everyone turns in their seat as Yasmeen makes her entrance wearing a stunning breath-taking mini spaghetti strap light gray dress that accents her toned gym body. Her hair is pined to one side with lose curls. Every step that Yasmeen take looks as if she's floating in her ankle strap stilettos and long chocolate legs. The light gives her a natural glow. Yasmeen smiles tossing her hair back from her face, not even Mahmoud can take his eyes off her. Yasmeen hugs her small waist as she makes her way over to Oscar. *"Well it's about time!"* Yasmeen looks around as Aaron knocks his drink over. *"I wasn't going to come but you guy kept calling my phone! So, where this mystery woman?"* Yasmeen takes a sip from a glass setting in front of her as she gives Brandon the finger.

"She hasn't come out yet."

"Well she had better hurry up I don't have all day."

"What?"

"Yes, you heard me I don't have all day Oscar! In ten minutes, I'm leaving!"

"You can't do that!"

"Oh yeah you just sit there and watch me!" Mahmoud is now standing in front of the room next to his family. Yasmeen can't help but to think how amazing they all look in their ceremonial attire. Her eyes start to burn with tears that she fights back. Mahmoud starts to speak. Yasmeen scans the room looking for Mahmoud's wife who's not standing with him. She can hear Mahmoud sweet voice. *"I want to think everyone for coming out to share this special moment with me but before we began I want to recognize someone who will forever have a special place in my heart. Someone who you all know all too well, Ms. Yasmeen Blake will you please come up here?"* Yasmeen whispers to Oscar. *"What in the hell is going on. I'm not about to go up there."* Yasmeen heart feels as if it's about to leap out of her chest. *"Yes, you are now get yourself up! I'll go with you just in case I have to fuck Mahmoud up along with his wife."* Yasmeen reluctantly makes her was to

the front of the room escorted by Oscar. She looks at Aaron as he turns to chase, they both laugh and point. Yasmeen knows that they are talking about her and not in a good way. She over-hears Aaron say. *"That good for her ass I told her that he didn't want her!"* Yasmeen has so many questions and she can't stop her legs from shaking for the first time Yasmeen fear meeting Mahmoud's wife. Mahmoud takes Yasmeen hand he can feel her shaking. *"Yasmeen I will never forget you. You have made me so happy. I just want to say thank.* Yasmeen squeezes Mahmoud hand. *The time has come for you to meet the love of my life."* A bright light comes on Yasmeen anxiously follows the light to the other side of the room with the anticipation of see Mahmoud wife. Yasmeen can hear the room gasp. She turns to look at Mahmoud who is down on one knee hold a small black box with the biggest and most beautiful diamond ring that she has ever seen. *"Yasmeen Blake will you do me the honor of being my wife? Will you marry me?"* Uncontrolled tears immediately start to run down Yasmeen face she looks to Oscar who is overjoyed with tears. *"O did you know about this?"* Oscar who is so emotional can only shake his head no. The room is silent waiting on Yasmeen to answer which seem to take hours. *"Yes, Mahmoud I will marry you, but what about..."* Mahmoud stands to his foot *"I only went home to tell my family that I could not marry her because I'm in love with you. I was planning this that's the reason for me not calling. I'm sorry my Queen!"* Mahmoud pulls Yasmeen to him and kiss her with the hunger and desire that he has had been holding in for months. Yasmeen welcomes Mahmoud sweet soft lips. *"I've missed you."* Mahmoud puts his strong arms around Yasmeen waist. *"Not as much as I've missed you Queen."* Painful tears flow down Rebecca's face like rain. *"I have to get out of here!"* Rebecca runs out without so much as a look back. The next three months Yasmeen and Mahmoud plan their wedding. Aaron is going out of his mind, there is no way he's going to let Mahmoud have Yasmeen without a fight. Aaron has never been so hurt before by a woman and he hates the fact that he can't let her go. Rebecca is stuck at the airport in Atlanta this is the second delay all she wants to do is get home. Aaron is Miami where he has been for nearly a week. He rubs his chest and smiles as he looks around his hotel room beaming with pride that he has not one but two beautiful women in bed with him when he remembers that there is something important that he needs to do. Aaron closes his eyes as he says to himself what could be more important than two bitch's sucking on his dick. Aaron just can't shake the since of urgent that he's feeling, and like being hit in his face with a brick. Aaron jumps out of bed scrambling to find his cell phone, but when Aaron finds it, it's dead. He started to panic. "I need to get home! I can't let this happen!" Aaron cry out in frustration as remembers that today is Yasmeen and Mahmoud wedding day and the only flight out of Miami isn't until that night after ten. Rebecca alarm goes off on her phone and the message flash stop Mahmoud wedding. She grabs her stomach in pain as fluid runs down her legs. Her heart breaks because at Two o'clock Yasmeen and Mahmoud wedding will take place. She frantically calls everyone that she can think of and not one of them answer because unlike her they are at the wedding ceremony. Rebecca screams out in pain. It's two o'clock Mahmoud is at the altar standing tall and proud in his black tuxedo with Maxwell and Wallace at his side. Mahmoud takes a deep soothing breath as Oscar sings a song by Michael Bolton" *I will take your hand, and I'll understand Share all your hopes and dreams. Show you what love can mean. Whenever life just gets too much for you. I'll be on your side, to dry the tears you cry. I'll love you forever, I promise you. We'll be together, our whole life through. There's nothin' that I, I wouldn't do. With all of my heart, I promise you!"* Just as Yasmeen enters wearing a long form fitting lavender gown embroidered with Swarovski crystal that fits her like a glove. Her beautiful black hair is braided with lavender flowers and Swarovski crystal under her long train. Yasmeen turns to Mahmoud and smile as to minister says. *"By the power invested in me I now pronounce you man and wife. Mahmoud you may salute your bride."* Mahmoud lefts Yasmeen veil *"You're so beautiful my Queen."* Mahmoud takes Yasmeen in his arms and kiss her for the first time as Mrs. Yasmeen Mahmoud Shashivivek.

CPSIA information can be obtained
at www.ICGtesting.com
Printed in the USA
LVHW090157160321
681658LV00011B/54/J